Copyright © 2022 by **Julia**

All rights reserved. No part of this text may be reproduced, transmitted, downloaded, decompiled, reverse-engineered, or stored in, or introduced into any information storage and retrieval system, in any form or by any means, whether electronic or mechanical, now known, hereinafter invented, without express written permission of the publisher. For permission requests, write to the publisher, addressed "Attention: Permissions Coordinator," at the address below.

Typewriter Pub, an imprint of Blvnp Incorporated
A Nevada Corporation
1887 Whitney Mesa DR #2002
Henderson, NV 89014
www.typewriterpub.com/info@typewriterpub.com

ISBN: 978-1-64434-245-9

DISCLAIMER
This book is a work of fiction. The characters, incidents, and dialogue are drawn from the author's imagination and are not to be construed as real. While references might be made to actual historical events or existing locations, the names, characters, places, and incidents are either products of the author's imagination or are used fictitiously, and any resemblance to actual persons living or dead, business establishments, events or locales is entirely coincidental.

IGNITING ICARUS

JULIANNA WRIGHTS

type
writer
pub

*For the woman who never found her soulmate
and raised me to settle for nothing less.*

Trigger Warning:
The following story contains strong language.
Reader discretion is advised.

CHAPTER ONE

In the sweltering heat, Alpha Superior continued to dig the trench for a well that would be placed later that day. Sweat dripped from his forehead, and he swiped it away with the back of his hand. He wasn't physically exhausted; digging was an easy task for him. But the heat was a fierce adversary. Hitting something hard, he threw the shovel down, clawing the large rock from its foundation in the dirt.

Above him on higher land was his beta working, laying the foundation for the house they were building for an elder. Why that pack elder wanted to live in the Dominican Republic, he didn't know. It was hot, uncomfortably so for lycanthropes as they were naturally warm, having evolved from the frigid climate of Romania. But his wolves could finally move and live wherever they pleased.

The idea that they were forever territorially bound to their place of birth was becoming obsolete. Traveling between cities was easier and quicker, allowing pack mates to go from one country to another without much difficulty. Their collective identity was still very much ingrained in their DNA, which was why when Superior received the call that elders wanted to build a home in Azua but were not strong enough to do so, he sent a platoon of wolves to help. He, his self-chosen brother, and a few other strong wolves worked hard for their elders.

He didn't want to be there with mud caked in his jeans and sweat dripping from his brow, but he would do anything for his pack. Wolves helped wolves, always. Still, he'd rather be in his grandiose home in Romania, where many pack members lived and congregated.

They were close to humans—he could tell—as he could hear schoolchildren playing soccer in the nearby dirt plain.

His confusion deepened as to why elders would want to live there. Humans were foreign to them. They weren't a part of their collective identity and thus didn't share a mind link with them. Humans were dangerous even though they were physically weaker.

The species that let their own starve in the streets and die in the cold, knowingly and willingly, made him uncomfortable. It meant they truly did not care and would do anything to maintain their materialistic lifestyles.

He shouldn't judge humans. Perhaps he was being a hypocrite. It was no secret that he lived a lavish lifestyle. Having a grand home, nice cars, fashionable suits, and so on, he definitely wasn't a minimalist. But there was once a time when he had to beg for food and sleep on hard floors. He convinced himself he was different. Yes, he liked his fancy accessories, but he would never trade the security of another wolf for a car or wealth.

Humans would, and that unsettled him.

Ironically, most saw him as a callous, cold-hearted lycanthrope. Even his own people viewed him as a strong yet austere individual. He liked that. He wanted that because no one would tread on his territory or position. And that meant his pack was safe. It meant he fulfilled his duty. Many pack mates envied positions of power, but that power came with great turmoil.

Alpha Superior nor Beta Superior had blood relatives. They were erased, murdered, removed. Their pack was their family. The beta and alpha, despite not being of blood relation themselves, grew up together fighting for their lives and honoring their species. Champions of Lycanthropes—that was what they called the adopted brothers.

Alpha Superior scoffed as he pressed his foot into the edge of the shovel, pushing it deeper into the ground. The shit he'd gone through wasn't something he'd wish on most.

"Thank you, Ana." Beta Kaius took a large, sweating glass of water from the tray the older woman was carrying.

Ana was a female with graying hair and fair wrinkles on her caramel skin. She lived there with a few others.

Ana walked toward the hole and then kneeled to present the tray to the alpha.

He took a glass.

"You're welcome, Alpha," she said sarcastically from his lack of gratitude, and he nodded once in response. She sighed, reaching out her hand to caress his cheek. "One day, that scowl will disappear." She stood up and went to the next lycanthrope and handed her a glass of water.

The younger female was Hasina. She had come with Dalmar, her mate. The male walked to her, taking her in his arms. The sight of the mates and that look of pure, unadulterated love and trust almost turned the alpha's blood cold. He would never have that. That was his curse, his punishment, his greatest sorrow.

He looked away, burrowing the blade of the shovel back into the dirt once again and then flicking it to the pile on the other side.

As the sun began to set, the elder females called the working lycanthropes for dinner.

Alpha Superior climbed from the hole, dusting off his hands on his pants. A hoard of wolves made their way into the small makeshift cottage that would be taken down soon once the construction was finished.

They sat on the dirt floor, being handed plates of raw meats and a bowl of stew. Meeting the eyes of the older female, Alpha Superior nodded—a silent affirmation of her work.

Alpha Superior rarely spoke. He didn't open his mouth unless it was to demand something or to insult another about their work. He was introspective by nature, a calculating and divisive leader of his species. He was a hardened man from years of fighting and having given a duty he never wanted but was punished with.

His brother was the opposite. Kaius was boisterous, filled with laughter and care. His brother wasn't liked by everyone but fervently loved, and his presence was asked for often. Even though the two shared physical similarities, their personalities and ranks within the pack were what differentiated them.

While Superior sat and ate in silence, his brother engaged in conversation across the small room. Others seemed to surround Kaius, enjoying whatever he was saying. Alpha Superior thought Kaius spoke too much, but it was fitting as Kaius was a practiced attorney. His mate, a human named Celest, said she loved Kaius' orations as much as the others did. She was a surgeon in the United States.

With full stomachs, the lycanthropes returned to their work. When the sun set, they laid out sleeping cots outside for the night. The alpha chose his spot in front of the small home, a silent announcement of his dominance and protection over the area. Lying with his forearm on his head, he let out a deep sigh as he gazed up at the stars.

After taking a moment to enjoy the darkness, he dug out a book from the depths of his sleeping bag.

His reading was interrupted, not by lycanthropes or even by another animal but by a cry—a loud, high-pitched shrill that made his ear twitch in annoyance. He would have ignored it if it hadn't been for the small hum of empathy that rang in his chest. Begrudgingly, he picked himself up from his cot and ignored how the others mirrored his actions, remarking on the annoying, never-ending screams of sadness.

They followed the noise that came from a shack far from their elders' on the periphery of the town. And when they entered, their faces wrinkled in discomfort as the pungent smell of sickness and death filled their nostrils. A woman lying unconscious on the uneven floor greeted their eyes.

Kaius checked her for a pulse, shaking his head, while Alpha Superior continued through the dilapidated shack, toward the dirty and ripped blanket on the floor, where a baby girl was crying vigorously in the corner. Against his better judgment, he leaned down and picked the babe up.

As he cradled her to his chest, something bloomed under his skin. A connection, as if he were her guardian angel, solidified in a singular moment. He realized—equally mortified and accepting—that this child would never be abandoned and harmed again. He would protect her, shelter her.

He tried to convince himself it was an act of kindness on his part; that even as he walked back to the elders with the girl in his arms and the looks of his pack mates on his back, he didn't care for the child. And as he handed the baby off to Ana and Hasina, he was sure that whatever protective instinct had developed would surely vanish with time.

When state officials came to collect the child, saying that they would place her in a good family, anger clawed at his chest. So he asked his brother for a favor, a big one. He was by no means a father figure, nor did he want to be. He didn't wish to take parental responsibility (in part, he knew a baby should never have him as a father).

Kaius and his mate took the child in, raising and loving her as their own in addition to their first daughter, Eveline.

CHAPTER TWO

"Congratulations, you two."

Celest and Kaius shared a smug look as their distant friend hugged them. They both knew it was only a social procedure. Both were very social and tried to maintain friendships at their children's school and community. Regardless, certain individuals just rubbed the mates the wrong way. Marie happened to be one of them.

"Thanks, Marie," Celest responded.

Most wouldn't see a difference in her expression or tone, but Kaius knew her better than she knew herself. He could tell, by the way her smile became taut and how her voice went up abnormally high, she was annoyed.

"Honestly, it's parents like you who are the heroes!"

"How so?" Celest asked.

"Well, because you're both so old, adopting a baby so young!"

Kaius had to wrap his arms around his wife to make sure she didn't hit the other woman. He pulled her away from the conversation, finding it amusing as she vocalized her annoyance in Spanish. Kaius was almost fluent, so he picked up a few things along the lines of "I'm old? I bet her vagina has cobwebs." He pulled her into the kitchen, where there were no guests.

Celest suddenly regretted begging to have a baby shower for Aella. She'd thought a party would be the perfect celebration after spending some quality time with the baby and her family. Now she wished she had taken the girls to the park instead.

Adopting Aella was an easy choice for her, almost an unspoken truth that she was theirs. Celest had the time, funds, and love to care for an adopted child. After having Eveline, she and Kaius decided not to try to have another one. The pregnancy had been difficult for Celest, more so for the average human or lycanthrope. And then like fate, Aella came into their lives. She was a beautiful, sweet baby. They could never imagine not having her in their family.

"I'm gonna fight that bitch," Celest threatened. "I'm telling you that right now."

Kaius nodded and put his hands up in surrender.

"I'm not old!" She balled her hands into fists. "I'm thirty-four!"

"Sweetheart, forget what they said."

She turned her head, knowing that if she looked him in the eye, she would cave in, and all her anger would go away.

"Do you think I look old?" She pouted.

Kaius always found her adorable when her bottom lip curled into a small frown, but he also disliked seeing her upset.

"Of course not. You're as sexy as ever," he whispered, pulling her into his chest.

Aella had been with them for three weeks. She slept through the night and ate regularly. She and her sister also got along well. Eveline seemed to love being a big sister.

Eveline ran to her father, covering her ears. "Daddy, are they leaving soon?"

"Soon, princess."

"My ears hurt." She pouted.

Celest sighed. She could never understand how sensitive their hearing was, but they shouldn't be uncomfortable for her amusement.

"Don't worry, *hija,* the party is ending now."

Eveline was lycan like her father. Her shift would not occur until after some years, but her senses were still hypersensitive. The family had to take measures to make sure she could live in the human world. It would be a little easier for her, though. She was born into this lifestyle.

They had her wear earplugs and showed her how to concentrate on one sound so her head wouldn't hurt as badly. They packed her sunglasses and fabric sheets in case any of her other senses got uncomfortable. They tried their best, but Celest still felt guilty. They could never move to pack lands because she was human. And now that Aella was in their family, she would never put her human daughter at risk. Humans couldn't live on lycan land. They could barely step a foot there.

Soon, the festivities ended, and the couple had put their older daughter to bed. The party was to celebrate the adoption.

"You're right. Humans are nasty," Celest commented in disgust as she picked up ham off her nice couch.

Kaius chuckled. He wrapped his arms around his mate, leaning closer to smell her natural scent. "Aella slept through the entire party. Too bad no one got to see her."

"I don't trust some of those people to hold her anyway." Celest turned, her arms around his figure. She rested her head on his chest and smiled, listening to his heartbeat; it always matched hers.

Kaius' ear twitched as he heard something bristle upstairs. He knew immediately Aella was awake, playing in her crib. "I think she's about to—"

Before he could finish his sentence, he and Celest heard the shrieking cry of their baby.

"I'll get her." His wife pulled away from him, then ran up the stairs.

As she came close to the door, Kaius' phone rang in his pocket downstairs, and the lycan sighed.

"Come home," said his brother on the other line.

Kaius raised an eyebrow. His brother was always concise and clipped. "What's happened?"

"The pack is getting anxious without their hierarchy. We both need to go home."

"When?"

There was silence, probably because his brother got distracted by other work. Kaius could hear him scribble something down on paper before laying his pen on the desk.

"Three days."

"That soon?"

"You are still a beta, brother. No matter how much you ignore your position, your duty remains."

Kaius didn't respond. His wife came down the stairs with his still-crying baby. He glanced at her, distracted momentarily by her sheer beauty.

Celest was Dominican. She was born in San Juan, but her parents immigrated to the United States when she was a child. She was a sight for sore eyes, the epitome of perfection to Kaius. Her long curly hair swayed down her back as she walked down the stairs, and he was—yet again—thrown into an appreciative mood.

Celest shifted the baby in her arms, murmuring something in Spanish. "Something's bothering her," she said. "I've changed her, but still she won't take her bottle. Can you hold her?"

Kaius put his brother on speaker, taking his daughter.

"Ridiculous . . . your need to procreate."

Kaius had to bite back a growl deep in his throat. His brother got on his last damn nerve. It was no secret that the alpha was a cynical, callous wolf. Alpha Superior didn't care for humans even though he worked for them. His duty in this world was to serve his wolves. He could live forever, but if he chose to, he could end it all. He knew the consequences, so he never would. He was bound to this Earth.

Kaius, on the other hand, was well-respected among humans. He could communicate and, at times, actually enjoy their presence in his life. He was far more approachable, and unlike his brother, he relished in entertainment and comedy. He enjoyed his life and had a mate, a family, and a career he loved. He didn't mind his existence.

"Some of us want to be happy."

"Some of you can be happy."

Kaius felt guilt creep up his throat. Sometimes he forgot how much had been taken from his brother.

"I can feel your emotions, brother," the alpha grunted. "It's unnerving. Come home. You have a responsibility." He hung up.

Kaius threw his phone onto the couch. He glanced down at his baby in his arms. Celest returned with a small baby swing in her hands.

"I found it! Oh—" She realized Aella was fast asleep. "Well, this is useless. What did you do?"

"Nothing. I was speaking with my brother when she stopped."

She hummed and shrugged. "Oh well, let's put her back in bed and finish up cleaning."

* * *

"I don't understand why he needs you now."

Kaius couldn't ignore the hurt in Celest's words. She was standing in the doorway with her arms crossed, watching him pack. Every time he had to leave her, they both felt the longing deep within their souls. It wasn't a particularly fond moment every time he needed to return to his pack, and in all cases, she was never allowed to attend with him.

He folded up one last pair of pants before walking to her and kissing the top of her head. He didn't say anything, and he didn't have to. They both hated being apart. Mates were meant to stay together. They could survive being apart for a few days, but after a while, the pain of being away from each other would be too strong that it would call them back together.

Leaving his mate wasn't simply leaving and missing her; it felt like drowning, only to be able to breathe again when they found themselves in each other's arms.

He could hear her sniffle against his shirt.

"What if you're needed there longer than we can handle? I wouldn't be able to move. We have children now, and they need their father."

"Then I'd fly back every day to see you."

"It's a fourteen-hour flight."

"So what? To see you for an hour would make it worth it. You are overthinking, darling. I will be back within the week. I am sorry I have to leave you so soon after Aella's adoption."

Celest didn't say anything and just allowed him to hold her.

That night, she drove him to the airport with the girls. They said their goodbyes and watched Kaius until he boarded the plane, then they went back home and had dinner before Celest put her daughters to bed.

"Mommy?" Sitting under her purple comforter with her favorite stuffed animal, Eveline was eager to get her questions answered.

She was an inquisitive girl, one who would accomplish great things. She looked much more like her mother than her father, with curly dark hair and hazel eyes. Her complexion was a bit darker than her mother's, and Celest always said it was the Dominican in her.

Celest closed the children's book and took off her glasses.

"Yes, Eveline?"

"Did Daddy go back to see Uncle?"

Eveline knew she was different. She knew that her father and she herself could see, hear, and smell better than an average human. The girl knew she could see the thread of her cotton sweater while her mother could not. They told her that once she was ready, she would go through a physical change that would alter her life. But she wasn't sure what they meant by that.

Kaius had taught her how to appear normal. They would often go into the woods for lessons on how to conceal their abilities and not get distracted by all their senses. She loved those days, and a part of her was worried that they wouldn't be able to do it with Aella.

Celest nodded with a slight furrow in her eyebrows.

"Why doesn't he visit us?"

"Do you mean your uncle?"

Eveline nodded, turning to get more comfortable on the bed. "I've never met him. Does he not like me?"

"He loves you, very much. You already met him. When you were younger, he came to visit. Has your dad ever spoken about him to you?"

"Oh, I didn't know that. No. I don't think Dad likes talking about him." She went quiet, a little pout on her face. She gently patted the ears of her stuffed bunny. "He hasn't come to see Aella. Does he like her?"

Celest knew the answer. The alpha didn't like humans. He tried not to associate with them. He believed they were inferior to his species and a nuisance to their society. Humans made impossible barriers for lycans everywhere, so the answer was no. He did not like her even though he only met her once. But Eveline was young, and Celest wanted to teach her kindness, so she told a small lie.

"Of course. She's family. He's just very busy."

"Oh yes, his business is very important." She giggled.

Smiling, Celest agreed. She pulled the comforter up to Eveline's shoulders, tucking her in as usual.

"Mom?"

"Yes, *mija*?"

Eveline seemed to fidget in her bed, contemplating if she should say what was on her mind.

After a few seconds, she spoke: "Sometimes I feel something in my head, l-like something wants to speak to me. Is that weird?"

Celest was shocked. She was definitely not the parent who should discuss this to her. Yes, that was her lycan, or maybe it was the pack mind link. She couldn't be too sure since she was human.

"No, baby. You should ask your father about it." Looking at the clock on the dresser, Celest smiled. "Should we call him?"

Eveline smiled brightly, nodding as she sat up.

* * *

Kaius landed at the airport in Romania hours later. He rented a car and drove a few hours to his pack. His species enjoyed being separated and secluded. They also loved the cold since the heat would make them uncomfortable.

Lycanthropes were around the world—including within the States, where Kaius lived with his family. He could feel the emotions and hear the thoughts of the lycans when he was in their pack. However, the farther he distanced himself from the original pack lands, the weaker his connection to them became.

Now that he was within the borders of Romania, their feelings and thoughts surged in his mind. If his mate and family weren't so far from him, it would be relaxing to be so close to his pack mates.

His brother had abilities that superseded his. Alpha Superior was the Champion of Lycanthropes, seen as a god with abilities that almost matched the title, and Kaius sometimes wondered how his brother managed to feel the emotions and hear the thought of every lycan without going insane. He heard and felt everything—every invasive thought and every earth-shattering feeling.

The car came to a stop at the metal gate that protected the entrance into the palace lawns. The beta put the car in park. When he stepped out onto the cobblestone, almost immediately, he heard the lock on the gate release and someone hollering, "Arrival!"

As the old dark gate cracked open, he returned to his car and then drove slowly up the paved driveway. He could hear the gate close again, followed by another shout from the curtain guard.

The drive up to the palace was long but enjoyable. Its driveway was lined with bristlecone pines.

The palace came into view, and he peered at the freshly cut lawn.

When he was younger, his pack would train there—in the large yet bare courtyard that served a military purpose.

The beta came to a stop under the stone awning buttressed by two pillars. Once he stepped out, another lycanthrope exited the palace, smiling at him.

"Caprias," Kaius greeted, handing over the keys. "How are you?"

"I'm good, Beta. Superior is inside."

Both nodded as they went their separate ways. Kaius walked up the stairs and into the large Victorian-style castle. It was beautiful, but it lacked the feeling of home. It felt more like a corporate building than anything else, not that it mattered to him. His real home was back in America, looking after his daughters.

He walked on the marble floor of the foyer. A few maids came and took his luggage, greeting him by his title. He could feel his brother's presence nearing, but he remained still. As usual, everything was pristine. The floors were polished, the windows cleaned, and the pieces of furniture dusted. But the place lacked any decoration on the walls except in the places where females asked to hang portraits of the Superiors.

On each side of the expansive room were staircases that led to the second level. A railing, twisted into the shape of vines, climbed up the edges.

Kaius felt his wolf tense within his subconscious, an instinctual reaction to a more dominant wolf drawing near. His defensive anxiety vanished quickly and was replaced with a sense of tranquility.

Alpha Superior was nearby.

"You've returned."

Kaius looked up. Stark silver eyes observed him from the railing above. Silver eyes were common among his species, but Alpha Superior's eyes were silver with golden flecks within the pupils. Kaius' eyes were the same. Those golden flecks signified they were a different breed of shifters, one that was rarer. The Superiors were stronger, faster, and more resilient than an average lycanthrope.

Kaius wore contacts more often than others because his life was very much integrated into human society. The lycans there didn't have to. They were free to be themselves in all ways. He did miss the freedom of pack life.

A charming smile graced his face. "I can't leave it up to an arrogant alpha to run my pack, now can I?"

The alpha smirked down, but it never reached his eyes. Kaius knew Superior enjoyed his presence, even if he never admitted it.

Advancing up the stairs, he came to a stop beside the other wolf. "It's been a long time, brother."

The alpha agreed with a silent nod.

"Why am I here?" Kaius asked.

Superior glanced down to the room below, a habit of an alpha to observe and protect. "Follow me."

The men walked down the hall until they came at Superior's office.

"My wolves are dying," the alpha said as they entered. He unbuttoned his suit jacket and then wrapped it around his chair. He grabbed a folder off his desk and handed it to Kaius, who took it with skepticism.

Kaius' eyes widened. "Impossible," he scoffed.

"My reaction too, but more wolves keep dying from it."

"Lycans can't get sick. We can't get illness. Who did this report?"

"Four different doctors have researched it. It seems infectious and presents no symptoms until it's at the most fatal. Then, the skin blisters . . . coughing begins, and the blood can no longer clot. All internal systems fail."

"How many have died?"

"The southern packs have fallen seriously ill. More than half have died, and another quarter have been infected."

"I'm assuming there's no cure?"

"We have been trying. No breakthroughs as of now."

"What do you plan on doing?" Kaius sat down on the leather couch and spread the file on the table before focusing on the images.

"You're the beta. Figure it out."

Kaius gave a bored expression. "You're joking."

Alpha Superior grinned. "We have quarantined the south, but you know they don't like isolation."

"You still haven't told me why you need me."

"I need to make a trip down, and because of the situation, I cannot leave the pack without a leader."

"How long?"

The alpha regarded him with a piercing gaze. "You're worried about your woman."

Kaius growled under his breath. "She is my mate. We cannot be separated for long."

The alpha rolled his eyes and walked around his desk to sit down in his chair. He leaned back, folding his hands on top. "One week. Two at most."

"Two weeks?" Kaius said, not being able to hold back his growl. "I can barely control myself for a few days."

"Control yourself. I will try to return within a few days, but I make no promises. You do your duty here as the beta. If necessary, you can fly your humans here and keep them close by to have your lycan under control. I'm leaving tomorrow."

"Leave tonight." The beta stood up.

Alpha Superior stared at him for a moment before glancing at his watch. "It's too soon."

"Leave, tonight," Kaius snapped again.

"Why? Because you cannot control your urges?"

"As your brother, I am asking you to be merciful."

Silence filled the room as the two dominant wolves stared at each other with dark, gloomy eyes.

Alpha Superior nodded once. "Very well."

CHAPTER THREE

It became clear that the alpha would not be returning any time soon a day into his travels. He then informed his beta and went back to work.

That same day, Celest packed her children's clothing and booked a flight to Romania. The separation was getting to both mates, and the pain was beginning to set in.

A day later, they landed. Kaius picked them up and brought them to the pack lands.

"We aren't supposed to be here."

Kaius turned to his mate. She was holding Aella while Eveline was holding his hand. He wrapped his hand around his mate's head and pulled her close, kissing her softly.

"It's okay. I need you here with me," he cooed.

"But, Kaius—"

"My pack does not favor humans. I do admit. But I will keep them in order."

Celest gave a faint smile as he led her through the castle corridors. She could hear the murmurs of the others around although they were not talking with her, ignoring her like the plague. Celest was used to it, yet it still hurt her that she wasn't accepted as Kaius' mate.

She would be staying with him in his room; the girls in the connecting room.

Kaius helped her unpack, and when she was finished, she sat on the bed. "Are you going to tell me what's going on?"

He looked at her with distant eyes, and she then knew the answer. He could never tell her about his pack politics—a bitter truth—but on some level, she understood. She was dangerous to their way of life.

"I'm sorry."

"It's fine," she whispered. "I assume we are going to be here for some time?"

"Just until things calm down."

"Does your brother know I am here?"

"Yes."

* * *

It had been weeks since Alpha Superior had left home, and he didn't know what the fuck was happening in his world. He was still in southern lands, dealing with the carnage of the spreading illness. Whereas the research regarding the disease was steadfast, many wolves continued to get sick and some died.

His body ached. His mind screamed. Every time he lost a wolf, he felt their death, as if he was living through it with them.

He pinched the bridge of his nose in aggravation as one of the scientists continued to speak to him in jargon he didn't understand.

"Stop," he ordered. "Explain in English."

The scientist looked frazzled as she fixed her glasses. She swallowed thickly. "What we are . . . experiencing is not . . . of this world."

"What are you saying?"

"I'm saying we don't know what it is because it's not from here, and we cannot cure it because it's godly."

Alpha Superior gave a cynical and unbelieving scoff. "Impossible."

"The best we can do now is prevention."

"Artemis hasn't descended in eons." The alpha bit back a sneer as he stood up. He hated discussions about gods and the other world, for it only brought back terrible memories.

"Alpha, I truly believe we are in the midst of war among gods. I do not know the part we play, but they have sent a plague to hurt us."

He shook his head. He had no time for trivial beliefs.

* * *

A month passed, and Alpha Superior finally returned to Romania. As soon as he set foot on his land, he could smell Celest and her children. He didn't necessarily mind their presence, but he could hear the ill thoughts of his pack. Luckily, he knew none would step toward his beta's mate. To pose a threat to Celest would mean expecting a brutal fight to take place—a fight Kaius would always win.

Alpha Superior got out of the car, then walked up the stone steps into his home. He went to his quarters, ignoring the pestering questions from the others. He needed time to think.

He entered the dark yet sleek bedroom, taking off his jacket. He set it on the medieval-style bed before taking a quick shower.

Alpha Superior glanced at himself in his bathroom mirror, his hands wrapped around the edge of the marble sink. He made sure not to use too much force so as not to crack the stylized features.

With droplets of water falling from his short dark hair, he leered at his reflection, his silver eyes focusing on his body—the armor of the lycanthropes. The color of his eyes almost made him sneer in irony; everything about him was tenebrous except those bright, icy eyes. His nose was straight, sitting between two average-set eyes and bushy dark eyebrows. His jaw was angular, laying the foundation for his regal-looking, high cheekbones.

He took his hand and rubbed the beard that had grown to a length. It made him uncomfortable, so he trimmed the disobedient strands of hair.

He was now donning well-groomed facial hair.

He knew Artemis had granted him a pleasing body—a body that allowed him to walk downstairs and choose any female he wanted and take her to bed—but it was rare of him to glut himself with sex.

His physical features told a lie of youth. He was by no means a child. However, he looked the same as he had been, when he was given his lycanthrope at twenty-seven. He was old, far older than most wolves.

There were two ways to obtain a wolf: the first was through birth, and the second was when the Goddess saw one fit to have it. The alpha was granted a lycan, and Artemis designated him Alpha Superior, Alpha of Alphas.

A knock came, and he groaned internally. He pushed himself away from the mirror, tightly gripping the towel around his waist.

As soon as he opened the door, an angry female stomped toward him, huffing and crossing her arms like a petulant child.

"You are ninety-five years old, Elena. Stop pouting like a goddamn pup."

"He brought that thing here."

"This is childish nonsense. Has she talked to you?"

"No, but—"

"Has she talked to any pack members?"

"No."

"Has she hurt you or Kaius?"

"No, Alpha, but—"

"But nothing, Elena. The only qualm you have with her is the fact that she's human. Instead of being a bitch and coming to my bedroom with this petty bullshit, remember that I can and will rip your vocal cords out with my hands. Get out!"

The female stifled her anger and left his office, slamming the door.

Alpha Superior rolled his eyes. He relaxed as much as he could, but that was until he heard the shrieking cries of a baby on the second floor. Celest was speaking soothingly to the child.

He growled lowly, feeling something arise within him. He got dressed and sought out the problem.

When he neared his brother's room, he heard him say, "Something has her upset."

"Maybe it's because you've brought her to a house of wolves."

Aella's cries quieted as Alpha Superior's voice echoed through the room like a cannon. Neither Celest nor Kaius noticed.

The alpha remained passive.

Kaius sensed his brother before he said anything, and he turned around to see the alpha in the doorway, his arms crossed.

"As happy as ever. I see," Kaius said sardonically.

Alpha Superior didn't respond. His eyes met Celest's. She was rocking the baby in her arms.

"We cannot be apart for too long. You know this."

Superior nodded once but still held a disapproving expression. "I'm back now. You can return to your home in the States."

"How was the southern pack?"

Alpha Superior didn't answer—an answer itself.

"Do you have a plan?"

"I don't know if we could call it a plan."

Kaius sighed and sat down on the bed in their room. Celest, sensing her mate's discomfort, sat beside him and rubbed his back.

"Go home, Kaius. Neither you nor I can do anything. Go be with your mate and children." He glanced at Eveline for a brief moment before looking at the baby in Celest's arms. He rolled his eyes and left to go back to his office.

* * *

Seven years later

"Come, Aella!"

"I'm coming as fast as I can! My little legs only go so fast!" Aella could hear Eveline's laugh as she struggled onward.

The two were enthusiastically navigating through their backyard. They lived in an upper-middle-class neighborhood. Kaius had been adamant about having some land for their girls to go explore. So behind their house was a small forest that was perfectly safe to venture in.

The girls had asked to go out after finishing their chores, and Eveline was quite happy about getting a little time to herself. She was old enough to look after her younger sister as long as they didn't go too far past the fence. She had promised her mother they wouldn't go too far.

Eveline smiled behind her shoulder. Although Aella technically wasn't related to her, Eveline was always protective. When Aella broke her arm when she was five, she slept in Eveline's bed for two weeks, a decision that was made by Eveline, not Aella. On nights when Aella was particularly scared, Eveline would tell her stories to make her feel better. They were practically inseparable.

"Wanna play princesses?" Eveline asked.

Aella tilted her head to the side with a cute thinking expression. Her tiny arms wrapped around her torso as she contemplated. Her lips parted when she thought of what she wanted to play.

"Can we be queens instead?"

Eveline grinned with mischief as she kneeled to the ground and picked a few daisies that were growing. She pushed Aella's dark hair behind her ear and stuck the flowers into her locks.

"What kind of kingdom are you queen of?"

"Hmm," she pondered. She smiled brightly, shrugging. "One with a lot of puppies!"

"I want to be a queen of fairies!" Eveline said.

The girls giggled as they bounded over fallen trees and growing moss. Aella fell a lot more times than Eveline, but every time her tiny knees hit the dirt floor, Eveline would return to her and help her up, telling her everyone falls.

Aella was out of breath, so they lay onto a small patch of grass, looking at the clouds.

"Can I ask a question?"

Eveline looked at her sister and nodded.

"Daddy always talks to someone on the phone in his office. I never hear what they say, and when I ask, he always tells me not to worry about it."

"Maybe it's Uncle Superior."

"Who's he?"

"He's Dad's brother, not real brother, but he doesn't visit much. He's pretty scary."

"He does seem scary." Aella rubbed the moss off her cheek. "But why doesn't he visit? He talks to Dad so much—"

"Mom says he's just busy."

"Why did Dad not tell me?"

Eveline smiled at her sister and held out her pinky. "I wasn't supposed to tell you. Pinky promise you won't tell Mom and Dad. They don't like talking about him much."

"But why? What happened?" Aella pouted as she rolled onto her stomach and played with the grass, breaking pieces apart and making piles in front of her.

Eveline shrugged, biting her lip. "I don't know. They just say he's weird."

"What does he look like?"

"Why do you care?"

Aella looked at her hands as she pondered for a second. She answered honestly, unsure as to why she was so curious. All she knew was what she felt, and she felt like she wanted to know his favorite ice cream, his favorite TV show, and what he liked to do.

All she felt was awe for someone she'd never met.

"I don't know."

Eveline stood up. She wiped her hands on her jeans, her nose slightly pointed to the sky to smell the familiar scent. Her senses were nowhere near as powerful as Kaius', but perhaps they would be when she was older. Her father was omnipotent in her eyes.

She held out a hand to Aella. "Come, let's get back home. It's about to storm."

Aella stood up and followed her sister. "How do you know that? You're always right about it too."

Eveline just chuckled and winked sarcastically as they neared their home. She could hear their parents speaking, but they quieted when Kaius sensed them nearing.

"Daddy!"

"Hey there, cutie," Kaius greeted, kneeling to pick up Aella.

This was his favorite part, and he loved coming home from work to be met with an excited family. His children were raised entirely different than how he had been, and a part of him was glad. His human childhood was unforgiving. In pack life, while it was loving, it was also brutal. One had to fight for their rank, and that rank was constantly threatened.

"How was work?"

Kaius adored his daughter's persistent curiosity, but at times, he had to lie to her, simply because she should never know about their existence. She was human. He didn't want to cause her emotional harm by telling her the truth. He couldn't answer her question with complete honesty. He couldn't tell her that every day his brother had new stresses on his shoulders, and it was Kaius' duty to alleviate them. He couldn't tell her that more lycans died every day, and they had no idea why. He couldn't tell her that some lycans wanted to see the downfall of Kaius and Alpha Superior. What he could tell her was that his firm was doing well, and he just got a new case.

"It was great," he responded. "Want to hear about it?"

Aella's eyes brightened, and she nodded enthusiastically, but as her father spoke to her, she couldn't seem to focus. All she could think about was what her uncle looked like and if he liked her.

* * *

Six years later

Alpha Superior preferred to remain in his homeland. He disliked the States. The wretched smell of humans and the fact that they lived so close together nauseated him. They were seemingly ignorant of the lycanthropes' existence. They didn't have a purpose or physical strength. They couldn't compare with lycanthropes.

But perhaps he was just sour. Perhaps life had fucked him over too many times for him to be happy for others. Perhaps the sight of humans walking with people they loved and birthing children to watch grow older made him remember the fact that he was destined to be alone.

Nonetheless, wolves from their native land had migrated over to the States, and he had to fly to his brother to handle pack business with other alphas. He never understood why some alphas chose their lands in the Americas.

As Alpha Superior packed his bag, he felt a small pain in his hand. Subconsciously, he rubbed the area as he placed pants into his black Armani suitcase. He prided himself on appearance, so his wardrobe consisted of finely tailored Dolce and Gabbana suits and black dress shoes.

There was hardly a moment where the alpha was indisposed. His hair always fell in the right place, his smile always pristine. Every part of him screamed dominance. The only part of him that could be considered unkempt was his facial hair, which at certain times he'd forgo maintaining.

A she-wolf neared his door and knocked once. He could smell her before even seeing her. When he realized she wouldn't leave him be, he rolled his eyes and closed his luggage, zipping it.

"*Come*," he said, in Romanian.

The alpha spoke many languages, but on his pack lands, they predominantly spoke the tongue of Romania—the oldest and most common language they shared. They were so secluded that English was of no importance, but many chose to learn it as well.

Elena entered and sat her ass on his chair. He stared at her with rigid, cold eyes until she finally stood up. She knew he could kill her with little effort. She also knew his pack was dying, and although his pack was large, he couldn't afford any more lives to be lost.

"You look pissed off."

"And despite the look on my face, you're still talking. What do you want?" he questioned, bothered by her presence.

She was unimportant in his eyes. He could tell by her lustful scent that she had come to prove something to him, but he was uninterested in whatever she had to offer. He'd had his way with many women, but even he would never touch Elena no matter how often she sauntered toward him.

"Alpha," she murmured in her native tongue, "have you thought about the offer?"

Ah right. He pulled his luggage off his bed and set it by the door. He didn't spare her a glance; she wasn't worth it. He had little regard for her.

She had come to his office a few weeks previously with her proposal.

"My answer is the same, no. Now move. Get out. I have shit to do."

The pout was evident on her face. She was a beautiful woman—even he had to admit. Her skin was flawless. Her hair fell in long brown waves down her back, and her almond-shaped doe eyes lulled most men to her in an instant.

He hesitated before he finally looked at her, watching as anger pierced her face. For a moment, her eyebrows knitted in apparent confusion, then she pursed her thin lips and nodded.

She paused as she neared his door. "You need a luna whether you like it or not."

There was some truth to what she said. The position of luna wasn't just for appearances in their world. The luna wasn't just the alpha's mate. They were another part of the hierarchical system, and his pack would never be at its best without one. Lunas were the heart, and a pack couldn't survive for long without them.

Admittedly, his workload was far more than he ever desired. Financial and political meetings filled his days, and his nights were nothing but paperwork and the occasional pleasure.

As the door shut behind the she-wolf, Alpha Superior sat on his bed, running his hand down his face. He was getting too old for this shit. The pathetic thing was that he didn't know when it would end. He didn't have a happy future for himself, and he'd accepted that a long time before. For others to be happy, he had to be miserable.

In the beginning, when he was proclaimed protector of wolves, he tried to persuade himself that mates weren't necessary to be happy; that his happiness was determined only by his actions, his mentality, his whatever. The truth was lycanthropes were dependent creatures who mated for life.

It's hard to believe happiness exists when the thing that guarantees such doesn't. He had no mate and never would. Artemis said he was the only lycanthrope without one.

He sighed again, and his shoulders sagged. *Fuck it,* he thought and stood up. Telling himself to suck it up, he finished packing.

* * *

Aella was thirteen now and attended school like every teenager. She was growing hair in places she didn't want. Her teeth were just freshly straightened. Her acne was atrocious, and she had an unwavering naivety. She was a sweet young girl with curly dark hair and creamy brown skin that beautifully contrasted with her deep-brown eyes. Her body was disproportionate as she was going through a very confusing puberty. To herself, she looked like an overweight walrus, which was unfortunate because she adored walruses.

"Aella."

She didn't hear her teacher call her name.

"Aella?"

She jumped slightly as the person sitting next to her nudged her on the shoulder. Aella looked over at Juliette with inquisitive eyes. Juliette gestured to their teacher, who was staring at Aella with a disappointed gaze.

Nervously, Aella looked up at her teacher and bit her lip.

"I asked you a question," Mr. Gregory said, walking along the row to her desk. "Are you not paying attention?"

She didn't know how to respond. All she did was shake her head and fidget with her hands on the top of her desk.

"I'm sorry," was all she could say.

"It's alright. Just try to keep your attention on me. I don't want to call your parents." Mr. Gregory walked back to the front of the class and continued his lesson on *The Divine Comedy.*

It wasn't that Aella did not have an interest in the discussion, but for months, it felt like she stuck out. She hardly made any friends throughout the school year, and she preferred to keep to herself. Sometimes, she let her mind wander off into distant lands; she was a dreamer at heart.

She twirled her pencil and, caught by another daydream, got poked in the palm by it.

* * *

"Dude, Mr. Gregory is so boring, right?"

Aella cradled her books to her chest as they walked out of the room.

She smiled. "I don't know how he doesn't bore himself."

Juliette's blonde hair and blue eyes were something Aella envied. She was so pretty and could hold a stimulating conversation. Juliette was fearless whereas Aella was full of fear.

They walked down the hall to their history class.

Aella sat down in her usual seat and took her books out, making an effort to rein in her wild imagination. She tried but at some point, her fantasies got the best of her, and she began daydreaming again. She had just finished a vampire novel, and it was safely hidden in her closet so her mother wouldn't find it. Celest didn't want her to read such novels, but Aella found them so tantalizing. She would never tell anyone about her secret books.

When class was over, she went to her locker.

She smiled at the photo of her and her sister that was taped up. She put her books away and grabbed what was necessary to do her homework before shutting the locker door and going to her bus.

That night, as she lay on her bed while doing her English homework, her father came in. He smiled down at her and sat on the bed.

Aella pulled her knees up to her chest and waited with apprehension as her dad went over her homework.

"How was school, sweetie?"

"It was okay, Daddy. How was work? Did you get any new cases?"

Kaius smiled and nodded. "Work was great. I'll take you with me again soon. Your homework looks good, but do you have any tests coming up that you need to study for?"

She shook her head. "I have some in a few weeks, but I think we can study later for them. Oh! Could you help me with this one book? It's Shakespeare, but I don't understand it."

Kaius smiled and grabbed *A Midsummer Night's Dream*. He asked her what she was struggling with and then explained the language to his young daughter. She didn't understand how he read the story so easily and so quickly. It was as if speaking like this was second nature to him.

While he was reading the next few lines, his phone went off. He distractedly took it out of his pocket and, Aella, for a brief moment, saw the name that popped up. It said *brother*, but that was all. There was no picture and no last name—nothing—but then she remembered Eveline telling her about her dad's brother. It had been years, but ever since, Aella had been fascinated by the man she'd never met and was never talked about.

Kaius' eyes narrowed at the caller ID for a moment. He answered the call, bringing the device to his ear. Aella couldn't hear exactly what was being said, but she could hear the man's voice; it was hard and calculated. She wondered what a man like that looked like.

Her father rose from her bed, saying he would be back shortly. When he stepped out of her room, Aella jumped off her bed and walked to her door, leaning outside. She strained her ears, but his voice never graced them again. She so desperately wanted to hear it.

Her eyes tunneled as she looked forward. Her heart raced, and the world seemed to erupt in sensation. She fell back, her body seizing uncontrollably, before she went unconscious.

Kaius was in his office when he heard the loud thump down the hall. He thought nothing of it, semi-distracted by his brother, who was growing increasingly anxious on the phone.

"How's the human child?" Alpha Superior asked, feeling his blood pressure rise steadily. He didn't know why he was asking. It wasn't like he cared. Still, he felt the undeniable need to check on her well-being. But again, it was just procedural and nothing else.

"She's turning fourteen soon. She's incredible. One day you should see her again."

"No time." The alpha's hand twitched with anxiety, and his leg bounced as they continued the conversation. Something felt wrong. He couldn't shake the feeling that it had to do with the girl. "Check on her."

"Why?" Kaius asked with a raised eyebrow. His brother hardly asked to check in on others, and he never asked about his human daughter.

"Just. Do. It."

Before Kaius could respond, he heard his mate scream.

"Kaius! Call 911!"

Kaius ran down the hallway. His eyes widened when he saw his mate on her knees, holding Aella's arms so she wouldn't injure herself as she seized. He hung up on his brother, immediately calling an ambulance. He could see his wife's anxiety soar as she tried to hold her convulsing daughter. He knew her better than anyone did—if she continued to be stressed, she would have an episode.

Since they had been mated, he learned how to understand her emotions. For the most part, what she felt, he also felt, and vice versa. She'd had multiple seizures, and each time he would experience the same cacophony of emotions, dizziness, confusion, and anxiety.

"Celest"—he reached out and grabbed his wife's shoulders—"you have to calm down, beautiful. You cannot help her if you seize. You know that. Take deep breaths."

* * *

Alpha Superior couldn't stop the rage that engulfed him. Pure annoyance and anger coursed through his veins. He stood up, his cellphone whining under his damning grip. It didn't make sense to him. Yes, he had a temper but never so suddenly.

Caprias glanced up at his alpha with a bored expression, as if saying, "This shit again?" They were at the airport, waiting to board their flight.

"Someone's happy," Caprias stated.

The alpha simply growled, then looked at his watch.

This damn plane had to hurry up. He had much more to attend to than just business.

* * *

Aella came to her senses but was disoriented. She'd had a grand mal seizure, though the cause remained undiagnosed. She had been taken to the hospital and had been told she needed to stay for a few days for some tests.

"You have epilepsy, yes?"

Aella watched as her father placed an arm around her mother to soothe her. Celest nodded, placing her hands on her hips. She got defensive when people brought up her illness.

"Yes, I do. But Aella is adopted, not biological."

The doctor smiled kindly. "Well, there could be many reasons why she had a seizure, but we are going to run some tests and find out what is going on. For now," she said, walking over to Aella, "make sure you get lots of sleep and drink a lot of water. If you need anything, just call the nurse, alright? Any questions?"

Aella shook her head. "Thank you, Dr. Stevens."

Doctor Stevens smiled. "No problem. No electronics for now and nothing too loud." The doctor nodded before slipping out of the door.

Celest sighed, pulling away from her husband. "I'm going to call Eveline to make sure she's alright."

Kaius sat in the chair beside Aella's bed and took her hand. She smiled at her father as he winked at her playfully.

"How ya feeling?"

Aella wiggled in her bed, stretching out her limbs with a yawn. "I feel fine. Honestly, I'm not sure what happened. I'm a little sleepy, though."

Kaius nodded. He sat back in his chair and crossed his legs.

"Get some rest then. We'll figure all this out." He watched her as she lay back down and turned on her side.

Her breathing evened out quickly.

Kaius sighed and ran his hand over his face. He loved his mate and daughter dearly, but their being human complicated so many things. They got sick, got hurt, and had illnesses they had to manage. It was exhausting to him—it saddened him. Celest and Aella would die years before he looked any older than thirty. It seemed ironic that they would die young yet had the most to worry about regarding their safety. Kaius rarely thought about it. He barely could. Every time he did, he threatened to shift.

He would never change his mate or his daughter because he loved their human nature, but he did wish he could spend eternity with both. Eveline would soon learn about her genes and what they entailed. He knew she wouldn't take it well, not after he explained the cost of lycanthropy.

He sighed again and watched his young daughter falling asleep.

CHAPTER FOUR

Alpha Superior landed in the States and immediately sought out Aella's hospital.

As he walked through the halls, the smell of disinfectant and diseases filled his nostrils. His nose wrinkled in disgust. He hated humans—hated how they lived and smelled.

A nurse tried to speak to him, but he went past her. He knew where the girl was and needed no assistance in finding the room.

He came to the door, his lycan rippling under his skin. He wanted to growl in frustration. He wasn't a pup who couldn't control his beast; he'd mastered himself decades before. *What the fuck is going on?*

He knocked once and then entered, shutting the door behind him. She was sleeping, curled into herself.

He held back a grunt as he walked further into the small hospital room. *Why am I here?*

Why did his lycan feel so concerned for a human child? He didn't know, and he wasn't used to being unsure.

She stirred. Instincts were a powerful thing very few learned how to use, and while she might not have understood what caused her to awaken so suddenly, he did. Her body was responding to danger, to the predator that stood in her room.

Even if her subconscious warned her, fear didn't appear on her features. She jumped, startled as she met his gaze, then sat up.

What made him question her sanity, what made him think just for a second she knew *what* he was, was when she smiled at him.

"You're Aella," he said, unbuttoning his suit jacket and sitting on the chair against the farthest wall. He didn't give her any fraction of emotion, nothing to show her that *she* caught *him* off guard.

For a moment, she tugged on the messy bun that sat on her head, barely containing those wild curls. She looked lost in thought, like she was analyzing him.

She once read an article in biology that implied dominant males often spread their belongings and limbs to assert dominance. If there was any definition of a dominant male, it would be this man. His sheer masculinity made her skin crawl.

She was always taught never to talk to strangers, so she became defensive. "W-who are you?"

He watched her, his legs now crossed, as she picked at her cuticles from nervousness. His hands flexed against his thigh while she cowered away from him. He knew he was intimidating to humans, and he liked it that way, but it didn't sit right with him that even human children feared him.

"Has my brother not mentioned me?"

She gasped, her doe eyes widening. She maneuvered above her covers and crawled down her bed, keeping a cautious distance. He watched her movements with bored eyes.

She shook her head quickly. "I thought you didn't like coming here? Mom said you're very busy."

"I am, but business called me back here."

"Oh, well, I'm glad we've finally met! Eveline told me about you, but there are no pictures or anything anywhere."

"Are you always so . . . animated?"

Aella grinned. "Mom says I'm just inquisitive."

He grunted.

Silence filled the room, and she awkwardly fidgeted. She wasn't the best at conversations.

"Well, what do you do?"

He looked at her like he didn't hear her.

"L-like for a job? You said you came back for business," she explained further.

"I'm the CEO of an IT company."

He rarely spoke openly, and when he did, it was only to certain pack members. He kept his life personal, and he was entirely uninterested in small talks, but when she looked at him with those brown eyes, he felt the need to quench her curiosity.

"Are you good with computers and stuff?"

Wordlessly, he walked closer to her bed. He gestured to her laptop, and after a moment, she handed it to him. He typed for some time. It was clear that he was focused on his task, although she didn't know what that task was. Once he was satisfied, he returned the laptop to her.

She could see all of her medical records for her entire life. He had hacked into the hospital's "secured" database in a matter of minutes.

"Wow," she whispered, looking up at him with a genuine smile. "And here I thought I was supposed to be good with tech."

"Are you calling me old?"

Her mouth fell open. She stuttered, trying to fix her mistake. She only ceased her worrying when she saw the playfulness in his eyes.

"Oh, you're mean!"

"So what's wrong with you, kid?"

"I'm not sure. I'm getting an EEG later today to see if I have epilepsy."

"Your mother has it."

She nodded. "Yeah. I'm nervous. I think it's going to be scary. I wish I could have a book with me, but they said I am not allowed because it would disturb the test."

He enjoyed reading as well, but he left that fact to himself. Kaius' voice from the hall filtered through his ears. He grabbed his jacket and wrapped it over his arm.

"Get well, kid."

"Why don't you come to our house?"

She blushed when she realized the answer was obvious: he didn't because he didn't want to.

"I'm busy like they said."

"Oh . . ." She cast her eyes to the floor.

"I'll try to come around more often."

"Really?" Her eyes lit up, and her entire frame perked up.

"Maybe," he responded with a steely gaze. He didn't know what possessed him to say that, but the look on his face was that of satisfaction.

"What is your name?"

He turned to her with a devilish grin. "People don't say my name." He pulled the door open, leaving her with a little hope in her heart that maybe everything would be okay.

"Brother?"

The alpha turned to the voice of Kaius and watched as the beta excused himself from the conversation he was having with the physician.

"What are you doing here?"

"The girl—what happened?"

Kaius was shocked by the question and couldn't answer immediately. He looked toward his daughter's room, then back at his brother.

"She had a seizure. Why are you here?"

Alpha Superior ignored his question. "Well, do we know why?"

"Uh, no. Don't you have a company to run?"

Alpha Superior never came to give best wishes to people, especially humans.

"Great. I'm attending her EEG. Her medical bills . . . are they taken care of?"

"Yes, brother. We are just fine."

Superior took out his phone and began texting someone. "When is the test?"

"Three. Why do you want to come?"

"Alright." The alpha turned on his heels and walked down the hall.

On his way, he noticed that all the kids in the pediatric wing had balloons, stuffed animals, and presents all waiting for them while the girl had nothing at her bedside. He brought his phone to his ear and made a quick call to someone under him in the States.

* * *

"Don't be nervous, mija," Celest cooed as she ran her hand down Aella's hair. "I had the test done too when I was around your age. I was nervous, but it was really easy."

Aella wasn't so sure if it was going to be the same for her. She sighed as she watched her father pacing in her room.

Her father was usually a calm man, but when his daughters or wife was ill, he didn't take it well. He was far more nervous than Celest, and if he was, Aella had every right to be as well.

She stood off her bed, rubbing her hands together from anxiety. She swallowed the lump in her throat as the nurses came in with a wheelchair. They helped her into the chair and wheeled her down to the basement where the test would take place.

It was a dark room and had a big machine she'd never seen before. They helped her out of the chair and walked her over to another and sat her down.

"Do you know how this works?" Doctor Stevens asked as she neared her. She sat down in front of her.

Aella shook her head. She played with her hands. Her leg bounced with apprehension as Doctor Stevens took out multiple bright, colorful wires and gestured to the end of the majority.

"These go all over your head, and they monitor what is going on in that pretty head of yours. The results will tell us about your diagnosis."

"Does it hurt?"

The doctor smiled politely and shook her head. "Nope, not at all. All you have to do is lie down on that bed and sleep. We will wake you up once the test is done."

Aella lay down on that bed moments later and focused on the ceiling as her doctor and nurse placed the wires on her head. They then shut off the lights and told her to try to relax.

"It will be okay," Celest said, kissing her cheek.

"I would never let anything hurt you, princess."

She looked at her father as he stroked her hair. "Not even a monster?"

He gave her a closed smile. "Especially a monster."

"It's time to go," Doctor Stevens spoke softly.

Aella watched as her parents followed behind the doctor, closing the door. As soon as she was alone, she realized just how nervous she was. Her eyes wandered around the room, and her brain started creating false perceptions.

That coat rack is a person, she thought.

> **The crazy thing about being told to sleep is that when you're told when it's necessary, the more you can't.**

The alpha walked into the observation room and stood beside his beta. Celest gawked at him, but he ignored her penetrating gaze.

Even though Celest didn't say anything, her mind raced with confusion. *He's never cared before, why would he now?*

She grabbed her husband's hand and squeezed it. Kaius looked at her. He gave her a reassuring smile, pulling her under his arm.

Alpha Superior ignored the stabbing in his heart. He just wished his brother wouldn't be so goddamn emotional with his mate; it was nauseating.

He rolled his eyes, then glanced at the doctor in annoyance. "What is it?"

The woman swallowed, clearly affected by the amount of dominance in the room. "Her heart rate is up. She can never sleep at this rate. Maybe if you speak to her, Celest?"

Celest listened and sat down in the chair next to Doctor Stevens, who then pressed a button that presumably opened the speaker in Aella's room.

"Hey, sweetie."

Aella jumped on her bed but started to relax once she realized it was her mother's voice.

"Hi, Mom."

"The doctor says you can't sleep."

"I'm really scared," she admitted, pulling the blanket up to her chin.

"Well, that's alright. Do you remember when we used to count sheep together?"

Aella nodded. Her mother started to count with her, but after a few minutes of counting sheep, Aella became frustrated and stopped.

"I can't sleep."

The alpha stepped forward and placed a hand on the back of Celest's chair. She looked at him, and that was when he gently nudged her from her seat. She got up and stood next to her mate.

Alpha Superior sat down and took his phone out. "You read?"

Aella's heart raced when she heard his voice. "Y-yes?"

"Is that an answer or a question?"

"Answer."

"What do you like to read?"

She couldn't tell him the answer, so she kept quiet as she thought of what to say.

"Mysteries, dramas, action, fantasy?" He listed several genres before sitting back in his chair.

"A-action," she stuttered out, her cheeks red.

"You're lying."

"Am not!"

"Right," he responded, unbothered by her fib. He thought for a moment, holding his head on his hand casually as silence engulfed both rooms.

He'd memorized the first few chapters of some of his favorite books and knew that he could recount the tales by heart. He chose one at random.

She listened with open ears as he began to read to her.

"Well, Prince, so Genoa and Lucca are now just family estates of the Bonapartes," he began.

She smiled to herself, and he watched as she turned in her bed and closed her eyes. Sleep came easy as he read to her. A person could fall asleep by taking medicine, counting sheep, or maybe drinking warm milk, but nothing could ever compare to falling asleep listening to the person that made her feel the safest.

* * *

Aella had epilepsy. It was confirmed rather quickly, and a small part of her was glad. At least she knew what was wrong with her. Celest kept telling her that her illness wasn't who she was; that it didn't decide her life, but she knew Celest was just trying to make her feel better. The truth was that it was a big part of who she was, and she would have to change how she had lived to adapt.

As she sat at the dinner table with her family, her mind still raced with thoughts. There would be no more movie theaters, no more loud music, and no more haunted houses for her. She couldn't eat certain foods and had to eat more of others. She had to take medication and had to be careful not to take certain medicines.

It was a lot to handle, but even having been diagnosed with epilepsy didn't cause her nearly as much confusion as the fact that the man left as soon as she had fallen asleep. She didn't know why it bothered her so much. It felt like he abandoned her when she needed him the most. Still, they weren't close, so his absence shouldn't have bothered her this much.

"Aella, you're daydreaming again."

Aella looked at her sister from across the table and cleared her throat. She wasn't daydreaming; she was thinking.

"Sorry, Eveline, what did you say?"

"I just asked if you could pass the salt."

"Oh yeah, of course." Aella passed the salt over to her sister and watched as her father came back in from the kitchen with a bottle of wine for himself and her mom.

Silence ensued, and curiosity burned the tip of her tongue.

"Dad?"

"Yes, sweetie?"

"That man who visited me in the hospital . . . he was your brother?"

Kaius stopped eating and laid his fork down. He rested his elbows on the table, forgoing the manners that he always maintained. "Yes, he is."

Aella swallowed and felt the room fill with awkwardness. "Why didn't I meet him before?"

"He's a busy person."

"But he came to my appointment?"

If she were the daughter of any other person, she might have thought her father was just as confused as she was.

"Yes."

"But why?"

It didn't make sense. Out of all the times to meet her—out of all the holidays and birthdays—he chose to appear at the hospital? It seemed less than ideal.

Kaius sighed and shook his head. "I'm not sure. Maybe he wanted to meet you?"

"Yeah, maybe," she muttered. "Are you close to him?"

"We used to be very close when we were younger, but we aren't anymore. We know we have each other's back if necessary."

"Oh," she mumbled, unsure how to continue. "Will I see him again?"

"Do you want to?"

She nodded immediately. She lowered her eyes when she realized her sister and mother were staring at her. She shouldn't have answered so enthusiastically, but he was just intriguing to her. He carried this aura of mystery around him and displayed it, unashamed.

"Maybe you will then," Celest spoke.

"Has he left already?"

Kaius shook his head. "He's leaving tomorrow."

Her eyes widened and brightened from that information. Excitement grew under her skin. "Are you going to see him again?"

"Tomorrow, yes."

"Can you give him something for me?"

Her father looked at her with his light-blue eyes. He sat back in his chair and ran a hand over his face. He nodded after some internal debate. She smiled. She put her fork down and went around the table to hug her dad.

"Thank you," she whispered in his ear. "May I be excused? I ate all my veggies."

Celest nodded, figuring it wasn't worth it to tell her no.

When Kaius heard her bedroom door close, he looked at Eveline. "Did you tell her anything? About us? About your uncle?"

Eveline shook her head. "I promise I didn't."

Kaius' eyes narrowed, and she immediately knew he could hear the lie in her head, filling her entire mind with the bitter taste of disingenuity.

She looked away, caught red-handed.

"Eveline, don't pretend you can fool me," he warned, his voice saying it all.

She relented, looking at him briefly and then at her mother.

"I told her about him when we were younger. She asked about him, but it's not . . ." she explained, fumbling for words. "It's just curiosity."

Eveline knew her father was not happy that she had spoken to her sister about their bastard uncle, but he seemed to have dropped his frustration about her blight.

"Do you know what she's giving him?"

"No, Dad."

Celest cleared her throat and smiled. "It's nothing to worry about. She just met her uncle for the first time all her life. It's natural for her to want to form a relationship with him."

"He's not the type of person she should form a familial bond with."

"He's your brother."

"That's why I'm worried."

* * *

The next day, Alpha Superior stood outside his private plane with his beta next to him. Kaius watched as his brother's bags were put on the plane by the aircrew.

"Ask what you want, brother. I can hear your thoughts."

His voice was dark and sounded unconcerned. He wished people would just say how they felt instead of forcing him to ask, although he had a feeling that if everyone began talking about their emotions, he would go nuts.

Kaius let out a breath. "Why did you come?"

"Business."

"You know what I mean." Kaius looked to the side with annoyance. "She wanted me to give this to you." He handed the alpha a small envelope that had something hard inside.

The alpha took it.

Sentiment—it was unsettling.

"Why won't you tell me why you came?"

"Make sure you look at those invoices I sent you." Without saying anything else, Alpha Superior walked away from Kaius and toward his plane.

As soon as he entered the aircraft, he dropped his briefcase on the other chair and sat down, gently rubbing his temples. He pondered his brother's question as the plane ascended. He didn't answer the question for one reason: he didn't know.

He didn't know why he needed to come, why his chest burned with protective instinct the farther away he went from her.

When he was fully in the air, he remembered the small package in his pocket. He took it out and laid it on the table in front of him, contemplating what he should do with it. He had no time for feelings, no time for little girls with infatuations.

He stood up. He threw away that silly envelope and then sat back down. He worked on some financial reports for a few minutes, but his eyes continuously darted to the trash can.

When he couldn't find peace, he growled. Giving in to his curiosity, he ripped the envelope open. He raised an eyebrow at the recorder, then pressed Play.

"Anna Pavlovna's reception was in full swing. . . ."

He couldn't resist the smile that graced his face as her voice went through the plane. There was a note under the recorder.

Atlas,

I've decided to call you Atlas because you look like you have the world on your shoulders. I think it suits you. My father says you probably won't visit us again, and a part of me believes him. I hope he is wrong. Anyway, you made me calm when I was really scared, and I hope this recording can do the same for you when you're scared or stressed. I was thinking maybe we could read the rest of the story together . . . when we have time. Maybe it's a stupid idea, and maybe you're way too busy, but I've read the first few pages of it. I hope we can read, together, War and Peace *by Leo Tolstoy—all 500,000 words of it.*

— Aella

CHAPTER FIVE

Months passed, and on her fourteenth birthday, Aella received a package.

"Happy birthday to you. . . ." her family sang as they entered her room. Her mother was carrying a small cupcake with a candle on it.

Aella sat up, immediately swiping off her bonnet. She smiled, locking eyes with Eveline, who was leaning against the doorframe. Aella obeyed her mother's command to blow out the candle.

"Did you wish for something?"

She nodded at her mother with a sweet grin.

"Alright, birthday girl, the day is yours. Get dressed and come down when you are ready to start the day."

"Alright, Mama."

"Good."

Her parents left, but Eveline stayed perched against that wall. After a second, she galloped to Aella's bed. Aella cocked her head at her sister, hoping she would let on to whatever made her stay.

Eveline grinned, rather devilishly. "I grabbed this before Mom and Dad could go through it."

"What?"

She took out a small envelope from her jacket pocket and handed it to her sister. Aella took it hesitantly, her excitement growing as she opened it and let the contents drop on her lap.

"What is it? It has Uncle's name on it."

Aella couldn't help her smile as she pressed Play and listened to his voice: "You are off to the war, Prince?"

Eveline did very little to quell her gasp of surprise.

As he read her chapter 4 over the recorder, she unfolded the note and read it with excitement. It had been months since she had met Atlas, and during those months, she didn't receive anything from him. It had saddened her more than she'd thought, but getting this recording brought her joy.

> *Aella,*
>
> *I fear you give me too much credit. Atlas was the name given to a titan who was punished to hold the universe up with his bare hands. This is not what I do. In any case, I do not mind if you call me Atlas, but please be aware that I am no titan. Do not fabricate a person of whom I am not.*
>
> *Thank you for the recording. It was nice to listen to. I will send recordings when I can, but* War and Peace *is a very long novel. Are you sure we can finish it?*
>
> *Happy Birthday, Aella.*
>
> *— Atlas*

"Wow."

Aella looked at Eveline and nodded. "Yeah."

"That's the most I've ever heard him speak!"

Aella grinned and ran her hand down the back of her neck, shaking her head in disbelief. "Thank you for grabbing it before Mom or Dad found it."

"I gotcha."

"Thanks, Eveline," she said sincerely.

Eveline laughed it off before walking out of her room.

With closed eyes, Aella listened to the deep, soothing voice of Atlas. He said the name didn't suit him, but she begged to differ.

She finished listening to him and hid the recorder under her pillow. She got out of bed and grabbed a pen and paper, then began writing a letter back. Unfortunately, her father called her name, and she had to wait to finish her next letter.

* * *

As she and her dad walked down the pathway of the zoo, Aella was licking her chocolate ice cream cone. They were in a comfortable silence that Kaius knew would end soon.

"He told me what you gave him."

Aella couldn't help but blush. The need to avoid his eyes was suffocating, so she stared at her shoes as they sat down on a bench next to the tigers. She didn't understand why this situation was so odd to her family when it was natural to her.

"Why did you write to him?"

She attempted to hide behind a curtain of hair. "I just wanted to say thank you."

Kaius nodded. He wasn't mad at his daughter, but she was walking a very thin line, and he didn't want her to be disappointed.

"Listen, Aella, our family is complicated."

"Why?"

"For many reasons," he said, looking at her. He took her ice cream so that she would focus on him. "My brother is the core of these complications, and I need you to understand that he is far too busy to respond to you regularly."

"I know." She cast her eyes away again. "He told me."

"Good, sweetie."

"Are you saying I can't send him recordings anymore?"

He wanted to say no, to say that it was dangerous to form a relationship with the alpha, but he couldn't say no when her eyes welled up with fear. It was important to her. So the beta shook his head but didn't elaborate. That was all Aella needed to know.

*   *   *

When she returned home, having had a great birthday, she sat at her desk and finished her letter.

> *Atlas,*
>
> *I think we can finish it, maybe not this year but within the next few. I've never finished the entire thing because I always get bored, but this will make me finish it.*
>
> *Do you know a lot of Greek mythology? I think it's cool.*
>
> *I'm not sure what my name means honestly, but I'm confused why you won't tell me your real name.*
>
> *Dad says our family is complicated. Why is that? He says that you're complicated.*
>
> *Thank you,*
> *—Aella*

She put the letter in an envelope and sealed it before placing it in her math book so she would be reminded to send it. She then took a shower and climbed into bed.

The next morning, she attended classes.

When she went to mail the letter, she checked the last letter from Atlas and wrote the same address on her envelope. She tucked her recorder into the envelope and sent the letter in with a small smile on her face.

If she had known she wouldn't get a response, she might have never bothered.

*   *   *

Two years later

The alpha walked through the wreckage with a scowl marring his face. The stench of blood caused his stomach to coil with unease. Usually, he would salivate from the scent because of his more primal nature to hunt prey and eat raw meat, but the smell of his pack members made his stomach churn.

Mixed in with the carnage was another smell that made his skin crawl. He would recognize that scent anywhere. It sent him into a barrage of memories that reminded him of the weight he carried on his back for his pack.

Caprias stood from his kneeling position as he felt his alpha nearby. He could feel the turmoil within his pack members and knew that what Alpha Superior was feeling was far worse. Being an alpha came with many benefits, but with those benefits came even more responsibilities.

Alphas were the leaders of packs. They were the first into battle and the last to return home. Their dominant personalities stemmed from a deep, carnal need to defend, protect, and feed the wolves on their land.

Alpha Superior was the last wolf to march onto the wreckage, which was common among their species. Alphas walked behind their warriors after a battle to survey for any possible threats.

"Do you smell that?" Caprias crossed his arms over his chest and looked over at the alpha male.

Even though Alpha Superior was far older than he was, he didn't look like it. His face conveyed the lie of youth.

Their lack of aging was one of the reasons they lived off the grid; people would get suspicious if none of them aged.

Alpha Superior nodded, not looking at the other wolf. His eyes scanned the bodies—pups, bitches, and males—lying on the ground. No one was left alive.

"It's him." The alpha was sure of it.

"Why has he returned?"

It had been centuries since he had made any contact with him.

"He hasn't gotten his revenge."

"It was centuries ago, Alpha."

"I killed the most important thing in his life. It doesn't matter how long ago it was. He won't stop until he hurts me as much as I hurt him."

"Does Kaius know?"

Caprias and Alpha Superior had a mutual understanding as they looked over the snowy field. Beta Kaius was not innocent in the blood-filled history of the alpha. Kaius was just as guilty as him. What they had done years before severely damaged a wolf, and this wolf would not rest until either the pack or their alpha fell.

Alpha Superior moved away from Caprias and phoned his brother. He walked into a ransacked small cottage.

He looked around the quaint home. It was clear that a struggle had occurred there. A male had his throat cut and bled out on the aluminum floor. Behind him was a woman—presumably, his mate—with her neck snapped. In the corner lay a child, who became a casualty in a war that should never have started.

The sight made Alpha Superior close his eyes in a moment of anger.

"Brother?"

The alpha looked out the window as Kaius' voice came through the phone.

"What is going on? It's three in the morning here."

"He's back, Kaius."

"What are you—" Kaius stopped talking, and enlightenment flashed through his voice. "How do you know?"

"He and a few of his mutts massacred a small village situated north of the castle. His scent is everywhere. Be on the watch, Kaius."

"Are there any survivors?"

The alpha shook his head. "No. Tell Eveline."

"She's too young to be mixed up in all this."

"She's stronger than the average wolf, brother. If you want your mate and human child safe, you need to tell your lycan daughter about what she is and what she can do. She can protect the girl at school when you are not around. It's time to tell her."

Kaius growled, waking up his mate.

Celest sat up on the bed and turned on the bedside lamp.

"Sweetheart? What's going on?" She watched with apprehension as her mate paced in front of her, talking to someone on his cell phone.

It was clear that her husband was annoyed.

Kaius looked at Celest and gave a sympathetic smile before continuing his conversation with his brother.

"Very well, Superior. What will you do?"

"I'll trace down more leads. I want to get this son of a bitch before he hurts anyone else."

Kaius nodded and sat down on the bed, rubbing Celest's leg through the covers. It calmed him down to show affection to his mate.

"He was a good alpha." Disdain and dejection laced his voice as he rubbed the back of his neck.

"That all changed when I killed his mate."

"Superior—"

"Call me if something occurs." He hung up.

Kaius threw his phone on the bed when the call ended abruptly.

"Want to talk about it?" Celest murmured.

Kaius sighed and gently caressed her hand that was resting on his shoulder. "Our past is catching up with us."

* * *

Aella was sixteen now. Her teeth straightened, her body grew, her hair curled into black shoulder-length locks, and she had vivid dreams that almost took her away from reality permanently. She grew into a kind yet determined young girl who would rather be alone than with others.

She had the incurable ability to make others feel heard, wanted, and safe. She didn't mind listening to others because she believed what she had to say was inferior to what they had to tell her. She liked listening—she preferred it. She was a hopeless romantic at heart and an irrefutable dreamer.

She felt a hand on her back, and she turned around to see Alex.

The cute boy handed her a note. She glanced at it and blushed softly.

Alex cleared his throat. "Can you pass it to Eloise?"

Aella swallowed and bit her lip as disappointment swelled in her stomach. She gave the note to the girl in the next seat.

Eloise wrote her response and then gave it back to Aella, who took it with a grain of salt before handing it back to Alex.

Crossing her arms, Aella listened to the rest of the lecture. After school, she went to her locker and got her books.

"Hey, girl."

She jumped as a face appeared behind her locker. "Alex?"

Alex offered her a charming grin and grabbed her hand. "What you doing right now?"

"I am about to head home. Why?"

Aella tried to play it cool like a cute boy wasn't talking to her. Alex had hardly ever said two words to her and never grabbed her hand before. He'd never showed any interest in her.

He shifted his weight. "I was wondering if you wanted to go to the park with me? I thought it would be cute, and maybe I could help you with your geometry homework?"

"Y-you want to tutor me?"

He smiled and looked past her for a moment with a dazed smirk. "Of course I do. You're cute."

"W-what?"

"I just never made a move because your sister would kill me and your dad is terrifying."

Aella smiled. She laughed and nodded, cradling her books to her chest. "They are pretty intimidating."

"Intimidating? Come on! That's putting it lightly." Alex laughed and held out his hands to take her books.

She handed them over hesitantly.

"So, what do you say?"

"What about your girlfriend? Eloise . . ."

"Did you read what I passed you?"

She shook her head. "It was for Eloise."

"It said I liked someone else, not her. I like you Aella, a lot."

And that was how they ended up at the local park.

Alex joked with her, and she laughed at his humor. He was sweet to her, and it made her heart drop in a good way.

They went up into the tree house, and he moved closer to her and then placed his hand on her thigh.

"I-I . . . I don't think I want . . ."

"May I kiss you, Aella?"

This was it. This was her first kiss.

He leaned close to her, his eyes shut. She did the same.

"This is my first kiss," she admitted.

Alex pulled back and gave her a cute smile. "Guess I should make it good then?"

She nodded. "I might not be any good."

"Just follow my lead," he whispered, pulling her close again. She placed her nimble hands on his shoulders, moving to sit on his lap. She could feel his hands on her back, along with her goose bumps. They kissed. His tongue attached to hers, and when his saliva started falling down her neck, she couldn't believe people enjoyed this. It was disgusting and uncomfortable.

Dizziness began to corrupt her. Oh no, she knew this feeling.

She pulled away quickly, and he could see the shock in her eyes.

"I think I'm going to—"

Before she could finish her sentence, she seized in his arms. He dropped her, clearly scared. He watched her as he stood up nervously.

"Oh God!" he screamed. He didn't have a phone, and Aella didn't have one either. "I'll get help! I promise!" He left her after.

* * *

"Your Honor, the evidence is staggering—"

Kaius was cut off when his phone rang. He cleared his throat and apologized. He continued his opening speech, but his phone rang again.

When he walked back over to his desk, he saw it was his brother calling. He ignored it. He would call him back later.

* * *

Alpha Superior threw the phone across his bedroom and watched as the screen shattered into shards. "Fuck."

Something was wrong. Every follicle in his body was on high alert. His stomach clenched, his muscles tightened, and his head swelled as his lycan grew increasingly anxious. If he were looking in the mirror, he would have seen his eyes brighten to a dangerous argent color.

He grabbed the landline in his room and called Celest.

She answered with her usual chirpy voice: "Alpha?"

"Where is Aella?"

"She should be home. What—"

"Something happened. Find her. Now, Celest."

Celest's body went taut. Alpha Superior may have been an ass, but he was a smart man. His senses were better than anyone else's, so if he said something was wrong, something was *wrong*.

She nodded, her phone tucked between her ear and shoulder as she ripped off her surgical gloves and gown.

"I'm at the hospital. I'll get home as soon as possible. In the meantime, I'll call Eveline to see what's going on. Bye, Superior." Celest ended the call, knowing the alpha wouldn't respond anyway. She called Aella's phone first but cursed when it went to voicemail.

She tried Eveline's phone.

"Hey, Ma. I'm at violin practice. What's up?"

"Hey, baby. Did Aella say she was going somewhere after school? Don't lie, Eveline. You won't be in trouble. I just need to know."

"No, she didn't say anything. Everything okay?"

"She's not picking up her phone. And Alpha Superior called," Celest whispered the last part.

"I'll meet you at home."

* * *

Kaius saw his mate's name pop up on his phone, so he asked for a recess from court. He was about to call her back when she called again.

"Celest?"

"Aella isn't at the house."

"What? It's four. Of course, she is."

"She's not. I'm here and Eveline is as well, but Aella is not. Something is wrong, Kaius."

"Calm down, Celest. I'm sure she is just studying somewhere—"

"Superior called. He knows something is wrong. You have to find her, Kaius."

Urgency rushed him. He nodded to himself, pulling the courtroom door open, then took his briefcase. "Stay in the house with Eveline."

The call ended.

His brother hardly talked to Celest and only called her when it was important.

Kaius wasted little time grabbing his belongings before racing outside. He had his car parked nearby, but he knew that he could smell Aella far better if he stayed outside. He was in the city, so he had to get closer to her school.

His breath was hardly labored when he arrived at the school. He could smell her scent from a certain direction, so he followed it.

By the time he reached the park, her scent was heavy. She was not there, but he could tell where she had been, judging by how thick her smell was. His phone rang again, and this time he didn't even check the caller ID.

"Hello, is this Aella's guardian?"

"Yes," he answered, jumping off the tree house and onto the ground.

"Hello, sir. Your daughter has been admitted to Saint Boulevard Hospital."

Kaius sighed in relief. "My wife and I will be there soon. Thank you so much."

He called his wife, and they met at the hospital.

They were immediately allowed to visit Aella, who had sustained a head injury from seizing.

"Oh my God, mija." Her mother ran into her room and immediately took her daughter in her arms, squeezing her.

"Ugh, Mama. I am okay."

Celest's tears fell on her daughter, and Aella sighed, hugging her mom. Aella realized that it probably terrified her parents when she didn't come home.

Eveline ran into her room and to the bed. "Jesus Christ, you scared us! Are you okay?"

Aella groaned. "I'm fine, everyone. I just had an episode. It's no big deal."

"Aella, you know you are supposed to go straight home after school."

"I know, Dad. I'm sorry. I didn't know—"

"You didn't think, Aella. You do not understand what could have happened!"

Her dad rarely yelled at her, so when he did, it affected her greatly. She was usually a good girl. She never sneaked out. She never had bad grades. And she never talked back to her parents. She tried to make them proud, especially her dad. It was obvious he preferred Eveline. They always went on secret trips together and had quiet conversations when they thought Aella wasn't paying attention.

"I-I know, Daddy. I just—"

"Just what? What were you doing at the park in the first place?"

"I was . . . I . . ." She didn't want to tell him. She didn't want to admit that a boy had a crush on her, and she wanted to spend time with him. She knew her father would flip.

Celest, seeing her daughter's discomfort, stepped in and put a hand on Kaius' shoulder. "Calm down, sweetie. It's alright."

Kaius gave Aella a stern look before leaving her room. Celest followed. It was instinctual for her to comfort her mate.

Eveline pulled a chair next to Aella's bed. She sighed. "What's going on? Why were you there?"

Aella sighed and looked at the corner. She told her sister everything, and Eveline told her most things.

"Alex asked to take me to the park."

"Oh my God! Hot Alex with the blue eyes?" Eveline's voice went up a few octaves as she spoke.

It was rare that Aella ever had juicy secrets or gossip to share.

"Did anything happen?"

Aella blushed and laughed nervously. "He put his hand on my thigh—"

"Oh my God!"

"And kissed me."

"Oh my God times two!"

"But as we were . . . you know . . . I had a seizure."

"Oh God! A hot guy wants to get in your pants and you fucking seize."

Aella blushed with a deep chuckle. "That's not—"

"Maybe it's not what you wanted, but it's what he wanted for sure."

"You're crazy."

CHAPTER SIX

Alpha Superior marched through the hospital. He wanted to be left unbothered. And he, again, didn't understand such a need to make sure the girl was alright. For days, he had sought anything to calm himself. He'd turned to work, physical exertion, and literature, but to no avail.

His brother mentioned the room and hospital she was at, so he was sure he could find her room, not to mention that her scent immediately struck him. She was on the third floor, room 323.

Kaius looked toward the door, sensing dominance that could only come from the alpha. He cleared his throat, wanting to warn his daughter of his brother's arrival.

"Aella?"

The girl shifted in her bed and looked at her father. "Yes?"

The alpha heard their conversation from outside her door. He didn't walk in, wanting to hear what Kaius had to say.

"He's coming to visit," her dad said.

"Who?" she responded. A beat passed before her black eyes lit up, and she sat up. "O-oh . . . when?"

The increase in her heart rate was intriguing to Kaius.

"Soon, Aella." He sighed, grabbing her hand. "You're excited to see him."

Aella didn't know what she should say. She nodded and looked away, embarrassed. "He never wrote me back."

"So that's it? You're excited because you get to have your questions answered?"

"Yeah, I guess."

Truth be told, she wasn't sure why she was excited to see him, but she figured the letters and recordings must have been why. It was then she noticed the handle of her door being twisted.

The door pushed open and revealed a man she hadn't seen in years. Still, all the familiar feelings resurfaced, and it was like she was the same girl infatuated with someone who didn't even want to visit her.

Her eyes widened as the dark-haired man appeared. She couldn't help but notice that he didn't look at her, just stared at Kaius, who held that steely gaze. It was clear they were having a silent discussion she wasn't supposed to participate in.

Kaius stood up. Surprisingly, he left her room. Aella looked at the man she called Atlas. It wasn't possible, but it looked as if darkness followed him, surrounding his robust form.

"H-hi," she greeted.

"Hello, girl."

She didn't say anything in response, but she watched as he took off his suit jacket and sat in the chair her father had been in. He had done the same the first time he visited her; he was a man of routine. He could make any room feel small.

"What happened?"

"I had a seizure and hit my head. I had to stay to get monitored for a concussion." She wasn't lying. She wasn't telling the complete truth, either.

There was a reason his wolf went haywire, but he didn't know why. He was certain of one thing, though: Aella was in danger.

"You were at the park. Why?"

"W-wanted to go and relax."

"You're lying."

"W-what? No, I'm not."

63

His eyes held disbelief. He was confident in his assumption. "You stutter when you lie."

"D-do not!"

He smirked at her. "Want to try again?"

She lay back down, giving up. "This guy took me there, and when we . . ." She stopped. "When he kissed me, I guess my emotions got the better of me. He went and got help, and that's how I was found."

His expression didn't change. Her admission was completely irrelevant to him.

He pulled his ankle on top of his knee. "Interesting."

She was going to die from embarrassment.

"You never wrote back." She fiddled with her hospital blanket.

He bit the desire to apologize. "There were developments in my . . . organization."

His nose wrinkled like he smelled something pungent. He stood up, finding his way to her book bag siting on the windowsill. He picked it up by the strap, investigating it. He brought it closer to his nose.

Strange.

"Developments?" she asked.

Her stomach growled low. He could hear it, his head tilting just slightly from the sound. Setting the bag down again, he reached into his coat pocket. He lofted a granola bar at her, which she caught easily.

She looked at what he'd tossed, her stomach growling again.

"You eat Chewy Chocolate Chip . . . granola bars?" She couldn't believe that such an imposing man would consume this type of snack. In fact, she could hardly imagine him snacking.

"Should I not?"

"I just . . ." She opened the snack. "I thought you'd eat raw eggs and, I don't know, spinach."

It was a joke—kinda.

If he had found her statement amusing, he didn't show it.

"I love these." She bit into the bar.

"Have any strange people spoken to you?"

She shrugged, her brows arching in surprise. "Besides you?"

"Funny." He rolled his eyes, and she smirked.

"No. If someone had, I would have told Mom or Dad. Why?"

He hummed, his finger pulling back the window shade. A second passed, and he walked to the bed, taking something out of his pocket. She realized, as he set it on the hospital table, it was a letter.

"I would like to stop making these hospital visits."

"Maybe you wouldn't have to visit me in the hospital if you came to visit more often."

He raised a brow. "Are you saying you would stop having seizures if I visited more often?"

She shrugged. "Maybe. Let's test the theory out." She looked up at him, a cheeky smile prying on her lips.

She could have sworn she saw an inkling of amusement in his eyes as he bowed his head before leaving.

Aella,

Perhaps I haven't been zealous in our efforts to finish it. My apologies. I was busy with work, and life became difficult. I've read War and Peace *multiple times. It's one of my favorite novels over the many, many years of my life.*

I'm sorry I missed your birthday. I hope this next present makes up for it.

To answer your question about Greek mythology, I studied it when I was much younger. It was fascinating to me just like it is to you.

> *My name is not of importance. The simple utterance of it reminds me of something that cannot exist. I prefer Atlas.*
>
> *As you can see, "complicated" is putting it lightly. Kaius is correct; our family is intrinsically complex. Most of our relatives live in Asia and Europe but, in recent years, have migrated all over South America and to some parts of the US. We have a large family.*
>
> *Aella—a whirlwind; a Greek Amazon who fought Hercules to protect her land.*
>
> *—Atlas*

Aella put the note down, smiling. She curled up into a ball and listened to his voice.

Kaius didn't understand it. In the hall, he waited for his brother to come out of the room. The alpha did so but never regarded him.

Kaius waited a moment before following Alpha Superior outside and onto the busy sidewalk. Celest and Eveline followed, standing to the side as the raven-haired men spoke.

It began to pour. Kaius had smelled it even before exiting the building. He felt the rain paint his shirt onto his skin. He watched as his alpha opened his town car door that was idling for him.

"What is going on?"

The alpha turned his head, looking at his brother. "I'm leaving."

"But why did you come? And how did you know she was in trouble?"

Alpha Superior shook his head, annoyed. He rested his hands on the car door. "I don't know."

"What do you mean you don't know?" Kaius dashed toward his brother with his hands in his pockets. "She's my daughter."

"I recognize that, Kaius. Why are you so angry?"

"I don't understand why you now suddenly care about my human family. You never have before. Something's gotten into you, and I want to know what it is."

The rain thickened. Kaius' blue dress shirt stuck to his chest and discolored. The alpha's suit jacket protected his white button-up. If it hadn't been for the hair that was sticking to his face, no one would have known he was drenched.

"He's back, Kaius. I loathe him more than I dislike your human counterparts. They are involved with us; they are targets. I will protect them no matter what."

Before Kaius could respond, the fire alarm inside the hospital blared. The lycans looked back at the building as humans ran outside for safety. A woman bumped into Celest, making her fall to the ground.

Eveline helped her mother up before Kaius could do so. "Are you okay, Mom?"

Celest smiled and nodded. Kaius ushered her and his daughter to the side, away from the stampede.

"Where's the child?" Alpha Superior asked, towering over the humans who were running out of the building. Then, as he smelled the same scent from the wreckage in Romania, it dawned on him.

He pushed through the crowd and went back to the hospital.

He bounded up the stairs and to the third floor, where Aella was. The hefty smoke almost suffocated him, but he couldn't see flames. He knew from the heat that they were close to him.

He didn't understand why the entire building was engulfed in flames so quickly. The sound of the fire alarm made his brain vibrate. It was a curse in this situation to have such a heightened sense of hearing. His one sense overwhelmed his other senses.

"Help!"

He stilled from her scream. With a new focus, he went to her room and saw Aella. She was handcuffed to the bed, pulling against the restraint and cutting herself deeply in the process. Her curly dark hair was out of her hair tie and down her back, frizzing from the heat.

When she saw him at the door, she cried harder. "I-I don't know what happened! I got really tired suddenly, and when I woke up, I was cuffed to the bed."

"Stop crying."

"W-what?"

"I said stop crying." He looked her in the eye and grabbed the chain of the shackle.

With one firm grasp, he ripped it off the post. He grabbed her by her upper arms and pulled her to the door. Even before he touched it, he knew the only thing that would greet them was flames. He growled, no longer hiding his animalistic side.

He bent down, grabbed her legs, and threw her on his shoulder before going to the window. He smashed it with one hand and leaped out, landing on the roof of the building beside them.

He set her on her feet but gripped her hand and dragged her down the stairs and outside the front door.

Aella's family was waiting for them, but she didn't have time to say anything as she was ushered into the car. Alpha Superior sat beside her and took her shaky hands. Tears streamed down her brown skin, her mind racing with everything that had happened.

"Y-you . . . you tore the chain l-like it was p-paper."

The alpha didn't respond as he broke the cuff around her wrist and inspected her wound that was profusely bleeding. Her blood pooled on his lap.

"Aella, you have to calm down," Celest said softly, touching her shoulder.

Aella shrugged her hand off and looked at her mother with blazing anger. "How can you say that? I was just shackled to a bed while the building was on fire. Someone tried to—" she shuttered, a rough cry leaving her chest. "He jumped onto a roof like it was nothing. What are you?"

"You have to stay calm, or you will have an episode," Celest explained with a calm, soothing voice.

Aella winced as the alpha wrapped her wrist with his suit jacket.

Celest inspected the cuff wound. "She needs to get this looked at and bandaged if the bleeding continues like this," Celest swallowed.

Kaius nodded at his brother.

Alpha Superior handed his phone to him. "Call Elena."

"She's here in the States?"

Alpha Superior nodded, still looking at Aella's injury.

Aella suddenly felt woozy, watching as the buildings blurred from the car window. "I don't feel well," she whispered.

Her eyes instantly fluttered shut, her body falling limp in his arms.

* * *

"We need to tell her, Kaius."

"She's a child! We can make up a story."

"She saw me. She is already suspicious. She won't take a story." The alpha's eyes glanced down the hall and to her room. He could hear her shift in her bed. "Enough, she's awake."

Eveline stood up and went to the door but stopped for a moment. She turned to her father and uncle.

"I don't want to keep secrets from her. She's part of this family, and she deserves to know everything. We all do. We aren't human, Dad. She needs to know that." Eveline opened the door and walked down the hall to Aella's room.

Aella heard her sister gently say her name. She sat up slowly and looked around. Her wrist was wrapped with gauze, but she didn't remember how she ended up on the bed. All she could remember was waking up cuffed to the hospital bed. She winced as daggers shot through her head.

Eveline sat next to her on the bed, and Aella smiled.

"How you feeling?"

Aella shrugged. She was never the type of person who complained. "I'm a little sore but alright."

Eveline raised an eyebrow. She knew that if Aella remembered anything, she would have said something. She leaned forward onto the bed and played with Aella's hair.

"Where are we?"

Eveline ran her tongue over her bottom lip and took a breath. She pulled her hand away from Aella's head and tapped her finger on her sister's hand. She was trying to figure out what to say, knowing very well that Aella would ask more questions the longer she was up.

"Our uncle was pretty worried about you. He bought this house."

"Today?" Aella asked.

Eveline grinned, shrugging. "Well, yesterday."

Aella winced as memories came flooding back. She brought her hands to her head, rubbing her temples to relieve the pressure. Flashes of Atlas flooded her. She remembered everything, and when she looked at Eveline, she gulped.

Eveline could hear the increase in her sister's heart rate. "You remember."

Before Aella could say anything, her parents along with Atlas walked into the room. Her mother and father came close to her while Atlas remained by the foot of the bed. Her eyes met his, and she swallowed.

"H-how are you not hurt? You j-jumped—" Instinctually, she shuffled up her bed, farther away from him.

"You must calm down," Atlas said. "We will explain everything." He looked at Eveline. "Take her outside. Explain it to her."

"Explain what exactly?" Eveline asked, and he looked at her and then back at Aella.

With his arms crossed, he replied, "Everything." He turned away and walked out of the door.

Eveline stood up and handed Aella her jacket and shoes. "Come. Let's go get some air."

And the two went outside.

Eveline closed her eyes, her nose pointing to the sky, smelling the trees. The house Alpha Superior bought was secluded for the most part, with a long driveway leading to the front door. He would be free there, and so would Eveline. She could shift if she wanted, jump from tree to tree, and even howl whenever her heart desired. She liked this. She had been forced for so long to act as human as possible. It wasn't hard for her, but sometimes she just wanted to allow her primal side to be free.

Aella turned to her sister and raised an eyebrow. "You've always enjoyed the outdoors."

Eveline opened her eyes and nodded with a soft smile. She looked at her sister, stuffing her hands into her pockets. Aella stood a few feet in front of her, enjoying the sounds of the trees swaying in the wind.

"Do you remember when we were children and we went behind the house? We played princesses, and I told you about Alpha."

Aella laughed, raising an amused eyebrow. "Alpha?"

Eveline smiled. "Yes. Alpha, our uncle . . . Atlas. Whatever you want to call him."

Aella snorted. "Why call him Alpha?"

It seemed as if the sun danced on Eveline's skin. Shrouded in sunlight, she was radiant. If Aella had always been the dreamer, Eveline was the doer—ever persistent, ever sparkling, and ever bright.

Eveline went quiet again, walking closer behind her sister. She rubbed her arm, clearly a self-soothing act. She wasn't sure how Aella would handle it all. Even Eveline struggled when she first found out.

"Do you like . . . ? Well, you see . . ."

Aella laughed softly. "You're nervous. Why?"

"Look, Aella." Eveline grabbed Aella's lower arm, seeing that she was becoming distracted by how the trees swayed. "Aella, look at me. Pay attention, please." She swallowed the nervousness that filled her throat. "Our family is complicated."

"Yes, I know—"

"Different. I mean *different*. You saw what Atlas did. He's different. I'm different. Dad's different."

"Different how?" Aella took a step back, hesitance creeping up her spine.

"We call Uncle 'Alpha' because he is an alpha. Alphas are the leaders of packs."

"Packs . . . like wolves? You're being crazy."

Eveline groaned. She let go of her sister. Her hand hesitantly went to her eyes, and with two fingers, she slipped out her contacts. Her bright eyes blinked at Aella. They were a stark sterling, bright—so bright that they almost blended in with her whites.

Aella took a step back, not understanding what just happened. She and her sister were always close to each other. They rarely had secrets. Why would she lie about something as trivial as her eye color?

"I can smell when it's about to rain. I can hear things from miles away. I am stronger, faster, and more agile than average people, and it's because I am different."

"But what does that mean?" Aella asked, her back hitting against the nearest tree. She was scared.

It was so unusual because her sister was always a safe haven for her. When she couldn't tell her mom or dad something, she could always rely on her happy sister.

"Please, you have to understand that I'm me. I am always me."

Before Aella could say anything, Eveline took off her shirt, shoes, and pants. Her chest heaved, then her bones seemed to break. She morphed into something Aella could only imagine.

The wolf stood in front of Aella, blowing air out of its nose.

Aella screamed and backed away, tripping over a root of a tree, and fell on her butt with a thud. She tried to scurry away, afraid that the wolf might attack her at any moment. She didn't understand. It was like her brain couldn't fathom the fact that she saw her sister change into a beast.

"S-stay away."

The wolf cocked its head to the side as if saying that if it hadn't moved at all, why would it move now?

After a few moments of practically nothing, Aella let the tension in her shoulders ease up somewhat. She crawled forward, hesitantly.

"Eveline?"

The wolf huffed and lifted its paw, hitting the ground.

Aella used the tree as a crutch to stand up. Her heart raced in her chest, and she found it difficult to breathe. Her breathing couldn't even out.

Eveline whined softly, knowing that if Aella got too emotional, she would have a seizure.

Aella focused on her surroundings and made sure she calmed down. She nodded once and coughed into her hand, breathing somewhat normally.

"Okay, okay," she said to herself. "My sister just shifted into an animal. That's okay, I guess. That's fine." She glanced at the wolf again and freaked out, hugging herself. "This is so weird. What the fuck? What the fuck!"

She paced for a moment. Then, she walked toward the wolf, sticking out her hand. It lovingly rubbed its head against her hand and purred softly.

Aella smiled. "O-okay," she whispered. "I'm okay." She pulled her hand back and walked past the wolf slowly, causing it to whine again.

She turned back. "You just told me our family is a bunch of wolves."

Eveline followed her into the house.

* * *

The older sister watched as Aella paced in the living room.

"Dad! Mom! Oh family of wolves, please, do me the honor of meeting me!"

Her father walked in first, followed by her mother, then her uncle—who ungraciously acted bored amid the entire situation.

Aella was biting her nails, still pacing. "O-okay, so let me get this straight. Twilight is real?"

"Not exactly, sweetie," Celest said with a sweet chuckle.

"Y-yeah I know. I-I just mean werewolves are real—"

Alpha Superior rolled his eyes, sighing. "Derogatory label humans gave us. We are lycans or shifters."

"O-okay," she responded, stuttering again. "S-sorry. So . . . all of you are like Eveline?"

"I'm not, sweetie. I'm human like you. Your dad, he's my mate."

"Mate?"

Celest walked closer to Aella. She took her hands and sat on the coffee table in front of her. "Mate is short for soulmate. You see, every lycan is born with a destined mate. Usually, they are also lycan, but I was the first known human who was paired with a wolf for a mate. It means that your father and I are soulmates."

"It's true love," Aella said.

Celest nodded. "Exactly."

Aella went quiet as she thought about it all in her head. She looked at Eveline—still in her wolf form—then at Atlas, who was carelessly watching the scene.

"You're Alpha, I'm guessing."

He nodded once. "How did you know?"

"You mean . . . besides the desire to cower away from you? Uh, Eveline called you that. S-so every pack has a beta also, so who is—"

"I'm the beta," Kaius interjected.

"O-oh." Aella looked over at Eveline, who hadn't transitioned back.

Aella felt overwhelmed, but she could accept this. She could learn to make this her new normal. Her family was still her family. It was shitty of them to lie to her, but she could understand the desire to keep her life as normal as possible. What was the alternative? Freak out and have her family never tell her anything regarding their species again? No, she refused. So, she nodded to herself, looked over at the wolf who hadn't shifted back, and gave a shaky smile.

"Can I pet you?" She grinned.

The wolf growled.

"Oh, come on! You've kept a family secret from me for years!"

The wolf huffed and lay down in front of the table, at Celest's feet.

Aella happily bent down and ran her hand down the wolf's back. "You're cuter as a wolf," she teased.

This was nowhere near normal. Her heart still beat a thousand miles a minute. Her mind couldn't wrap around the entire ordeal, but she knew she loved her family and that they would never hurt her.

It was strange, yes, but she'd read about this in all sorts of books. It would be ironic for her to freak out when she had dreamed about something happening like this for so long.

CHAPTER SEVEN

Celest insisted that Aella get back to sleep, and Aella acquiesced to the demand. She lay down in bed, her family surrounding her. She had so many questions, but she stifled them. Sleep seemed so much more important.

"Ask them," Alpha Superior encouraged. "I know you have questions." He sat the farthest from her, a book in his hands. His dress shirt sleeves were rolled up to his elbows, his top buttons undone.

Aella caught herself staring. She cleared her throat and looked away, her eyes on her sister.

"W-what happened at the hospital?" Her throat was so dry.

"My past is catching up with me," was all he said.

"Our past," Kaius corrected.

"What does that mean?" She looked at her father.

"The person who attacked you . . . his name is Ansan. He has a vendetta against me."

"Why?"

Atlas shrugged and then rose from his chair.

"This is a lot for you," he said. "You're taking it well."

She gave him a worn-out smile. "I wish you had told me. I'm hurt that all of you hid such an important part of your lives." She flattened out the duvet on top of her, yawning. "Are the books true?"

Kaius grinned from the end of the bed. "What parts?"

"Are you guys immortal?" she joked with a dismissive chuckle. Her laughter died instantaneously as she noticed Kaius and Atlas sharing a bemused look.

"Not exactly," Kaius answered.

"W-wait." Aella sat straighter and looked between her father and Atlas. "You were both born in the twentieth century, right? Please say right because I might go crazy."

"I was born in 1615."

She gawked at her father. "If you say BC, I'll lose it."

Kaius gave her a fatherly grin. "No, Aella, AD. Alpha was born a few years before me."

She ran her fingers through her locks in anxiousness. "This is crazy. This is crazy!"

She could tell that her entire family was amused by her reaction, but she was so overwhelmed. Her breathing became shallow, her hands gripping her blanket to steady herself.

Her sister noticed her discomfort.

Eveline sighed. "I think Aella needs some rest. And I think I need food. Anyone else?"

Celest and Kaius huffed an agreement, following Eveline out of the bedroom. Atlas was the last to leave.

* * *

Aella rested her head on her arms as she watched her father and Atlas work behind the desk. Her mom and Eveline were busy playing chess in the corner, clearly uninterested in whatever the men were doing. She, however, was fascinated. She wondered what they were signing and why they were signing it.

"So," she began, her eyes landing on her father, "how does it work?"

"How does what work?" Atlas murmured, not looking at her.

"The whole part-human, part-wolf thing? There has to be a dominant and a submissive personality, so which is which?"

"We share one body," her father stated. "We are one wolf and one human. Neither is submissive, just like neither is dominant. We can choose which part of us we want to focus on at any given moment."

"So, you never . . . wolf out?"

Atlas finally looked up from his papers.

She blushed with embarrassment as the two stared at her like she was silly.

"Wolf out?" Atlas asked.

"Like . . . I don't know. When your wolf side takes over your humanity?"

"Why do you assume humanity is better than inhumanity?"

She stayed silent.

"If you ask me, humans have proven to be the most inhumane of all the species. Genocides, mass extinction, disrespect for the land on which they live . . ."

"I'm sorry I didn't—"

"You're associating inhumanity with cruelty. Yes, we protect what is ours. Yes, we fight to claim ranks within the pack. But that isn't cruel to us; it's natural. Perhaps lycanthropes are more 'human' than humans themselves?"

It knocked the wind out of her. She was speechless as she looked into his deep bright-blue eyes. She began to fiddle with her shirt. She didn't mean to offend him.

"I'm sorry," she whispered. She could feel her face heat up from embarrassment.

Atlas didn't understand why he felt such a need to make her feel better again. "It's not your fault."

Kaius almost broke his neck from looking at his brother so quickly. His brother never apologized, and he never put the blame on himself.

"You're inquisitive. Ask whatever you want. I will try to answer nicer."

Aella bit her lip, looking up at him. She gulped, her eyes dropping to her hands for a brief second. "Mom said every lycan has a mate. I was wondering who your mate was?"

The atmosphere in the room immediately intensified. She could feel the tension building up as her father looked at Atlas. She could tell by the slight pout on his lips that the question was a tough one to answer.

Kaius knew he wouldn't want to answer her question. "Aella—"

"They don't exist."

She swallowed from the response. Her heart fell into her stomach. "W-what?"

"When I became a lycan, I was told I would never have a mate, for I am the first of the species."

As they shared a hard stare, she realized it wasn't anger that filled his eyes but a pain of desolation. She couldn't imagine what it would be like to watch as everyone around him fell in love and had children, and him knowing that he could never have what they had.

Atlas looked away, stuffing a folder under his arm. He straightened out some papers before leaving his office. His back disappeared into the hallway, and she knew she shouldn't have asked such a question. Looking at her father, she could tell he was frustrated by what just happened.

"I'm sorry." She was starting to hate the phrase.

"He's a very complicated person."

She sat and put her head down, contemplating her next moves. She felt like the world around her was as fragile as glass. Every question she asked was wrong, and everything she did caused problems. Every part of her world was changing, and she didn't know how to navigate it.

* * *

Aella walked down the hall of the house as her mother called her name from downstairs. They were going back home. She passed his office and noticed the door was slightly ajar. She wriggled her hands in anxiousness before gently knocking on the hardwood door.

"Come."

She knew it wasn't English, and she wasn't sure what he said, so she just waited outside.

English came easily to him. He was young when he learned it. Still, he preferred his native tongue. He made a mental note to teach Aella simple Romanian phrases.

"Come," he repeated in English. He could see her hesitantly dip her head into his office, clearly unsure of his reaction of seeing her.

He watched as she nervously slid inside before pushing her back against the door. Her hand fidgeted with the doorknob, her reluctant brown eyes gazing at him.

"I wanted to apologize. I didn't mean to . . ." Her sentence fizzled out. She tried again: "I was just confused because I was told every lycan has a mate, but I didn't see a woman come with you, so I wasn't sure if you had found her yet or maybe it was a guy, hey I don't discriminate, love is love you know? I'm rambling. I know I am, but I can't stop. So this house?"

His expression didn't change. "Was that sentence?"

"Definitely a run-on," she said with a small chuckle.

If he were a better man, he would have chuckled.

He closed the book in his hands. "Your question was valid. I am not angry with you. And in regard to this house, yes, I bought it. I will need it when I am staying here."

Her eyes widened. "Y-you're staying?"

He nodded.

"Why? I-I mean, don't you have work?"

He nodded again. "You and your mother need protection Kaius is unable to provide by himself."

"O-oh, well, will your pack be okay? Without you?"

He gave another nod.

She realized he was probably much more introverted than her, or maybe he just didn't find the conversation interesting. She was in a way the same, but she could be quite loquacious when agitated.

After several awkward seconds, she delved into the small satchel on her side. She took out an envelope and laid it on his desk beside him.

She left shortly after that.

Once he heard the door of his new home shut, he played the recording. It left off right where they had stopped. She also had another note for him. Her handwriting had gotten significantly better within the few years.

Atlas,

You're a few centuries old, which explains how you had the time to read War and Peace *so many times. Now, it seems like we don't have to finish it, considering that you've read it already.*

Thank you for the birthday wishes. When is yours?

I have to admit, all of the new information is . . . insane to me, but part of me is glad that fairy tales are real. Do vampires exist? What about wizards, and pixies? What does being an alpha exactly entail? And how good is my dad's hearing?

You said you were cursed . . . why you?

— Aella

* * *

Aella stuffed her books in her locker as the bell rang through the hall. She suddenly felt a tap on her shoulder, making her jump. When she turned, she smiled with a deep red on her cheeks.

"Hey, Alex."

"Hey, Aella. I just wanted to see how you were doing."

"I'm okay." She pushed a strand of hair behind her ear. "I have epilepsy and had an episode. I wanted to apologize. I bet that was scary for you, but thank you for getting help and not leaving me until the ambulance arrived. I suppose it kind of turned you off from hanging out with me, huh?"

He smiled boyishly as he shook his head. "Actually, no. In fact, I was wondering if you wanted to go to the park again after school tomorrow, as a date."

She tried to contain her excitement, but the smile on her face was a dead giveaway. "S-sure."

"Awesome," he said. "Hey, I got basketball practice. I'll see you later, alright?"

Aella nodded as he walked away. She leaned against her locker with a soft sigh. Boys never seemed interested in her, especially the cute ones, so it was a nice change to be the focus of someone's attention.

Eveline jumped to her side with a knowing grin.

"Hey, *chica*. What's with the blush?"

Aella walked past her sister. She couldn't wait to tell her what happened. "Alex asked me out."

Eveline gasped and hit her softly. "No way! Again? He's so cute! When? Where? Give me details."

Aella couldn't stop her laughter as they neared her sister's car. They both got in when Eveline looked at her, wiggling her eyebrows.

"Now you gotta tell Mom and Dad."

"Do I have to? Dad will freak." She groaned as she put her seat belt on.

Eveline shrugged. "Oh definitely, but you gotta. He'll find out as soon as you come home."

"What if I lie?"

Eveline feigned shock. "You're telling me that my sister, my angel of a sister, is thinking about lying to her father?" She laughed, then her expression sobered. "It wouldn't work regardless."

"Why?"

"You do realize your father is a lycan, right? Did the whole 'heightened senses' thing not make sense to you? Dad will smell him on you as soon as you walk through the door."

She groaned in frustration. Eveline was right.

Aella looked out the window as her sister drove them home.

* * *

They pulled into their driveway. Eveline froze as soon as she shut her car door. Aella, seeing her discomfort, looked strangely at her.

"What's wrong?"

Eveline looked at her with clear disgust. "Nothing. You know what? Why don't we go get some ice cream?"

"Why?"

"We can't go into that house." Eveline slid back into the car.

Aella got back in as well, and suddenly it dawned on her.

"Oh God! They're doing it, aren't they?"

Eveline didn't answer as she pulled out of the driveway.

"You can hear them? What happens if you're sleeping or something?"

"Let's just say they never ever do it with me in the house."

"But me?"

"You can't hear," she said with a grin.

"It's the principle! Oh God, gross!"

"Yeah. You're not the one who hears everything. Everything, Aella."

Both shivered in disgust and dropped the topic the farther they drove away from their home.

After an hour, they returned and walked through the living room as quickly as possible.

"Hey, girls," Celest greeted, and both kept their heads down and said hi back. "How was school?"

"Fine. Gotta study." Eveline ran up the stairs with speed that Aella had never seen before.

Aella cursed under her breath when she realized her sister abandoned her, leaving her with her mom and dad downstairs.

"Aella? Everything okay?" Kaius asked.

Aella crinkled her nose and nodded, keeping her eyes down. "Yeah, I gotta study too. Bye!"

As she passed Eveline's room, she glared at the door and then she went to her own room. Shutting the door, she sighed. She dropped herself onto her bed. She smiled when she saw an envelope on her desk. She knew it had a letter and recording in it, and excitement buzzed through her. It had been a few weeks since she had seen Atlas.

She jumped up off her bed and went to her white desk to pick up the envelope. To her happiness, she brought it to her chest and sighed softly. She hid it under her shirt as she walked down the hall and to her sister's room.

She knocked once, and the door flung open.

"Oh good, you escaped."

"No help from you," Aella whined, walking in. She shut the door behind her. She played with her hands and lowered her voice as she spoke, "Do you think he can hear us?"

"Dad?" Eveline asked.

She nodded.

Eveline nodded and grabbed Aella's wrist, pulling her out of the room. They went to the bathroom and turned on the shower and the sink faucet.

"You should be good now. What's up?"

Aella pulled the envelope out of her shirt and sat on the floor. "I want to play it, but Dad always gets weird about Atlas."

"Why do you call him that?" Eveline sat beside her against the tub.

"He seems like an Atlas, doesn't he?"

Eveline just sighed as his voice filled her ears.

Aella's love for literature was so strange to her, but she liked that her sister had someone to talk to about it. She watched as Aella's eyes zipped through the letter and then closed as she listened to his voice as if he was the only one she focused on.

It seemed as if . . . Nah. It's impossible.

Eveline shook the thought away.

Aella,

To be frank, I do not remember the day or the month of my birth. I do not know exactly how old I am. All I know is that your father is younger than me. Birthdays are unimportant to me. However, yours is a different case. Each year you grow older, smarter, and bigger; each year, you get close to the inevitable. Your birthday is important because your days here are numbered. Your father's lifespan—if his mate weren't human—would last centuries longer. When one mate dies, the other does as well, so when your mother passes on, so will your father.

I have read the book many more times than I remember. It's been years since the last time, so it's fine to continue it. After all, you do have to read it.

You have taken everything we told you really well. It makes me wonder just how wild your imagination is.

> *Vampires are very few and far, but they do exist in small numbers. Wizards do not exist, although some have unusual powers. Pixies do not exist, either. But faes do.*
>
> *Your father, Eveline, and I can hear a sound of a tree falling from miles away if we focus, so your father has very good hearing. Why do you ask?*
>
> *An alpha is a pack leader. We are responsible for the protection, financial advisement, and security of all pack members. There are many alphas and lunas in the world, many of whom organize their pack however they wish. Honestly, it's a tedious job; one might think it to be boring.*
>
> *I'm considered the oldest lycan because when my species was first created, I was chosen by the Goddess Artemis as their protector. It's a long story.*
>
> *– Atlas*

She exited the bathroom and got ready for bed.

She could see the moonlight streaming in from outside. She relaxed into her covers and stared at the desk that held all his notes.

Aella smiled to herself.

CHAPTER EIGHT

Aella awoke to a tapping noise on her window. She yawned into her palm and got out of bed. She opened the window and looked down. Seeing nothing, she sighed and shut it. But as soon as she did, she caught sight of Atlas. She jumped, looking at his reflection in the glass.

"Atlas," she whispered breathlessly.

He didn't say anything as he stepped forward. His eyes were cast down, but she knew they held so much pain, and it made her heart break. He placed his hand on her hip, pulling her flushed against his chest.

She swallowed nervously. His grip was harsh, but she liked it. She liked how dominant he was. It made her feel something. He was taller than her by many inches, so she could easily rest her head on his chest.

All other thoughts about her feelings and her family dissipated when he raised her shirt, his fingers touching her bare skin.

A painful expression crossed his face as he looked at her reflection.

"Come," he said, almost too quietly. "Let me read to you."

She did not attempt to hide her reaction from him. She felt something she'd never felt before, and it piqued her curiosity. She nodded, regretting she'd responded as he pulled away and went to the side of her bed.

She lay down. He kneeled beside the bed, his calloused hand on her stomach. His eyes, she realized, were no longer blue. Staring back at her were bright sterling-silver eyes. It surprised her, but it did not startle her because he felt safe.

His eyes left hers and shifted to the book in his free hand. He started reading—quietly, hoarsely—and his voice lulled her into deep relaxation.

After what felt like a minute, he stopped, and that voice of his morphed into a blaring alarm.

The dream vanished as soon as Aella opened her eyes. She grabbed her phone and turned off her alarm, feeling two simultaneous emotions she couldn't yet wade through at that moment.

"Oh God!" She cringed into her hands. "What is wrong with me?" She sat up and ran a hand through her dark hair, feeling frustrated. She looked toward the door, seeing her sister run past.

"Aella, hurry up. We are gonna be late for school!"

"C-coming!"

She groaned with a palm over her eyes as she realized how terribly she phrased her response.

*   *   *

Alex found her in class and asked about their date, but Aella felt weird. It felt wrong to go out with him after fantasizing about someone else, let alone her father's alpha. So she told him that her mom wouldn't let her go out because of the impending storm, and Alex was understanding.

They sat next to each other for the rest of class.

She didn't know how to feel. She'd never had a dream like that before, and even if she had, it couldn't have been about him. Aella felt so gross. Her hormones were going crazy, and she didn't understand why.

Maybe it was just a fluke. Maybe it wasn't gross. It wasn't like she could choose what she dreamed about. But it scared her because it wasn't just the dream that made her feel sick but also the fact that she enjoyed it and wanted to have another.

She came home late at night and finished her homework in her room. Eveline knocked once before walking in.

"Hey."

Aella smiled and put her pen down. "Hey, what's up?"

Eveline grabbed Aella's notebook and pen and wrote down something for her to see.

Dad is down the hall.

Aella just nodded and wrote back, What's up?

What's going on? What happened to your date?

Aella bit the inside of her cheek. She didn't want to tell the truth, so she wrote, I got scared.

Understandable. I just wanted to make sure you're okay.

"Thanks. I really do appreciate you. I'm okay . . . just got cold feet." Aella sat up. "I've been thinking about what Mom said about Dad. Do you think about your mate sometimes? I think I would be excited knowing I had someone meant for me."

Her sister sat on her bed and nodded enthusiastically. "I think about them all the time."

"Do same-sex mates exist?"

"Yes, of course. They may be less common, but we can't choose who we are destined for. They're actually a really important part of our world as they adopt many pups whose parents already died."

"Pups?"

Eveline chuckled. "Babies. Children."

"Oh, that makes sense," Aella said, embarrassed. "What happens once you meet them?"

Eveline fell quiet, and Aella knew the importance of the topic.

"If they have a higher rank than me," Eveline finally spoke, "I will follow them to their pack. If they have a lower rank, then they will come to this pack. We'd get a home"—she smiled to herself as she thought about her future—"have pups, and be happy for centuries. I'd finish school, run the pack, and teach my children how to be beta. One day . . ." she trailed off dreamily, shrugging.

"Beautiful."

"It really is. And I am very excited to experience it, but I'm in no rush. When I find them, I find them. Hey, do you want ice cream? We can still talk more, but I want something sweet."

* * *

Eveline sat on the counter, eating butter pecan ice cream. Aella was standing, having cookies and cream. Their parents were at the table, talking about something Aella and Eveline didn't care about.

"So, I'm assuming, because you have destined mates, your species pop out babies quickly, right? Or pups, like you said."

Eveline chuckled. "Usually, yes, unless a couple doesn't want pups."

"So you meet your mate, fall instantly in love, then what? Marriage?"

"We don't marry. Once we meet, we mate."

"So you and your mate will mate?"

Kaius sputtered into his hand, clearly angered by what she said.

Eveline blushed, grabbing her sister's hand. "You're killing me, sis."

"Why? What's mating?"

Eveline stared at Aella for a long moment before it clicked in her head.

"O-oh. Sorry. I didn't know. But why call it mating? It's just sex?"

"It's more than that," Eveline explained. "It's so much more. It's . . . it's so difficult to explain. Mating means you solidify the bond. It means you get marked by your mate."

"Marked? Like in the books?"

"What do your books say?"

"A mark is given by the male to the female to show others they are mated."

Eveline nodded. "Yes, except both mates may mark each other, if they are lycans. Mom could never mark Dad; her teeth aren't sharp enough."

"Wait, wait, wait. You're telling me a grown-ass wolf-man comes at you with big ass canine fangs, and you're just supposed to . . . accept it?"

Eveline and Celest laughed. "Yes, Aella, but when you have a mate, you want them to mark you."

"I'm sorry. I just don't understand how! Well, what happens if you don't want your mate?"

"It's rare. And in all known cases, both mates always accept each other. But if a wolf doesn't accept his mate, I guess eventually the female's heat will come."

At this point, Kaius must have gotten sick of the conversation because he got up, kissed Celest, then left.

Aella focused on her sister. "Heat?"

"It's a phenomenon that happens to force the mating to occur. Usually, heats only happen after the first mating to increase the chance of pups, but if a lot of time has passed without mating, it happens."

"So a heat is like a period?"

"Kinda, but way worse for most. Periods and heats usually happen at the same time for females."

"Then why call a period a heat? What's the difference?"

Celest stood and walked to her daughters, leaning against the counter next to Aella. "Because a heat causes the female to feel hot until they become physically ill. The pheromones they release are like a drug to their mates."

"Oh, I understand."

"Do you?"

Aella looked at her mother, then shook her head with a chuckle. "It's so confusing!"

* * *

She didn't write back to him. She didn't know how she could, knowing very well she'd had a dream about him. She wasn't sure how she felt toward him. Maybe she was just fascinated by him. Maybe it was just a crush that would eventually go away. Either way, she didn't want to focus on it.

As she sat at her desk in her room, scrolling through her Facebook feed, she saw a post about Atlas. He was on a list of "The Top Twenty Most Eligible Bachelors." She looked behind her to make sure her door was shut before clicking on the article. His picture popped up on the screen as number three. He wasn't smiling. He was fixing his cuff link with a particularly icy gaze toward the camera. The article didn't say his name, but it mentioned his business ventures and successes.

"Aella?"

She quickly shut her laptop and turned around, completely unsuspicious. She coughed into her hand and stood up quickly, fidgeting a little.

"Uh, h-hey, what's going on . . . pal?"

Eveline lifted her eyebrow in suspicion and leaned against the doorframe with her arms crossed.

"Pal?" She waved the question away. "Never mind. Let's forget your weirdness. Can you read this essay and give me feedback? You're better at English than I am."

Aella nodded.

Eveline was always better at math and sciences while Aella was better at humanities subjects. So when either of them needed help, they would go to their sister. They preferred each other to their parents as they didn't like disappointing them.

Eveline handed the papers to Aella.

Aella grabbed them and jumped onto her bed, lying on her stomach. "Shit, I need a—"

Eveline grinned and suddenly appeared right next to her with a yellow highlighter and a blue-inked pen.

Aella chuckled. "It's not fair." She blew her hair out of her face. "Why do you get super speed?"

"Oh, shut up. You're smarter than me." Eveline sat next to her sister and waited as Aella went through the essay, marking it with verb-subject corrections, tone commentaries, and other important fixes that should be considered.

Aella finished and sat up, handing the papers back timidly. She bit the pen apprehensively while looking at Eveline.

"You're graduating this year."

Eveline chuckled. "Yeah, I am."

"Are you excited? Do you know which college you are going to?"

Eveline shrugged. "I have some options. So, we shall see."

There was silence.

"I wanted to talk to you about something," said Eveline.

"What's up?"

"You know how Dad is a beta, right?"

Aella nodded, listening carefully.

"It's a very high rank in the pack, and as his daughter, I must make a public appearance after my eighteenth birthday."

"You mean because you're like Dad . . . so I won't have to, right? Because I'm human?"

Eveline sighed, instantly feeling so guilty. "I'm sorry, Aella. Our pack isn't exactly accepting of new ideals and customs."

"It's fine, Eveline. So they're throwing a party for you?"

"Yes."

"Alright, I'll just stay in the background."

Eveline looked at her with an even bigger guilty expression.

"What, Ev?"

"You aren't allowed to go. If the pack knew a human was attending, you would be relentlessly ridiculed. Mom barely gets to go, and the only reason she may is that she's Dad's mate. When I get into power, I promise you I'll fix it."

Aella could feel the tears all up in her eyes and her face heating up. She knew it wasn't Eveline's choice.

"I won't be alive by then."

Aella regretted saying it as soon as it spilled from her lips.

Eveline's face dropped, and Aella could see her taking a step back.

"That's not . . . I didn't . . ." She sighed and pulled Eveline into her chest. She knew it wasn't anything personal from Ev's end. She also knew Eveline was probably the one who wanted to tell her.

She pulled away after a few moments, mustering a smile that reached her eyes. "It's alright. Really, it's no big deal. I hate socializing anyway."

Eveline looked hesitant to respond.

"It's at Alpha's house," she spoke. "But you have to keep your phone on with you because I'm going to be texting you like crazy."

"When is it?"

"Next weekend."

Eveline left shortly after.

Aella looked at her laptop, taking a deep breath. She'd always told herself and others that she hated socializing, saying she disliked having to greet and be nice to people even if they weren't the nicest to her. The truth was that she was always nice and rarely disliked someone. She told such a lie because it was harder to admit that she was terrified of social ostracism and afraid that people would hurt her. It was easier to say it was a choice rather than a deep-rooted insecurity.

* * *

The week came and passed. Her father and Eveline left early in the afternoon to go to their alpha's house while she and her mother stayed at home. But Celest would be attending later because Kaius would become agitated by not having his mate. Celest had insisted she spend the day with Aella, knowing very well how it felt not to be invited to such an event. She knew how it felt not to be accepted.

Celest gently knocked on the open door.

Aella smiled at her. "Heading out?"

Celest nodded. She was in a long black dress, her curly hair cascading down her shoulders. She looked beautiful.

Aella stood from the bed and hugged her. "I love you, Mom."

"I'm sorry it has to be this way."

"I know. I bet it's hard for you too."

Celest gave a smile that conveyed all the hurt she felt. "We will be back soon, alright?" She sighed. "There's money on the table for food if you want to order something."

"Have fun. Can you send me a picture of Eveline? I bet she looks beautiful."

"I will." Celest backed out of the room.

Aella shut the door and leaned against it to control her emotions. She wanted to be strong. She wanted to act like she wasn't hurt. But she was. She was adopted, and it felt like that made her less of a part of her family.

She sniffled and pushed herself off the door and walked toward her window, her arms crossed. She watched as the trees swayed with the wind. She couldn't hold the tears as they streamed down her face. She wished she had been like Eveline. She wished she had been as pretty, as smart, as lycan.

"You never sent me a letter."

Aella jumped. She turned around. She swiped away her tears and leaned back against the window, blushing furiously.

"I-I didn't think you enjoyed them," she lied.

He was dressed to the nines, in a complete suit and with bow tie. His dress shirt clung to his frame, displaying every muscle on his toned body.

She dropped her gaze.

He raised an eyebrow and walked into her room. He didn't know why he was there. He shouldn't have been there. He was a host and should be greeting the alphas and betas arriving at his house.

"You'd know if I didn't." He rubbed his chin as he took in her appearance.

He'd heard her crying from downstairs. Her eyes and nose were red, and she looked exhausted. She wouldn't look at him, and it frustrated him beyond comprehension, beyond rationality.

"Shouldn't you be at the party?"

"It can wait. Don't cry."

"It's hard when you're the black sheep," she scoffed.

He rolled his eyes. "They're unimportant. Not worth crying over, so don't."

Her tears kept falling, but she held back her sobs and just looked at her feet. He wanted her to stop crying. He didn't like it. He didn't know why.

"Come here."

She hesitated for a moment before she walked over to him.

He looked down at her, his eyes turning gold for the slightest second.

"Stop," he ordered harshly. It was an "alpha command."

She couldn't help but obey. Her body listened, and immediately she felt her sniffles stop. "I just feel left out. I wish I was like Eveline."

"You mean you wish you were a lycanthrope." He walked around her room, wanting to gag from all the pink and purple.

She was simply so bubbly. It was foreign to him.

"It's hard for her too. You and your mother will die even before she gains her first wrinkle. She thinks about it more than you think."

He was right, and she had thrown that in her face the other night.

He was busy staring at the pictures on her desk, and she didn't notice him opening her laptop.

"Wait!"

Before he heard her, the screen brightened, and he turned to her with an amused expression.

"Curious, I see."

He sat down in her chair and read the rest of the article.

When he was finished, he turned back to her. "This is wrong."

"W-what?" she asked, completely puzzled.

"My net worth is a lot more than this, and if you want answers, you can ask."

"I hardly see you."

"You hardly write to me too."

"It was one letter! You are not one to talk! I do write you!"

He enjoyed watching her become flustered. It was humorous to him and better than seeing her cry.

She huffed in frustration. "I did write you, okay? I just never gave it to you."

"Do you not want to finish the book?"

"I do. It's just . . ."

"Just what?" he asked, standing up.

"Nothing," she squeaked, backing away from him.

He watched her retreat from him, and before he could respond, he felt Kaius pushing against his mental boundaries, wondering where he was through their mind link. He had to return even though he didn't want to. He disliked hosting; it was a pain in the ass.

"I have to go." He turned around to leave.

"W-wait, uh . . ." She went to her desk and opened her drawer. She handed him an envelope and backed away, looking nervous. "I do want to finish the book."

He didn't respond. He left her alone in her room, with just a little more happiness in her heart.

CHAPTER NINE

He had a lot on his shoulders. Staying up late and waking up so early were frequent in his occupation. But he enjoyed being an alpha, and it wasn't a position he took lightly. He wouldn't change his rank. He'd fight anyone to death if they tried to steal it from him.

He walked into his room, dragging his feet. She shucked off his suit jacket. He sighed as he sat down next to the fireplace. He was stressed, overworked, and hardly had enjoyment. He watched the flames rise and fall.

As he took off his jacket, his pocket crinkled with the letter Aella had given him a few days prior. He laid his jacket down and placed the envelope on the table. Staring down at it, he realized just how much he looked forward to their recordings.

Atlas,

I think we should choose a birthdate for you. How does April 19 sound? If we don't celebrate, it makes each year less valuable, right? Just because you will live for a very long time, it does not mean that time isn't important.

You were right all those years ago—action is not my favorite genre. Can you guess what is?

Thank you for visiting me that day. Somehow you made all the fear go away. It was like you were fighting off all my bad and scary thoughts.

The fact other species exist is super cool! I want to meet a vampire so badly. You said some people have powers. What type? Faes exist?

I asked how far you can hear because sometimes a girl just doesn't want her father to listen in. It's embarrassing. It's invasive.

Lunas? What are lunas? You mentioned alphas and lunas in your last letter. I've read many books explaining this topic somewhat, but they were considered fiction, and I probably shouldn't get my information from those.

You became protector of lycanthropes. I hope one day you will tell me the story, even if it's long. I have time, even though it's much less than yours. So what do you say? Can we finish War and Peace *and the story of Atlas?*

– Aella

"Atlas, here is chapter 6: *'Having thanked Anna Pavlovna for her charming soiree, the guests began to take their leave. . . .'*"

He sighed and leaned back in his chair, listening to her voice. Somehow, he became less stressed the more she read, and when the recording was over, he was frustrated that she didn't read more.

He finished some paperwork and took a shower before going to bed.

* * *

Two years later

Aella's dreams didn't stop. In fact, they became more vivid the older she got. She ignored them as best as she could, and she never told anyone about her secret fantasies.

Eveline graduated from high school and decided to attend college near their home. She took public transit, and she preferred it that way. She felt like it was her responsibility to keep her little sister safe. Deaths piled up in the pack, from the disease and Ansan, but little progress was made with both.

Aella knew what was going on because Eveline told her what their father wouldn't. Still, there were large gaps in her knowledge. She couldn't know much.

It seemed that the worse the situation grew, the farther the alpha was from their family. He was nearby, physically, but he was constantly busy. They rarely saw him—only when necessary—but he always made sure to write and read to Aella, who longed to see him.

She sat up on her bed and took off her bonnet. The previous night had been another seven hours of constant dreaming about Atlas. She didn't understand it. It nauseated her.

Her eyes moved to the window as her sister appeared outside. Aella smiled and walked to the window, unlocking it to let her sister come into her bedroom.

"Heads up, Beta coming through," Eveline warned.

"What?" Aella gawked as she saw her father jump from a tree and onto her window. She backed away with a hefty laugh.

"As the young people say, 'Sup, Aella.'" Kaius smiled.

Aella rolled her eyes and shut her window. "You know, you think I'd get used to the whole jumping-through-the-trees thing?"

Eveline crossed her arms with a mischievous smirk.

Aella raised an eyebrow at her.

"Get dressed. We are going out."

"Dress warmly," Kaius affirmed. He wrapped his arms around her head and brought her into an embrace. "Happy birthday, sweetheart."

"Thanks, Dad." Aella beamed.

Kaius left with Eveline, who winked at Aella before leaving.

The birthday girl sighed happily and dropped herself onto the bed, then she quickly got dressed.

* * *

Aella skipped down the stairs to see her mother dancing in the kitchen with a birthday cake while singing "Feliz Cumpleaños."

"My beautiful daughter, happy birthday!"

"*Gracias*, Mama."

"Good, you're dressed warmly. Let's go." Celest took Aella's hand.

The entire family walked out of the front door. Aella started for the car, but Eveline pulled her hand and guided her around the house.

Aella was confused as they led her to the backyard. Her mother stood behind Kaius, and before Aella could say anything, he already lifted and carried her mother on his back before jumping up to the trees.

Eveline grabbed Aella. "Get on my back."

"Ev, I'm fat as fuck."

"If you don't shut your ass up—just get on."

Aella cursed as she wrapped her legs around her sister, her arms around Eveline's neck. Eveline didn't jump up like her father. Instead, she took off from the forest floor through the trees.

Aella laughed as the wind blew through her hair and the trees blurred. She couldn't see anything in focus, but she knew Eveline wasn't going as fast as she could.

They stopped at a clearing.

Aella got off with a bad set of giggles. "That was so cool!"

Kaius and Celest landed with a thud beside her. There was a soft sheet of snow on the ground, and Aella watched as her mom laid down a thick blanket. They all sat and had a cold lunch.

Aella didn't mind the cold so much. She enjoyed the time with her family, and she could tell Eveline and her dad liked being outside and being able to show their true selves.

"You'll get your gifts once we get to the house, but we knew you'd want one thing."

Aella looked at her mother strangely.

"You get so happy when you see him," Celest continued, her eyes on someone behind Aella.

Aella turned around and gasped softly when she saw him. She turned to her mother with a huge smile and stood up. She ran to him, then wrapped her arms around his waist and hugged him with all her might. Atlas didn't hug her back. He didn't know what to do. But she didn't care. She just enjoyed his presence.

This was the closest she ever got to him. She hadn't seen him in months, and the last time she did, she didn't react this way. This time, she couldn't resist throwing herself into his arms.

"Happy eighteenth birthday, Aella."

She smiled against his chest. "Thank you."

He gently coaxed her away from him, his hands firm on her shoulders. He didn't smile at her, but his gaze was soft as he went into his suit jacket and pulled out a small rectangular box. He handed it to her gingerly, as if debating with himself whether he should give it to her.

She smiled. "You can wrap presents?"

"No, but I'm rich enough to buy someone who can."

A fond laugh left her chest. Something about how serious he sounded struck a chord within her. He was funny but didn't try to be.

The box contained a bracelet—sterling silver—with two pearls on the ends that didn't connect. Its design was simple, but she loved it. (There is beauty in simplicity.) Engraved underneath were words in Romanian.

She looked up at him. "What does it say?"

"*Adormim până ne îndrăgostim.*"

She raised an eyebrow. "In English?"

"Life did not stop, and one had to live."

Her eyes brightened. She knew that quote from somewhere. With knitted brows, she suddenly remembered where she read it.

"*War and Peace.*"

He nodded. He didn't translate it correctly. If she had asked Kaius, she would have caught his lie.

"This seems very expensive," she muttered. "I can't take this."

"I collect jewelry. There's a safe where the best of my collection are kept. This bracelet was in it. It would please me greatly if you accepted it."

"Thank you. It's beautiful." Her heart raced at his kind, candid words, and she nodded in gratitude. "Although, gold has always been my color," she teased.

His eyes darkened. "No." His response was immediate. "You belong in silver."

For the rest of her birthday, she watched her sister and father play an extreme version of catch game. She couldn't help but laugh as Eveline slipped and fell on her ass.

"You're shivering."

Aella smiled up at Atlas. "It's cold out."

"You'll get sick. You should be wearing a heavier jacket." Atlas reached for her hand, shocking her. His brows knitted together. "Jesus, you're freezing." He pulled away from her, regrettably, and took off his jacket, handing it to her.

"Won't you get cold?"

He looked at her as if to say, "Obviously not."

"Oh right, stupid question." She wrapped the jacket around herself, rejoicing in the oversized warmth. It smelled like him—pine and mint. It was intoxicating to her, and she wanted to be cocooned in his arms, but she had to bite back the urge.

A yawn caught in her throat as she felt his penetrating gaze on her.

"You're tired. Why?"

"I haven't been sleeping well."

In part, it was the truth.

"You're lying."

"Am not."

"Yes, you are."

"A-am not." She saw his eyes light up with amusement, and she sighed in frustration. "I know, I know. I stutter when I lie."

He rolled his eyes and stalked toward the blanket on the ground where Celest sat, taking a video of Kaius and Eveline.

Aella followed, sitting down beside him.

"So"—he sat down—"why can you not sleep?"

She swallowed and leaned forward. "Why do you not come around? You confuse me."

Celest's laughter resonated throughout the forest. Eveline asked her to come play with them, and Celest happily went to play with her family, leaving Aella and Atlas.

Aella had expected he wouldn't answer, but then his voice slithered into her ears like the wind that circulated around them: "It's hard being around your family."

"Why?"

He looked at her with those piercing bright-blue eyes. "Your mother and father are incredibly happy. Do you know why that is?"

Her eyes slid over to her parents, who were sharing a look of longing for each other. Kaius reached out his hand, and Celest took it, pulling him into her. They were happy, almost impossibly so. Perhaps it was impossible for humans to feel such happiness.

"They're mates," she whispered.

He nodded, his eyes on the mates now kissing. He looked away.

"Seeing them is hard because you will never have a mate," she whispered to him. "You don't like watching them looking happy because to you the only way to be happy is to have a mate."

His silence unsettled her.

"But maybe you could be happy just loving someone, unconditionally," she continued. "Humans don't have soulmates, or maybe we do and just can't recognize them as easily. Nevertheless, some of us are happy and are in love. You can be too."

He shook his head. "You don't believe that. Or maybe you do, but you aren't being honest with yourself."

She cocked her head to the side, wondering if he was going to explain.

"When you say the word mate, your heart races. You want one," he said, barely above a whisper. "And that's why you are tired. Do you stay awake thinking about it? Or do you dream about it?"

She averted her gaze, shying away from him. She watched as Eveline jumped with Celest on her back. "Do you think I could have one? Do you think I'm worthy?"

"Your self-worth is not hinged on a mate. But yes, I do."

"Then, what is?"

"Your mate." When he saw her confusion, he elaborated, "Mates are created for each other. You are perfect for your counterpart. You were made for someone, and someone was made for you."

"Do you think I have one?"

I hope not, he thought, because he didn't want to confront the contradictory, illicit feelings that ran through his head. But he didn't think he could stand a look of disappointment on her face again.

He nodded. "I do."

And he did. He knew that no male would be deserving of her, ever. She was the kindest, brightest, most earth-shattering soul he had ever met. She radiated something he'd never witnessed before in his life.

It startled him.

It liberated him.

It ignited something that was already so burned out.

* * *

Aella felt him beside her on the bed, but he was not actually there. She sat up, longing to feel someone next to her. She pulled off the covers and rolled out of bed, only to realize it wasn't her room. She saw a light on behind a door and heard the steady stream of water splashing against a hard surface.

She pushed the door open and bit her lip, seeing him standing under the showerhead. She crossed her arms as she watched him while he smiled to himself, sensing her presence.

"Aella."

She stepped in the shower. Atlas grabbed her hips and turned her around, and she could feel every facet of him against her back.

"You're still in your nightgown."

Her skin crawled as his fingertips caressed the curvature of her thighs. His hand delved under her soaked sleepwear and palmed her ass. Her head lulled back against his chest, the water cascading down her skin.

"You're beautiful, Aella."

She could feel his hands move up her arms and pull down the strings of her nightwear, which soon fell to a puddle by her feet. He turned her around and pushed her back against the wall, leaving a trail of warmth down her neck that made her moan softly.

"Atlas," she whispered.

"That's not my name."

Before she could say anything, she heard her name over and over again. She sat up, startled to see Eveline shaking her shoulders. She cursed into her hands and looked at her sister, who looked like she was going to pass out from laughing.

"I don't know who you were dreaming about, but damn! I want what you're having."

"Oh God! I am so sorry." She was completely mortified that her sister woke her up amid a sexy dream. "Was I loud? Do you think Dad heard? Oh God," she groaned into her hands.

"Nah, I wasn't asleep. That's the only reason I heard. So?"

"So?" Aella saw the excitement on Eveline's face.

"Oh, come on. You hardly have sexy friends. Tell me everything. Who's popping your cherry in your dreams?" She looked like a child on Christmas morning as she jumped on Aella's bed, laughing out loud.

The sun was about to rise, but it was still dim in her room.

"I've been having them for a while now."

"About who?"

Aella shook her head. She didn't want to tell Eveline who it was about because it was so weird! She should harness any feelings for Atlas.

Yet, every part of her wanted him.

"I-I don't know."

"Oh my goddess! Do you know what that means?"

"What?"

Eveline grabbed Aella's shoulders and shook her with eagerness. "It could mean that you have a mate!"

Aella paled. "W-what? What do you mean?"

"Well, depending on the situation, but it isn't unheard of for mates to dream about each other. I think Mom had dreamed about Dad for a long time before they met."

"O-oh. Well, I don't think it's that, honestly."

Eveline sat up and crinkled her nose in disgust. "Oh no," she whispered as Aella's door began to rattle.

Aella looked at the door and then at her sister.

"Oh no," Eveline repeated.

"Are they . . . ?"

"They're old. Shouldn't they . . . not like it anymore?"

Eveline groaned into the air.

"Eww—"

Eveline stood from the bed and put her finger over her lips, shushing Aella. She walked to the window and opened it.

"Get dressed," she whispered. "Let's blow this popsicle stand."

Aella nodded and, as quietly as possible, got dressed in warm clothes. She grabbed Atlas' letter as she passed her desk, then stuffed the envelope into her pocket and walked behind Eveline. She wrapped her legs around Eveline's waist and held on as she jumped out of the window.

Aella chuckled again from the butterflies she got in her stomach.

"Wait, let's not go too far. Mom and Dad would be pissed."

Eveline agreed, and they went to the small clearing they had gone to on Aella's birthday.

* * *

Eveline put Aella down.

Aella took out the envelope and opened it.

"Hey, let's go sit in a tree," said Eveline. "That way, you don't have to rest on the snow."

"How will we get up there?"

Eveline gave Aella a bored, knowing look.

"Oh," Aella muttered.

Eveline helped Aella into a shorter tree.

They sat on a branch, and Aella read the letter carefully and listened to the recording.

Aella,

Happy eighteenth birthday.

You are persistent in learning about my past and the story of my existence. In every letter, you ask, and in every other letter, I tell you that I do not want to tell you. However, it has come to my attention that an eighteenth birthday is important these days. It signifies a coming-of-age event. So, I will tell you, but only in person. Have you decided where you will attend college? What will you study? What gives you joy?

– *Atlas*

"What chapter are you two on?"

Aella looked at her sister as she folded the note back up.

"Fourteen."

"You guys have gotten far. I thought you two would have stopped by now."

"I'm glad we haven't," she admitted. "On bad days, it's the only thing I look forward to."

"Let's get home. Mom and Dad are up."

"How do you know, Ev?"

"Dad mind-linked with me."

"Oh, I forgot you could do that."

Eveline grabbed Aella again and hopped down from the tree. She helped her sister all the way back to the house.

* * *

This time, they walked through the back glass doors into the kitchen.

Celest looked up from the stove. "Where did you two go?"

"Anywhere that wasn't in this house," Eveline said curtly. She walked past her mother and ran up the stairs, to her room.

"She didn't get much sleep," Aella said, to ease the tension. "And we were kinda awake when you . . . well . . . hid the sausage, if you know what I mean."

"Alright! Enough of that!" Celest yelled, embarrassed. She finished making breakfast and set the table for everyone.

Aella bit her lip softly as she reluctantly put her fork down.

"Mom?"

"Yes, mija?" Celest didn't look up from the book in her hand but was definitely listening to her daughter.

"Before you met Dad, did you have dreams . . . a-about him?"

This caught Celest, and Kaius, off guard.

Celest looked at Aella. "Yes, I did. And the longer we went from seeing each other, the more I had them. They didn't stop until we mated."

"Oh God TMI!" Eveline groaned.

Kaius and Celest ignored Eveline's outburst.

Kaius cleared his throat. "Are you having dreams about someone?"

Aella gazed at her father, then quickly shook her head. "No. I was just curious."

Kaius and Celest shared an unbelieving expression.

"I know you're lying," Kaius muttered, leaving the conversation at that.

* * *

Atlas,

A couple of years ago, I chose a birthdate for you, April 19. You said you didn't want a gift. This year will be different. Your birthday is in a few weeks. Be prepared for the celebration. Hopefully, you can also tell me your story.

I've decided to stay close to home like Eveline. With Ansan still around, Dad won't let me go too far. I have also decided to study animal behavior and biology, with plans on attending veterinary school.

You asked me what gives me joy. I'm not quite sure.

Atlas, I have been having dreams about a man. Is it normal to have such vivid dreams most nights?

– Aella

* * *

Eight weeks later

"Hey, where you going?"

Aella finished zipping up her coat and turned to her sister. She untucked her hair, shrugging. "Just out for a little."

"You're going to see Alpha, aren't you?" Eveline crossed her arms.

She gave in and nodded. It wasn't an oddity anymore. She often found herself at his house.

Eveline exhaled slowly. "Alright. I'll stay away from Dad so he won't know."

Aella hugged her sister. "Thank you. I appreciate it."

"But you have to be back soon. You're graduating tomorrow!"

Aella chuckled and nodded, walking quietly down the stairs and yelling a quick goodbye to her mom.

She got into her car and drove away.

* * *

The drive to his house was fifteen minutes. She would hardly call his house just a house; it wasn't a home, either. It was a fortress of stone and glass, carefully constructed in the depths of the forest where her own home was standing a few miles away.

As she came to the garage, she pressed the garage door opener button on her mirror and drove in next to Atlas' favorite car. It was a sleek black sports car, but she never cared enough to pay attention to the model. She had never driven in it, and it was always carefully stored away in his garage.

It was never a surprise when she came to visit him, and he never sent her away. The only time he said she couldn't stay was when he was running out of the door looking pissed as hell. Something had happened that day. She still did not know what.

As she skipped up the steps that led to the kitchen upstairs, she was pleasantly greeted by the smell of banana bread. The house was open and bright, lit well by floor-to-ceiling windows that overlooked the canopy outside. Those windows were never covered by blinds, and the view was one of her favorites.

Her stomach growled as she cut two pieces of bread and set them on one plate. She coated hers in plenty of cream cheese and left the other plain. Immediately, she sought his office, finding his door cracked open.

She held her breath as his gaze locked onto her.

"Aella," he greeted, unsurprised by her visit.

She walked in and gently shut the door behind her. She set the plate on his desk, taking a seat.

"Hungry as usual."

"I once watched you eat an entire chicken breast by yourself," she teased.

He rolled his eyes, jutting his chin toward the bread. "Do you like it?"

"It's so good. Tell your baker they did well."

He nodded, a small grin coating his lips, as his eyes moved back to his work. Taking the silence as a cue to move, she went into her satchel and pulled out an ornate, wrapped present. She had chosen to wrap it in red paper with blue ribbon around the width. On the top right corner was his name in big black letters.

She knew his eyes were on her even before she looked up. When she did, his gaze was focused on the present in her hands. She gently set it on his desk beside his lamp.

With stoic eyes, he regarded the present and then her.

"Happy birthday, Atlas."

"No one has said those words to me in centuries."

"Everyone deserves a celebration, even hardworking old alphas."

He raised an eyebrow. Amusement filled his eyes. He'd grown accustomed, even fond, to her taunts.

"This old alpha can still hear better than you."

She laughed. "You never wrote back." she said, playing with her hands.

"I didn't know what to write," he replied honestly.

"Oh."

"When someone in our species dreams about another, it means their mate is near."

Aella nodded. "Eveline told me that."

He looked away from her. She watched his hands grip the file harshly, making it crinkle and tear on its sides. He brought his bright gaze to her, not looking at her, investigating her. She fidgeted.

His kind gaze seemed to have been replaced with something in a quick exchange of emotion. She watched, instead of the familiar blue eyes, his contacts disappear into silver orbs. It was like they weren't enough to conceal the brightness of his eyes. She knew her family had silver eyes—that it was a facet of their species—but she had seen them only on Eveline. Atlas and her father always wore their contacts, and that usually worked.

She didn't understand. It was like he morphed into something else—someone else that was him yet different.

"Who is he?" He stood up from his chair.

She couldn't dismiss the way the room seemed to darken. He was simply so imposing, a creature that not only wanted to dominate but needed to.

"Who do you dream about?"

"I-I don't know," she whispered, her throat so dry.

"You stutter when you lie."

She didn't think it was possible, but he consumed the room.

She wasn't scared of him. She held her ground, swallowing her nerves. He was beautiful. Every part of him was perfectly crafted. She had never seen such an attractive man.

Her stomach twisted from the grip of desire as she looked at his hands placed on the desk. They were those of a craftsman: large, strong, and intricate. His arms were just as consuming, and she watched as a vein throbbed through his forearm.

"Who do you dream about, Aella?"

As her eyes trailed up his frame, she realized he could see nothing else but disgust and guilt in them. She hated herself for having those dreams about him. Even worse, she hated how she didn't want them to stop.

He inhaled deeply from the revelation. He didn't need her to say it.

CHAPTER TEN

"Me?"

She looked up at him and saw his eyes flicker with emotion she couldn't read, then she nodded, unable to speak.

"Impossible." He pushed himself away from his desk and ran his hand through his hair as if the movement would wipe away what he'd just learned. Whatever emotion had filled the room was now replaced with clear disbelief.

Aella looked at her feet. She shouldn't have told him. He must have thought she was insane, repulsive even. She couldn't blame him.

She turned around and left him. He didn't call for her.

She drove away but didn't go home. She just needed time to think. She didn't understand why night after night, day after day, year after year, she thought about him constantly. It wasn't a crush—it was an obsession.

The desire she had for him forced her to forgo any other long-term romantic relationships. She had dated Alex for a few years and had willingly and enthusiastically given her virginity to him. He was a sweet boy, someone who treated her with respect. She liked him and felt sexual desire for him, but she couldn't live with herself, couldn't continue seeing him, when she realized that the man she fantasized about wasn't him.

So, she broke it off.

Aella went to a small ice-cream parlor and ordered a cone. Her phone went off multiple times, but she ignored it and kept to herself.

* * *

"Sweetheart, are you okay?"

Aella looked at her sweet mother and nodded. "I'm fine. I just wanted some ice cream and left my phone in the car."

"For five hours?"

She knew Celest didn't believe her, but her mother had no proof that she was lying.

"Yeah, Ma."

Celest stared at her for a moment before nodding away her accusatory tone. She walked to Aella and pulled her into a loving embrace.

"I can't believe my youngest is graduating tomorrow."

Aella smiled in her mother's arms and sighed away all of her unnecessary thoughts. "I'm glad. I can't stand high school."

Celest laughed and pulled away, stroking her daughter's hair. "Dinner will be ready shortly. Why don't you go make sure your gown and dress for tomorrow are ironed?"

Aella nodded and disappeared upstairs.

As she walked into her room, she smiled to herself. The decorations had changed drastically since her childhood. The pink on the walls was gone, replaced with a dark purple with some yellow pops of color here and there. And instead of posters on her wall, she had bookshelves and a bookcase that wasn't quite filled yet. Aella grew up in this room.

She sat on her bed, saying to herself, "I know you can hear me, Dad." She released a breath. "I just wanted to say thank you for everything—for adopting me, for giving me a home, for raising me. I don't say it enough, but I mean it." She stood up and took off her jacket.

While setting it on the back of her desk chair, she felt a gush of wind behind her. She knew immediately that her dad was at her door. She turned around and walked to him, hugging him with all her might.

"Aella?"

"You'd love me no matter what, right?"

"First, you're thanking me, and now you're asking about how much I love you? Sweetheart, are you okay?"

She chuckled and nodded slowly.

Kaius smiled down at her, his eyes scanning her face for any semblance of a lie. "I'd love you even if you hated me. I'll love you when you fall down. I'll love you when you reach your dreams. I'll always be here for you, my little girl."

"I love you, Dad."

"I love you too, Aella."

As Kaius walked out of her room, he gave her one more glance. He knew her mind was running wild with thoughts, but he didn't know what those were. He figured it must have been due to the fact that she was graduating.

Aella took a bath and put on her pajamas.

As she entered her bedroom, she looked at her bed, reluctantly. It didn't feel like a place of rest anymore. Every morning she woke up restless, and every night she went to bed anxious. She knew that her dreams wouldn't stop. She knew she would see him again, in her dream.

She wanted nothing more than to stay awake all night, but that moment quickly passed and was replaced with the longing to hear his voice, even if it came only from her head. She hated that she dreamed about him, and yet if she was asked if she could live without ever dreaming of him again, she'd say no.

A deep, resigned breath left her chest as she crawled into bed.

*　　*　　*

Aella could smell the beach as she rolled over. She smiled, seeing the curtains blow in wind coming from the double door being opened. She sat up and realized that she wasn't wearing anything under the light sheet that covered her. A feather was stuffed in the ends of her curly locks, and she chuckled as she took it out and then threw it on the bed. That was when she saw the floor was littered with many of them.

"You're awake."

She turned to the origin of the voice. Atlas was standing by the double door, his large arms crossed. He walked in, leaving the doors open. He sat on the edge of the bed and gazed into her eyes, then his hands grabbed her arms and hoisted her up and sat her on his lap.

She blushed as she felt him harden underneath her.

"Be careful. I might take you again."

Her eyes met his, and he smiled.

"You want me to, don't you?"

All she did was nod and bit her lip.

He threw her down on her back and climbed on top of her, spreading her thighs so he could fit between her legs. He quickly moved against her, the button of his dress pants rubbing against her clit. He held her hands above her head and captured her eyes once again.

"You're mine," he said with a growl. "No one can look at you. No one deserves to cast their eyes on such a jewel. No one can touch you. No one can make you come as I can. No one will ever have you the way I do because you are mine. And you know what?" He leaned close to her ear. "You love knowing that I would end the world to save you."

Aella sat up, startled by the honking of a car outside. She groaned into her hands. She could feel her underwear was soaked from her dream.

Eveline came barging in. She looked at Aella with a knowing expression. "You had a dream again."

Aella only nodded and eased herself back onto her bed.

Eveline laughed at her sister's pain. "I'm sorry if I woke you up, but you're graduating today!" She threw a hairbrush and a curler on the bed. "We have to get you dressed, your hair done, and makeup on point. We must start now if you want to be on time!"

Eveline was a master beautician, apparently because Aella thought she never looked prettier.

* * *

Aella joined her friends in the processional line outside the venue. The music started playing, and her class began walking into the large gym. They sat down in rows, in alphabetical order by last name. Aella's last name began with a *K*, so she was right in the middle.

The ceremony became dull until awards were announced.

Aella twisted the papers in her hand as nerves began building up the closer it got to her speech.

"And ladies and gentlemen, please welcome this year's class president, Aella Knight."

Applause echoed throughout the gym as Aella walked up to the podium with a smile. She was glad her hard work paid off and was being recognized, but there was a reason why she was so good at her studies: it was all she did. She didn't enjoy going out or being with people. What she enjoyed was stuffing her nose in a book.

It irked her that extroverts seemed to have their charismatic large public-speaking hands on every part of life. Aella didn't want to give a speech. Why couldn't she just write a newspaper article or something?

She smiled and swallowed as her teacher put her pin on and then gestured to the podium. She was for sure going to vomit.

Those poor people in the first few rows were going to get a shower they never wanted.

Her stomach twisted. Silence filled her ears as she set her speech on the lectern and cleared her throat. She didn't want to start. She just wanted to finish, preferably without spewing chunks.

"To say that I am honored is an understatement," she began with a nervous tilt in her voice. She hated how her voice wavered. "But I must admit that as I stand before you, I can't help but feel overwhelmed. Truth be told, there are probably many others that are just as qualified as me, perhaps even more so...."

The more she talked, the more nervous she became. She looked around for her family and saw her mom recording her speech with her phone. Beside Celest was Kaius, and next to him was someone Aella didn't expect to see so soon. She smiled and blushed, unsure how to continue.

Eveline looked at Aella and then at her alpha. In a subtle glance from Alpha Superior to Aella—and Aella's evident blush— Eveline just knew.

"It proves just how subjective this award is and education in that of itself. What I mean by this is that everyone has the potential to do great things, and even if someone beats you for a job, a title, or even an award, that does not mean you are any less capable, intelligent, strong, brave, or courageous. It just means that your hard work hasn't been recognized yet."

Her speech was five minutes long, and she was glad that it ended quickly and she could sit back down.

Soon, they were lining up to receive their diplomas. Aella's name was called, followed by her sister's obnoxious voice.

"Let's go, sis! You get that diploma!"

When the ceremony was over, Aella realized Atlas had left but had made sure to give Eveline the recorder. Eveline eagerly stuffed it in her hand as she hugged her sister in the foyer.

"Your speech was incredible. I know you hate public speaking, but you did so well!"

* * *

Later that night

After talking for a while, Eveline asked Aella to take a walk with her.

She turned to her sister with a reluctant gaze. "You and Alpha have been reading that book for years."

Aella looked down at her feet. "Yeah, we have."

"And you always go to his home when he allows it, and you always ask about his well-being, and your heart always races when someone talks about him, like it is now."

Aella didn't know what to say, so she just kept quiet.

"I see the way you look at him," Eveline continued. "I always thought it was just some infatuation that would eventually go away, but it hasn't, and I have a feeling that it won't." Seeing her sister's discomfort, she lifted Aella's chin now covered with tears. "Is he the person you've been dreaming about?"

Aella only nodded, unsure how Eveline would react—but probably with disgust. She shouldn't feel such a way toward her bastard uncle.

Eveline inhaled and swallowed. "Have you told him?"

Aella nodded.

"What did he say?"

"He said it's impossible. He's right. I shouldn't have these thoughts about him. I shouldn't feel the way I do, but I don't know how to stop."

Eveline hugged Aella. The reason why she wanted to take a walk was that she didn't want their parents to hear. She didn't know why Aella felt so strongly, but it must have had something to do with a bond of some sort.

Alpha Superior didn't have a mate; he couldn't. So it wasn't plausible.

"It's alright," Eveline whispered.

"Really?"

"Yes, Aella. He isn't related to us at all. He's family by choice, not blood. He's not Dad's real brother, and you aren't Dad's blood daughter. Don't feel so bad. I'm sure whatever it is will go away."

Eveline tried to make Aella feel better, but truth be told, she wasn't so sure what was going on. She had a feeling that whatever it was, it wouldn't end well for both Aella and the alpha.

Aella pulled away from her sister. "How did you find out?" she asked, her voice raw from tears.

"The way you looked at him today . . . You were so nervous before you saw him and then you just mellowed out. Please don't be afraid to tell me anything again. I will mostly always be on your side. Unless you're acting like a bitch, then I'll call you out," she joked. "I'm the person you can tell anything to. You know I love you, right?"

"I love you too."

CHAPTER ELEVEN

In the envelope was only a recorder. There was no letter.

He read her the first chapter of the third book, and when she thought he was finished, he began talking about her letter:

"Aella, congratulations on graduating. It's an important success in your life. I wanted to apologize for my behavior. I shouldn't have lashed out." (He sounded like he took a deep breath.) "Truth be told, there is no importance to your dreams. It is nothing to analyze. I have business in Romania and will not be in the States. Your mother's birthday is coming in a few months. I will see you then."

Her hear plummeted. She wouldn't see him for four months, and that was almost enough to make her cry. She put on a bright smile and forced herself into bed. She had an inkling that if she had never said anything, he wouldn't be escaping to another continent for months. This was her fault. He needed space from *her*, not to do work.

The next day, she woke up early and got dressed. She had plans for the summer that she wanted to get ahead of.

"Where are you off to so early?"

Aella smiled. "I have an interview."

"Ooh. Good luck!"

"Thanks, Dad!"

* * *

"We have these interviews just to make sure our applicants are determined and will be successful in this environment. Honestly, after getting to know you, I think you'll have no problem joining our group."

"Thank you so much! I'm very excited. Because of school, I never had the chance to do something like this."

"I'm glad you are here. So the next steps are training and certifications. CPR training, intervention training, conflict and resolution training . . . You have to go through these steps because of the sensitivity of our work. Unfortunately, this is a volunteer position—"

Aella smiled. "Yes, I know."

"Alright. Well, let me show you around. The soup kitchen is down the hall. Treatment is down the other way, and cots are in the room across from here. You wanted to work in our domestic abuse sector, so when we receive a case, we will forward it to you. You will act as a counselor of sorts . . . a friend if need be to those victims of abuse seeking help. And if you need a break when the work gets heavy, you may always work in the soup kitchen or clinic."

Aella loved her job at the center. She worked with people who went through domestically violent situations, helping them talk through their pain, by being their friend, and finding them a place to hide out. And when they were ready, she helped with job interviews.

* * *

The work she did was emotionally draining, but she loved seeing these people transform into independent, confident individuals. She had been working in the program for four months when her mother's birthday party came around.

Aella smiled at her aunt even though she wasn't interested in what she was saying. Soon, her dad, sister, and mother joined in the conversation.

"So, I was walking around town yesterday, and I saw you having lunch with some lady at Greg's Diner. Who was she?"

"Oh," Aella said, "she's a friend."

Her aunt laughed. "Your friend looked like she needed a good shower."

Aella didn't appreciate such disrespect, but she bit her tongue. It wasn't her place to tell her aunt exactly what that girl had gone through.

"She needed a friend," was Aella's only reply.

Truthfully, the lady her aunt was talking about was Genevieve Langosta. She had been in a relationship that had started blissfully but progressed into beatings at night. She stayed with her husband through years of physical and emotional abuse because his words became a fact to her: She was ugly. She wasn't worthy. She was stupid. She wasn't good enough. Genny finally came to the clinic after a brutal beating. Her husband had hurt her so badly that she miscarried.

Aella's eyes drifted over to Atlas, who just entered. He didn't look happy and didn't look even the slightest interested in the party. She smiled at him, and she could have sworn his gaze softened.

She excused herself from the conversation and walked into the kitchen, needing a break from everyone.

"The party is out there, you know."

She smiled at her hands as she poured a glass of water.

"Exactly why I am in here."

"You're antisocial," he commented, sitting down at the table.

Aella scoffed and turned around. "I'm antisocial? We hardly see you." She sat down at the table in front of him.

A moment passed, then two, and she relented.

"I'm sorry," she blurted out.

"What for?"

"Telling you . . . I-I didn't mean to make things awkward."

"You didn't."

She fidgeted and started picking at her cuticles. He noticed it but didn't say anything.

"It feels like I did."

He grabbed her hand but immediately retracted it as if she had burned him. He looked at his palm with knitted brows. After a long pause, he gazed at her again, his eyes burning bright.

"You did nothing wrong," he whispered.

Aella only nodded. Silence hung between them.

"Atlas?" she finally spoke.

He winced, making her recoil instinctively.

"Are you okay?"

"Those dreams . . . what are they about?"

God, his voice is so deep, she thought.

Anxiety climbed up her spine, and she stiffened.

He locked eyes with her, holding her in his pull.

Pull—that was what it felt like. Every day for years, she felt pulled to him, drawn to him. But just recently, she felt more. She felt his intense gravity pulling her closer to him.

"You already know."

It was a shitty response, and he wasn't having it. "When you"—his Adam's apple bobbed—"dream of me, what are we doing?"

For once in eighteen years, she saw his cool, collected attitude waver into hesitancy. Her chest heaved.

She shook her head.

"Don't lie, Aella."

"Everything," she said quietly.

The sound of laughter entering the kitchen slipped her out of his gravitational pull. She looked away, flushed and hot, absolutely brimming with embarrassment.

"I forgot her gift," she mumbled.

It was an excuse, anything to get away. She knew it. He knew it.

As she entered her room, her phone rang. She picked it up. She grabbed the gift and heard someone's voice.

"Aella! Aella?"

She was on high alert and instantly focused on the call. "Genevieve? Genny, what's going on?"

"H-he came back. Oh God, Aella, I'm bleeding badly. E-everything h-hurts."

"Listen to me. I'm coming right now. Call an ambulance."

"I-I can't afford that."

Aella could tell Genny was becoming tired the longer she talked. She took off downstairs and ran through the party to her car.

"You must! Genny, do you hear me? Are you at your house?"

"Yes."

"Put pressure on your wounds. Hide if you must. I will be there soon. Stay on the phone with me."

If she had had a clear head, she would have been smart. She would have told her mother and taken her with her. She would have brought Kaius and Atlas. But she was so wholeheartedly scared and concerned about her friend that all she could think about was getting to her immediately.

Aella turned on the car engine and sped down the street. Genevieve's house was about ten minutes away; five if she broke the speed limit, which she did without reluctance.

More so than anything else, Aella was a good friend. She tried to be. Family and friends were all she had. Strangers had rescued her as a child, and she made sure to do the same to others.

Eveline watched Aella. Kaius looked at her with a questioning gaze. Eveline shrugged as her alpha pushed through her mind.

Where is she going?
I don't know, Kaius responded.
I don't know, Eveline repeated.

    * * *

  Aella pulled up to Genny's house and ran up the porch, noticing the door was kicked in, and there was a blood trail leading to the living room.
  "Genny!" Aella didn't know what to do, but she knew her friend was in desperate need of attention.
  She could see broken glass and holes punched into the walls. The entire stair banister was also broken. She saw Genny's bloody handprint on the wall leading upstairs. She ran up the stairs and followed the broken glass into the bedroom, where Genevieve was lying on the floor, bleeding from her head. She rushed to her and checked for a pulse.
  Genevieve was unconscious but still alive.
  Aella took her phone out of her pocket, but then she suddenly remembered that Genevieve couldn't afford an ambulance, so she called the only person who could help.
  "M-mom?"
  "Aella?" Celest was in the kitchen, making another plate of finger sandwiches.
  "I-I need your help."
  Celest didn't need to look for Kaius because he and his brother were already running into the kitchen. They could hear Aella's distress.
  "Baby girl . . ." Celest trailed away.
  "I need you to come to 35 S. Amsterdam Drive. Now, please! M-my friend has a really bad wound to her head, and she's . . . unconscious. Mom, she needs help. I can't call an ambulance—"
  Atlas immediately grabbed the phone from Celest and brought it to his ear. "Aella."

"Atlas," she whispered. "You need to get—"

He could hear Aella screaming in the background before the phone dropped. He immediately took off outside.

Kaius grabbed Celest's hand, pulling her onto his back, and followed.

Alpha Superior hated being bothered. He hated having to deal with trivial shit. However, as he ran through the trees, it dawned on him: she wasn't trivial. If he ever thought she was in danger, he would not hesitate to drop everything to go to her. But why? Why her? Why an innocent, young, easily breakable girl?

He ignored the way his heartbeat increased as he thought about the fact that she dreamed about him. He didn't bother researching it. What he had told her was the truth.

Mates do dream about their counterparts in some circumstances.

He immediately erased that line of thinking from his head. It was impossible, and he couldn't deal with such foolish thoughts.

* * *

With a hard thud, Alpha Superior landed on the greenery in front of a small home.

"Do you smell that?" Kaius asked, landing beside his alpha.

Celest hopped off Kaius' back and immediately marched forward.

Kaius' instinct took over, and he followed her.

The sight of blood, cigarettes, alcohol, and whatnot greeted their eyes. Atlas surged forward and pushed Celest behind him, going into the house first. He heard Celest gasp, but he ignored it. As he climbed the stairs, he could sense Aella. She was here, bleeding. He could smell it.

"I'm going to kill you, you little bitch!"

"Get off!"

Atlas marched into the room, immediately drowning everyone in a coat of darkness. He was an alpha no matter where he was.

A man was on top of Aella, gripping her hands above her head.

Alpha Superior didn't know what overcame him. He sent the man flying to the other side of the room.

He stood inches from the man, who was now lying on his back. He had kicked the bastard hard in his side, causing his body to slam into the wall.

Aella sputtered, dazed and in pain. She could hear the sickening crack of bone coming from somewhere.

The alpha grabbed the man by his neck and hauled him up.

"L-look," the man gasped, "I have no problem with you. Let me just deal with what's my business, and we don't gotta fight. They're my problem."

Atlas grinned, dropping the man on his ass. He took his contacts off and kneeled before him. The man tried to scurry away from him, only to be forced harder into the wall, and as soon as he got a look at Atlas' violent silver eyes, he started sobbing.

The alpha glanced over his shoulder, seeing Celest and Kaius taking care of the two women on the floor. He wanted to make sure Aella wouldn't see what he would do next, so he turned around. Then, he forced his hand into the man's chest.

"She's not yours," he whispered, ripping his heart out.

If he were a younger wolf, such action would have nauseated him. He would have felt regret. He would have mourned the life he had taken. Now, he only felt the pride of success and the relief of protecting her. He would always protect her.

He stood up, pulled out his pocket square, and wiped his hand.

Aella clung to her father as Celest checked the other woman.

"We have to get them both to the hospital."

His eyes couldn't be torn from her. She was safe. She had to be safe.

She didn't have to even try to break his walls down. She was simply within them, effortlessly, like she belonged there. Anything she ever wanted would be hers.

He saved her. He'd saved her many times before, now that she thought about it. He always knew when she needed help. Granted, when she showed any type of emotion, he always left, but he was always there.

* * *

Genny was alright. Well, Aella wouldn't call it "alright," but she was alive. She had to stay in the hospital for her post workup, and to be monitored.

Aella sat on the couch, watching Genevieve's chest rise and fall. She wouldn't feel okay leaving an abuse victim by herself in a scary hospital. She looked up as the door opened. She smiled and waved to him.

"What are you doing here?"

Atlas gestured to the sleeping woman.

"Oh, she's knocked out. We won't wake her. They gave her some heavy sleep meds."

Atlas didn't sit. He stared at her with luminous, anger-ridden eyes. "How do you know her?"

"Uh, well . . . I volunteer at a clinic for abuse victims in town. It's hush-hush, which is why Mom and Dad didn't know about it. I provide comfort, or at least I am someone to talk to for people who need it. Anyway, her name is Genny, and her husband is an asshole. She was about to be placed in a temporary home, but she needed things from her house, so she went back home while he was at work." Aella sighed and shook her head. "I should have advised her against it."

Aella had enough time to think about all her mistakes. First, she should have vehemently said no to Genny's proposal to go home. She had vocalized her disapproval but said it was Genny's choice to do what she wanted. She didn't want to take away her freedom. She didn't want to suffocate Genny like her husband had. Second, she should have forced Genny to tell her when she planned on going. She should have gone with her and with someone from her family. Genny should never have gone alone. Third, she should have checked the fucking room before rushing to Genny on the floor.

She felt the burn of tears. She sniffled. "C-can I have a hug?"

No?

Before he could say anything, he found her against his waist, firm and unmoving. He stood there, unsure what to do. He decided to allow her arms to stay around him—for her comfort, not his.

"I've brought you something," he spoke.

She pulled away, and he stuffed a book with worn-out spine in her hands. It must have been bound many years previously. She ran her finger over the leather cover and looked up with clear confusion.

"It's a very old book." He opened it in her hands. "It contains information about lycanthropes—mates, illnesses, anatomy, etcetera. It's in my native language."

"Romanian?"

He grinned, though it was counterfeit, forged by the feeling that it would make her feel good. "Yes."

"I don't know Romanian," she said more to herself than to him. She was fascinated by the book, completely engrossed in it even though she couldn't understand it. "How many languages do you know? Are you a polyglot?"

He shrugged, finding her questions unimportant. "You'll have to learn Romanian to be able read it."

133

She pouted. She knew English and Spanish, and now she had the motivation to learn a third. Still, she wanted to know about his world right away, not later.

Deep in thought, she didn't notice he was already holding a candy bar in front of her.

She smiled gratefully. "Thank you."

She felt his gaze on her as she nuzzled herself back in the uncomfortable hospital recliner. She did not get the chance to eat the candy.

Moments of trying to decipher another language passed, then she heard him speak: "Where do you go?"

She looked at him, confused.

"You go somewhere when you read. Where is it?"

"Do you not daydream when you read?"

"No. I read the words. That is all."

"Oh, I didn't know people read like that. I guess"—she closed the book on her lap—"when I read, I can see the scenario in my head. If it's fantasy, I'm the heroine. The best books are the ones that take you there but let you imagine the specifics."

"You're an escapist."

She nodded. "I suppose I am." And then she smiled—that bright, effervescent, genuine smile. "One day I'll take you with me on a literary odyssey."

"Is that a promise?"

"Do you want it to be?"

He stayed silent, his eyes on the book on her lap.

"I want to go where you go," he said, his eyes shifting to hers.

Atlas walked to the door, but as he passed her clothing sealed in a plastic bag in the chair, he stopped in his tracks. He stared at her as she eagerly looked through the old pages of the book, looking content.

He decided to stay and look after her, but if he was completely truthful with himself, he knew he would stay even before entering the hospital. He had gotten out of the room but stayed close.

Aella slept in Genny's room while he stayed awake outside the door.

* * *

"His scent was on her clothes."

Kaius grimaced. "How would he know her—" He stopped once Alpha Superior gave him a disdainful look from behind the office chair. "You think he's following Aella, us?"

"He's closer to us than we thought. He was closer to *her*, Kaius. He would have touched her for the scent to be so strong. We thought the hospital went aflame because he knew we were in it, but so was she." His hand flexed by his side. "I think he is scheming. If he wanted to hurt us, he would have done it. Your mate and Aella are perfect targets, and whereas it is rare that they are alone, he could have killed them if he wanted to. He could have killed you, hurt me, but he hasn't."

"What do you think he's planning?"

"I don't know, Kaius. What I do know is he doesn't want to hurt us; he wants to destroy us. Our legacy, our fortune, our everything."

"Killing Celest would kill me and would hurt the pack." Just the mere thought made Kaius' skin crawl, his heart beating enormously.

"Killing Celest would hurt, but it wouldn't raze us. He aims to wound us with immeasurable pain."

"And how will he do so?"

"I am not sure, but his plan must be aimed primarily at Aella and your family. Celest is safe because you look after her. Eveline is strong. She will fight. Aella—"

"Aella is my daughter. She will be safe. I will—"

"If you had to choose between your mate and Aella, do you know who you'd save?" Atlas watched as Kaius clearly had an internal debate. "You don't have to choose," he added. "He's getting too fucking close to her."

Kaius' jaw clicked. "So what do you suggest? Someone goes with her everywhere she goes? Someone stays with her at all times?"

* * *

"This is ridiculous!"

"Aella, Daddy, and Alpha have enemies—enemies that could hurt you and Mom. This is the only way."

"You shouldn't change your major, your choices, because of me. I don't like being . . . a nuisance."

Eveline smiled and grabbed her sister's hand. "My duty as your older sister, your friend, and your family, is to protect you. If something were to ever happen to you, I wouldn't be able to forgive myself." Tears welled up in her eyes. "Do you understand that? I only have a few decades with you and Mom. I want to do this. I want to spend as much time with both of you as I possibly can."

Aella hugged her sister. She didn't want to be selfish. She wanted to be better. She just didn't know how because she felt like whatever she chose, someone got hurt.

"Alright, Eveline."

"I'll attend classes with you. I'll change my schedule accordingly. I'll join the clubs you're in. I'll go with you everywhere during school hours. On Tuesdays and Thursdays, you'll go to Alpha Superior's company after class and work with him because I have violin practice. On Mondays, Wednesdays, and Fridays, we will go to Alpha's house. I need to begin training to take over the beta position."

Aella's eyes widened and lit up as she looked at Eveline. "All week I'll be with Atlas?"

"Yes, Aella." Eveline smiled, nodding. "I don't understand why you like him so much. He scares me. He's gloomy."

"He's *interesting*," she argued.

Eveline grinned and walked away from Aella. "You say that because he turns you on."

"H-he does not!"

"You stutter when you lie," Eveline reminded her, walking out of her bedroom. "Mom and Dad will be home soon."

CHAPTER TWELVE

After her classes, Aella went home. She knew Ansan was keeping a close watch on her, much closer than her parents had assumed. She knew her parents loved her, but the reality of the situation was that she wasn't in line for a pack rank. She wasn't someone's mate and didn't possess any abilities that would innately make her important, and sometimes she wondered why they put so much effort into protecting her.

Perhaps, everything would be much easier if she wasn't there.

She didn't know what to wear to a business as big as Atlas'. She had not had any clue just how prolific his company was.

She decided to wear dress pants and a nice blouse.

Someone clearing their throat made her jump, and when she saw him, she smiled nervously.

"Hi." She fumbled with the brush in her hands as she stared at him.

His eyes held amusement. "Hello."

She gestured to her outfit. "Is this okay?"

He nodded and turned around to leave.

She followed behind him to his car.

* * *

The ride was silent. He didn't play music, and it made her uncomfortable. She had wanted to get so close to him for so long, and now that she was, she wasn't sure what to do. She looked out of the window, at the skyscrapers, as they were driving into the city.

He pulled into the parking garage under the building. It was filled with cars, but there was a spot with **S U P E R I O R** painted on the floor, and he parked there. He then took off his seat belt, glancing at her as she reached for hers.

"Wait."

She looked at him.

He got out of the car and opened her door, then reached across her lap to undo her seat belt. Her breath labored. She could feel his hand as it graced her side, making her feel something. She knew what that something was, but she refused to admit it to herself.

He held out his hand, and she gingerly took it, stepping out of his expensive car. "Thank you."

He shut the door as soon as they entered the building and walked in front of her to the elevator. They got in and stood in silence as it moved them up—holy shit!—one hundred flights.

Another set of doors to an expansive office opened, reminding Aella again of the prestige Atlas had. The room had tiled floors, high windows, and contemporary furnishings. It was so put together, open, and strangely very masculine that she couldn't seem to know how an office could be described as such.

"This is yours?"

"No. I just brought you here." He sat down and looked at her.

She rolled her eyes. *He's being sarcastic.*

"I don't read sarcasm well," she said.

"I can tell."

"I didn't realize how large your corporation is. This room is huge, and it's just your office."

"I have buildings in major cities across the globe—in Moscow, New York, Tokyo, London, etcetera." He didn't look at her. He was far too engrossed in whatever files were on his desk in front of him.

"What about," she began, lowering her voice as she sat in a chair in front of his desk, "your pack?"

He found her carefulness charming. "This office is soundproof. No need to whisper. Many members of my pack work in this firm as it provides expendable money for them. Others work elsewhere."

"It must be a lot, bossing a pack and employees around?"

"Bossing around?"

She shrugged cutely. "You're a little bossy."

"You're wrong. I'm *very* bossy."

Aella laughed, agreeing. He rarely joked with her.

"Well, how do you deal with it?"

"Deal with what?"

"The stress," Aella explained.

"I don't."

She thought he was lying, but seeing his shoulders hold a regal position, she knew he was telling the truth. It made her sad that he had all of this but enjoyed none of it. He worked so hard for others.

She walked over to his bookcase and looked at the titles of his books.

"May I?"

He looked up and caught her dark eyes.

She blushed as she remembered his inhuman silver eyes that were discreetly covered by blue contacts. She liked his natural eyes; she preferred them. Now that she thought about it, those silver eyes were so bright that blue contacts couldn't conceal them. She pondered that he wore dark-brown contacts, but his eyes turned the brown tint to a light blue.

He nodded.

She chose a book she'd never read before, then sat down on the couch. About an hour later, a tall woman walked in. She was in a tight pencil skirt and a white blouse that flaunted all her curves.

Aella had curves too—at least she thought she did—but why didn't she have the confidence to wear something that highlighted them? Why was she now feeling insecure?

The woman stopped and glanced at Aella in pure disgust. "You're not supposed to allow the help to sit."

"Don't, Elena."

Elena rolled her eyes and waltzed over to Atlas' desk. She leaned over, allowing a perfect view of her cleavage, and touched his shoulder.

Aella hated how Elena looked at him, how she touched him, how badly Elena wanted him. Even more, she hated how even though Atlas shrugged off Elena's advances, it was obvious he thought she was beautiful. Elena placed a new file load on his desk, then walked out of his office. Aella watched as Atlas' eyes remained on Elena as she sashayed out of the room. She swallowed, having realized something: he dealt with *stress* the same way any other man did.

She didn't know why it bothered her so much. She especially didn't know why she wanted him to see her as a woman. Maybe what she wanted was for him to do with her what he had done with so many others.

* * *

"Okay, tell me what's up."

Aella looked at Eveline and threw her pencil down in frustration. She got off her bed and ran a hand through her hair. "Nothing's up."

Eveline looked at her with suspicious eyes. "Yeah, nothing is wrong. Nothing is so wrong that you're biting your nails and pacing."

Aella turned to her. "Is that sarcasm? I don't read sarcasm well."

"Yes, it was."

"Oh my God, is that sarcasm?"

"*Carajo*, just tell me what is running through your head."

"You should see the way they look at him. It's so frustrating!"

"I'm lost."

"Atlas. He's attractive, okay? Even you know that. And this woman, Elena, kept touching him, flaunting her oversized, jumbo shrimp—"

"Oversized, jumbo shrimp?"

"Boobs! Big ole titties, like massive."

Eveline smiled, putting her pen down on her notebook.

"Ah," she said as if she finally understood. She stood up and crossed her arms. "You're jealous."

"Am not."

"Oh my God, you definitely are."

"I just don't understand why she had to touch him. And you know what? He has a lot of sex, like a lot of sex—which is fine, you know? I'm all for having safe, consensual sex. Like . . . you do you, you know? Not literally, though, clearly."

Eveline watched as Aella continued pacing. "You're rambling."

"I am not. I'm speaking, quickly."

"Aella, you're jealous. You're jealous because you don't want him touching other people. You don't want him to feel things for them."

"That doesn't make sense!" Aella argued.

But she knew Eveline was right.

"You don't want him touching others, feeling for others, caring for others because . . . you want him to touch you, feel for you, care for you. You only."

"But why?" Aella groaned, dropping herself onto the bed. "I barely know him. We don't spend much time together."

Eveline bit her tongue as a thought came to her. *It's impossible.*

* * *

"No, Kaius, immediately! I do not have time to wait for your feelings to align with your duty!"

Aella watched from the doorway as frustrated Atlas spoke to Kaius. A few wolves in the east were attacked, and Atlas could not leave his post. Kaius was next in line, and he would be able to manage the situation better than anyone else in the alpha's absence.

Kaius only nodded. He stood up and then walked out of the door, ignoring Aella, who was standing to the side.

"Take Celest if you need to," Alpha Superior added.

Aella leaned her head against the doorframe as he sat down behind his desk. She could tell he had the weight of the pack on his shoulders, as usual. Aella wasn't allowed to touch pack materials because she was human, so he confided in her and counted on her to be there when he needed her. The company was hers, though.

Aella walked in and shut the door after Kaius left. She went behind Atlas and wrapped her arms around his shoulders, rubbing his chest gently.

"You're doing great," she whispered.

"Sometimes, I'm not so sure."

"I always am. You're an amazing alpha. I will always be on your side."

Atlas grabbed her by the arm and pulled her onto his lap, then he ran his hand down her hair and kissed her nose.

"You're the only thing that brightens my soul."

Aella leaned her head against his and smiled. "You always said you were filled with such consuming darkness. You always pushed me away, telling me that I was too bright to be in your gloomy world. The truth is . . . I want nothing more than to be consumed by the darkness within you."

"Aella," he growled softly against her lips.

"You're stressed," she said, almost in a whisper. "I know how you deal with stress."

Aella woke up to her room being flooded with sunlight. She groaned when she heard a knock on her door.

"They're getting more frequent."

Aella sat up and only nodded at Eveline, who must have heard her from the hallway. She'd been working with Atlas for months, and each day they grew a little closer. She had just turned twenty, but it seemed like the older she got, the more infatuated she was with him. When she wasn't working, she was attending classes for her bachelor's degree.

The thought that he was not thinking of her, or dreaming of her, angered her. She didn't like that he was probably with other women, thinking that she was a child.

Aella wanted to gag. Whatever she felt was unrequited, and that sucked.

"I have an idea. Let's skip class today," she suggested, shutting the door. "Mom and Dad won't know. Let's go shopping, pick up something more . . . adult-like?"

Eveline sighed and rubbed her hands. "The family sees you as a child."

"Why? I don't dress completely modestly. I wear tight sweaters and jeans. I'm normal."

"Aella, you're beautiful. You have such a beautiful, curvy body. You're thick with three *c*'s. Let's flaunt it. You don't have to, though. I want you to be comfortable in your own skin. You're beautiful the way you are. I was just thinking because of what Elena wears on the regular. You could wear what she wears and draw everyone's attention the way she does."

It wouldn't hurt to try something new, so she nodded. And that's when Eveline pulled her out of bed, literally.

*   *   *

Alpha Superior was sitting at the head of the boardroom table, listening, as his consultants advised him.

"Our revenues grew by 30 percent this year," he spoke. "Money is not an issue, but it is clear greed is on this board. We will continue with—" His eyes darted to the window as he spotted Aella walking in.

She stopped at the receptionist's desk and handed over a wrapped box with a large ribbon on top. He could hear the receptionist, an older woman, thank Aella profusely and hug her. Apparently, Aella was the only one who remembered it was her birthday.

Aella was always so bright, so perky, so kind, so sweet, and so *innocent*. The alpha would never admit that sometimes he wanted to drown himself in her suffocating, palpable, and undeniable luminosity. Her radiance made him breathless. She was beautiful. She was young. She was his brother's daughter. He could never touch her, and he never would. Even the thought of it repulsed him, he couldn't help himself at times.

Aella is . . . he thought. *Wait, what the fuck is she wearing?*

Aella carried her peacoat in the crook of her arm, trying to ignore how the room became quiet. She tried to ignore how a few men walked behind her with their eyes traveling up her body. She didn't usually dress like this, and she wasn't sure if she liked the attention, but she wasn't sure either if she hated it. Eveline had insisted on picking out her outfit for the day and selected a tight long navy pencil skirt, a white blouse that revealed some cleavage, and a navy suit jacket. The heels Aella was wearing were also navy.

Clark, a man from the finance department, walked over to greet her. And just before his hand could grace her back, Atlas was immediately between them. He didn't look thrilled, and before she knew it, his suit jacket was already on her shoulders.

"Office. Now."

She looked at him, shock lacing her face. They walked down the hall to his office, where he slammed the door shut behind him.

"Is something wrong?"

He loosened his tie and cleared his throat. He walked to his chair and sat down, gesturing for her to also take a seat.

"No," he said. "I just needed your help with something."

Her eyes dimmed, and he wasn't quite sure why. She nodded as he handed her a few documents.

"I need you to run over these advertisements and check for errors."

"O-oh alright." She smiled and looked down at the files in her hand. She sat back in her chair, crossed her legs, and started working.

She was totally unaware that Atlas couldn't focus. He was distracted by how deliciously tan her legs were. He'd never realized how smooth her skin was. He'd never realized how full she was. And now it was all rearing up in front him as if she was an untouchable present for him: his idea of perfect femininity, the perfect woman.

Her waist was slim but not too much for his hands to fully lay themselves on her. Her breasts were deliciously more than a handful.

Tan skin, dark eyes, curvy body . . . He was in so much fucking trouble.

Her personality was something he always admired. Her body was something he had never even glanced at, but not anymore. Both were impossibly divine.

Sick—it's sick. She is twenty. Your brother's adopted daughter.

He had fucked countless women, and he was sure he could please her, and he would be pleased by her. But she was off-limits; she would always be off-limits because she was the adopted daughter of Kaius, his brother.

He would never ruin that relationship by choosing to start another with Aella. And he knew that he couldn't simply fuck someone like her. She was pure and kind and deserved a world of love, which he couldn't give. She should be worshiped and be made love to, not fucked for a few hours and be discarded afterwards.

CHAPTER THIRTEEN

Aella continued to read the files. Atlas had left. Eventually, she became bored and began looking at other files on his desk. She stumbled upon a file with Genny's name on it, and it piqued her curiosity.

After what happened with Genevieve, Aella texted her daily, but Genny moved away, and now after reading the file, Aella understood why.

Atlas walked back into the office but stopped in his tracks. He didn't do well with feelings. "Why are you crying?"

She threw herself in his arms again. "You sent her to school."

"What?"

"Genevieve . . . she always wanted to go back and get her GED. She always wanted to go to college. I saw that file. Y-you paid . . . for her to go to the coast and go back to her hometown. You're paying a tutor to help her—her rent, even her therapy."

She saw it when she pulled away and looked at him. She saw it in his light, contact-covered eyes. He wasn't gloomy. He wasn't mean. He wasn't a bad person. He was dealing with his circumstances the best he could. He wasn't all beast. He wasn't all alpha. He was hurt. She felt her lust change. It wasn't just lust, but she wasn't sure what it was.

He nodded, gently taking the file from her hands and filing it back into his cabinet. "She's doing quite well, you know. You'd be proud."

Hours later, he gestured for his jacket, and Aella gave it to him.

"Your father won a big case. He wants to celebrate."

"How do you know?"

He gave her the look.

She looked down. "Oh mind-link thing."

He grabbed her peacoat and held it up, and she gladly put it on.

"Do you want to change?"

She raised an eyebrow. "Should I?"

He stifled a groan of frustration and shook his head. "Let's just go," he said, walking to the elevator.

* * *

Lights blurred as they drove on the highway.

"Why did you do it?"

"Do what?" he asked, keeping his eyes on the road.

"Sent her to school. Got her to safety."

He didn't answer for the longest time, and she assumed he really wouldn't, but then he finally broke his silence.

"She reminded me of my mother. Everyone deserves someone who gives them a chance to succeed."

Aella's mouth hung open in surprise. "You have a mother?"

He gave her the look, and she laughed.

"I just kind of thought you just sprung from the foam of the sea."

"You think you're hysterical."

"Oh, I don't think it. I know it. Where is your mom?" Then it dawned on her, and she stopped laughing. "O-oh. I'm sorry. I-I thought she was . . . like you."

"No. She was human. She died a very long time ago."

"How did Genny remind you of her?"

"My mom had an arranged marriage. My father was a cruel man. He hit my mother until she couldn't take it anymore, killing her."

Her eyes dropped. "I'm so sorry," she muttered.

She was quiet for a moment.

"He didn't only hit your mother, did he?" she spoke again.

His hands tightened on the steering wheel, and that was her answer. She placed her hand on his arm, and he loosened his grip.

She smiled at her little victory.

"When Artemis granted me my lycan, I killed him."

She wasn't fazed that he murdered his father. She would have too, probably. "You couldn't turn your mother?"

"You can't turn someone into lycan. You can either birth them or be blessed with them. The Goddess chooses who deserves to inherit such a legacy." He switched his turn signal on. "Your father, Eveline, and I are different. Those granted a wolf are a divine connection to the Goddess herself. We are stronger, faster, larger . . . And your sister is the offspring of such power. She's like us."

He parked the car and then got out and opened her door.

She didn't step out of the car right away. She turned to him. "I'm starting to think the big bad wolf isn't so bad." She slid out of the car, and they began walking into the building.

* * *

Celest's laugh died down when the waiter came over and laid their food on the table. He smiled at Eveline and Aella before leaving.

"He's cute, Aella! You should get his number."

Aella gawked at her mother, then shook her head. "Not my type."

"He has blue eyes and blond hair. What is your type if that's not it?"

Eveline started dying of laughter, pointing at Aella, who was blushing like a tomato. "Please, make my day. Please, tell Mom what your type is!"

Aella rolled her eyes at her. "Can we please change the topic?"

Celest and Eveline shrugged and soon talked about something else. Aella kept her eyes cast down for the rest of the night.

After a few hours, everyone decided to leave Celest and Kaius so they would have some alone time. Atlas offered to drive the girls back home.

Comfortable silence filled the car until Atlas decided to speak.

"What is your type then?"

Aella looked at him. "What?"

"You told your mother that waiter was not your type. What is?"

She was like a deer caught in headlights. She didn't want to answer. She didn't know how to answer without giving herself away.

"Would you believe me if I said girls?"

He gave her a look.

"I'll take that as a no," she mumbled.

"She likes older guys."

Aella's head whipped back to look at Eveline, who was sitting in the back. Her wide eyes only made Eveline laugh harder.

"Just kidding."

Aella rolled her eyes and refused to look back at Atlas.

"I hardly ask you questions," he said, "and you ask me many. It seems only fair that you give me an answer."

She fiddled with her hands as she thought.

"I'll answer this question if you answer one of mine," she replied.

"Fine."

She glanced at him. "What is your real name?"

His hands tightened around the steering wheel. His jaw clicked in annoyance before he shook his head at the question.

Aella knew it wouldn't work, so she asked another: "What do you desire the most?"

He exhaled. "A mate."

Aella could hear his uncertainty. "But?"

"I don't deserve one."

"So if you had one, you wouldn't accept her?"

He fell silent. "I'd have to make sure," he spoke again, "that her being with me doesn't damage her more than being without me." His voice was hoarse.

"Why do you think you're so toxic? Dominant and bossy maybe, but you aren't the only one. Have you met my father?" She let out a soft chuckle.

"We said one question. Your turn. Your type. Go."

She looked out of the window as she thought.

"Someone with a pulse," she said cheekily.

"That's not a type. That's a quality."

"Yeah, okay," she scoffed. "I like dark hair, and I prefer someone taller than me."

"You're 5'2. That doesn't take much."

"Are you calling me short?"

He smirked at her, taking her breath away. "Yes, I am."

"I have to let you know that we prefer to be called fun-sized." She looked ahead, then back at him. "What's your favorite color?"

He shrugged. *An uninteresting question.* "I don't have one."

That was the last of their discussion.

He pulled into the driveway and shut off the engine. Eveline got out quickly, sensing the impending awkwardness. Atlas remained there, wondering if he should ask what had been on the tip of his tongue.

"How did you know?"

Aella looked at him as she unbuckled herself. "Know what?"

"My favorite book. The first time you gave me a present for my birthday, you came over and told me . . ." He swallowed. "Told me about your dreams. You gave me a present. It was *Les Misérables*, translated in English. It had all your notes in it."

Again, she smiled, nodding. "I made sure to read it before giving it to you. I figured you'd like to know someone else's thoughts about your favorite book."

"But how did you know that it was my favorite?"

"I saw it in your library. Its cover was pristine—looked brand new—but the pages were worn and torn. I just took a guess." She gasped, realizing she forgot something. "I'll read the next chapter. It's upstairs. I'll be right back, alright?"

When she went back inside after giving him the recorder, her sister was standing right by the door with a Cheshire grin.

Aella's smile fell as she looked at her. "What?"

"Do you guys normally talk like that?"

Aella went into the kitchen and took out a cup from the cabinet. She wanted a glass of water. She was so thirsty.

She nodded.

Eveline sat on the barstool behind the island. "H-how do you feel when you're around him?"

Aella blushed. "Safe."

"Anything else?"

"I don't know." She didn't know how to explain it. "I feel nervous, calm, and exhilarated all at the same time. I feel as if breaking down his walls would give me the greatest satisfaction."

"Do you . . . do you . . . ?" She couldn't believe she was saying this out loud. "Do you think maybe he could be your mate?"

Aella shook her head. "He said it's impossible."

"But what if he was?"

"Wouldn't he know?"

Eveline hummed. "Sometimes it takes a while. Dad didn't know right away, either. Think about it: if he's spent centuries believing he wouldn't have a mate, then it might take a lot to make his lycan recognize it."

Aella shook the thought away. "We can't be mates, Eveline. Not everyone gets a happy ending."

CHAPTER FOURTEEN

He was always so sure he'd live forever by himself, in solitude. The thought made his stomach churn and his heart lurch, but he'd become used to it. He'd accepted it. However, after centuries, why was he just questioned what had always been a fact? He thought when one found their mate, their wolf signaled the bond. Admittedly, he ignored the topic of mates in all his books. It was painful to him, and all that pain calloused his heart.

He shouldn't let these thoughts consume him. He had work to do and a murderer to catch.

He parked in the driveway of the beta family, then made his way inside. As their weekly routine demanded, he was there to pick up Aella for her shift at his firm.

She came down the stairs in a skirt and frilly blouse, looking as if going to a nine-to-five job was a normal thing for her. No. She looked as if she owned that nine-to-five company.

She greeted him with a sweet smile, and they exited the house.

In the car, he increasingly became stressed. His hands tightened around the steering wheel while he stared at the road as though it was his enemy. *Why did she have to change how she dressed? Before it was loose sweaters, jeans, and the occasional crop top. Now, every time she comes to the company, she is in a pencil skirt and cleavage-showing blouse, or in tight dress pants.*

He stopped that line of thinking. It was dangerous. It was frustrating because every day she tempted him a little more, and he hated to admit that one day he might just lose all control.

His hands tightened more around the steering wheel as her skirt slithered up her thighs. She crossed her legs, inching it up further.

He swallowed the desire that suffocated him.

* * *

Celest was very intelligent. She was fifteenth in her class in high school, tenth in undergrad, and second in medical school. When she was younger, she tended to minimize her accomplishments and maximize her faults. She wasn't pretty. She was too fat. She wasn't smart. She would hear these insults in her head repeatedly. It led to her taking some time away and going to the hospital for some much-needed therapy, and took her many months to accept who she was.

Her mental health got much better once she finished her degree in medicine and later met Kaius, who reinforced what she had to believe; that she was beautiful and smart and should love herself.

Oftentimes, she wondered what would have happened if he had found her earlier. Maybe if she had met Kaius when she was younger, she would have gotten better quicker. But then, she would tell herself it was her own journey to take. Relying on herself and getting help from medical professionals made her stronger.

She closed the file in her hand and walked out of the hospital room. She slid off her latex gloves and threw them away. She smiled, seeing her handsome mate down the hall with flowers in his hand.

"*Mon amour,*" he greeted, pulling her into his embrace.

She laughed and kissed him before pulling away. She took the flowers, blushing. He still acted like he was trying to get her to date him. To him, she was the most beautiful creature—human or lycan—he had ever laid eyes on. She made him want to be better, do more, and be someone she could be proud of. He wanted and loved the parts of her she had been so convinced no one would ever love.

His loving eyes contorted into pain and turned vibrant red. Celest looked at him with wide eyes, barely understanding what just happened. She heard a gunshot, and moments later, all she felt was pain. Time stood still as Kaius lowered to the ground, bracing for her fall.

Looking down, Celest gasped. She placed her hand over her wounded side. Blood stained her fingers slowly as the shock wore off. She had been shot; someone had shot her.

Kaius eyes widened in shock. He yelled something, but she couldn't hear it. She reached for his arm and forced him to look at her.

"Listen to me," she whispered, breathing harshly. "It's only a flesh wound," she reassured him.

She was a doctor. She knew she would be fine, but it didn't seem like it to him. He wouldn't listen as he frantically put pressure on her wound.

"Kaius, I'm going to pass out from blood loss, but I am fine. It's a flesh wound," she repeated. She noticed a gurney coming her way and some medical staff screaming at Kaius to move away.

It didn't make sense to Celest. Whoever shot her had the perfect chance to kill her. They wouldn't have missed.

If it was Ansan, he wouldn't be so sloppy . . .

She gasped as she realized, hitting a nurse by accident.

They began wheeling her down the hall, to the operating room.

But Celest needed to tell Kaius: "It's a distraction. F-find Aella."

* * *

"She was shot!"

"What?" the alpha growled over the line.

"That son of a bitch..."

Alpha Superior stopped listening as he glanced over at Aella, who seemed unaware. She sat, looking over some files. Time slowed, and his chair fell back as he stood up, dropping his phone from his hand. He ran to her in a flash, a gunshot ringing in his ears.

Her body contorted, and she felt herself waver on her feet. She looked at him as if she couldn't understand what just happened.

He couldn't, either.

The windows had shattered around them, and before he lowered her to the floor, he made sure to move all the glass away from her. He could see blood soaking her blouse, covering her chest.

"Aella, stay awake. Stay awake!"

She choked on her own blood, struggling to ignore the searing pain.

"It hurts," she whispered, tears filling her eyes.

"You're strong, Aella. Stay with me, please. You have to stay with me."

She smiled softly, pressing her palm lightly on his cheek. She sighed as she rubbed his cheekbone, feeling light-headed. She didn't want to stay awake. She was too tired.

Curiosity arose within her as she remembered something she always wanted to know. "What is your name?"

"No, don't ask me that. Not now."

"Why not?"

"Because the only reason you are asking me that is because you think this is your last chance. It's not. You will not leave me! You are mine, Aella!"

Her eyes shut, and he shook her, trying to get her to wake up. His heart fell into his stomach, unable to contain the emotional turmoil he felt. He hadn't felt something so raw, so strong, in centuries.

He cradled her in his arms and brought her to his chest. "Icarus." He ran his hand down her hair. "My name is Icarus. My name belongs to you, Aella." His lycan pushed through his head, forcing his canines to elongate. His eyes widened, his worries lifting. And in that moment, only she mattered.

As he stared down at her, it dawned on him how truly beautiful she was—every part of her was intricately designed—but she was bleeding before him, dying in his arms. He couldn't handle losing her. He just couldn't. He looked at her like he just realized what love really meant.

What was he the most afraid of? Not being alone, not dying. No. What he was terrified of was losing the human woman in his arms. All he could focus on was her face, her smile, her eyes, her voice. Her. He couldn't lose her, not when he just found her.

His world and her soul collided, and all he could see were stars. It became clear, as the paramedics came in and asked him to move, just how she ignited his world.

He stilled and his heart felt like it stopped. His lycan roared in his mind, whining in pain, calling out for Aella.

Mate . . . my mate.

PART TWO
This is the story of how I died.

CHAPTER FIFTEEN

The sound of wheels running over the treads of tile into the operating room was a sound Kaius would never be able to forget. He had thought that after years of rushing Celest to the emergency room whenever she had epileptic episodes, he would be able to control his emotions better.

Yet, he still felt as if his heart was on the edge of failure. And then he felt guilty—guilty because his mate and daughter were injured, and his first thought was of his mate. It should have been about Aella. For a good father, their daughter would always be the priority.

"Kaius."

He didn't answer. He couldn't. He knew he was on the verge of transitioning.

"Brother!" Alpha Superior forced Kaius' back against the hard ceramic-tiled wall, his forearm under his chin. "You cannot lose control here. Think of your mate."

Icarus was always a calculative, infallible man. His voice held a cool edge to it.

"You have no idea, brother—"

"Yes," Icarus snapped, his arm pushing tighter into Kaius, "I do. Calm down. Not here."

"What?" Kaius regained a moment of clarity. "What do you mean?"

The alpha didn't respond.

"What do you mean you understand?"

Icarus dropped his arm but still did not say anything.

"What the fuck do you mean you understand?"

"Not here, Kaius."

"My mate and child are now lying on hospital beds, and you say you understand? How could you possibly understand?"

"You're deflecting your anger."

"Am I?"

"Yes."

"Then leave." Kaius sneered.

The alpha's eyes narrowed as he stepped away from the other man.

"Leave," Kaius repeated. "You'd never cared about my family until recently. You should leave. You do not have to deal with our drama." He paused, narrowing his eyes. "But you can't do that, can you? You can't do that in the same way that I can't."

Heavy silence reigned as they stood still. The realization didn't hit Kaius; it fell on him. All the memories of the years entered, webbing together. Even as a baby, Aella found solace in his brother's presence. It was why, as a girl, she was infatuated with Icarus; why she seemed to be everything Icarus was not. They were soulmates. She was made for him. He was made for her.

The thought nauseated Kaius. *It is sick. They are related.*

"No, we aren't." Icarus firmly said as Kaius' thoughts wafted into his head.

Kaius glared at him, the contacts masking his silver irises failing.

"You're thinking it. Say it, Kaius."

"I can't!" He gasped. "Aella—say this is some sick joke."

Icarus remained unmoving.

"Do you plan on accepting her?"

"Yes."

It was an easy answer to a silly question.

Icarus knew his brother would punch him before Kaius swung, but he allowed it. He would have done the same if he had been in Kaius' position. It hurt but didn't handicap him.

His gaze returned to the other lycanthrope as he wiped the blood from the corner of his mouth with the back of his hand. "I deserved that."

"You're not mating my daughter!"

"What do you expect?" Icarus took a step back. "You expect me to reject her? You know how that will end."

It would end with Icarus dying, if not both of them.

"She's good, Icarus. You're—"

"I'm not. I am the worst possible thing that could happen to her. You think that don't you?"

"Fuck!" Kaius tangled his hand in his hair, turning away from the conversation. "We are magnets for death. She deserves a normal life. Aella could never survive the dangers of being a luna, let alone being mated to someone that doesn't know how to love."

If his brother's words hurt him, Icarus didn't show it.

"Do not underestimate Aella." Icarus didn't care about the insults thrown at him, but an insult toward his luna was unjustifiable. "You accepted Celest."

"Yes, and I had to move out of the pack land!" Kaius took a moment to lower his voice, turning around to stroke his jaw. "If you pursue a relationship with her, you will kill her, Icarus—if not by your enemy's hand, then because you are incapable of giving her everything a female mate needs. The best thing you could do for her is to stay away. Let her find love; a human man she can have children with. I am asking you, as your brother, not to mate her."

Icarus never responded. His stupor broke when Eveline rushed into the hallway.

"Dad? What happened? Are they okay?"

"They're in surgery now."

"What the hell happened? This was Ansan's doing, wasn't it? What are we going to do? She turned toward Icarus. "I know you don't care much, but we have to do something. They need to be safe," she whimpered.

Eveline looks like Aella, Icarus realized.

He never looked at both closely enough to see the resemblance. They had the same dark and curly hair, almond-shaped eyes, and an upturned nose. The notable difference was their face shape. Aella had a rounder, heart-shaped face—a shape that reminded him of a doe—while Eveline's was narrower. Her features were sharp whereas Aella's were delicate.

An emotion washed over Eveline. Her expression morphed from worry into confusion and into astonishment in seconds. "Is something different? I feel different. I feel . . . something."

"What do you feel," Icarus asked.

"I . . ." She shook her head. "I don't know."

But Icarus did. He knew. Even if Kaius didn't want to admit it, Aella was already connected to her rite. Eveline felt the shift in pack dynamics. No longer was there one leader of Pack Superior, but two: a mated pair.

* * *

Aella didn't wake up. She didn't move. It was strange to watch her sleep for days on end, but he couldn't bring himself to leave her. He had pulled her into his world of danger and chaos, and he felt guilty. She wasn't safe—Kaius was right. Aella was human and always would be. Anything minor to him would be catastrophic for her. He could not risk her life. He wouldn't, now that he realized what she was to him. She was the most important person in his life.

He scoffed at himself, already fawning over a human who did not have any idea they were mates. Silently, he leaned forward, enough to brush a curly dark strand of hair behind her ear.

"Anything you will ever want is yours. A wise wolf once told me that the most important member of the pack is the luna, and I remember thinking how untrue that was, but he was right, Aella. I would do anything for you. How dangerous you are."

She needed to wake up. He needed her to wake up.

He was told he would never have a mate. He was born without a counterpart. He was the start of a long lineage and had been alone in his world—at least that was what he had always thought—after making a deal with Artemis that he would forgo a mate so that every wolf could have theirs. It felt selfish for him to accept her. She had her life to live.

But he was a selfish man, and he wanted her painfully.

He briefly regarded Celest and Kaius, who slowly entered the dimly lit hospital room. Kaius made the couch with a blanket and helped Celest sit.

"You aren't supposed to be out of bed."

"Our daughter was dying, Kaius." Her eyes were bloodshot from crying, the bags under them evidence of her lack of sleep.

None of them slept peacefully. Icarus didn't sleep at all.

"Hand me her chart," Celest said.

Kaius reluctantly walked toward the edge of the bed and grabbed the clipboard. Celest took it and skimmed over the information, humming.

"She should be waking up soon. Everything is looking great," she said.

Eventually, the rest of them went down to the cafeteria to get something to eat except Icarus.

He grabbed the book lying on the table beside Aella's bed and opened it. The lights were off, but his eyes were well-adjusted.

They were on chapter 28, the last chapter of the first book: *Andrew did not speak; he was both pleased and displeased that his father understood him. The old man got up and gave the letter to his son.*

* * *

Aella felt a dull ache in her chest, but the pain wore off when she realized a low voice was speaking to her—no, reading to her. He was reading to her. To open her eyes felt like the hardest thing she would ever do. She blinked slowly, ignoring the slight sting behind her head. Her eyes landed on the large wooden door with emergency evacuation instructions posted on it. She groaned almost inaudibly as she tried to shift.

"Stop moving, Aella," said a voice in Romanian.

She knew that rude-toned Romanian. With a soft grin, she slowly turned her head to look at her side. She watched as Icarus placed the book down on her bed. His eyes brightened to sterling silver before reducing to a smoky gray. Both colors were intoxicating to her, and although she could not read the emotion that clouded his gaze, she had seen this very expression a few times before; they were fleeting, but this time it seemed to last.

He hesitantly lifted her chin and stroked her cheek, rubbing his thumbs over her high cheekbones. She could fall asleep again.

"I heard you reading to me."

"I should get the doctor."

"Wait." She grabbed his hand. She knew that as soon as he left, the moment would vanish, and he would never be so warm to her again. "I just need a few moments, please." She relaxed when he nodded and sat back down. "How bad is it?"

"You'll have a scar and will need to stay in the hospital for a few more weeks, but you'll live."

"Was it Ansan?"

He nodded.

"Do we know where he is now?"

"No, we don't."

Silence filled the room again. Icarus turned on the bedside lamp.

She laughed. "Thanks. Not all of us have lycan vision."

Having realized that she was his mate, Icarus understood why Kaius pined after Celest. Aella's laugh could make his heart fly. It was calming to him. It was beautiful.

The grin on his lips fell as he remembered what he needed to talk to her about. He had to tell her the truth because she deserved nothing less. However, considering her state, she was still too fragile.

"Aella," he began.

She shifted on the bed and tried to sit up.

He growled, standing up and coaxing her back down. "Don't move."

"Bossy," she muttered.

"You can't tear your stitches. We must be cautious."

"We?"

His eyes faltered. His hand ran up and down her messy, matted locks of hair. "We have a lot to talk about."

He would tell her. Of course, he would.

A mate was the only thing he ever wanted. He would cherish her more than anything, a privilege he had never imagined he would have. Kaius' words rang in his head, and he felt conflicted.

Her heart began to race, fearing the worse. "Is it bad?"

He sighed, harshly. "I think you know that what happened is making us change some things."

"Oh no, are you hiring a bodyguard?"

He smiled as she laughed again, which was incredible. She had almost died two days previously, but she acted like nothing bad had happened. Nothing stopped her radiance. She was light.

"Don't give me ideas. We are moving to Romania, where the majority of the pack members are."

Her eyes widened. "W-what?"

"Ansan won't attack there, considering how many of us there are. It's safer there."

"But Mom and I . . . are human. We aren't allowed, I thought."

He simply gave her a look. He was an alpha, a king. He could permit it.

"Your family has been worried. Relax. I'll go get the doctor."

As he neared the door, she called his name—his real name.

"Icarus?"

He stopped. His back straightened and tightened in a swift motion. He turned to look at her. His right hand tightened into a fist.

She forgot what she wanted to say, distracted.

"Icarus—it suits you. It's better than Atlas. Thank you, Icarus."

"Don't. If it weren't for me, this would have never happened."

* * *

"Aella, when we arrive, keep your head down," Celest reminded her.

The drive from the airport to the house in Romania was going to be long. She had been told it would be a few hours since pack lands were isolated from the wilderness, and her parents took this time to advise her on how to behave once they arrived.

After waking up, she was hospital-bound for two months more, undergoing physical therapy and routine checkups. She was ecstatic when she was finally discharged but was immediately piled onto a plane and transported to another continent. All her clothes and belongings were being shipped.

Aella readjusted herself in the back of the car.

"You okay?"

She nodded at Eveline, who was next to her. "Yeah, just in a little pain. That plane ride and now this car ride fucked up my chest."

"Language, Aella."

"Sorry, Ma."

"Baby girl, we will give you your medication as soon as we stop," Celest said. "But I was serious, keep your head down. They do not like humans. We are not a part of their pack, so they will naturally feel more nervous around us."

"Why? They clearly have the upper hand."

"There's a history of humans hunting us," her father answered. "And sometimes they were successful."

About an hour later, the car stopped at a black iron gate with a wolf insignia on the front. Icarus undid his seat belt. He pinched the bridge of his nose for a second. Kaius looked over from the passenger seat.

"Are you okay, Icarus?" Aella questioned.

He nodded, but it clearly was a lie.

"There are a lot more wolves in a concentrated area here. The mind link is growing stronger, and it's giving me a migraine." He raised his head to look at her through the rearview mirror. "How are you feeling?"

"I'm fine. I'm nervous. I'm hungry."

He nodded. "Eveline, Kaius, and I are getting out now to run next to the car while Celest drives," he spoke, his hand going into his suit jacket pocket. He turned in his seat, handing Aella a Crunch bar.

She took it gratefully. "Why?"

"Sensing humans enter the pack lands will aggravate them. They'll attack."

"W-what?"

"Don't worry. Nothing will happen to you."

Eveline gently brushed back her hair. "Alpha can't command them not to. Well, he can. But if he did so, it would greatly offend them. If it makes you feel better, they could do such to any lycanthrope to exert their dominance in the pack. They like strict hierarchy."

Kaius, Icarus, and Eveline got out of the car. Celest got into the driver's seat while the three stayed outside the Escalade. Eveline and Kaius were at the front; Icarus at the back.

Celest slowly drove up the winding, snow-covered driveway. She stopped at an old metal gate that opened almost immediately as the car approached. The sound made the hair of her arms stand up. Inside pack lands, nothing had drastically changed. Large pine trees surrounded the narrow driveway.

A sheet of fog blurred her vision as she continued to drive. Snow littered the ground and trees—a beautiful sight.

Celest asked, "Not what you expected?"

"Actually, it's exactly what I expected," Aella answered.

Nothing seemed out of the ordinary until the majestic home came into view. Sitting at the end of the driveway behind a switched-off fountain was a castle with Baroque architectural features. It was reminiscent of the Château de Chambord in France.

The car stopped at the rotunda before the palace, and Celest did not move for a long minute before she undid her seat belt.

She turned around to look at Aella. "Ready?"

Aella nodded.

The back door opened, and Celest held out a hand to Aella.

Aella gulped as the door slammed behind her. A circle of humans started swarming around the car. They were far enough for her not to suffocate but close enough that she could see their features. They were clearly disagreeable with her and her mother's presence.

Looking up, she watched as others came to the balconies of the ascending floors, looking equally unenthusiastic. Elena, the woman from the company, smiled brightly at them and took a step forward.

Eveline moved in front of Aella, her arm extending toward her.

"I wanted to fight something today." Elena's smile was sinister.

Aella didn't understand why. She wasn't shocked to see so many faces from the company. Icarus had explained that many of them worked there and traveled back and forth every few months.

She had been told to keep her head down, so she did not respond.

Before Elena could say something else, a male rushed to the car, getting close to Celest. Kaius was quick. A sickening crunch of hands against the chest resonated through the forest as the man was launched into the air. He landed, not as a human but as a wolf.

Aella gasped. The shift was so swift that it was over once she blinked.

The male was the first of a line of wolves that started their assault.

Kaius turned toward Aella before looking back at the rush of pack members as he shifted, tearing his clothes. Aella had never seen her father or Icarus shift before. It was more startling than watching Eveline because it was slower, and she could see each bone break and reform.

When he finished, a brown wolf—larger than the other—stood in front of them. He was far bigger than Eveline.

Eveline stayed as human even after some landed on the roof of the car and shifted around them.

Celest grabbed Aella's hand, pulling her close. As Kaius was defending Celest and Icarus standing his ground on the other side of the car as human, Eveline began to usher them closer to the door. Someone gripped her hair and pulled her away, giving enough time for them to surround Aella and Celest separately.

Aella was pushed to the ground, the bodies of others towering over her secluding the sun. A hand wrapped around her throat and lifted her to her feet. She winced, stridor parting her lips. The pain from her wound made her dizzy.

A growl—a growl that seemed to make the world around her shake—echoed in her ears, and instantly she was dropped and fell on her back, coughing. Icarus parted the crowd with another growl, making his way to her. They cowered from him. He stepped over her, his foot on either side of her hips. He stared down the other wolves, and they whimpered, backing away from Aella and then from Celest.

"Enough!"

The amount of dominance in that tone elicited a sudden urge in her to genuflect before him and lower her eyes. But she didn't. She didn't submit to him. She couldn't say the same for the others.

One by one, the people around them kneel, their heads pressed into the ground. Those who shifted lowered their beastly heads, their snarling ceasing. It was disturbingly quiet.

Just as Aella thought the storm was over, Elena screamed, "No! It's impossible!"

Icarus gently helped Aella up by her waist, his one hand bracing her neck. He ignored Elena. His hands then roamed over the top of her head.

Aella realized he was checking for injuries.

"Are you alright?"

She had never heard him speak to her so gently, filled with so much care and worry.

She nodded, unable to speak.

"No, she cannot be the luna!" Elena protested. "She's unfit! She's human!"

Icarus ignored her and guided Aella into the home. He settled her in the foyer. Eveline, Kaius, and Celest came in, each wearing individual expressions. Celest looked morbidly shocked while Kaius looked angry. Eveline—she looked vindicated.

"What's a luna?" Aella asked no one in particular.

Eveline came to her. "Let Mom look at your stitches and then I'll take you to the library."

Aella's eyes widened. "Library?"

"Oh, it's great. You'll be allowed to read all the boring shit all day long."

"Are you going to tell me what a luna is?"

Eveline turned toward Icarus and then looked at her father. "Dad, you knew. You never said anything. How did you hide it?"

Wolves that weren't alphas or lunas could not close their links to the rest of the pack, so it did not make sense that her father hid it from her. He must have been old enough to have mastered it in a short time.

"Knew what?" Aella asked.

"You knew, Kaius," Celest said with an angry tint to her voice. "And you kept it from me?"

Kaius went to grab her arm, but she pulled away.

"Don't touch me, Kaius! How long have you known?"

"Celest, I—"

"She's my daughter too. I can't know about your pack life, but anything and everything about our daughter I have the right to know about."

Aella had never seen her mother so livid. Her question still wasn't answered, but Eveline already ushered her out of the room.

* * *

"No, you are not talking your way out of this one this time, Kaius. I am not some attorney you're up against in court."

Celest was furious, not only at the fact that her mate kept this secret but also that he felt he could control their lives.

Kaius remained seated as she paced. They were in Icarus' office. Icarus was sitting behind his desk.

"I am sorry—"

"No!" she shot out. "You always have the physical and financial upper hand in this relationship, and the only thing I could ever consistently rely on was that we were raising our daughters together. You don't get to make decisions for our adult daughter or for our family."

"I will not allow our daughter to—"

"To what, Kaius?" Celest placed her hands on her hips. "Be with her soulmate? If you loved her, you would never ever deny her such happiness."

"She's twenty-one, Celest."

"I was twenty-six. So what? It should be her decision."

"He's a monster," Kaius ripped out.

Celest took a second. "How could you say something like that about your brother? What happened that has made your relationship with each other so sour? Regardless, he's the person that not only found Aella but also saved her, twice. If anyone deserved our daughter, it would be him simply because of that. What did you say to him? Why hasn't he told her?"

Kaius was silent.

Celest turned toward Icarus. "What did he say to you?"

"He has a point, Celest."

"So what? You don't want her as a mate? You think she isn't worthy? If you are rejecting her, say that—"

"Aella is"—he took a moment, his hand flexing on top of his desk, curling and then uncurling to ease the tension—"important. I can't and will not risk her life."

"So, what does this mean?"

"It means," Kaius interrupted, "that I've asked him not to mate her. She deserves more."

"She deserves a choice! Even more, she deserves a mate."

"You're right, Celest. If anyone deserves one, it would be her but not me. I have blood on my hands and older than her by centuries. Kaius is right; I am a monster."

"You've made your decision then, for you and for her."

Icarus shook his head. "No, just part of it." He pushed himself off the shelf he was leaning against, then walked out of his darkened office.

He walked down the hall to the left and up some stairs, stopping at the library, where Eveline and Aella were talking. He could hear them behind the doors.

"Eveline, what is a luna?"

He pushed the doors open, a scowl on his sharp features. "A luna is a term in our world."

"Like calling someone a bitch in ours?" Aella asked.

Aella knew that both lycanthropes could hear how her heart picked up, but she was used to everyone in her family knowing how she felt.

Icarus could not hide his grin.

"No, not like calling someone a bitch." He went to the second level of the library, the third row on the left, and took out a large book. He tossed it in his hands before descending the stairs.

He laid the book on the table in front of her. "This book explains everything in our world. It's used to educate pups as soon as they reach puberty. This one, unlike the other, is in English."

She locked eyes with him for a short second and then picked up the book. "This . . . this is your handwriting."

He was not surprised that she recognized it. They had written back and forth for years.

He nodded. "I wrote it. Page 180."

She quickly caught on what he just said and flipped to the page.

"Mates? That's the heading"—she looked up at him—"which . . . you already know."

She began reading. Eveline had already explained the broad strokes of mates, but this specific chapter explained them much more in-depth.

She must have been taking too long to finish because Icarus spoke again: "Do you remember anything when you were shot?"

Aella watched closely as he seemed to become livid at it. His fists flexed, and his jaw clicked.

She shook her head. "I remember talking, and I remember you telling me your name. After that, I passed out." Looking around, she realized Eveline was no longer in the room. "Why?"

"Keep reading."

"I hate it when you do this. You're so bossy and cryptic that it drives me insane." Nevertheless, she buried her head in the pages again.

A small gasp left her lips, and she read this sentence out loud, "The only lycan not granted a predestined mate is Alpha Superior."

She could tell by the indentation on the old paper that he had struggled to get through this sentence, and her heart fell into her stomach. She knew this already, yet it still made her feel horrible.

"I am so sorry, Icarus," she whispered, putting the book down.

"Keep reading."

Reluctantly, she continued: "The only ranks of designation are given to the mates of those at the top of the hierarchy. The mate of the delta is Delta Female. The mate of the beta is Beta Female." She raised her head. "So that's Mom? And what's a delta?"

"Keep reading, Aella."

She sighed. "Finally, had Alpha Superior been granted a mate, their designation would have been Luna Superior," she read, stuttering. She held her breath. "This is all mates of alphas take the name of L-Luna." Her heart stopped in her chest. She lowered the book once again and set it on the desk as silence started to suffocate her.

Icarus looked unfazed, curious even by how she reacted.

She wished she had worn a looser shirt because the cropped sweater she had decided on suddenly felt too tight. This meant that every dream, every feeling, every second glance, and every heart flutter was not wrong. It was not a testament to her sick, delusional mentality.

She did not understand, though. When Eveline spoke about it, she said it was an exciting, romantic moment. She said mates could not wait to be with each other in every way. However, Icarus looked as if he were trying to stay away from her.

He didn't seem shocked by the sudden revelation, and her eyes widened as realization came over her.

He knew—how long has he known I am his mate? And why doesn't he seem enthusiastic? He said the one thing he'd ever wanted was a mate. What's changed?

"What are you thinking?"

His voice almost startled her. "Are you saying I am your mate?"

"Yes."

She looked away. "But you aren't happy with it?"

"I wish the circumstances were different."

"W-what? That I was a lycanthrope or that I came from a different family?" Averting her gaze, she stared daggers at the chair legs. She felt the familiar burn behind her eyes, and she knew that the instant she let a tear fall, he would smell it. But she didn't want to be weak. She felt humiliated.

"Aella—"

"So what? You're rejecting me? I-I thought—"

"Don't say that word," he snapped. He quickly closed the gap between them. "You are my brother's daughter."

"Adopted daughter."

He sighed. "I am not rejecting you." His strong finger lifted her chin, then he dropped his hand. "I . . . I am sorry, Aella."

"Is my father making you do this?"

"Your father is right. You deserve more." He pushed himself away from her, swiping his hair back as he walked away.

"Look, I . . ." He sighed. "I don't know how to do this. I don't know how to be a mate, and I don't know how to have my mate and not hurt my brother. Kaius saved my life, and I will forever be indebted to him. I will not—" He stopped as if the utterance of such a word could burn his tongue. "I will not take you."

"You don't want me?"

"It's not that."

"Well, it must be." A stray tear fell down her cheek. "I'm human and I'm adopted, and that's not something you can get past."

"I don't care that you're human—"

"How can you say that? You despised my mother when my father mated her because she's human."

"I've gotten over it. I don't care that you're human. It doesn't change how much I want you, and it doesn't change how much I want to protect you. It doesn't change your pack status, either."

"So, then what? I don't understand."

"I am giving you choices." He turned again to look at her. "The first one, you could reject me. You could reject me, and I'd die, giving you the freedom to marry whoever you want. The second is we wait for five years until you turn twenty-six."

"Twenty-one, twenty-six, what difference does five years make?"

"By the time you're twenty-six, you will have graduated from a university and in theory will have worked for a couple of years. You'd still live here but would have your own life. This way, you can be sure about what you want. Celest was also twenty-six when Kaius mated her. Hopefully, your father has had a change of heart by then."

"And if he hasn't?"

"Then, by that point, hopefully, my care for his opinion will have fallen."

She struggled to understand her emotions. She was frustrated, angry, sad, disheartened, and insecure. But she also realized that a part of her was proud. Icarus cared enough for Kaius that he would forgo mating immediately for the sake of his feelings. It seemed to her that her father was more of the insensitive wolf than Icarus.

Icarus wasn't selfish. He was in all ways a caring, loyal male.

"Why do my father's feelings matter more than mine?"

The room froze as Icarus stared at her. She watched as his contacts failed to mask his emotions, blinking between colors. She learned that his eye shade was an indicator of his emotions, and they showed more than just anger. They revealed his confusion, sadness, and frustration.

"They don't."

"If he wasn't in the picture," she started, taking a breath, "if he had never adopted me and I was just some human who happened to be your mate, would you wait?"

"No." It was an immediate, sure response. "But those aren't the circumstances, Aella."

"You're expecting me to live my life for the next five years: go to college, work, travel, date—"

"Don't say that."

"All the while my soulmate is right here!"

"Do you think this is easy for me?" He was startlingly cold. "Do you think," he forced out, "you're the only one who has dreams? That I can watch you live a life without me? That when I see the way men look at you, I don't get homicidal thoughts?" He placed a finger into the loop of his tie and ripped it down and off his neck. "Do you remember when I told you about my mother?"

"Your mom was arranged to marry your father," she said softly. "Your father killed your mother, and in retaliation, you killed your father."

She gave him a silent nod as he played with the silver ring on his right forefinger. "When I was younger, I was a small boy. I wasn't a great fighter. One night, my father admitted that he'd gambled his wages for the week and that my mother and I would have to forgo food. He sat in front of us eating," he sneered.

Aella could tell that he couldn't, or wouldn't, look at her because he was furious. "I'm so sorry—"

"The next morning, I stole some bread at the market. I got caught. My father flogged me and took me to the town's square so everyone could watch my embarrassment." His hand flexed at his side. "Kaius was there. He saved me. He helped me back to his home and convalesced me until I was able to return to my mother.

"Kaius was not well-off, but he was in a better situation than my family. When he could, he would bring my mother and me food and help heal our wounds. At one point, he fought my father for hitting my mother, and Kaius won. My father was more reluctant to do so after that."

"I didn't know," she whispered.

"Kaius saved me and my mother when we needed it the most."

"And now, you feel that if . . ." she trailed off, and her dark brows furrowed as she tried to articulate what she meant. "If you were to mate me, would it be the greatest form of disrespect?"

"Yes. Do you blame him? It's wrong." He looked to the ground before dragging his eyes to meet hers. "I am wrong."

"You didn't get to decide. I didn't get to decide. It wasn't our choice."

Icarus tried not to let his emotions show on his face as his heart dropped into his stomach. As he asked himself whether he would have decided differently if he could, part of him thought he would.

The other part—the guilt-ridden half—knew that in every lifetime, it would always be Aella.

CHAPTER SIXTEEN

Aella sat rigidly as the scraping of silverware and ceramic plates filled her ears. The long dinner table was filled with the members of the pack, who were eating as if they had been starved. Kaius and Icarus were not seated yet, and it made Aella feel even more uncomfortable, but they had coveted their dominance. No one would lay a hand on her again.

Eveline was seated beside her, looking more relaxed.

Aella was tired. She was annoyed. She was sad. She had thought that if she had to live among people who hated her, the trade-off would be a mate that was affectionate toward her. Yet , somehow she ended up in a segregated house with a mate who wanted nothing to do with her. It seemed unfair. After all the shit she had been through, she wanted peace.

"I thought the day the pack received a luna would be one of the most jubilant celebrations. Tell me," Elena continued from down the table, "how does it feel to know that your mate has been in every woman at this table and yet refuses to do the same with you?"

Aella stared at her through eyes burning with hatred. She felt her stomach dip, but she refused to give in to the subtle dominance that emanated from Elena. She wondered if it was true.

A short laugh from Eveline caught Elena off guard.

"How does it feel to know that a human is of higher destined rank than you, Elena? Everyone knows that you've been begging to become the luna and Aella beat you at a game she wasn't even trying to win."

Elena bared her teeth.

Eveline stood from such blatant disrespect. "I am not a human, Elena, nor am I a pup that you can bully into submission. I am stronger than you, and to be honest, I've been looking for a reason to kick your ass."

Pride resonated within Aella. She felt safe knowing Eveline would always be on her side and would fight for her honor.

Elena's confidence wavered, and she lowered her head. Eveline's rank was higher than hers. It was natural for her to submit to Eveline.

Eveline sat again, and everyone continued to eat except for Aella. She could not get what Elena had said out of her head.

Eveline nudged her after a while. "Don't listen to her. Alpha wouldn't touch her with a ten-foot pole."

Aella nodded in uncertain agreement. "I'm tired. I'm going to head to bed."

As she climbed up the stairs to her room, Celest caught up to her and wrapped an arm around her shoulders. Aella couldn't help but suffocate in her mother's arms. She prayed that they were far enough so that no one could hear her pathetic sobs.

"I can't imagine how hard this must be for you. I am so sorry that they're so stubborn."

"I thought you would be against it too."

"It's still weird, but I believe that you should get to feel what I feel with your father. It's a magical, beautiful thing that I want both of my daughters to have one day. It's not fair to deny you that. I will try my very hardest to change your father's mind."

Aella's sobs were somewhat silenced by Celest's shoulder as she felt her mother freeze around her, and that familiar pull tugged at her heart. She knew her mate was behind her, watching as she crashed and burned in the embrace of her mom.

Pathetic. Childish. Infantile.

Celest ushered her down the hall to her room, then she put her to bed and stayed until her sobs turned into a gentle murmur.

Coming out of the room, Celest wasn't surprised to see the lycans at the door. She stopped before them, shoulders locked and head held high. She spotted Icarus, and a slight relief burned through her.

He looked pained—guilty.

Silence reigned.

"We have to get used to hearing her cry," Celest finally spoke. She shook her head at her mate. "How could a luna ever learn to be a great one if she doesn't have the support of her mate and family?"

"Celest, I can't—" Kaius started. His hand flexed at his side. "You expect me to allow them to . . ." His nose wrinkled in disgust.

"Yes, I do. You're being so selfish that I hardly recognize my mate anymore."

*   *   *

Aella couldn't sleep. She tossed herself to her other side, staring at the door. With a huff, she sat up and wrapped her robe around herself.

She exited her room and ventured down the hall to the library, to which Eveline had brought her. Her steps stuttered as she saw a lit lamp. Icarus was reading in the chair next to it.

He looked up, and she hated how he took her breath away.

"I'm sorry. I can leave."

He looked at her heavily. "Can't sleep?"

She shook her head. "You can't, either?"

He nodded and gestured for her to come in.

She picked up the same book he had shown her before and sat down on the couch against the bay window on the other side of the library. She glanced out of the window longingly. A sight to behold—the large conifers were heavy with rich white snow that glistened under the moon. Just behind those trees were mountains that peaked in succession from one another. They, too, were blanketed in snow.

She turned her eyes back to the book.

There was a time and place where alphas and lunas congregated with their packs to participate in pack games, which reminded her of human Olympics. They would spar, and the last remaining member would receive designation, and so would their pack, getting a higher world ranking.

Pack Superior never participated, but it seemed to Aella that this was a specific location, in which many pack leaders chose to remain throughout the year to receive advice and training from the more experienced leaders.

Aella wondered if she was allowed to go. Living in this house, with a mate who didn't love her and pack members who didn't respect her, would end up with her killing herself. She didn't know how long she could do it.

"What happened tonight at dinner?"

His voice startled her.

She looked at him and shrugged, struggling to see his entire face under the shadows. "You already know. You can read Eveline's thoughts, and Elena's for that matter."

"I didn't."

"What?"

"I didn't sleep with any female in my pack."

She let out a heavy breath. She didn't respond, but she was relieved. She dipped her head back into her book.

A mug was set on the table in front of her, and she looked up.

"You left?" she asked.

"You need to get better at being aware of your surroundings."

She grabbed the mug and took a sip of the sweet chamomile tea. She moaned softly. "Thank you."

"I don't think you can call that tea with how much milk and sugar you like in it."

She smiled at his disdain. "I didn't know you knew my tea order."

"I'm starting to realize I pay closer attention to you than I thought." His brows furrowed. "How are you feeling?"

"Sore," she admitted.

Icarus sat beside her, but far enough so they weren't touching.

"I won't bite, you know," she quipped.

"I know, but I might."

She laughed, shaking her head. "Surprisingly, I've had men say worse to me."

"Doubtful."

"Oh really?" She straightened. "I once had a man say his favorite amendment was the thirteenth."

She was surprised at the sound of laughter that came from Icarus. It was a deep, boisterous, hearty laugh. She couldn't participate as she was far too distracted by the way his eyes glistened and how this was the first time, she saw him look happy.

"Well, did it work? Did it sweep you off your feet?"

"Can't say it did, but it did make me question if I liked women more."

They fell into a comfortable silence.

Aella continued with her book. She untucked her feet and stretched them over Icarus' lap. She expected him to push them off him, but he only rolled his eyes and relaxed further, his one hand settling on her ankle while the other holding his book up. He was reading *Les Mis*, the one she had gotten him.

She peeked over her book, and she watched as he stared intently at one of her annotations on the edge of the page. It made her content to see him interacting with her notes. It gave her some type of tranquility to know that they both got lost in between the pages of fictional worlds. When she couldn't keep her eyes open any longer, she sighed and put the book down on the coffee table in front of them. She removed her legs from his lap and sat upright for a moment, contemplating.

"What are you thinking?"

She leaned her head slightly. "I want to touch you," she admitted. "Not like that," she added on with a shake of her head, embarrassment flooding her cheeks. "I mean the desire to be near you is so intense that I cannot breathe sometimes, and it's only gotten worse. As soon as I turned eighteen, I felt this constant vice-like grip on my heart. I had thought for the longest time that there was something wrong with me, and I was ashamed. Does it not feel the same for you?"

A drawn-out silence ensued.

She knew he was listening, judging by how still he was.

He placed a bookmark between the pages and set the book on his lap. "I'm ashamed, not of being your mate but of the fact that I believed years ago that I could live life without someone like you in it. My day doesn't begin until I see you, and I can't fall asleep without knowing you're safe. Every day I walk restlessly, aching to touch you, but every night I get relief by dreaming of you. It doesn't feel the same for me; it feels worse. Never think this is easy for me."

"I think this waiting thing is not completely about Kaius." She looked at him. "I think, in part, you are doing this because you feel that you don't deserve love and to be loved. It's some sort of self-punishment, but in doing so, you're also punishing me. You're forcing me to live unhappily and uncomfortably, and that's not fair, Icarus." She stood, frustrated by his stubbornness—and even more so by how her body reacted to his sweet remarks.

* * *

Aella could feel the steely gazes on her as she walked into the kitchen. Their coldness froze her, handicapping her into submission.

She understood why they had to move. Kaius and Icarus felt more comfortable there, but it was no secret that if her life was threatened, no one would choose to protect her. In fact, she was partially sure they would give her to Ansan if given the chance. They didn't respect her, didn't trust her, and didn't want to make friends with her.

After grabbing an apple, she turned from the island to see the pack women talking about Daria's soon-to-be-born child. Daria was the only pregnant woman there.

One thing Aella couldn't help but respect was the pack's treatment of their pregnant wolves. Daria was royalty. She never lifted a finger, never waited for anything, and never went out unprotected. Her sweet mate—Ferhat—pandered to her every whim, showering her with gifts and compliments, which was refreshing to see.

Aella, on the other hand, was treated so poorly. But she knew that if she were a wolf, she would be treated just as well.

"I just wish I could have a luna birth."

Aella's focus shifted to the conversation.

Elena scoffed at Daria as she patted her hand. "Don't we all wish we had a real luna?"

"You shouldn't . . . you shouldn't speak about her that way, Elena," Daria muttered. She was a kind-hearted woman and the only one thus far to have said something nice.

"She's human. Get a backbone."

"You wouldn't like any luna even if she were a shifter."

Aella could tell by the way Daria couldn't hold Elena's gaze that she was more submissive, but she tried to stick up for her point.

The conversation fizzled out, and Daria's argument was muted by another conversation.

"Daria?"

The room turned to Aella. She rarely spoke out of turn around them. It had been about three weeks since their arrival, which was long enough to teach her etiquette.

Daria looked over at her, shocked. Her pouty mouth turned downward in confusion. "Yes?"

"What is a luna birth?"

"Oh." She set the deck of cards down in front of her in a neat pile. "It's a tradition within the pack. The luna usually acts as a midwife. They assist in labor and birth and then welcome the pup officially into the pack."

"Lunas are trained in midwifery?"

She nodded. "They're trained in many areas: communication, diplomacy, accounting, husbandry, combat . . ." She chuckled to herself. "Well, now that I think about it, there isn't one aspect of pack life that lunas aren't a part of. Alphas rarely assist in birth and husbandry."

"I was always told," another woman, Catina, chimed in, "that the only thing an alpha is good at is helping his luna run the pack." She smiled coyly. "Well, that and making sure she's in a good mood."

The table chuckled except for Elena, who was scowling.

Aella didn't understand until Daria winked at her. Her cheeks burned a dark crimson, and she found herself smiling beneath her curls.

"We shouldn't talk about fantasies," Elena carped. "After all, Alpha made it very clear he would never touch Aella."

Aella's smile fell with her heart. She felt a moment of kindness and humor, but Elena did everything she could to squash it.

Aella sighed deeply, removing herself from the kitchen.

She ran up the stairs. Then, down the hall, she walked past Icarus' office. His door was open, and she saw her father sitting in the chair in front of the desk. She tried to walk away unnoticed.

"Aella?"

She stopped and stifled her sigh of disappointment. She slowly went back to the door and looked at her adoptive father.

"How are you? We haven't spoken in a few days."

She always thought she was a kind and fair person, but she couldn't control the bitterness that erupted in her chest every time she spoke to him. She felt that it was his job to make sure she was at her happiest, and yet he denied her that. He was the only reason she couldn't be with her mate.

"It wasn't by accident." She leaned against the doorframe, crossing her arms. She almost felt bad as she watched his face fall.

She straightened to give off less hostility. "Mom said she's going to take me to the library today to get some different books. Pretty boring around here, no offense. We're in the middle of nowhere."

Her father's wrinkles seemed to fade, as if he was instantly regressing to his younger age. He already looked younger than his age, but when he was relaxed, he could pass as someone in their late twenties.

Icarus was the same, although those moments of relaxation were few and far between. His constant scowling aged him into his mid-thirties.

She wondered what he would look like when happy. She bit the urge to look at her mate, trying to keep her eyes fixed on her adoptive father. She flexed her hand and then made a fist to ease some of the pressure in her chest. She ignored how their eyes instantly trained on her movement.

"Yeah, I'm sorry about that. Take Caprias with you when you go," Kaius said. "And tell your mother I love her."

She raised an eyebrow. "Why don't you just tell her yourself?"

His face fell again, and his eyes conveyed a kind of sadness she was getting much more accustomed to.

"She is upset with me. We haven't spoken more than a few sentences in the past few weeks. We are close enough that the bond doesn't weaken or hurt. But, well—"

"Oh."

Aella didn't realize her mother was taking a stand with her. It made her feel much better to know she was on her side. She knew Eveline was also very expressive of her opinion around the pack house.

They were her family and always would be. They routinely chose her and put her feelings above their own. She knew her mother must have been feeling the need to be near her soulmate, and yet she fought against it. She was much stronger than Aella ever gave her credit for.

"So, the mating bond only hurts when you aren't in proximity? In theory, if I went away, as long as I came back every week, we wouldn't feel the pain?"

"Every two days," Icarus answered. "And the mate bond doesn't matter because I won't let you leave."

"Even if I went to sleep at a friend's house? Oh, come on. I should have some flexibility."

His eyes narrowed, but he dropped his disagreement. "You could go, but you would be expected to abide by very strict protocols."

"Such as?"

"Hey, Aella. I heard Elena was giving you shit again."

The young luna turned to look down the hall toward Eveline, who was walking with Celest.

She nodded. "Yeah, nothing new."

"Yeah, but I heard Daria was nice to you. I listened in on the conversation. Did you want to learn more about the birthing process? She's due in a few weeks. You could read up on what you can . . . Hey, Dad."

"Hey, Ev." Kaius looked at his mate, who refused to meet his gaze. "Hello, beautiful."

Celest hesitantly looked at him, sucking in a breath as she did so. It was a struggle seeing him and being near him, but she held strong.

"Hello, mate. Aella, are you ready to go? Ev, would you like to come?"

"Where you going?"

"To the library and then shopping." Celest gave a wide smile.

"Library, boring; shopping more, my speed. Sure, I'll come."

"Celest," her father started, standing up to take out his wallet.

She held up her hand. "No. I will use my own money."

Aella and Ev held their breaths. Their father loathed it when Celest insisted on supporting herself and the children financially.

"Go, girls. Caprias is waiting with the car."

They nodded, then practically ran away from the awkward scene.

Celest sighed deeply. "Do you feel that?"

Kaius didn't need to ask what she meant.

"Every day Aella feels the same, and so does Alpha Superior. If she has to go through it, we will too."

CHAPTER SEVENTEEN

Late at night, Aella found herself in the library again. Instead of seeing Icarus, she saw her mother sitting in the same spot, reading. She looked tired, which was a stark contrast to her usual, bubbly disposition.

"Mama?"

The older woman looked up, startled. Her senses weren't as strong as the others in their family, so she didn't hear Aella come in.

Aella hated how sullen her mother looked the recent days. Celest's age wasn't masked by the ageless effects of lycanthropy like her father or Icarus. She was fifty-five. Her hair had started to fade into gray, her eyes were framed by subtle wrinkles, and her smile was between two large smile lines—a testament to the joyous life she lived. But it wasn't her aging that upset Aella. It was the fact that Celest rarely wore a genuine smile now. Her features were worn out by her putting distance between her and her mate.

"Hey, mija. Why are you still up?"

"Couldn't sleep. You couldn't, either?"

She nodded.

Aella grabbed the old, handwritten book Icarus had given her and then sat down next to Celest. "You can't sleep next to Dad, can you?"

Celest was surprised to have heard her daughter say something so spot on. She nodded. "It gets easier."

"You're lying."

Celest's eyes dulled. She didn't try to dispute her. "I'm okay, I promise."

"Thanks, Mom. Thank you for taking a stand."

"Of course, baby girl. Your father is used to being the most dominant one in the room, and I have given him that for the most of our relationship because I thought he would always respect me. In this instance, he does not, and that is unacceptable."

Aella nodded, opening the book to finish the section on lycanthropic medicines.

Twenty minutes of silence later, she sighed. She laid the book on her lap. "I found out today that lunas are supposed to do, well, everything."

Celest didn't say anything but turned slightly to show Aella she was listening.

"And I am sure there are things beta females are supposed to do that Dad and the pack haven't told you."

"I'm not a real beta female, Aella."

"Then I am not a real luna, either." Her heart fell at the prospect.

Maybe she wasn't. Maybe she was an imposter. Maybe the universe fucked up and gave Icarus the wrong mate. She was weak, fragile, and human. All these aspects of her would not make her a great luna.

"Not the same."

"How is it not? We are both humans with nonhuman mates of rank. Our circumstances are not different. If you think I am a real luna, don't disrespect yourself by saying you're not a real beta. You know there's a place—not sure where—but new beta females and lunas go there to learn about their duties. If I were a wolf, I'd go there. But being a human, I don't know if they'd accept me."

"Where did you read about this . . . place?" Celest gestured to the book on Aella's lap and gingerly took it. She leafed through the pages and turned to the end of the chapter Aella was reading.

She hummed as she then flipped through the last pages of the large, practically falling-apart book. "There's an appendix. Maybe you can find contact some information here and ask—send a letter maybe."

* * *

In her desperate attempt to pinpoint when her life turned upside down, Aella thought about every major event. Her life began in mortality, surrounded by poverty. Maybe this was when things started to spiral out of control—maybe order couldn't come from a beginning so chaotic—or maybe it was in that forest behind their home in the States, when Eveline told her about their distant uncle.

Perhaps it was that stupid date with that boy in high school, who tried to kiss her, and she had the first epileptic episode that sent her to the hospital, where she met Icarus for the first time. Icarus was cold and at times brutish, but he provided her with much-needed comfort, doing so effortlessly and efficiently. He left just as easily, though.

Maybe it was when she hit the deep cusps of puberty, making the damage irreversible—when she got butterflies at the thought of Icarus, and her most intimate parts yearned for his attention. It was during this time that her self-loathing skyrocketed in tandem with her guilt and shame.

Maybe it was on graduation or at that restaurant; in the car, at his workplace, or any other places where Icarus was around or mentioned.

However, none of it mattered anymore. It would have been the same, maybe not the circumstances but the conclusion. In the end, she would always desire him, and he would always be the one she was soul-bonded with.

* * *

The psychological bullying toward Aella and her mother continued in the house. Elena was ruthless in her torment, and no one else cared enough to stop her. Daria was a sweet woman but tended to submit to Elena without much fight. It was all beginning to become too much for Aella.

Aella read over the parchment in her hands once again, checking for spelling errors. Then, she folded the letter and stuffed it in an envelope with the address written on the front.

She delivered the letter later that day.

As the pack house declined into nighttime rituals and murmurs, she retired to her bedroom with Eveline. They decided to watch a movie, picking *Eclipse*, one of Aella's favorites but one of Eveline's least favorites.

"If you ask me," Aella chirped, "I think all lycanthropes should remain shirtless at all times."

"Including the women?"

"Especially the women, Ev."

Her sister laughed as she lounged on her side, the popcorn flakes scattering around her waist. Aella snatched the bowl and threw a few pieces into her mouth. Eveline suddenly stiffened as she stared at the door opening.

Icarus cocked his head a little, looking at the TV. "This is entertaining to you?"

"Don't say you don't love this cinematic masterpiece of a series," Aella warned. "I might have to kick your ass."

His mouth turned slightly, his eyes training on her.

"Violence is never the answer," he said.

She snorted, which was unbecoming of her and completely not feminine. "You once said to me that violence is always the answer."

His eyes softened, and he gave way to a deep sigh that somewhat relaxed his stiff frame. He was never one completely at ease.

"I know you swapped all the books in my office for sappy romance novels. One of note is *Fernanda's Exploration*. I don't want to know what's being explored. Even more so, I don't want to know how you have so many copies of romance books."

Aella laughed again, throwing her head back against the headboard. She winced from her mistake and held the back of her head, only to go on laughing through the pain with Eveline.

"You should thank me. Your life would be so very boring without me. Plus, you should read up on how to be romantic. You'll need it in a few years, if you ever want to win me over again." She winked at him.

Icarus' eyebrow rose, his coy grin still plastered on his face.

"You give a hard bargain, female. But you shouldn't prank someone ten times your age—"

"Ten times is a conservative estimate, Mister I-Was-Born-in-Sixteen . . . blah blah—"

"Because I have honed decades of knowledge and skills, by which I can drive people insane while entertaining myself."

"Oh, I'm shaking," she said, feigning disbelief.

"I also wouldn't mess with a CEO of a big tech firm. I thought you'd need new music to listen to when you work out, so I took the liberty of downloading 'Friday' by Rebecca Black on your Spotify."

"You know I know how to delete a song off my playlist, right? Some prank—"

"I didn't delete your playlist. I'm not Satan. But that song is now added to your playlist, after every other song. And unfortunately, someone tampered with your phone, so now you can't edit it or skip songs."

Her jaw dropped, and she quickly moved toward the edge of the bed to grab her phone that was charging. "How . . . ?" she started, unlocking it. "How did you even get into my phone?"

He shrugged, a smile growing on his face as he backed away from the door. "Oh, and Aella, I'd suggest never choosing 66666666 as your password again."

"Ass!"

"Be nice, Aella, and I might mandate all wolves to walk around shirtless for your birthday."

* * *

Aella couldn't help but want to be near her mate, and Icarus never complained when she came in to read as he worked. However, if he needed to speak with someone about pack relations, she had to leave.

She noticed Caprias hesitantly enter Icarus' office. He stood with his arms folded behind him militarily. She could feel his uneasiness coming in waves. She put her book down and rose from the couch.

"Don't hover, Caprias," Icarus spoke.

"Superior, a letter has arrived."

"Very well. Lay it on my desk."

Silence followed. Caprias held the letter in front of him.

"It's not addressed to you," he said, shaking his head.

Icarus' eyebrows knitted together in realization, marred with confusion. Aella figured he had read his mind.

"The letter is addressed to Luna Superior Aella and Beta-Female Superior Celest," Caprias continued, a chilly tint in his voice.

Aella felt her skin warm as the men looked at her inquisitively.

It was apparent that Caprias was waiting for Icarus' instruction.

Icarus lifted his hand toward Aella. "It's her letter. Why would you not give it to her?"

"It says—"

"She is Luna Superior. I want to make myself clear." He readjusted himself in his chair, his one palm laid flat on his desk. "I do not care if anyone in the pack does not want a human as a luna. Eventually, she and Celest will take over some duties of the pack. She is my mate." He fixed Caprias with a stony gaze.

Caprias lowered his eyes in submission.

Aella held her breath as the envelope was handed to her. The letter inside was thicker than the one she had sent. The postage stamp was an ordinary flag, except it wasn't Romanian; it was Swedish.

She ignored how the men clearly wanted her to open it in front of them, but this letter was not addressed to her only. So she stood and left the office, venturing downstairs and to the kitchen.

She saw Daria sitting with her mate, eating breakfast.

"Hey, Aella," Daria greeted.

"Hey, Daria. How are you feeling?"

"Like a stuffed pig."

"You look beautiful. Have you seen Celest?"

"I think she's giving Kaius a hard time in their room."

Aella nodded, gently tapping the letter in her palm. "Thanks." She bounded up the stairs, her mate and Caprias following behind her easily.

By the time she reached the fourth level, her breath was coming in pants. She rolled her eyes when she turned around and saw Caprias grinning.

"Hey, you get shot and then jog up three flights." Caprias held his hands up in mock surrender.

Aella hid her smirk as she came to Celest's room.

"She's a child, Celest."

"No, Kaius. She's a beautiful young woman, a young luna at that. Are you really asking for your alpha, your *brother*, to die before he takes his mate?"

"She does have my support." Kaius sounded dejected.

"In order to be a luna, she needs comfort and security that only her mate can provide."

Aella knocked before she could invade more of their privacy. The door swung open with great force that it made her hair lift from the wind. Kaius barked out a *what*, then instantly softened. "I'm sorry, Aella."

"It's okay. I'm sorry . . . uh, Mom?"

Celest was by the window, her back to the door. Aella could tell that she had wiped away tears before turning around. She wanted to convey that everything was perfectly fine, but this was hard for all of them.

"What's up, baby?"

Aella held up the letter, and Kaius sucked in a breath.

"They responded, I think. Your name is on it too," said Aella.

"I never wrote them. Did you put my name in it?"

Aella nodded. "Do you want to open it?"

"No. You were the one sending them a letter. You should read it."

She nodded, flipping the letter in her fingers a few times. She turned it on its front and ripped the sleeve open with her nail. She discarded the envelope on the end table, but something fell at her feet. She glanced down.

Celest picked up three items and laid them in her palms. All of which were oval-shaped silver brooches with marquise and pear-shaped diamonds encircling the largest oval jewel in the center. At the bottom were three gems hanging from three separate ropes of silver. On the outermost left side was the smallest gem of the three with a small rose image in its center while on the outer right was a larger gem longer than the left rope of silver but had the same flower. In the middle, hanging from the longest rope was the biggest gem with the largest rose.

"We need to get Eveline," Celest said, staring down at the pieces.

"Where is she?"

Celest shrugged but turned to Kaius and Icarus.

"She's hunting," Kaius answered, his eyes on the brooches in his mate's hand.

Icarus' eyes were just as focused. He and Kaius both seemed to be distracted by what Celest was holding.

Aella went over to the window and unlocked it, pushing it open.

"Eveline, come home," she called.

"She's coming," Icarus announced. Eveline must have mind-linked with him.

"They're beautiful."

Aella walked over to her mother and nodded.

"I think . . ." she started unsurely. "I think they're our crests."

Celest looked at Aella asking silently for her to explain.

"Whenever the mate of one of the upper ranks is found, or for whatever reason a pack member is put in one of the upper-rank positions—alpha, beta, gamma—they receive their pack's crest. It's the symbol of the pack, but I don't understand why they've given us."

It did not add up because neither of them was accepted as an actual, permanent member of the pack.

"Maybe the letter explains it."

The crest was only given to mates when the couple officially mated. She and Icarus had not consummated their relationship, nor had she been designated as Luna Superior.

Aella stayed quiet, sharing a subtle look with Icarus, as if saying, "What does this mean?" His response was something along the lines of "What did you do?"

There was a loud thump on the outside wall of the pack house, and seconds later Eveline whipped her head in front of the window. She climbed inside, huffing, clearly from running back from where she was hunting.

"What's happened? Is everything—" She stopped mid-sentence when her eyes landed on Celest's hands. "Why do you have Superior's crest?"

"What?" Aella asked.

"It's Superior's crest. Well, wait." She stepped closer, examining the crests. "Wait, these are luna crests. How . . . ?" Her eyes widened. "Oh God! You did it, Aella? You sent the letter? You bad bitch, I'm surprised you grew the balls to do it."

"Language, Eveline." Celest sighed.

"Well, did they give you something else?"

"A letter." Aella held up the unrefined thick paper.

"Dude, did you read it? What did it say?"

"I haven't read it yet."

"What the fuck? Why are you taking so long?"

"Eveline," Celest harped.

"Sorry, Ma, but still."

Aella swallowed the ball of nerves in her throat, then unfolded the letter. She read aloud:

> *Luna Superior,*
> *It is with the utmost excitement that I welcome you to the Luna Council. However, I am saddened to be writing to you under the circumstances outlined in your letter. I have the greatest respect for Alpha Superior and Beta Superior.*

Aella couldn't help but look at Celest, who was glaring at Kaius, then she took a shudder breath.

> *Kudos to you and your beta female for being exceptional. Please send my formal acknowledgments to Beta-Female Celest and*

Gamma Eveline. I am upset to have just been notified of Celest's existence; there was never an announcement that Beta Superior was officially mated despite the rumors.

Your letter leads me to believe that you may not know much about me or the Luna Council. My name is Luna Alita Sok. I am the High Luna of the Luna Council. I am mated to Alpha Sok. The majority of our pack lands are within Cambodia.

The Luna Council is a global congregation of all lunas and is headquartered within neutral territory in northern Sweden. This is where upcoming pups and pack mates are trained for their respective duties. This is also where wolves who disaffiliate from their pack are allowed to seek a different pack. It is where your delta, who will be in charge of your training and protection detail, will be chosen.

Aella didn't understand what the letter meant by it. She was human. The lycanthrope rules didn't apply to her. She couldn't choose a delta.

There are fifty lunas within the council (you can find their signatures at the foot of this letter). All of us are very enthusiastic to meet you. We want to extend an offer for you, for Beta-Female Superior Celest, and for Gamma Superior Eveline to come and be apprentices under me, my beta female, and my gamma female. It is important to note that your respective mates are not allowed on the territory at this time.

The Luna Council is under the sole protection of lunas. No mates of upper ranks are allowed within the lands. However, in three months, the pack games begin, and for a week your mates are allowed to attend and meet the new additions to their packs.

I understand that the distance and time away are difficult for mated pairs. This will be exceedingly difficult for Beta Superior Kaius and Beta-Female Superior Celest since they have consummated their mate bond.

"How does she know that?" Aella was startled by the personal information expressed in the letter.

"Her human recognizes you as a luna, but her wolf does not. However, her human and wolf recognize Mom as a beta female. The wolf always knows the truth," Eveline explained. "Keep reading."

> *However, there is a solution, and I hope that you consider this. Below is the recipe for a remedy that will assuage the effects of the mate bond caused by distance.*
>
> *I think it would be an excellent experience to train and learn. I am also selfish and would love to meet the first human mates.*

Aella shared a look with Celest.

> *In this envelope are three brooches. These are yours. They are your pack crests. Wear them with pride. Your mates were already given theirs centuries ago. These were crafted in his image when Alpha Superior created his pack, but more importantly, Luna Aella, he specially made yours by hand. Your crest was regularly cleaned and protected by the most secure vault within the Luna Council. Your brooch is not only a sign of your status but also a note to Alpha Superior's . . .*

She stopped. She didn't want to read the rest of that part out loud. She would not finish it herself because she knew her body would react, and everyone would know.

She swallowed again, then proceeded to the next paragraph:

> *We had always thought that Icarus would not be given a mate. Artemis had explained that he had to live mateless for all of us to live with ours. He is and always will be the protector of our species. Because of the reality of his being mateless forever, Alpha Superior*

spent decades building a library and jewelry collection that would, in theory, please his mate. I believe he did this to . . .

She took a shaky breath. She couldn't read this. Her hands shook as her mouth dried up at the saddest sentence she'd ever read: *He did this to ease the pain of never having a mate because—to him—his mate existed within the contents of his library.*

"Aella? Here, I'll read the rest." Celest carefully slid the letter out of her grasp. "Where should I start?"

Aella pointed to the next paragraph. She tightly gripped the edge of table for support, her knuckles turning white. Her eyes were downcast; she couldn't look at Icarus. It broke her heart that he was always deemed selfish and cruel. He did not sugarcoat his opinion and, for the most part, did what he wanted when he wanted, but he had given up the most important thing to him for the better quality of life of his wolves.

Aella knew he spent nights working, alone and unenthused in his office, just to repeat the same during the day. He also gave up what he wanted—her, his mate—for the well-being of his beta. He was the most selfless person of them all.

Although he was brutal to everyone, he was the most so to himself. And it wasn't fair. It wasn't fair to her, and it wasn't fair to him. She was sure she could make him happy. He deserved to be happy. He worked so hard every day with no relief and no end. She knew he must have been exhausted.

She was resolved to help, if not romantically, then professionally. She had been able to take on some of the workload, and she still would. She would learn to be the luna the pack did not deserve because Icarus did.

It was clear she could not do it there. No one would teach her and read about the protocols that paled in comparison to practicing such things. "Hands-on" was always the way she learned best.

"Aella, Aella"—a hand shook her shoulder—"you're not listening."

"Sorry," she said distractedly, looking at Eveline. "I'm sorry. Yeah, I'm listening."

Celest bit her lip, then continued:

> *If you choose to come, all the other lunas will be in attendance, accompanied by their brigade. You will be given your pack lands and pack house here, and new members will be added to your pack if you accept them. The entire council is protected—with twenty-four-seven security provided by a neutral squadron of wolves. Arguably, this is the safest place for a new luna, beta female, and gamma. Please know that your arrival to the Luna Council would remain strictly confidential and only those within the council would know of your presence. Only upper-rank wolves will know, and their secrecy will be bound by my order.*
>
> *Please consider this offer. Affixed to this letter is my phone number and email address.*
>
> *With love,*
> *Luna Alita*

It was quiet right after Celest finished the letter. She folded it back silently and set it next to the brooches on the end table.

"It's nice that Luna Alita sent you a letter," Kaius started. "I am glad she's more accepting than I thought she would be."

Aella and Celest looked at each other.

How do we tell them we're going? was their unspoken question.

"I want to go." Celest stood next to Aella, looking at her mate, whose face darkened.

"Absolutely not."

"You think you get what you want because you love me, but you don't, Kaius."

"You're not going. End of discussion."

Celest laughed.

"The reason why we brought you here," Kaius continued, "was so the pack could protect you."

"The pack would throw me to Ansan if given the chance. It seems that the Luna Council is far more enthusiastic about my protection than anyone else here."

"Aella," Icarus interrupted, "what do you want to do?"

"I think I'm tired of feeling . . . this way."

She couldn't explain the deep-rooted insecurity and sorrow she felt in the pack on a day-to-day basis.

"I think it's only three months, with a protection detail and secrecy of our location, so that covers Ansan. I think there's a way to be gone for so long without feeling the pain of being separated. And I think the pros outweigh the cons. I could learn how to be the luna I want to be. Celest could learn how to be the beta female she's always wanted to be. And Eveline, if she wanted to go, could learn how to be an efficient gamma."

"You wish to go, then," Icarus concluded.

There was a darkened pause.

Icarus raked his eyes over Kaius and then back to Aella. His Adam's apple bobbed. "Would it make you happy?"

She nodded.

"There would be rules, Aella. You break them, and I haul your ass back to Romania."

"Yes, sir," she joked.

"And Eveline would have to go with you."

"It should be her choice—"

"I'll go." Eveline shrugged. "Superior is kinda boring anyway."

"Watch it, pup."

She held her hands up in surrender.

"Absolutely not," Kaius restated. "This is absurd. My mate will not move halfway across the—"

"What would change, Kaius?" Celest asked. "We aren't close anymore. We aren't romantic. We spend our time fighting about our daughters or talking about things that don't matter so we don't bite each other's head off. We are mates, but we don't act like it. We haven't for a while." She shrugged. "And I think I need space, away from you."

Aella felt Icarus' eyes on her, but she couldn't keep his gaze. He made her nervous—he made her hot. She couldn't stand that, not when he wouldn't handle the problem between her legs.

"Get out."

She was shocked by Icarus' command as it came out of nowhere. She walked past him to leave, but he grabbed her arm, holding her back.

"Not you."

Kaius paused beside them, pain etched on his face. He left reluctantly, leaving the mates to themselves.

Aella jerked her arm from his grip.

"You're leaving me."

"No." She shook her head. "I'm not leaving you."

"You are."

"Well, you're not choosing me."

His face contorted into something she couldn't decipher. He opened the door and gestured for her to leave. He led her away from her room, down the hall, and into his office, where he shut the door behind him.

She stood awkwardly as he faced the door.

His hands palmed the dark wood, and he sighed.

"Icarus?"

"What am I going to do with you?"

"I can think of a few things."

She was nervous to say something so risky but fuck it. Things were already tumultuous. She should not make anything between them worse.

She watched as the muscles in his back rippled.

He stood straight, rigid. "Anything you've thought about, anything you've read in those filthy novels, has already crossed my mind."

She was expecting him to roll his eyes, to scoff, to tell her off. What she was not expecting was him to tease her back.

"I—what?"

"Do you think I don't know?" He turned, his eyes trained on her.

"Know what?"

"That you read those books because the men remind you of me? Or that when you disappear upstairs, it's because you finally got to that chapter and need to be alone. Doing what? Well, that's easy to assume."

She blushed. How the hell did he know any of that? She had never told a soul. She never realized he paid so much attention to her.

He walked to his desk and sat down.

She desperately tried to ignore the way her underwear rubbed against her clit as she turned toward him.

"Come."

Damn, I just might.

Begrudgingly, she walked behind the desk and stood in front of him as he reached into his drawer and pulled out a small velvet box. He handed it to her. His crest was in it, and while hers was very similar to that, there were distinct differences between them. Whereas hers contained sparkling sterling silver with a delicate rose, his was darker silver and had a wolf's eye.

He took the box from her hand but left the brooch in her palm. His hand was large and warm under hers, and she gulped from the proximity. His legs were opened around her, his head right below the valley of her breasts. He closed his eyes and inhaled.

She knew she was in trouble, but she remained frozen in her spot.

His grip tightened. "Fuck."

Yes, please.

"You smell so sweet." His voice was hoarse. He cleared his throat. "I want you to put my crest on me."

Her eyes met his. She had a feeling it was a very important thing in his world. She closed her palm around the object and then removed the magnet in the back.

"Stand up."

He obeyed.

"Can I touch you?"

He raised an eyebrow.

Her eyes left his silver orbs and went to his black belt. She laid a hand on his lower stomach, and it was firm to the touch. She inhaled sharply. His palm ran up the length of his torso, going to the lapel of his suit jacket, delving underneath it, while her hand with the brooch stayed on the outside.

She latched the magnet to the crest. It was so hot. She was so hot.

"Don't you dare move. What little restraint I have might break."

She stayed motionless as he commanded. She knew that once she was far from his presence, she would turn on the bath and enjoy the showerhead.

* * *

"Do you remember the rules?"

Aella sighed, nodding.

They had gone over the rules six times since arriving in Sweden. She recited them by heart as they came to the giant bronze gate of the Luna Council. Icarus had to leave the car as was mandated by the lands.

He gripped the car handle so hard that she feared he would break it.

"Hey," Aella whispered softly, reaching for his hand. She uncurled it from the handle and cradled it in her lap. She could feel his pulse beneath her pointer finger and a hardened scar just below his right thumb as she rubbed circles on his skin. "I know you don't like this."

"I hate this. I hate that you won't be near me. I hate that you won't be there to read on that couch next to my desk. I hate that I won't be able to smell your disgustingly sweet coffee in the morning. I hate that I won't be there to protect you, and the thought of something happening to you again sickens me." He couldn't look at her. His voice was hoarse and tired as he spoke like he was pulling the words from his throat.

"But I know being around me without . . ." he trailed off, but she understood. "I know this is difficult for you, and I know you crave independence. I know that you were unhappy at home, and the fact that you will be safe here helps me. I will see you in three months."

He said the last part more to himself than to her. He was motionless. Then, his hand wrapped around the back of her neck, pulling her close to him. Forehead to forehead, they breathed in each other's scent. She couldn't help the way her lower stomach warmed, or the way she felt herself instantly prepare to take him. She blushed from the embarrassment.

"I'm sorry," she whispered.

He shook his head, eyes closed and pained. "It's okay. I understand. Aella, tell me the rules again, one last time."

She nodded. "No leaving the council territory even if escorted."

"I mean it. Not even to go sightseeing."

"No venturing alone in the council lands. Eveline always has to be with me."

"Even if you get a delta, I do not trust them the way I trust Eveline."

"I have to call you every night."

"I will always answer."

"My phone has to be left on at all times."

"And lastly?"

"If I am ever in trouble, our sentence is 'Tell Rebecca Black I love her.'"

He smiled and pulled away. "Be safe. I will always find you. Do you understand? I . . ." he trailed off again.

She smiled. "I know."

She did. She knew how he felt about her because she felt the same way. He didn't have to say it for her to feel it.

"Good bye, Icarus."

"I'll see you in ninety days. Don't ask me anymore to give you up because I won't."

He opened the door and got out. It was then she realized how badly she didn't want to leave him.

Celest and Eveline slid back into the car. Celest was crying. Eveline was enthusiastic. And Aella was trying to pretend that leaving Icarus wasn't affecting her as much as it was.

Aella and Celest watched out the back window as the car drove into the gated community.

CHAPTER EIGHTEEN

The civil hall of the council lands was grandiose and ornate. The outside had stunning, well-maintained gardens with beautiful cobblestone roads and lantern-strung trees. Supported by six Corinthian columns was a classical pediment engraved with words *Non ducor, Duco* (I am not led, I lead). On top of the adage was a sculpture of a woman and a wolf.

The car door slammed once they exited the car.

Eveline whistled at the lavish lifestyle. "Damn fancy, ain't it?"

"I guess we go inside?"

Aella nodded at Celest. She struggled to start to move as the weight of her decision came upon her. What if this was yet another mistake? She wasn't sure if she could handle more rejection.

Before she could pull the doors open, they automatically extended outward, allowing them to walk onto the marble floor of the entrance hall.

Displayed on the corridor were portraits of women dressed in their finest apparel, their names carved below.

Luna Earheart
Luna Black
Luna Cho
Luna Abayo

At the end of the hall, where two doors were closed, was a spot with no portrait. There was a placard, however, which said in bright, powerful, not-at-all–ashamed words: *Luna Superior.*

Arms wrapped around Aella's shoulders, a hefty laugh echoing throughout the hall.

"Dude, you're going to be on this wall one day."

Aella laughed, leaning into the embrace of her sister.

"It's . . . good to see," she admitted. "But what if the pack was right? What if I can't be what they need? All of these lunas are beautiful, and I am sure they're strong, eloquent, intelligent young women. How could I ever compare?"

"Well, I wouldn't exactly say young," a lower, feminine voice spoke.

The women turned to look toward where they had come from to see a middle-aged woman with dark, curly hair held up in an updo, two stray curls framing her face. Her gown—a deep, forest green—hugged her curvaceous figure. Proudly hanging around her neck was her crest, which was far different from Aella's.

A smile made Aella feel more relaxed.

"Luna Earheart is the youngest of us, at eighteen years old, so she fits into your assessment. But I am two hundred and fifty years of age, which I think makes me older than all of you combined."

The sound of heels clicking on the marble floor broke Aella out of her stupor. The woman was beautiful, confident, and seemed to be genuinely nice. When she reached them, she held out a hand to Celest and Eveline, who took it without argument.

"Luna Aella, Beta-Female Celest, Gamma Eveline, my name is Luna Alita. I am the High Luna of the Council. It's an honor to meet you all."

Aella's brain went fuzzy for a moment. She had never met a luna before.

Luna Alita then curtsied.

Am I supposed to do the same? How should I introduce myself?

A laugh took Aella out of her head.

"Oh, you're an overthinker. Aren't you, Luna Superior? But no worries. Did Alpha Superior not explain the customs?"

"Uh, no. He's . . . he's very busy."

"Ah yes. I hear he spends most hours working hard. Well, it is customary that lunas shake the hands of the higher females, nod to the higher males, and curtsy to the alpha and luna. Come here, child."

Aella stepped forward. Luna Alita lifted her chin and placed a gentle hand on her stomach to force her to stand straight and tall.

"Lower your head just a tad. Place your right foot behind the left while placing all of your weight on your right—excellent. Bend your knees and lower yourself to the ground. Allow your knees to lightly tap the marble and then come back up—yes, good." Luna Alita chuckled. "It takes some getting used to."

Aella wobbled while trying to stand up straight, and she blushed from the slight embarrassment.

The luna smells like lavender, Aella realized, and it was an inviting scent that wasn't too strong.

"None of you are wearing your crests. Were they not to your liking?"

Aella could tell by the tone that she was a bit offended, but it was not at all supposed to come off that way.

"No. I'm so sorry—wait, yes. I mean yes. I mean"—she took a breath—"we weren't sure if wearing the crest would be accepted or expected of us. Within the pack, we never wore it because we were afraid that the wolves would purposefully remove it."

"You were worried about what?" Luna Alita tried to hide her shock. "And your mates allowed this fear?"

"The pack did not like us being human," Celest stated with a tint of shame in her voice. Still, she held her head high.

"Ah, I see. Well, it is ironic, isn't it?"

"What is?"

"That they probably consider you both weak, submissive women, yet you both hold the highest of roles within our society. You will not face such adversity here. I would love to show you the lands, but there is something very important we must handle. Are you all up for a bit of a shopping spree?"

"Did she say shopping?" Eveline chimed in. A cheeky smile graced her face. "We are always down for some shopping."

"Good, because it is time for all of you to dress as your roles."

* * *

"Allow me to introduce you to my beta female and gamma female," Luna Alita said.

They were in a couture house.

Aella stood on a small pedestal next to Celest and Eveline. Behind them were floor-to-ceiling-length mirrors which reflected the ornate chandeliers high above them. Before them, standing in front of the double doors, was Luna Alita, the beta female, and the gamma female.

"Apologies to Gamma Eveline. Unfortunately, my lead gamma cannot come onto these lands as he is a mated male. I will be sure to make a time where you can train with both of them."

The other women came forward, shaking the hands of Celest and Eveline before coming to Aella and curtsying. Aella wasn't sure how to respond. It made her a little uncomfortable.

"Oh, it's really okay. You don't have to."

So fucking awkward—she was so awkward.

"Rise," said Luna Alita.

The bowing women stood straight once more, sharing a confused look with each other.

"It's an honor to meet you, Luna. I am Beta-Female Alexis."

"Yes, very nice to meet you, Luna. I am Gamma-Female Genesis."

"It's so nice to meet you as well. I am Aella and"—she paused, but then she remembered that they all had titles that were rightfully theirs—"to my right is Beta-Female Celest and to my left is Gamma Eveline."

"Before we can introduce you all to the others, we must prepare your wardrobe. There are three outfits of note that all of us must have. The first is your business professional attire. The second is your cocktail attire used for celebratory gatherings. And the third is your regalia. We are currently wearing our regalia. All of these outfits are in the colors of your pack and have matching jewelry. Pack Superior, of course, is silver. There are also lingerie choices that must be made."

Three separate tailors worked on each woman's outfit choice, and for the first time, Aella felt as if she were royalty. They donned her *her* every whim, and when she was not sure about a stylistic choice, they would give her three other options.

For her business attire, which she wasn't so sure was necessary, Aella elected on a black midi pencil skirt and white button-up blouse with two rows of ruffles along the buttons. For her undergarments, Aella chose nude pantyhose, a black silk-like thong, and a matching cute yet efficient bra. However, her favorite aspect of her ensemble was the red bottom heels.

"Luna Aella, is this to your liking?"

Aella turned to face the mirror to get a full glimpse of herself. She looked at Eveline—who chose a pantsuit—and then Celest, who chose a shorter skirt with a sleeveless blouse.

"Do you think it's too much leg?" she asked Celest.

"No, baby. You look . . . you look like you're about to go to a meeting and kick ass. But if the outfit makes you uncomfortable, choose something else."

Aella sighed. She had a feeling any outfit she put on she would have comments about. The outfit had no fault. It wasn't what made her feel so desperately like an imposter. It was herself. It was the fact that she had no idea how to be a luna. She plastered a smile and faked enthusiasm toward her designer, Lia. It was time for the cocktail attire.

She was particularly fond of a V-necklined, sequined silver dress that finished just above her knees. It was fitted to her body, hugging the curvature of her frame. She was by no means a slender woman. She was naturally curvy with a slightly athletic build, which was highlighted by the dress. Her pair of nude stilettos fit like a glove. She loved the dress, and she liked the way she looked in it. She just wasn't sure if it was the dress for her.

Finally, the regalia was hand-tailored and could not be tried on during this time. However, the women were allowed to choose the style of their gown and coordinate the intricacies of their attire. Aella was most excited to see this particular outfit.

"When are these dresses worn?"

Luna Alita, who was gracious and kind throughout the fitting, put down the fabric in her hands to give Aella undivided attention.

"They're worn when visiting other pack lands or when new additions are added to the pack. Special ceremonies, matings, congressional galas, etcetera. When your gowns are finished, we will introduce all of you to the rest of the council. It should only take a few days to make if the tailors work around the clock."

"Oh, wait, they shouldn't have to work so long." Aella fidgeted on her pedestal. "Aren't there other gowns that we could wear just to meet everyone?"

Luna Alita paused, then she walked over to Aella. "You are a very kind woman, Luna Aella."

"Thank you, Luna Alita."

"Please, call me Alita from now on, but in our world, image is very important. You shall wear the gown of your dreams in the color of your mate's pack. It's an exquisite rite of passage for a luna."

"Luna Aella," Lia interrupted gently, "it's truly an honor to be able to give you this dress. We love what we do and feel no annoyance by the quickness."

"Well"—Aella bit the inside of her cheek—"is there something we can do to make it easier for you?"

Lia looked confused for a second. "Would it be alright if the alterations you need to your dress pants took a few days longer?"

"Oh yes! Do not worry about it. Thank you so much. I am very happy to have you as my tailor."

Lia's eyes reddened, and she sniffled softly.

Aella felt the sudden urge to apologize for making her cry.

"Oh God, Lia. Did I say something to upset you? I didn't mean to."

"Aella, I think you'll do just fine."

Aella looked at Alita, puzzled.

* * *

Aella's eyes dwelled on the stack of books on the desk in front of her. She coughed from the dust coming from the aged novels. Alita was moving around the office space, humming to herself about lessons that need to be taught. Celest and Eveline were in different rooms with their mentors, undergoing similar lessons as Aella.

"What does it mean to be a luna?"

Aella parted the sea of books blocking her view of Alita. The question was puzzling. She knew that a luna was the mate of the alpha, and she learned from the books she read and Daria that the luna had a role in every aspect of pack life. But what did it mean to be a luna?

Aella wasn't quite sure.

"To be a luna means to support your alpha, and work toward the progression and happiness of the pack."

Alita hummed, a signal for Aella that she had answered incorrectly. "That was a good answer if I were testing you."

"Are you not?"

"Nope. Being a luna is something that you have to internalize. It's something you have to figure out for yourself. Right now, your definition of a luna is what you have read and been told about. By the end of this, it will be what you want to be. And by the end of your life, it will have been what you have told to your successor."

"Why are you not against me being a luna?"

"Why would I be?" Alita laid down yet another book on the table, smacking her hands together to get the dust off. She responded like it was a stupid question, as if it had never crossed her mind that she would ever be against Aella being of the same stature as her.

"Because it puts us at the same status."

Alita laughed. "No, it doesn't. Your mate is Alpha Superior. You're of a higher rank than me."

"I—" Aella wanted to disagree, but she bit her tongue in respect. "And doesn't that bother you?" she pressed.

"No."

"But I'm human."

"And I'm a Libra. Does that mean I shouldn't be a luna?"

What the fuck does that have to do with anything?

Alita pulled the chair out and sat down, sighing heavily.

"I am a firm believer in the mate bond. I am a firm believer that Artemis and the universe make no mistakes. She chose you to be the lifelong companion of the Great Superior. Look"—Alita reached forward, grabbing Aella's hands—"I was surprised to have learned that you are human, and while this limits you in certain areas, being human is not a negative thing. It does not make you lesser a luna than any other one.

"The adversity you have gone through should empower you. I can tell that your pack treated you in a way I could never understand, and this has damaged your confidence, but you are no longer a scared, powerless girl. And you never ever will be again. You were made for Alpha Superior as he was made for you; you are the perfect counterpart for each other. Now, are you ready to gain the knowledge of a luna?"

Aella never realized how desperately she wanted to be accepted as the mate of Icarus and in the position of a luna. It made her feel as if she could actually do it.

She took a shaky breath. "Absolutely."

"Great. Accounting and economics first."

Fuck.

* * *

Aella felt like her head was going to explode as she crawled into her bed in the building she arrived in. A knock at the door was all the warning she got before Lia and Alita walked in. She turned her head to see them with their bright, perfectly awake grins.

"Tomorrow you will choose your pack house and see if you have a delta and other wolves that wish to join your pack. Lia will help you get undressed for bed."

"Huh? I can do it myself. Lia worked harder than I have today."

"Really, Luna Aella, I would love to assist you. It's an honor."

Aella sat up and nodded.

"Luna, your day starts at 6:00 tomorrow."

"PM, right, Alita?"

"In your dreams," she responded as she waved a goodbye.

Once the door shut, Aella looked at Lia. "How do you feel about Twilight?"

After bathing, redressing her in the nicest pajamas she'd ever owned, and brushing through her hair, Lia left her to get to sleep. And Aella took the time to call Icarus.

One ring.

"Aella? Are you okay? It's been hours. Do you want to come home?"

"Were you hoping I'd call and say I want to return?"

"Honestly, yes. We just landed in Romania. Kaius is being a dick."

She laughed. "I'm starting to think you're getting comfortable with me, Alpha Superior."

There was silence, then a heavy breath.

"Does this mean you aren't coming back?"

"No, not yet. It's been . . . good so far. Luna Alita is incredible. She is very welcoming. Genesis and Alexis are great as well, but honestly, I am exhausted. I don't know how you look at those figures all day. I had one lesson on accounting, and I wanted to scream."

He gave a low, sexy chuckle.

Aella gulped.

"It gets better," said Icarus.

"Does it?"

"No, but I thought it would make you feel better."

"It's rude to lie to your mate," she joked.

"It's rude to move to another country without your . . . mate."

"It's rude not to mate with your mate," she said.

It was meant to be a joke, but the heavy silence that followed was anything other than humorous.

"I was joking, Icarus."

"What else did you do today?"

"I was fitted for my regalia today and for an entire wardrobe. It was, honestly, one of the most fun experiences of my life."

"Oh yeah? What did you choose?"

"You are never one interested in women's fashion."

"Maybe not, but I am interested in you."

Not in the way I want, clearly. "Your color is silver, so the dress—"

"Ours."

"Is a long—what?"

"Ours, Aella, *our* colors."

"You've never . . . I . . . You've never seen me as the luna of the pack."

"Aella, you're the only person I ever see as the luna of the pack. I have always seen you as my luna."

"But why make me leave during pack discussions?"

"Because I knew that it would be too much to handle at first. Putting the workload on you when we aren't . . ." He paused again. "It is a lot for a young woman to take on. I never wanted you to feel like you're a slave to the desk."

"Like you?"

"Like me," he agreed. "Tell me more about the dress."

"You can't seriously be interested," she joked.

"Maybe not too much, but your voice is the only thing keeping me from killing Kaius."

She snorted. "Yeah. What's he doing to piss you off?"

"What isn't he doing is the question. I can hear his thoughts, you know. If I have to hear one more apology mantra to Celest, I will lose it. He's already punched three holes at the airport."

"He sounds like a Kyle."

"A Kyle?"

She smiled. Of course, he didn't know. "Doesn't matter. Do you know if Celest called him?"

"She hasn't."

"I'll ask her to tomorrow. Remember to take that cocktail Alita gave us. If we forget to take it, the pain will be excruciating."

It was Valium—a liquid medication that could relieve some of the pain caused by being separated from one's mate. It would work only for short periods of time, or in this case, three months. Taken every day, the pain wouldn't occur.

"Don't worry. I will remember. I want to see pictures."

"Of the dress?" she asked dumbly.

"Of you."

"What? Why?"

"You're gone for three months. I need something."

"You know the last time a man asked for pictures, he wanted—" She stopped, realizing who she was talking to. "I'll send photos. I want to see the baby when Daria has it, okay?"

"Deal. So, the dress."

Smiling, she placed a forearm on her forehead. "The top has these beautiful silver beads that border the top and go down the bodice to a sharp point. The dress is white underneath a layer of smaller gems. At least, that is what Lia told me. What does yours look like?"

"Well, my dress is shorter—"

She laughed. "Oh? I bet you wear it better than me."

He gave another light chuckle. "I rarely wear my regalia now, but it's a three-piece light-gray suit."

"I never see you wear your crest."

"I don't. They're meant to be worn in pairs."

She stayed silent for a moment. "Now that I wear mine, will you wear yours?"

"Only if you're the one who puts it on me."

She smiled. "Wait, is that why in your office you had me put yours on?"

"It's a tradition that when the crests are worn, the mates are the ones to put it on each other. I enjoy how often you wear yours, but I will only wear mine after you put it on me."

She tried to tell herself her stomach didn't flip from arousal. Somehow, the thought was so tantalizing even if it was just an innocent act.

She changed the conversation because she didn't know how to respond without expressing her sexual interest.

"How are those romance books?"

"I am really quite concerned by what you read. Particularly, one book about robots is disturbing."

She laughed, her chest practically heaving. "Did you read it?"

"Of course not."

She waited.

"Okay, maybe the first few pages."

"Uh-huh," she teased. "What can I say? I got a thing for stoic men."

He chuckled. "Clearly."

Silence hung again, a question burning in the back of her throat. "Why haven't you shifted around me?" she finally asked.

"Do you want me to?"

Yes, she absolutely did. "I'm curious. What do you look like? Like my father?"

"My wolf is darker than his. I'm larger. I never shifted around you because there was never a need."

"Eveline needs to shift frequently, or else she gets agitated."

"She's young. Sometimes I feel the need, but it's less often. I've learned to control the frustration."

She hummed in understanding. "I am so tired, Icarus."

He sighed softly. She could tell he was hesitant to hang up.

"Alright. Get sleep."

"Will you be sleeping tonight?"

There was no response.

"Do you not sleep often because of the workload or due to nightmares?" she asked further.

"Nightmares?"

"I know you have them. I think they're about your father."

"Some of them are."

"And the others?"

Silence again. He took so long to respond that she had to make sure the call was still active.

"The others are about you dying. I see the blood, and I remember how your eyes were so peaceful like you were accepting that you would leave. I hear your pants and your desperate attempt at knowing my name."

Her heart lurched. She sat up. "I'm alive. I'm right here, Icarus."

"I let you go because I know"—he sighed—"I know that you need this."

"I need this because your pack hates me."

"They crave the hierarchy. They need to be reminded of their place."

"They were still mean to me after they submitted to you."

"Were they? Or was it Elena?"

She sat, her back against the headboard. "They follow Elena like she's . . ."

"What?"

"Like she's their luna."

She heard him swallow.

"What she's done to you is inappropriate and worthy of disaffiliation. I've thought about it."

"Then why didn't you?"

"Do you want me to?"

"Y-yes!" she faltered. "No?"

"I didn't because I knew that the taste of disrespect would linger. You need to establish your power, your place. You should be the one to disaffiliate her."

"I don't understand."

"I'm the one who gave you the book."

"Yes."

"The book that gave you information about the Luna Council."

"Yes."

And then it clicked: he'd done it on purpose.

"I needed to see if you were going to seek your own future. I knew you would."

"You wanted me to send that letter."

"I wanted you to go and be taught, away from me, away from this. Never let the bastards get you down."

"You wanted me to learn."

"Yes, and not by me. I know nothing about being a luna, but there were other reasons as well."

"Which are?"

"Everyone thinks you're here in Romania."

"Even Ansan."

"Even Ansan," he agreed. "So you're safe; you're secured. You're welcomed, and you're going to learn. That's all I care about. When you come home, you will have all the skills and knowledge to put the others in their place."

It was a lesson *she* needed to learn, an action she needed to do.

"Why didn't you tell me about all of this?"

"Wasn't sure it would work. It hasn't yet, technically."

"I was wondering why it was so easy to convince you to let me go only with Eveline."

Silence ensued.

Her eyes narrowed. "Icarus, it's only Eveline and Celest who came with me, right?"

"I think Eveline is a very skilled fighter, but I would never trust her by herself to guard the luna and beta female of my pack."

"What are you saying?"

"I'm saying there are people I trust around you."

"You trust no one."

"I trust some."

"So you're saying you have spies here? It's neutral territory, Icarus. How did you even—" She sighed.

"Be glad I didn't move to Sweden with you. I was about to."

She rolled her eyes, a yawn interrupting her sentence.

"Get some sleep, young Luna."

She didn't. She woke up in a cold sweat, fear and dread consuming her and making her feel like she couldn't breathe. As she gasped for air, only then did she realize that those feelings weren't her own.

CHAPTER NINETEEN

The Knight ladies were told that under no circumstances were they allowed to present themselves anything other than composed women. They were allowed to feel the pressure and to become emotional, but they could not break down in front of others. No one should ever know their weaknesses. After all, their world was still filled with wolves.

Aella tried not to convey her nervousness as she sat next to her mother in the back of the town car. She gazed out of the window, at the passing trees, once again shocked by how large the estate was. The others were able to travel easily if they shifted, but Aella and her mother could not navigate hundreds of acres of land by foot.

Uniform houses blurred in her vision as they came into another area that resembled that of a small middle-class town in the United States. It was a big day for her.

She pulled her pencil skirt down as the leather made it slither up her thighs. She investigated her pantyhose to make sure she didn't accidentally rip a hole into them.

"I have extras," Celest murmured. "If you did rip them, I have extras. I also have an extra outfit in case you need it."

Aella looked at her with a thankful expression but didn't say anything. She was afraid her voice would give way to how she was really feeling—anxious, unsure, and erratic. She suddenly wished she were wearing a shorter-sleeved blouse. She felt like she was sweating through the linen.

Don't fucking trip, Aella. How embarrassing would that be? You're going to see if you have more pack members, but you end up stumbling your way out of the car.

Alita explained that it wasn't she or Aella who would decide who could be added to the pack. Naturally, Aella's presence would call to lone wolves, and they could choose to either accept the pull or disregard it and choose another pack. This would be the same for her delta. Aella would not choose who would serve under her, but if she did have one, they would instinctually seek her.

It was like the mate bond—how Icarus found her without knowing her and how she knew Icarus was her favorite person. It was an innate circumstance crafted by fate. Some lunas, Alita explained, did not receive a delta. Some did not even get new members. It said nothing about the quality of the luna. It simply meant the pack was as it should be.

Aella hoped that wasn't the case. She wanted people on her side. She wanted comrades. She wanted wolves that actually wanted her. Maybe it was selfish. Maybe that would be the reason she would receive no additional pack members.

As the car slowed, Aella held her breath, waiting for the back door to open for them. Eveline was the first to get out, followed by Celest and then Aella.

Rule number two: always entertain the crowd.

Aella smiled politely and raised her right hand to wave. She knew there was a crowd of people cheering and shouting at her in excitement, but it barely registered because the sudden urge to blow chunks was far too grand. Eveline, on the other hand, was a natural figurehead. She was enthusiastic in her friendly assault. She laughed and waved, and the wolves loved her.

Eveline smiled back at Aella with a wink.

Celest seemed to be naturally gifted as well, though in a much more demure sense. She waved slowly with grace and nodded to the crowd with a kind, reserved smile. She stepped toward a woman and complimented the pup she was cradling to her chest.

"Would you like to hold her?" the woman asked excitedly.

Aella chuckled at the scene. She thought she was flailing like a bird in the water. After a few seconds, she made her way down the mulch path to the grass field. There was a dais on the side closest to her with three chairs aligned next to each other.

She sat in the middle chair while the other ladies sat on either side of her. All of a sudden, with quickness she did not quite expect, the field was filled with crowds of people. She knew the men weren't of rank, which was why they were allowed on the lands.

Aella held her breath.

You do not need to do anything. Just sit there. Do not look bored and take in the crowd. If there are more members to be added, you will know. In this circumstance, you will stand and take the ribbon from your beta female and then tie it around their wrist. They will pledge themselves to you, and you and the pack will say the following . . .

Ten minutes passed, then fifteen. Aella was starting to believe that she really called to no other wolf here. She took a long inhale. The urge to look to her left was indescribable. It was like a silent, unseen creature was forcing her eyes to move to the side, meeting one's bright eyes that stared back at her. The same urge assaulted her, and she looked away to her right.

Another urge to the front, another to her diagonal, another to the other—another and another and another assaulted her senses. She knew she must have looked insane.

"Oh my Goddess," Eveline muttered.

Aella was vaguely aware of her exclamation.

A large man came forward, stopping just before the scaffold. His expression was earnest and hard, as if he were embarking on the greatest journey of his life that he took with the utmost responsibility. He was a tall man, one of the tallest on the field, with dirty-blond hair and an angular jawline. His hands were folded behind him, militarily.

Something akin to a magnetic pull solidified, and Aella knew. She stood gracefully. Then, she walked down the stairs, followed by Celest and Eveline.

The male bowed to her, lowering his head, before he went to his knees. "Luna Aella."

"What is your name, wolf?"

"My name is Machiavelli, Luna."

"Do you recognize Pack Superior as your new pack?"

"With the utmost sincerity, Luna." His eyes remained downcast toward her feet.

Aella turned to Celest, who opened a small chest in her hands. Displayed in neat, organized rows were thick silver ribbons with a rose insignia at the bottom. She took one and lowered herself to the ground, balancing on one knee. She took his hand, laid it palm up on her other leg, and tied the ribbon tightly around his large wrist.

"It is with the greatest confidence that I welcome you into Pack Superior. I will protect, care, and provide for you as I can. I will treat you as a comrade and as my child, and with the utmost sincerity, I appreciate the promise you make today. For any wolf willing to give their life for their alpha and luna is a wolf I am willing to do the same for. I thank Artemis for providing me with another wolf. You may rise."

Fourteen other wolves were added to Pack Superior, and while their connection was felt by Aella, Celest, and Eveline, Eveline explained that they would not be added to the pack link until after their official acceptance into the pack. It was also difficult for them to be fully initiated due to the distance between them and their new homeland in Romania.

As Aella and Eveline walked to the laid-out blanket under the willow tree a few meters away, Eveline wrapped her arms around Aella and Celest. Aella was glad to have such formidable new pack mates, but the fact that she had not recognized a delta ate at her silently. A part of her was upset.

What does that say about me as a luna? Do I not deserve one? Am I never destined to have one?

Her thoughts were interrupted by Eveline.

"Alpha knows."

"You can hear him this far away?" Celest asked.

"Superior is a strong wolf." Eveline grinned. "And believe it or not, I can hold my own."

The women laughed.

The young luna stopped to glance behind her, at the others following them. "We don't bite, you know."

Machiavelli gave a Cheshire grin.

Aella was told that for the next few hours, they would have time to get to know one another. They were all one pack now, but the feeling was still disconnected. It was like a new team being drafted. They weren't exactly close, but Aella hoped they would be one day.

As the sun faded behind the trees in the distance, Aella found herself sitting, running her fingers through Eveline's hair.

"Let's play a game," Celest suggested. "If I can remember each and every one of your names, Aella will pay for lunch. If I can't, Aella will *still* pay for lunch."

There were laughs.

"So it's a lose-lose situation for me. I see." Aella chuckled.

"It would be a privilege to eat all of Luna's money away," a female named Rowena shyly said.

Aella Knight nodded in agreement.

"That was funny," Celest remarked, trying to remember the woman's name. "Fuck."

Aella enjoyed how their relationship seemed to shift away from maternal to platonic. It made her feel like she could speak to Celest about anything.

"In my defense, I didn't remember Kaius' name for like three days. The only reason I did end up remembering is because of the orgas—"

"I am so dangerously close to killing myself every day. Please don't finish that sentence," Aella pleaded.

"One person and she already lost the bet." Another male grinned. "I look forward to betting against you again, Beta Female."

"In her defense"—Eveline sat up—"I don't remember, either. All of you look like assholes."

"You don't even know us," another woman piped up.

It was all good fun.

"Yes, but any wolf who is chosen to be in Pack Superior has to be a dick. It's a prerequisite, actually."

Aella smiled at the group.

"Do you?"

Aella looked at Eveline. "Do I what?"

"Remember their names."

Aella looked at her sheepishly. "I think so."

"No fucking way. New bet. If you can successfully name every single one here, I will not send Alpha that picture of you looking like you're about to puke getting out of the car today—"

"Celest, you gave birth to Satan's spawn," Aella jested.

"But if I win, you have to tell Gamma-Female Genesis to give me a break."

"We have been here for a day." Aella laughed, throwing her head back.

"One day and my back already hurts from carrying the success of the pack."

Aella narrowed her eyes for a second before nodding, accepting the bet. "Alright, from left to right: Machiavelli—sick name by the way—Rowena, Edeline, Delilah, and Jasper." She continued, "Nicolas, Aasir, Ade, Breton, Amilia, Katrina, Kathleen, Charles, and"—Aella stood up—"Christopher. Get wrecked, Eveline." She took a dramatic bow. "And delete that stupid photo."

"Let us see it first, though," Machiavelli said.

*   *   *

"We have fourteen new pack mates!" Aella couldn't help but pace in her room as she spoke to Icarus on the phone. "They were all so nice. I was nervous, but everything ended up great. We had lunch on the field and then I had to go back to my lessons with Alita, but we all met up for dinner. They're great, Icarus. They're so different—" She stopped. "They're just . . . nicer to me."

"I understand, Aella. It sounds like you had a good day." He sounded genuinely happy for her.

"It's not over yet, but it was a great few hours. The first one who recognized the pack was Machiavelli. He's super tall, and has very broad—"

"I have very little restraint when it comes to you drooling over other men, Aella. Tread carefully."

"I'm not." She chuckled. "He's not my type."

"What is your type then?"

Her heart raced as she remembered that conversation in the car.

"Women," she joked, smiling. "Oh, Rowena! She's pregnant, but her mate isn't here. He doesn't know she's pregnant. She came to train as an enforcer when she found out, and she didn't want to leave her studies early. I told her, of course, that her mate has a place in Pack Superior, but that I'd understand if she wanted to go back to where her mate is. I asked her to stop training until she has the pup, and she agreed, but I made sure to tell her she can continue training once she has recovered from childbirth. Oh, and oh my God, I forgot to tell you!"

There was a knock on the door, and she paused the exciting recount of her day.

"Come in," she announced, in Romanian.

"Good job, young Luna." She faintly heard from Icarus.

She had been practicing the language since their arrival there. The native tongue of the pack was vital. It was traditional. It was something she would accomplish one day.

Machiavelli entered. "Luna, Alita says it's time to return. Something about a lesson on the liberal international order. Not sure what exactly that is."

Aella nodded. "Icarus? May I call you back?"

She barely heard his response before she said goodbye.

*   *   *

Don't yawn. It's rude. Don't yawn. It's rude. Don't—fuck!

"Am I boring you, Aella?"

She gave a sheepish look toward Alita. "I'm sorry. It's been a long day. I think I am just sleepy."

Alita hummed in dismissive understanding. She switched off the pointing device in her hand and set it on the desk beside her, then turned off her computer that provided visuals of pack separation and demarcation of land.

"How many days has it been since your arrival?"

Aella perked up. "Five."

Alita looked at her watch and then gestured for Aella to stand up. "That should have been enough time."

"For?"

"Come now, child. Follow me."

Aella stood quickly, earning a scowl and wave of disapproval.

"Stand straight."

Aella quieted, and they left the office that had been their classroom for a few days.

She was brought to another room down the hall which was a bigger conference room. Eveline and Celest were already waiting, both glancing up as she entered.

Luna Alita smiled.

Celest sat behind the oblong table, a book in front of her. She was focused on the words on the pages while Eveline seemed bored, playing something on her phone. Both women stood to acknowledge Luna Alita.

"As you know, Aella looked at a few open homes and chose the house she could see herself in. This will serve as your pack house. Your control over it will remain even after you return to Romania. Decorate, fix, and change what you want. It is yours."

Aella took the keys with a Cheshire grin. "Get the others."

The house from the outside was an established colonial home with similar Corinthian pillars to the town hall. The lawn was bright green and freshly mowed but had no flowers. There were, however, beautiful willow trees in the back right next to a small creek. Up the driveway, past the silver gates, were proud oaks.

Aella knew there were no personal touches because she was meant to make it her own—their own.

She looked at Celest and Eveline. The ladies walked up the porch steps and into the foyer. The home was a crisp, almost startling white with silver fixtures. All pack houses were acres away from one another to give any resemblance of privacy.

Aella couldn't hear anything until laughter invaded her ears as Rowena, Delilah, and Kathleen surrounded them.

Rowena wrapped an arm around Celest's shoulders. "Nice crib."

"I draw the line at pink walls," Kathleen said.

"Damn," Aella cursed. "I was thinking I wanted nipple pink everywhere."

"Bigger problem there. Your nipples are pink? Get that checked out for sure."

Rolling her eyes, Aella sighed contently. "Where are the others?"

A calm, collected silence settled over the group.

"We were told that you guys never received the celebration you deserved," Delilah stated. "We wanted to do something special to celebrate this moment."

Aella could smell fresh paint with a hint of something—flowery?—wafting through the air. The sun was setting, decorating the white floor in a wash of orange. She was acutely aware of Celest's hand, clutching hers for some comfort.

"If you don't like it, we can always redo it."

Machiavelli seemed nervous as three easels, each draped with a black sheet, were brought to the center of the foyer. And when the sheets were lifted, Celest instantly teared up. Eveline squeezed Aella into her side.

"They're beautiful," Aella whispered.

In front of her were three portraits—of her, Celest, and Eveline. They were all in their regalia, each with beautiful silver gowns highlighted by diamond jewelry and beautiful makeup. They were each wearing their crests, proudly. And Aella was donned with a crown, royal scepter, and an orb in her hand. There was no greater feeling than to be accepted by people one respected.

"Thank you guys," Eveline exclaimed. "We love them."

"I never thought anyone would ever accept my position as Kaius' mate," Celest said. "It feels really great to be in this position with you all, and I will do anything and everything to convey how special this means to me."

Aella never realized it, but Celest had been facing the same struggles she faced for much longer. Celest had no one for years. She was always at the mercy of Icarus, who could be quite prejudiced toward humans. He was a stubborn man who could never understand the plight of a human in a ranked position. Celest was far stronger than any of them gave her credit for.

A testament to her strong will was her coming all the way there. She was a woman with a mate who was not embarrassed or ashamed of her, a mate to whom she was happily married. Leaving him was probably the hardest thing she'd had to do in a long time, but even more so, Celest denied his affection for the sake of supporting Aella.

Celest wouldn't allow Kaius to touch her romantically, nor would she humor him with his advances. She did this so that they would feel what Aella and Icarus felt. She did this to change Kaius' mind. She did this for Aella. All of this was for Aella no matter how much she tried to cover it by saying it was to prove a point of equality in their relationship, and Aella's love for her intensified.

"Shall we choose rooms?"

Hefty laughter filled her ears once again as everyone ran off to fight for the best rooms. She never thought the echo of happiness through an empty house would fill her with so much contentment.

* * *

Aella didn't have the comfort of Eveline or Celest. She stood behind the large, almost overbearing doors, her heart beating profusely. It seemed silent besides that resistant, monotonous thump. She could feel her heart in her stomach. She was so nervous that she thought her vision would blur from how high her blood pressure must have been. Suddenly, she wished the bodice of her gown were looser, but she was infinitely grateful she had chosen an off-the-shoulder design. She had a feeling if it went higher up, she'd suffocate.

Her hands palmed the ornate silver gem embroidery that ran from her waist to her chest. It was what grounded her. Her skirt shone with the brightness of the stars from all the intricately designed small jewels, but she wished she could see her legs. She felt like she was going to drown in the amount of tulle and cotton around her.

Just behind the doors were dozens of lunas—lunas that were experienced, confident, and maybe a little judgmental. How could she ever compare? Alita said she was ready to meet the council, but Aella doubted it.

"Luna Aella."

She closed her eyes, drinking in the voice, replaying rule number one in her head. *Never let them see weakness.*

She turned toward Luna Alita, plastering a tight smile on her features.

"You got used to that, didn't you?"

"What do you mean?"

"Plastering on that smile. To most people, it would seem sincere. It's good that you have already learned how to fake it." Alita scanned her from head to toe. "Come with me, child."

They went down the stairs and to the lowest level of the hall.

Alita took a key from inside her bodice and unlocked the door. Inside was a walk-in safe, and she easily pushed its large door and gestured for Aella to step in. Aella couldn't help the sharp inhale once the bright lights flickered on. On perfectly polished tile were pedestals and counters of jewelry of varying sizes and colors. She could hear the sound of her heels on the floor as she walked forward, admiring the collection.

"What is this?"

"This is his sadness."

Aella looked at Alita.

Alita walked toward her. "This is what he has nurtured for his mate. It's the only space untainted by anyone or anything. It's what he fostered solely for his nonexistent mate. You, Aella. All of this belongs to you. Every jewel was carefully picked by your mate. Some were even hand-forged, and every book in the library behind those doors was read and organized in your vision. This is the most expensive part of this entire community, and it is under your command."

Her heart swelled, and suddenly her sweaty palms from nerves dried.

Alita went to the back of the room and input a code to lift a glass casing. She came back to Aella with a crown. She gently placed it on the younger luna's head.

"Try not to move your head too much." And then she went back to the case and returned with earrings and a necklace.

As she clasped the diamond around Aella's neck, she said softly, "Behind every strong alpha is a stronger luna. I once asked you what it meant to you to be a luna. To me, being a luna means you live a life of luxury. You're pampered, revered, cherished. Turn around."

Kind eyes looked into Aella's. "But you only get this lifestyle at a very high price. For each and every pack member, you must be willing to lay down your life for them. They submit because of this. You have to always maintain your pack's priorities above yours. You will stay up, working for hours on end, only to find out there is more work to be done. You will be blamed for the hard decisions. You will be threatened. You will be envied. You will be tested. But you are a smart, genuine woman. I have faith in you. If you can't do it for yourself, then do it for your mate. Do it for me, for your mother. You can be the change. This is your birthright."

* * *

Aella learned that her nerves were all for nothing. Most of the lunas were kind to her, welcoming her to their council with warm embraces. It was clear, however, that some individuals did not like her existence, nor did they respect it. They made snarky comments, scoffed at her statements, and made her feel weak. But she held her head up high and hit back with equally damaging yet more eloquently articulated remarks.

By the end of the celebration, Aella was thrilled to be able to return to her pack house. As she ventured to leave, someone called out to her.

"So, what's with the not-mating thing?"

Her steps faltered. She turned around to see a taller, blue-eyed luna with golden-blonde hair in a pale orange taking off her heels. "Excuse me?"

"I know you're a luna, but my wolf seems to be confused. Only one explanation." She shrugged, then she sighed in relief. "These fucking heels are tiring me!"

"I don't think it's any of your business."

She didn't seem fazed by the lack of an answer.

"Touchy, Luna Aella."

"Luna Ilsa, I—"

"Sorry. I know I can ask very invasive questions. My therapist says it's because I hate small talks. I'm working on it. But still, I'm curious."

Aella gave her a look, as if saying, "In your dreams."

"Okay, okay . . ." she trailed off. "What—he can't get it up or something?"

Aella gaped at her. *How is she so brazen with her comments? Where is the decorum?* She was confused by how she felt about them too. Part of her thought they were funny.

Laughter took her out of her thoughts.

"You should see your face. Anyway, call me Ilsa. I'm the mate of Alpha Earheart of Ukraine. It's very nice to meet you."

"It's . . . nice to meet you too. You remind me of my sister."

"Oh, is she stunningly beautiful too?"

She gave another kind smile before a woman walked in, wearing the same shade of orange as Ilsa, who then waved at her and started walking away.

"I'll see ya, Aella."

"You," Aella started, "you're a very confusing woman."

"Keeps things interesting," she called back.

CHAPTER TWENTY

Five weeks later

Aella sat next to her beta female and gamma at the large maple table in the conference hall. The women, donned in their business professional clothes and pack crests, were silent.

Celest had really come into her own as beta female. She wore her crest proudly and no longer hesitated when presented to other high-ranking officials. She helped Aella in whatever way she could. They spent many hours together going over financial records and accounts and budgeting plans for the next four years. They became partners, friends even—a bond that seemed to eclipse the fact that one raised the other. Together, they ran a well-oiled, well-financed, and emotionally supportive house.

Eveline, bless her heart, was having a fantastic time. She was the fighter of the three of them. She enjoyed the grueling training of a gamma and would actively ask Jasper or Machiavelli to spar with her. She focused on hand-to-hand combat and the organization of Aella's security detail. Since Aella had never received a delta, Eveline took on the responsibility of protecting the luna.

Eveline was naturally a gifted fighter, but Aella had an inkling that Icarus had trained her when she was younger, knowing she would be the next gamma of the pack.

The three of them made a good team. They learned each other's tricks and memorized the expressions of the other. They could silently communicate with one another with one look. They felt like they were on the same wavelength.

They sat here with the other upper ranks of the world. Each luna sat in between their beta female and gamma female. Others were not allowed in these meetings, only ranked officials. There were no males in this meeting, which was odd but understandable. Many of the deltas and enforcers preferred to spar or work on strategic performances.

Aella played with the glass in front of her, spinning it. She focused on the reflection of the lights above in the water. Another luna was speaking about their qualms about the southern territory. There were many disputes, most of which were due to greed or territoriality. It was stupid, senseless, even. She quickly learned that wolves liked to fight each other, but she couldn't be bothered unless it was a danger to her pack.

She'd learned to squash some of her morals. She would always fight for the underdogs—the impoverished, the minorities, the helpless—but these pointless wars between packs would not be solved by her meddling, not yet at least. So, she persevered despite the shouts among lunas, the diplomatic roller coasters, and the tedious addendum to treaties. She did so to win the war, not the battle. She did so to put her pack first.

"Another point of contention," Luna Alita announced, "is within Pack Barnes. They have stated that 3 percent of their pack will be forced into servitude due to their inability to pay their levies."

This was the only discussion Aella was being interested in. She didn't show her interest, though—not yet.

Always stay calm and collected, was her reminder to herself.

In truth, the mere prospect that such a law could be enforced made her blood boil. Her eyes met Eveline's and then Celest's to convey a singular message: *focus.*

"Due to the sickness that plagues our lands," Luna Barnes started, "our finances have fallen. We cannot afford to take care of our members. Our members do not take care of us. Their inability to do so should be punished."

The disease that ravaged the lycanthrope world did so unforgivingly. It sickened lycans, razed packs, and forced the strong into weakness. There was no cure, no medications, no end in sight. The mortality rate was 21 percent, and she'd learned that the number steadily increased each year. She was twenty-one. She'd turn twenty-two soon.

"You want your pack members to pay the price of your ineptitude," Luna Earheart stated bluntly.

Luna Barnes bristled, her teeth flashing momentarily. She wouldn't snarl. A snarl would end up in a brawl. "We punish wrongdoers all the time."

"Yes, criminals," Earheart continued. "Rapists, thieves, murderers . . . not the poor."

"Tax evasion is a crime," Luna Barnes justified. "It's a crime, and this is the punishment."

"Is?"

Aella's—that was her voice.

"Is?" she repeated, cold and emotionless. Her eyes met Luna Barnes'. "If you were thinking of enacting such a law, you should have used the conditional tense. Is?" The word was hot on her tongue. "You've already forced your people into slavery."

It wasn't a question.

Luna Barnes sputtered, trying to backtrack her statement. When she realized there was no getting out of the labyrinth she put herself in, she resorted to ad hominem attacks.

"I do not take judgment from a luna whose mate refuses to touch her."

A snarl was heard, along with the sound of a chair scraping against the tile, and Eveline was out of her seat, prepared to teach the luna a lesson on respect. Eveline wasn't worried about the

244

status differential. She was a wolf born from a Superior. She would always have the advantage.

"Stop."

Eveline halted from Aella's soft command. Her back went rigid. Aella knew she would hear more about this later from Eveline, about how respect needed to be taught. However, Ev would always listen to Aella; she was Luna Superior.

The room was leery, cold, and silent—intrigued by what Aella would say, except it wasn't her who spoke immediately.

"Everyone knows that you despise Pack Superior because he wouldn't fuck you before you became a luna."

Eyes went to Luna Earheart—Ilsa.

"Because you're a spiteful, vindictive bitch," Luna Earheart continued. "We can do whatever we want within our pack lands!"

"No," Aella said, chillingly. "Every part of this world is under Alpha Superior's reign, my mate's reign." She wanted nothing more than to say *their* reign, her and Icarus', but she wasn't a lycanthrope. She couldn't physically protect the land.

She stood, the air around her seeming to cover her. "I promise you, unless you release every slave, every servant, and every wolf you deem . . . worthless, Pack Superior will make every effort to defend the lives of the poor."

Luna Barnes snarled her response: "You're threatening war—"

"For the sake of peace and freedom."

"You can't be serious." She seemed genuinely shocked.

"Pack Superior supplies the majority of your resources. Our lands nourish yours, and we do so because your pack needs it."

"We trade with you—"

"Your exports are minuscule to us. I can and will place trade restrictions on you and provide asylum to refugees. I will cripple you and your power."

"You can't do this."

"I'm the mate of Alpha Superior. I can do whatever the *fuck* I want."

She wasn't surprised to see Delta Barnes enter the room. It was natural for a luna to call out to her delta in times of distress.

Delta Barnes stopped next to his luna, scouting the room. It was cool, chilling even. The atmosphere was precarious.

What Aella wasn't expecting, however, was the collective growl of annoyance. Confused, she followed the gaze of every luna to the top of the overarching balcony in the boardroom. Her brows knitted.

Eveline leaned over to whisper in her ear, "That's not a delta."

Aella looked at Ev and then Celest.

"That's a beta" Eveline continued—her nose turned upward.

She sucked in a breath. Her eyes went to the male again, whose hands wrapped around the railing firmly. An air of authority wafted from him as his cold, dead eyes scanned the room. He was wearing his crest, the powerful sign of a beta. She could see it on his chest. She couldn't see the symbol or color of it, so she had no idea which pack he was from, but that didn't matter. He wasn't allowed to be there. Alphas and betas were not welcomed there.

And boy, she was definitely not expecting how Luna Alita rose to her grandiose size, a snarl leaving her lips. She was furious, her strong and genteel facade crashing away like glass. She jumped over the balcony, her dress snatching on the railing, draping itself, but not strong enough to stop her sturdy form. Her dress ripped.

"Beta—"

"Luna Alita," he answered chillingly.

Her hand wrapped around his neck. Her delta appeared beside her along with her upper-ranked females.

Aella was acutely aware that the room was filling up with her pack mates and those of the other lunas'. Her mates surrounded her, cocooning her, protecting her, sheltering her—not only her but Celest too. Eveline's hand was firm on both of their wrists.

"This is sacred land, Beta!" Alita snarled again. "You are not welcome here."

Startling to Aella, the Beta only grinned; it was a slow, feline grin. He was not at all concerned by the Luna's physical threat.

"Alpha Samir—"

"Has no mate. He does not have any ties to these lands. What are you doing here, Cyril?"

"Seeing as Alpha does not have a mate, yet all of you are discussing issues regarding Pack Barnes. He wanted a representative here."

Luna Alita's canines retreated into her gums, and her hand around his throat relaxed. Cyril stood to his natural height and then bowed to her. Aella realized then that Cyril respected Alita but was massive in physicality. He looked like a brute with his wild dark hair and dangerously cold eyes that seemed to stab daggers. His skin was as dark as Aella's.

Cyril blinked through a curl that fell over his eyes as he straightened the sleeves of his dress shirt.

Yellow—his shirt is yellow. No, wait. It is darker than yellow. It is supposed to be gold. His pack color is gold. Aella felt like she got kicked in the gut. *Pack Samir.*

Pack Samir was located in Egypt, but Aella had never met any of their representatives. This was because Alpha Samir didn't have a luna and never met with Icarus when she was around. That was intentional. Samir was a cruel alpha, ruled by a code similar to Hammurabi's.

Aella was taught of their history of relentless persecution and violence motivated by greed. She'd never seen pictures of them, never asked to, and never wanted to. They were distant from her. She was not the one to manage the relationship with them. She was glad that Icarus never wanted her to. This beta looked feral, unhinged even.

"We all know Pack Barnes has been encroaching on our territory. We wanted to send a message."

And that was when all hell broke loose. Cyril was on the lower level of the boardroom at an instant, surging toward Luna Barnes with speed Aella could barely witness.

"We are leaving," Eveline ordered, grabbing her arm.

Pack mates filed on top of her, ushering her out of the room. She heard a piercing scream and then a grunt, but she was already forced out of the room by her protection detail that she couldn't see what was happening.

* * *

Aella was pacing, biting her nails. She couldn't believe she threatened such a thing. She did so when she was emotional and angry. She did so knowing that a war could kill her and others. She gambled with the lives of others, of her pack. She gambled on the fact that Icarus would agree with her. She felt disgusted with herself.

Her intentions were pure, her argument justified. But she should have never threatened war. She should have stuck to what she knew best: economics, trade, and finance.

Calm down.

"I can't," she whispered. "I threatened lives, your lives." She stopped, facing her sister, beta female, and Jasper.

You did what was in your right as a luna.

"No," she groaned. "We are a team. I should have spoken to you about it."

We aren't mad at you. We are proud. Alpha would be proud.

"No, I . . . I am so disappointed in myself."

Eveline stood, surprise and excitement lacing her features.

"Aella"—her voice was so much stronger than before, louder, more concrete—"do you understand what you just did?"

"Yes, I just threatened another pack."

"No." She gripped her shoulders.

"You mind-linked with me. You heard me."

"What?"

"Do you understand what this means?"

No, she didn't at all.

Her phone blared throughout the kitchen of her pack house. She knew even before she picked it up that it was Icarus, but she was so overwhelmed by the gravity of what she had promised that she couldn't speak to him. She was a ball of nerves and regret. She wouldn't be the one fighting in the war she seemed to start, and that sickened her.

Her phone stopped ringing, then Celest's phone started going off.

"Aella," Celest began.

"Don't," Aella begged.

"He'd make you feel better."

"No. He's going to be disappointed in me. I—"

Eveline's phone started ringing. Eveline silenced it, and she winced, bringing her fingers up to massage her temples. "He wants to know why you aren't answering."

"Tell him I'm fine."

She nodded.

"Yo, why am I getting an international call?" Machiavelli strolled in, a buzzing phone in hand.

"Wait—"

But he answered and brought it to his ear. He paled. He had never spoken to his alpha, and it showed as he stuttered just slightly from surprise.

"Yes, Alpha. She is alright. Luna is right here."

Aella shook her head profusely.

"I mean she's dead?"

"That's the lie you choose," Eveline hissed. "How stupid can you be?"

He held up his hands in mock surrender, and Aella grabbed the phone from him.

"I'm fine." She walked out of the kitchen and up to her room.

"No, you aren't. And you broke all the rules."

"I did not—"

"Why didn't you answer?"

She remained quiet just for a moment, sitting down behind her desk. "I thought you would be angry at me."

"I am angry because I could feel that you're upset, and you didn't answer. Do you understand"—she heard him growl—"how insane it made me when I felt you uneasy, and you wouldn't pick up the damned phone? For fuck's sake, Aella!"

She whimpered. She didn't mean to, but she didn't want him to be mad at her. He stopped immediately. His anger dissipated.

"Aella, what's wrong? What happened?"

"What do you know about Pack Barnes and Pack Samir?"

"Pack Barnes—their alpha is power-hungry, greedy, conniving. Did he do something to you? I know about Beta Cyril. I am coming to you."

"No, not me. I am fine, really. Cyril was handled. We had a council meeting this afternoon, and we were discussing their levies—"

"They're poor excuses of leaders. They sent me a policy memo about their idea of how to decrease their debt. Stay away from Cyril, Aella. I am coming to you."

"When? Why? He looks—"

"Rabid. I know. Stay away from him." He let out a breath. "A few months ago they sent me a brief about servitude. I denied it."

"They enacted it anyway, Icarus. Today, Luna Barnes used the present tense, and now that I have said it out loud, it sounds ridiculous. But I know I'm right." Her gut turned into a ball. "I told them that Pack Superior would do anything to preserve freedom, even if it meant war."

There was silence, and she almost winced from it.

"Alright. I know servitude upsets you as it absolutely should, but I do not understand why you didn't want to speak to me."

"I thought you would be mad at me. I overstepped my boundaries. I wouldn't be able to fight—"

"Even if you were lycanthrope, you wouldn't be fighting."

"Okay, we will unpack that later—"

"I am not angry at you, young Luna. I am proud of you. Not only were you able to detect a lie, but you also stood up for your pack. You're possessive of what's yours. That's what being a wolf is all about, not your ability to shift. Lycanthropy comes from the heart, and you have the heart of any wolf."

Her heart swelled, and if she were being honest with herself, his voice made her feel so much better, her nerves ebbing away. His voice coated her in contentment.

"Why is Beta Cyril like that? Why does he look like that?"

"Do you remember when you were younger, when you just found out about what we were, and you asked if we ever 'wolfed out?'"

"Yeah, and you bit my head off."

"Some wolves do. He's more wolf than man. Stay away from him."

"I don't even know where he is. What do you mean?"

"I mean he can't control himself."

"I don't understand."

"He's dangerous, Aella. From what I heard, Luna Alita let him go shortly after he arrived. He didn't do anything to Luna

251

Barnes, and the only punishment for trespassing once is immediate removal."

"Why did he come?"

"He was ordered to. Alpha Samir wanted to prove he could easily enter Luna Council lands and get close to Luna Barnes."

"Are you still coming?"

"No."

She narrowed her eyes. "You're lying."

"Absolutely, but I won't step a foot on Luna Council lands unless it's absolutely necessary. Now, it's late there."

She heard something in the background and then he shooed someone away in Romanian.

"What are you doing?" she asked.

"Being bothered by people as usual."

"You're so happy, I see."

He gave a rough chuckle. "Go to your room."

"Bossy. I'm already here."

"It comes with the title. Keep me on the line as you get ready for bed."

"I have to shower, Icarus."

"I'm sorry, were my instructions unclear?"

She smiled as she entered her en-suite bathroom. "No, not at all."

"Take a shower, get dressed, then turn on the camera. I'll read to you."

"I would love that."

"We are almost done with the second book."

"I know, and it makes me a little sad."

"What book do you want to start next?"

She laughed. "How do you feel about the Twilight Saga?"

"I would rather burn in hell."

CHAPTER TWENTY-ONE

Aella was typing on her phone as she made her way through the halls of the municipal building. She was so consumed in her texts. She didn't hear Luna Earheart's beckoning to her until Celest tugged at her arm and made her stop.

Her eyes wandered to the other luna. "Luna Ilsa, how are you?"

Truth be told, she had far more pressing issues to address than to chitchat, but Ilsa was a kind, strong, morally right woman and did not deserve a bitchy Aella.

"Do you believe Pack Barnes has already started enslavement?"

Right to the chase. Aella didn't mind it. She nodded. "I do."

"I do too. My mate . . . he doesn't believe me. He said he met with Alpha Barnes, and that there were no suspicions. He believes that I am on to something but does not believe there is enough evidence to do something about it."

Aella knew what she was asking already. She nodded.

"I'll talk to Icarus."

Luna Ilsa winced at the name. "That's his name? Pretty dramatic, don't you think?"

"He's always had a flair for dramatics." Aella winked.

"I would like to invite you to my pack house tomorrow for tea. Let's say noon?"

"Actually, I have—"

"Luna Superior, please."

Something urgent in her voice made Aella hesitate to reject the invitation, so she nodded. "Of course, Ilsa. I'll be there."

* * *

Unlike Aella's pack house, Ilsa's was far more modern, with large floor-to-ceiling windows canvasing the front of the house. The driveway was lined with a white picket fence that led up to a beautiful fountain with a Greco-Roman statue in the middle. Around its circumference were bright-orange and white flowers. Strung along the perimeter of the large windows were bright-colored string lights. The house itself was white, with orange accents.

Ilsa was waiting on the porch. She was wearing a light-orange blouse and white slacks, a magazine in her hand. She put the magazine down and smiled at Aella as she approached with Celest and Eveline at her side.

"Luna Superior." She curtsied just slightly.

"Luna Earheart." Aella showed the same respect.

Celest and Eveline bowed, their knees touching the ground with respect. Then, they rose and shook Ilsa's hand.

"Please, come in. My upper ranks are away for a while, but they promise to meet with all of you soon."

"It is alright. We follow Aella everywhere."

"Even your pack mate Machiavelli? He's on the edge of my lands."

Aella looked away sheepishly.

"I get it," Ilsa said.

She led the Superiors to the back patio where a pot of tea was already waiting on the glass table. There were four chairs, and each woman took a seat.

"There is a reason you invited us here," Celest spoke. "What is it?"

Ilsa poured three cups. "Milk? Sugar?" Setting the pot down, she clasped her hands on her lap. "My pack is landlocked, Luna Superior."

Aella nodded. "Yes, I know, but your commerce is strong. Your debt is minimal. Your laws are fair and just."

Ilsa nodded.

Aella continued, "I'm afraid I am confused. I thought this was about Pack Barnes, but it seems I was wrong. And then I thought this was a request for a loan, but I am wrong about that too. What is it, Luna Earheart?"

"We can't take in any more pack mates. We will offer financial assistance if the situation with Pack Barnes escalates, but we cannot offer asylum."

"This is distressing to you," Aella responded. "It is okay. We will find asylum elsewhere. Pack Superior has space. Please, don't worry."

She smiled tensely. "There's more. The other day, my mate found a pup freezing in the outskirts of our pack—a human child, more like."

Suddenly, it was starting to make sense. "I see."

"She's staying here for now, but we cannot keep her permanently. She's an incredible little girl, Luna Superior. She's funny and kind. She doesn't remember her family. She doesn't remember anything."

"And she's human," Eveline chimed in. "So you think Pack Superior is the best fit."

"It makes sense," Celest muttered.

"Of course, we will house her. No need to be so nervous about something like this next time." Aella placed her hand in Luna Earheart's. She smiled. "May we meet her?"

As they came to the door with the small *Princess* sign hanging, Luna Earheart knocked, and the door opened—too slowly. A small face hid behind the frame, peering out at the woman.

"Hello." Aella kneeled to be at her level.

Celest and Eveline did the same.

"My name is Aella. What is your name?"

"M-my name is Malia."

She had a very thick accent, and sounded reluctant as she spoke in English, but she was speaking, and that was a great sign.

"This is Celest and Eveline. May we come in, Malia?"

Aella liked to think she had at least one maternal bone in her body. She read that lunas were supposed to be able to soothe and comfort any child or pack mate and that they exuded peace, but Aella was starting to doubt that. She wasn't a mother, nor did she babysit often. The only time she babysat was when she was sixteen, and she never did it again after the toddler fell and bruised his eye.

Malia slowly opened the door more, and the women walked in. Aella turned toward Celest; she was a mother, so she could spearhead this situation.

Celest nodded and kneeled back down, this time going toward the girl's dollhouse that was in the corner. "Do you like dolls?"

The girl nodded enthusiastically.

"Will you play with me, then?"

"Yes! You can be Ariel, and I'll be Moana, but you can't be a mermaid because I want to be the mermaid."

Aella and Eveline chuckled.

"Malia, how old are you?" asked Eveline.

"I'm six!"

"Six? Wow, almost an adult."

"No, silly. I'm baby!"

Aella glanced at Ilsa. "Shall we go file her transfer papers?" She nodded.

As they walked in silence, Aella took in the modern, stylistic features of the home. Everything seemed neat and inviting in some way. She liked the decoration, and she was taking mental notes of it.

"You're doing well," Luna Earheart began.

"Excuse me?"

"With being a luna, I mean. You're confident but humble. You don't overstep, but you honor your code. You're smart."

"Thank you. I appreciate that sentiment."

"But I don't know how you do with the whole not-having-sex thing. I'd lose my mind."

She chuckled. "Yet, you've been here for three months."

"Eh, I go home regularly." Ilsa opened the door to her office.

If Aella didn't know, she would have never thought this was her office. It was too clean, too pristine. Not a paper or book was disorganized.

"Ilsa, are you a neat freak?"

"What gave it away?"

She smiled as Ilsa went behind her desk and placed a manila folder on top of it. She sat down, grabbed the pen Ilsa had handed to her, and opened the folder, spotting Malia's photo.

"And for the record"—Aella unbuttoned her suit jacket—"it works perfectly fine."

Confused for a moment, Ilsa stopped writing. Then, she smiled brightly with a laugh of a hound, and Aella joined in.

"Between you and me, you got shot. You're on someone's murder list, and you were thrown to the wolves, literally. The least Alpha Superior could do is make you orgasm."

Down the hall, Aella heard a response: "Hell yes!"

Fucking Eveline heard everything.

* * *

Three weeks later

Aella sighed softly as she sat behind her desk. The office and the rest of the pack house had been decorated. Her office was far more feminine than Icarus', with a lighter color scheme of white and gray. The rest of the home was much more inviting than the other in Romania—she liked to think. She had spent hours carefully choosing her furniture and decorating it as she desired. Celest favored the gardens, spending hours a day, carefully nurturing and maintaining the greenery.

A little sound of laughter resonated down the hall, which was the only hint that Aella's door was about to be thrown open by an excited child. The door slammed against the wall, and a bright-red face laughing so hard—Aella feared it would pop—appeared before her.

"Luna, Luna! Christopher and Machiavelli said if they catch me, they're gonna tickle me until I pee!" The child threw herself onto Aella's lap. Her tiny hands fisted her blouse as she tried to burrow herself into Aella.

Aella laughed with the little girl. "Do you deserve it?"

"I would say so," Christopher muttered.

Aella tried hard not to laugh out loud, but she snorted as the two men came in, covered in red paint from head to toe.

"What did you do, Malia?"

"Well," she started nervously, "I wanted to see if red and blue make purple! But I couldn't find paper. I found balloons, so I kinda . . . I kinda put the paint in the balloons and threw them, but I didn't see Christopher and Machiavelli—"

"And now we look like Smurfs!"

"The Smurfs are blue," Aella corrected.

"Yes, because that's the important part of this conversation." Christopher deadpanned.

"You're staining my floor with the paint, you two." She turned to the child. "But you, little girl, say sorry."

"I'm sorry, Uncle Machiavelli, but I think red looks really good on you! And I am sorry, Christopher, but . . . the red brings out the color in your eyes."

Aella cooed, cradling the child to her chest. It was a sincere apology.

"I guess I can accept an apology from a pretty lady," Machiavelli relented.

"No, don't give in. She's evil," Christopher warned.

Malia jumped off Aella's lap and chased after the men, who quickly ran away, screaming dramatically.

Aella was left smiling in their wake. An anxious Eveline stomped her way past the others into the office. It felt like her office door was revolving with pack mates. She didn't hate it. She actually loved it.

"We have a huge issue, not being dramatic at all."

"Oh please, do come in, Eveline," Aella said sarcastically, picking up a pen. "I'm not working or anything."

"You're not busy, right? So listen. Luna Black is on my dick."

"Do you listen when I speak?"

"She wants me to go train with her gamma, and I definitely want to at some point, but you remember Alpha's rules. Not that I totally don't want to stay and watch over you. I just—hey, you're not gonna eat this, right?"

Aella watched as Eveline took the biggest bite of the apple on her desk. "Actually, I—"

"I love it here too. I don't want to leave yet. We only have a few weeks left here, and new additions are added every day! See, like if I had left to go train, I would have never met Malia."

"I'm talking to a wall," Aella said. "Hey, Eveline, I'm having a really bad day. Can we talk about it?"

"Still, it's an incredible opportunity. Gamma Black is one of the best, I hear."

"Eveline, I'm pregnant."

"Still, if they want to train me, the offer should stand for the next few months."

"I think I'm going to bleach my hair blonde."

"But they're doing me a favor. I should—"

"Icarus and I had sex."

There was a hard stop, then Eveline exclaimed, "Fucking finally!"

"Really?" Aella looked at her, concerned. "That's what your selective hearing is trained to hear?"

"What can I say? Your love life, or lack thereof, is paramount on my priority list."

"What is wrong with you?"

"How much time you got?"

Celest entered, clearly having come from somewhere far judging by how hard she was breathing. "Hey, what's going on?"

"Talking about our trauma," Eveline responded.

"Wanna join?" Aella added, stuffing her hands under her chin.

Celest chuckled. "Maybe later. I don't know if this changes anything, but Daria is in labor."

Aella stood, the landline in her office already in her hand. "Do we know how dilated she is? What is their plan for the birth?"

"Kaius just said that her water broke a few minutes ago."

"Pack your bags. Tell the others we are going to Romania."

"Wait, for realsies?"

Aella nodded at Celest. "If I know Icarus at all, he doesn't bring in a doula. And since I've ascended into the role of luna, it's important for me to be there."

"You're going to birth the pup?"

"Yes," Aella answered sternly. She held the phone to her ear. "Daria wanted that—hey, Luna Alita, it's Aella. I need to request a favor."

* * *

Six Escalades drove into Superior's land. Aella's stomach twisted from the prospect of returning to the Romanian pack. She bit her tongue to steady herself. It was no secret the pack in Romania disliked her. She didn't favor most of them, either. Daria was the only kind one to her, and Aella felt she deserved the luna birth she wanted.

Aella's gaze met Machiavelli's in the rearview mirror.

"We're going formal here," he said to her.

Aella's brows furrowed. "No need. I know all of you respect me."

"We know how they treated you and Beta-Female Celest. It's time to show them how a true pack treats their female leaders."

"You're a sweet man," she responded. "You will please your mate one day."

The cars continued up the driveway and parked side by side one another in two straight lines. As customs demanded, Celest was in the car behind Aella, and Eveline was in the car behind that one. There was one car with no leaders at the front and two in the back. Aella was supposed to remain in the car as well until Machiavelli and Eveline ran the perimeter, checking for security issues.

Aella heard two doors shut from the car in front of her. She watched as Machiavelli and Eveline sprinted in opposite directions and shifted into their wolves. It was quicker for them to finish the security detail when they were in their lycan form. Behind the two enforcers, another pair of guards followed. The rest stayed with Aella and Celest, shielding the cars on both sides.

A lock of hair fell over her eyes. She tucked it behind her ear, suddenly feeling the weight of the tiara on her head. She was surprised how easily she had gotten used to the dress code of her position. If it wasn't the crown, it was the tiara. If it wasn't the tiara, it was the diamond beret. She would be lying if she said she didn't want to make a lasting, respectable example of herself to this part of the pack. She wanted to prove to them that she was a luna and a damn good one at that.

Ten minutes later, there was a knock on Aella's window. Machiavelli opened her door and held out a hand. She got out, immediately feeling the eyes of her mate on her. The others in the pack house were standing on the porch, clearly surprised by the level of organization and respect given to the humans.

Eveline ran up the steps first, hugging the pack mates that she had missed. Aella looked at Celest, who looked at Kaius with a painful longing. She turned toward her beta female.

"I love you, and I love what you have held steadfast on. I love how supportive you are, and you have proven yourself as a beta. But Celest, our lives are too short, for you not to spend every moment with your mate. I am permitting you to be with him. I will not be hurt."

"Are you sure? He's—"

"He raised me, Celest. He's a dad. It is natural to be protective—"

"He's the reason why Icarus won't—" She sighed. "You deserve to have what we have, Aella."

Aella agreed. She knew the pack could hear their discussion, but she disregarded the discomfort. "Celest, please, you've been so bitchy lately. You need to get laid."

Machiavelli and the others laughed around her. Celest couldn't help, either but chuckle. She nodded, and Aella gave her hand a final squeeze before letting her go. She watched as Celest ran up the stairs and embraced her mate. Aella took a steadying breath, dragging her eyes to meet her mate's.

She swallowed. "Where is Daria?"

"She's in her bedroom." He, at least, had the decency to look conflicted. "Aella."

It was like he was saying, "I wish."

She understood. She nodded at him. She was so close to him, yet she felt so emotionally far.

"I know," she responded, walking past him.

A shout of pain came from upstairs, and Aella rushed to Daria's room. The pregnant she-wolf was in the middle of the bed. Her mate was behind her, soothing her hot head with a cold towel.

Daria's eyes opened heavily. "Aella"—she smiled—"you came."

"Of course. Are you ready to bring a new Superior into the world?"

"So ready," she said exhaustively. "So tired of carrying them."

Birth in the packs was a household event. The arrival of pups was a celebration of great proportion.

The rest of the pack filed into the room until it became too crowded. Aella had a feeling they all wanted to see if she was actually going to be successful.

"May I?"

Daria nodded, the look of hesitation draping over her soft features.

The luna gently laid her hands on her pregnant stomach, closing her eyes. Warmth drowned her palms, the sensation reminding her of cupping the flame of a candle in the dead of night. A gentle sigh parted her lips, and she found herself smiling.

"She's a very happy baby."

Bright-silver eyes locked on her, warm and moist with unshed tears. "She? You can tell she's a girl?"

"Yes," she said, although she didn't know how she could. It was an instinct like how a mother knew her child was up to no good. "She is very excited to meet you. You're going to make a wonderful mother. I have to check your dilation. Is that alright?"

About five hours later, the house was flooded in the painful cries from a laboring mother. Daria's desperate, pain-filled screams echoed in Aella's ears as she gently maneuvered the baby out of the birth canal. The matured screams turned into sobs, and the sobs mixed in with the loud, high-pitched squeals of a newborn baby.

She felt small limbs kick her forearms as she turned to Eveline, who gently wrapped the pup in a warm, clean towel. Aella's heartbeat started to slow as she brought the child to her chest. Sweat made her hair stick to her forehead, and she blew past a curl, forcing it out of her eyes.

"Hey, baby girl," she marveled. Glancing at Daria, who was tiredly lying, she said happily, "She's healthy."

"Can you—" Daria stopped with a gulp. Exhaustion lingered on the woman's features. "Are you able to . . . ?"

She knew what Daria was asking, but the truth was, she was unsure if she could. Daria wanted her baby to get a luna's confirmation, the process of a luna accepting the pup into the pack and bestowing their goodwill onto the child.

Aella had only read about it. Never in her studies had Luna Alita explained the process. It was never of great importance, and she never thought to ask, but Alita was vehement that Aella could do almost everything any other luna could.

She licked her lips before looking back at the crying pup. She knew the process. She'd studied it.

She brought the pup's forehead to hers, releasing a quiet breath against the delicate skin of the babe. Moments passed, and Aella's hands grew cold as she held the pup's head steady. In a silent moment, her hands grew warmer, and those cries soon turned into a sweet babble.

"Welcome," Aella said in Romanian. She sighed.

That singular word—a radiant salutation—washed the room in comfort. Calmness swept across the wolves in a final wave as another thread of mind link strengthened into place.

"Thank you, Luna."

Aella swallowed her emotions, placing the pup into Daria's arms. "You're welcome," she responded in Romanian.

* * *

Aella could smell blood on her blouse. It was an uncomfortable scent, but she couldn't find it in herself to be upset. It was a natural aspect of childbirth.

The pack buzzed in excitement, and the hall outside Daria's door was filled with happy lycanthropes. She moved out of the way so that others could get into the room to see the newest addition.

"There aren't enough rooms for everyone to have their own, so we will have to share," she stated and locked eyes with Christopher. "Christopher will sleep in Breton's room. Amelia and Katrina." The list of roommates concluded with, "And Machiavelli will share a room with me."

Leaden, dark laughter brushed against her back.

"There is no way in hell you're sleeping in the same room as him."

She resisted the urge to turn to him, forcing him to maneuver in front of her. "What do you suggest then?" she inquired.

He cocked his head, a maddening grin etched on his face as he pulled at the sleeve of his dress shirt. "You'll stay in my room. I don't care where the others sleep."

She did everything in her power to hide how her body grew excited. She relented with a nod before turning to Christopher once again. "I'll show you guys where your rooms are in a second. I have to change."

* * *

The smell was starting to turn her stomach. Her room was exactly as she had left it. Then, realization hit her like a ton of bricks. This was no longer her room. This room was nothing more to her than a place of sleep. It only represented the woman she already outgrew.

Machiavelli, Christopher, and Edeline crowded the room. They made themselves at home, arguing over something trivial.

Aella unbuttoned her shirt as she made her way into her bathroom. The buttons hit the marble sink first, and her hand went to turn on the warm water. She carefully removed her pack crest, once again admiring its beauty before setting it aside. When the sink filled, she soaked her blouse and watched as the water turned into a blush.

"So, Aella, you excited?"

The door to the washroom remained open.

"About?" she called out.

"Staying with Alpha," Edeline teased.

"Don't say it like that."

"Like what?"

Aella was glad she didn't have to look anyone in the eye. She tucked a piece of hair behind her ear. "Like I'm going to get laid."

"Who knows?"

"No, Icarus isn't . . ." she stammered. She bit her lip, looking at herself in the mirror. "He isn't attracted to me that way."

"No offense, Luna, but you aren't really this stupid, right?" Machiavelli quipped.

Judging from Machiavelli's ouch and the sound of a slap, Aella knew someone had hit him hard. She didn't mind. She knew he was just joking with her.

"Aella, we are going to go see the baby again. You okay?"

She went to the entrance of the washroom and nodded. "Okay, take pictures!"

She watched as her pack mates left her, then she pushed herself away from the doorframe and returned to the water. She watched it slowly fill the sink, which she soon started to refill once again.

As she rubbed the blouse with her hands, images slithered into her head—images that weren't hers. She winced at the vivid, explicit scenes of Kaius in her head. Those were Celest's thoughts, she realized. That was what she saw. Neither Celest nor she could expertly navigate mind linking yet, and sometimes things not meant to be sent through the link escaped.

She turned, resting her back against the counter. "Oh God, make it stop." With eyes squeezed shut to the point of pain, she pushed her nails into the marble. She silently begged for Celest's strength to waver.

Their ability to communicate telepathically was weaker than that of a lycanthrope, and they could only hold the thread open for some time before it had to drop. She just had to wait until Celest could no longer bridge the mind link.

She pressed her fists into her eyes and cursed. "I'm never going to unsee this."

"Unsee what?"

She jumped from the voice in front of her. She must have been so distracted that she never realized Icarus had come in.

"Celest and I can mind-link, not for long, and it's not very strong, but we can," she articulated, frazzled.

His brow knitted. "I can't feel your presence."

"We can both turn it off. Well, sort of," she grumbled. "We're still human. Alita thinks it has something to do with being the mates of Superiors."

He stepped further into the washroom and turned off the sink before it overfilled, and she mumbled a thank-you.

"You won't get the blood out," she said.

Of course, he knew that.

She was growing frustrated.

"I take it Celest isn't great at closing the link," he surmised.

When she opened her eyes, she could have sworn she saw amusement glimmer in his own eyes.

"No. She sucks, and I don't want to see."

"Show me."

She raised a brow. "You want me to show you Kaius and Celest having sex—"

"No," he said emphatically.

She bit her tongue to hide her laughter.

"Show me what you can do, through the link. Try it with me."

Her chest raised at the challenge. "What do you want me to say?"

He shook his head. "Show me the dress."

She cocked her head, confused. "My regalia dress? Why?"

He swallowed.

Her focus shifted to his neck, and she watched as his muscles flexed from the movement.

"If I said it's always been a fantasy to see . . ." He wasn't sure if he should expose himself. "To see my mate in my colors, would you believe me?"

Her brown eyes softened as she looked up at him. She wanted him closer. She wanted him to touch her, to kiss her.

"Yes," she said. "You"—she wet her bottom lip—"you created an entire vault filled with the most beautiful jewels for your mate."

Pain flashed through his eyes as he nodded. "Yes, I did."

"And that's where that bracelet you gave me for my eighteenth birthday came from?"

He nodded.

"But you didn't know I was your mate by then, and those gems were saved for her."

"You were special to me even then, and I knew that I needed to give you something from me."

Another image flashed, and she groaned, the palms of her hands pushing into her eyes.

"Here," he said.

The images were forced from her head, sucked away like they were being vacuumed out. They stopped almost immediately.

"Sorry it took me so long." He shrugged. "I had to find her mind thread."

"You can put her own shield up?"

He nodded. "It was easier than usual. She's distracted and human."

"Thank you." She sighed in relief. "So you want to see the dress? It's beautiful. It might take your breath away," she warned jokingly.

"Without a doubt, it will."

"I have to focus hard. Don't laugh."

"It's a miracle you can link as a human. Even if it's a fragment of an image, I won't laugh."

She nodded. She closed her eyes and imagined herself in that tailor's room, standing on the pedestal. It was easier because she'd lived through it. She remembered the time she first saw her dress and how she wanted to cry over the beauty of it. She remembered how she felt—regal and accepted.

And then when the image was so crisp in her head, she pictured it floating, wafting around her. She found his mind thread and followed it until she hit a wall. She gently nudged the image in, and in an instant, it felt like she was being pulled within him, like he himself was pulling the image toward him. He was so strong. His link was impressive, dominant just like him.

When she opened her eyes, she saw something cross his features. His gaze was fixed on her wrist that had the bracelet on.

"You're beautiful, Aella." His eyes shut and then opened again. "I am so proud of you."

* * *

"Dinner is ready, Luna, Alpha."

Aella looked up from her paper-scattered bed. She had taken a shower and changed into dress pants and another blouse. Her hair was put up and held by her pack beret. On her chest remained the crest of Superior.

Icarus sat in the chair by the wall, working on his own files.

She looked up at Katrina and then at her watch. "Oh shit, I'm sorry. I should have helped."

"You have enough on your plate. Come on, let's eat."

Aella waited for Icarus to walk beside her. Those at the table rose as they entered the dining hall.

"Luna, Alpha," they said in unison.

She noticed that some of the older members didn't address her, but she tried not to let it affect her. She smiled at them.

"Good evening, everyone," she greeted.

She realized she didn't know where to sit. Usually, she would sit at the head of the table, but this wasn't the Luna Council, and there was only one chair at the head of the table.

Playing with her hands, she elected on the chair next to the head, leaving it for Icarus. However, before she could sit down, a hand grabbed her arm, keeping her standing. With furrowed brows, Icarus pulled out the chair at the head of the table—for her, she realized. He was doing it for her.

She didn't waste time. She didn't want to make it awkward. She sat there, and as he pushed her seat in, she looked up at him. "Thank you."

He sat beside her. "You're welcome."

The table erupted in conversation.

Once her plate was filled with chicken breast, potatoes, and asparagus, Icarus gently picked it up and inspected it, *sniffing* it. This wasn't the first time he did so. She had asked him before why he did it, but he shrugged her question off.

"Luna?"

"Yes, Malia?"

"Machiavelli said that *that* pup was put inside Daria because she had sex."

Machiavelli coughed from the unexpected mention. He tried to appear innocent when Aella looked at him.

"She was gonna find out at some point," he spoke.

"What's sex?" Malia inquired.

Aella's stare at Machiavelli grew more pointed.

He laughed. "See, I didn't tell her everything."

"He said to ask you."

"Yo, kid, stop spilling the beans."

Malia ignored him. "So, what is it?"

Aella broke her stern face with a chuckle. She threw her hands up. "I wouldn't know."

The table erupted into laughter, and Aella couldn't hide her amusement, either.

"Wait, what's so funny?" Malia huffed.

"You know what? Next time you see Beta Female, I think you should ask her," Aella suggested, noting that the said woman was still not at the table.

"But why can't you just tell me?" She pouted.

"Because I don't know."

"But," she heaved, "Eveline said the other day that you would be in a much better mood if you and Alpha Superior just had se—"

"Wooooah," Eveline interrupted, covering the girl's mouth. "Not only are you annoying, but you are also a snitch."

Edeline redirected the conversation. "So, Luna, we were wondering if we could celebrate. You know, because of the new pup and all."

"Oh?" She sat back in her chair. "Any excuse to get drunk, huh?"

"Absolutely, Luna."

Aella nodded at Edeline. "It's not my decision."

Edeline's eyes looked wearily at Icarus as her voice filtered through Aella's head: *He scares me.*

He won't bite.

No, he'll kill me instead, which is much worse. Please?

Aella sighed, looking up at Icarus. "They would like to know if they could go out to town tonight."

As she finished her statement, Kaius and Celest walked in bravely and not at all ashamed. They sat in their respective spots next to Icarus.

"I'd say welcome to the party," Machiavelli spoke, "but it looks like the party already happened."

"Yeah, it did," Celest agreed. "Over and over and over and over—"

"Oh God, make it stop," Eveline cried.

The table chuckled.

"You all may go out. The town is about an hour away, so I suggest you get ready now if you want to be back before four in the morning," Icarus said, cutting a piece of meat.

Aella hardly heard the hoots of excitement as Icarus returned his gaze to her. She sucked in a deep breath. He was gorgeous. It wasn't fair. She looked away, feeling her body react to him in a way most women probably did.

"Luna, you coming?"

Aella looked at Machiavelli.

"Oh, come on. You haven't gone out in years," he groaned. "Please?"

"Only for a few hours," she relented.

* * *

By the time her makeup was finished, and she was dressed, it was 9:00 PM. Downstairs was already crowded with the partygoers of the evening.

Machiavelli watched as Icarus played a game of chess by himself in the corner. The alpha remained pensive, eyeing his pieces as he would anyone in war, except this war was one of only himself.

"I don't think you have thought this through," Machiavelli stated, lounging against the wall next to Eveline.

"How so?"

"You really think he's going to let Aella out of the house?"

"Why wouldn't he?" She placed the cap on her lipstick, looking at the male.

"Well, for one, someone wants to kill her. Kinda a buzzkill on the getting-wasted thing, don't you think?" He downed a shot of tequila. "Secondly, because she looks like that. You can fight, right? Might have to; guys'll get handsy."

"What are you—" Edeline stopped mid-sentence as she turned around to see Aella walking down the steps.

There are two things to know about the luna. One, she proudly wore Superior colors, and two, she had the body that would make any straight man salivate. Wait, there was a third: she absolutely, 100 percent, wanted to die because there was no way in hell Alpha Superior was letting her out in that very low-cut short silver dress.

Edeline watched as Icarus' face morphed dangerously. Laughter started—not hers, not Mac's but Icarus'.

Alpha Superior stood and went to her, towering over her smaller frame. "No."

She crossed her arms in defiance. "Excuse me?"

"You're not going out like that."

"You don't get to decide what I wear. You'd never hurt me."

Mac never saw the alpha's face turn so dangerous so quickly.

"You're right." He leaned down to her ear. He pressed his hand against her lower back as he whispered, "But you're wrong to assume I am a rational man, and you're too kind to accept that I will kill anyone—*anyone*—just for looking at you like they want to fuck you."

She paled. "You wouldn't."

"I've done worse with far less of a reason."

She gulped.

He released her. "Go. Change."

Aella broke eye contact with him before ascending upstairs again.

"God, they need to get laid." Edeline snickered.

* * *

She slammed her door shut and pushed herself against the cold wood. She felt so very hot. She turned, her palms against the door as she tried to regulate her body heat. She was naturally a very sexual person. Maybe it was because she was unmated. Maybe it was simply her natural state. But she could control herself. She could masturbate and please herself, and even in the worst of moments, she could wait until she went home to her pack house.

But she did not think she could wait more. She needed to orgasm. She ached for him. Her body wanted her mate.

She rushed to her luggage, throwing the contents onto the floor. She found that one small purple item she craved satisfaction from. She lay on her bed, her hand fumbling to push down her underwear, and she felt her clit quake from the anticipation. She was so caught up in her pleasure that she forgot she lived in a house with fucking wolves. When her head cleared, maybe she would feel embarrassed—not now, though. All she needed was that sweet, addictive vibration against her swollen bud.

She gasped from the familiar sensation. Her stomach coiled but not enough to make her come completely undone. Her free hand roamed under her dress, encircling her nipple. She imagined him. She imagined he was with her. She imagined he had told everyone to get out as soon as she came downstairs. She imagined him fisting her hair and grabbing her neck as he kissed her senselessly. He'd say those words again, his silver eyes glistening to their true dazzling radiance: *I will kill anyone—anyone—Aella just for looking at you like they want to fuck you.*

His hands would burn her skin from how quickly they roamed over her. He'd kiss her here—she touched her collarbone—and nibble her ear as she ran a finger over her bottom lip.

She focused on the vibration. Almost, she was almost there. She imagined that through the haze of kisses and harsh nips at her lips that he'd move them to her nipple, push her dress up to her hips, and yank her underwear down to her ankles. And then ruthlessly, hard and without an apology, the way a wolf would take its mate, he'd fill her.

She felt herself ripple, her body becoming rigid as her orgasm ripped through her. She made a noise; she knew she had, but she couldn't stop herself, nor could she take the time to care. And suddenly, going out was the last thing on her mind.

CHAPTER TWENTY-TWO

Breakfast was entertaining, to say the least. Between the constant grunts of pain and the excessive swearing, it was clear that everyone who went out regretted their existence. The savory smell of French toast with powdered sugar made her salivate as two pieces were placed onto her plate. She gave a polite thank-you and dug in as she held the budgeting plan for the following week.

"Oh," Machiavelli started, picking his head up. "Alpha Xavier is pissed about the amendments to the tariff proposal. He wants to speak with you, Luna."

"Rough night?" she responded, glancing just slightly over her stapled papers. With a small smile, she nodded. "I'll talk to his luna when we get back. If he wants to speak with me—"

"He won't," Icarus concluded. His jaw ticked as he ran his hand over it. "In no universe will she ever be speaking with an alpha without me present. I'll deal with him."

She looked over at Icarus, and they shared an unspoken conversation.

You're being possessive.
I'm being protective.

Maybe one day she would admit that she liked this aspect of his personality. She liked feeling treasured but not kept. She would not admit that to him, not yet at least. It would go straight to his already enormous ego.

"We're leaving today," she announced.

"Luna, I am so sorry," a rushed voice piped up, "but Gamma Graydon is on the phone. He says it's urgent."

Aella heaved as she forced herself to stand.

"No," said Icarus.

Before she knew it, a hand burned her wrist. It wasn't a forceful grip, but whenever he touched her, it made her feel warm.

"You didn't eat much," he continued. "You didn't eat much yesterday, either. You have to eat."

"You heard the woman—"

"Gamma can wait."

"What if—"

"Even if someone were dying, it can wait."

Her eyes widened. "You can't possibly mean that."

"Sit down and eat. I will take the call."

Before Icarus could go, she bit her lip in hesitation and then gave a lopsided grin. "Thank you."

* * *

Aella watched from beside Machiavelli as their belongings were packed into the moving van. Her eyes wandered behind him, to the woman gossiping with the other females of the pack. She forced herself to focus on her conversation even though in the pit of her stomach, a ball of anger grew. She hated Elena. She couldn't stand her. During this visit, she had ignored the taunts and the disrespect that Elena spewed toward her, but it was getting old.

It was getting old real fucking quick.

She had told her pack mates not to intervene, not to feed her fury. She told everyone not to engage with her. She did so because she knew anyone who came with her would kill Elena without a second thought. She was ashamed to admit that sometimes she thought about how good it would feel to have Elena gone, but she refused to stoop to such lows.

The rest of the pack seemed to be slowly accepting her. It was helpful that those who came with her presented the standard for how she should be treated. She knew that by seeing others respect her so easily, the others would follow suit. Sure, she knew that people were still wary, and she didn't expect them not to be, but she did expect a level of consideration and mutual respect. She was okay with her orders being questioned but not her intentions for the pack. The pack went above all else—she was taught that, and she would honor that code.

She wanted to see Daria and the baby before leaving, and as she waved goodbye at the mother and pup, she shut the door behind her.

"Does it not bother you?"

Aella bit back a sigh of annoyance at that voice that filtered through her ears. Her lips formed a straight line.

She held out her arms in defeat. "What, exactly?"

Elena stood at the end of the hall, a smug smirk on her painted lips. She was a beautiful woman. Even Aella couldn't deny it, but her personality was so fucking awful.

"That even though you have taken over the responsibilities of a luna and have presented yourself as a gracious, understanding, and perfect luna"—her voice slowed somewhat, condescension lacing her statement—"Alpha Superior still finds his way into my bed at night?"

A rough, low growl ripped through the hall. Machiavelli was quick to assault Elena, his hand around her throat.

"If I were you, I'd watch how you speak to Luna Superior." His canines elongated as they neared her ear. He spat his words at her, pissed at such blatant disrespect. "Let me be clear. I don't care if you are a woman. I will kill you for such an offense. The only reason I haven't yet is that our luna protects you, although the reason eludes me."

The hall began to fill with pack mates watching the scene, but no one stepped in to rescue Elena. No one would challenge Machiavelli.

The woman clawed at the wrist at her neck, tears welling in her eyes. A red shadow clouded her skin as she looked at Aella for help.

```
Ironic.
```

"Let go of her, Machiavelli."

Machiavelli clearly disagreed with her choice, but he respected her position enough. So he dropped his hand, grunting, and retreated to Aella's side. Elena melted to the floor, her rough coughs breaking through the thick silence. The young luna squatted down before her.

"Maybe you tell the truth," Aella said in a soft whisper. "Maybe my mate finds your bed every night. Maybe he pity-fucks you." She smiled, but it was marred by smugness.

"But do not be mistaken," she continued. "The only reason he does so is that he can't have who would actually please him. Next time he's on top of you, inside you," she sneered, "remember that the only way he can come is by thinking of me. You are no more than a vessel that he uses. You are inferior to me, Elena, and I'm a *human*." She allowed the atmosphere to settle before standing. She straightened the sleeves of her suit jacket as she looked down at the woman.

She turned and walked away and wasn't surprised to see her mate and Kaius standing among the crowd. She stopped before her mate, practically toe-to-toe. If she stood on her tippy-toes, she'd be able to feel his breath on her skin. He saw through her facade. She knew he had, but she kept that mask up, showing no weakness.

Her eyes softened. *Please tell me she's lying.*

He never broke eye contact with her.

"I want the truth," she stated. "I will know if you lie."

He remained emotionless.

"Have you . . . ?" She struggled to get the words out. "Have you been fucking that thing since finding out we were mates?"

If he was surprised that she was so crude, he didn't show it. His response was quick and sharp: "I have never slept with her, not even after finding out you're my mate or before." He finally turned his gaze and looked at Elena, who was now struggling to her feet.

He focused his gaze back to her. "Do it," he said. "Do it, or I will because I can't take it anymore."

Aella looked up at him with scrunched brows. She didn't understand at first, then her eyes raked Elena's pathetic form. She looked back at Icarus.

"You can do it," he encouraged.

Damn straight she could. "Elena."

Wild eyes looked at her, startled.

"Pack your belongings. You're coming back to the Luna Council with us to choose another pack to affiliate with."

"What?" Her voice was weak.

"I am renouncing your affiliation to Pack Superior. You are no longer one of us."

"Please, I didn't—"

"You heard your Luna Superior," Icarus interrupted. "You are gone, Elena." His eyes moved back to Aella.

In his gaze, she swore she saw something akin to pride?

She had to bite the inside of her cheek as her heart leaped in her chest and her stomach did somersaults. She hated how a look, a touch, or a sound from him made her feel like she was about to combust.

She broke the contact first, stepping aside. She couldn't be in his presence for too long. She didn't trust herself.

* * *

"I'm telling you, Luna's a bad bitch. You should have seen Elena's face," Machiavelli barked out in laughter.

They had arrived back to the council lands a day previously, and Elena was placed into the disaffiliate house to receive another placement. Aella didn't keep up with where she was placed; she couldn't care less. She was just glad Elena was gone.

"Why are you acting like this wasn't a known fact?"

Aella gave a demure smirk from behind her desk. Scattered across the deep mahogany were stacks of papers, ranging from financial accounts to personal memos for her next meetings. Celest was studying a file on the other side of the desk, folding the back page so she could hold it in one hand.

When the two worked together, they shared one desk even though Celest had her own office. It was easier to communicate when they were in the same room.

The young luna's eyes became glossy as she felt that familiar tingle of arousal erupt in her belly. She remembered how effortlessly she had worked beside Icarus in Romania. She imagined pushing away his work and distracting him.

She ignored the wetness that started to soak her underwear, locking her horniness away for a later time when she could handle it.

"Pack games are coming up," she said through a hoarse throat. "We need to decide who's competing in the solo matches."

"I know there are many younger wolves that want to prove themselves," Machiavelli stated. "It could be a good chance for them."

Aella nodded in agreement. "I don't know if anyone from Icarus' house wants to participate, but I'll ask."

Although she tried not to let her hesitation show, it was evident to everyone that something else was on her mind.

She sighed. "This may be infantile, but this is our first pack games with me as your luna. There are many rumors that I am not . . . equipped to be in the position."

Machiavelli scoffed. "Fuck them."

She nodded in distant agreement. She opened her mouth to say something, but then closed it again.

"You want to win the games."

Aella looked at her beta female, nodding. "I think it would be the most efficient way to prove ourselves. Of course, you and I will not be the ones fighting, so it shouldn't be my decision."

It ate at her that she couldn't defend her pack or participate in the games. She hated feeling inferior and inadequate, but the reality was that she absolutely was at a disadvantage, so she overcompensated in other ways—in knowledge. She memorized pack bylaws, studied international economic trends, and could even recite every name of every member in her pack and the surrounding packs'. They could beat her physically but never mentally.

"Oh come on, Aella. You know we would all fight for Pack Superior."

"You shouldn't have to because of my need to prove myself."

"We would because pack games are an important event and honestly some of us need to get some energy out."

"Could someone get me Eveline?"

* * *

"I don't doubt your ability. I have seen you train, and Luna Black has stated that you show great promise and skill."

"Aella, you're in your head." Eveline sighed, pinching the bridge of her nose. She stood near the bookcase in her sister's office, her arms crossed while looking at Aella as she leaned against the desk.

"I just . . . I need to make sure that everyone who fights is doing so because they want to and not because they feel they must because of my position," Aella said.

"No one is. And even if they were, it's under your authority to make such choices. Alpha Superior would make the decision."

"I am not him," she replied. "He is very good at order, punitive measures, tactical plans . . . well, he's great at everything except empathy. He is cold, and I know what I can and cannot do. But as I said, I don't want to force anyone to do anything."

"We want to fight, Aella."

She nodded, staring heavily for a few long seconds toward the floor. "Icarus and Kaius won't fight. They aren't allowed to anyway due to the nature of their wolves."

"Nature of their wolves?"

She nodded at Edeline. "They were given their lycans, not born with them. They're larger and stronger than the average wolf, and Icarus has alpha command over the lycanthrope population. They're prohibited from participating because it would be unfair." She watched as Edeline's eyes widened. "Therefore, the alpha and beta matches and the luna and beta female matches are already forfeited, as well as the delta match considering I don't have one. We need to win every other match, including the pack match, to come in first."

"Easy shit." Machiavelli shrugged.

Aella smiled at his lackadaisical response. "Eveline is participating in the gamma match by herself. Machiavelli will fight in the random selection while Edeline will participate in all-female. For group matches, Eveline will be selecting the participants," she concluded, straightening herself. She played with her iPhone in her hands. "Alright. Tomorrow, training starts for all of us. Get some sleep. Everyone is dismissed."

* * *

Aella climbed into her king-sized bed. She brushed a wild curl out of her eyes and sat motionless for a moment. She knew she gave off a facade of confidence and happiness, but she was miserable. She honored her position and was enthusiastic to become a great luna, but she still felt broken. She felt utterly and completely alone. She felt like she was drowning, allowing herself bursts of air now and again.

She hated it. She hated herself. She hated Artemis. She felt like no matter how much she studied or how well she did, she could never be good enough in Icarus' eyes. She knew that if she were better—prettier, smarter, and less-human—his relationship with Kaius wouldn't matter. If she were the epitome of everything Icarus wanted, he wouldn't be able to control himself. He would choose her and wouldn't regret it.

She felt tears in her cheeks, and she wiped them away. Her heart was so full of Icarus that she couldn't even call it her own anymore. Maybe that was the problem. Maybe she needed to realize that she was her own before she was anyone else's.

Aella.

She practically jumped out of her skin from the deep, baritone voice that fluttered through her head. It was big and domineering, eclipsing her own conscience. She didn't understand how he was able to link her from so far. The link only worked within a few miles, less with her because she was human. The link between them wasn't supposed to last long; she couldn't hold it open.

I want to show you something.

She nodded although she didn't know to whom. That voice set her body aflame. Only Icarus' voice had that capability.

A montage flew across her head, drenching her in the feelings and thoughts of Icarus, but they weren't sour or angry. They were nothing like she thought they would be. They were calm and loving—peaceful, tranquil, bright. They were of her.

There she was, smiling while helping Daria pick out baby furniture; reading in the car, in his office on that couch; laughing, fixing her hair, biting her lip, doing perfectly mundane things. Yet, she looked effervescent. She knew this wasn't how she usually looked, but this is how he saw her—she realized.

She watched herself from his point of view and saw a woman she always wanted to be. She felt the confusion he felt, the feeling of wanting her so badly yet feeling so guilty. She felt the love Icarus had for Kaius, but beneath it, she felt the sour feeling he had for himself. Then, it dawned on her that he was so guilty for being her mate. She felt that he knew so concretely that he could never please her; that she deserved better. He felt much worse than she felt.

"Oh, Icarus," she murmured, her palm lying flat on her chest. "It breaks my heart that you see yourself in this negative light."

What you were thinking about me, about yourself . . . none of it is true. You were never supposed to exist. I was never supposed to be granted a mate. I never forced myself to love you. I drown in it, and I've been drowning in it since the moment I realized you are mine. I would walk a thousand miles to untangle all the doubts you have about yourself, and I would fight a thousand battles to show you a fraction of the beauty you bring into the world. The happiness of our pack is created by you. You have no idea how your smile encourages me to go on another day, or how your laugh warms my chest. I hate that I have made you feel this way. I hate that I hate myself so much that I can't love you the way you deserve.

She tried to focus on the sweetness of his words. She felt her soul light up from his admission. She swallowed, realizing her hand fisted the sheets so tightly that they wrinkled. She let go of a shaky breath, inhaling one that was just as quivering.

No more, Icarus, she promised. *No more of this. No more staying away. No more secret glances. No more guilty touches. No more wondering what will happen. No more hesitancy. No more hating yourself. No more punishing yourself. Enough is enough.*

She released her fist as her heart jumped in her throat. She suddenly wished she had chosen a different set of pajamas instead of the baggy shirt she'd thrown on after her shower. She found herself lying on her back, eyes closed as she reveled in the mental presence of her mate.

I know what you're thinking.

She nodded. *I know.* Her hands fisted the hem of her shirt that had slid up her thighs. She was acutely aware of the fabric rubbing against her.

I can see what you're doing, said a strained, low voice in her mind—a voice that was almost in pain, a voice with an edge that said, "Don't stop."

I love your voice. I know you said you wouldn't touch me. This isn't breaking your promise. You aren't touching me. Her hand found the lining of her underwear, and she trailed the cotton with her finger before hesitating for just a moment.

She knew she was wet. She knew she'd come quickly and quite possibly the hardest she would ever have. She felt her clit pulse in trepidation.

You were right. I do come to you, but you were wrong about something else.

The pad of her finger lightly traced over her fabric-covered pussy, a moan of approval getting lost in her throat. She swallowed. She could never finish just from her fingers, but she enjoyed teasing herself.

What's that?

I have not been with another woman since I found out you are my mate.

"Oh God," she mumbled, forcing herself onto her elbows. She shakily opened her side drawer and fished out the familiar purple toy.

Please, don't go, she begged.

There was only silence. She couldn't feel him anymore, and she mourned the loss of him but savored what he had given her. She slid down her underwear, too impatient to remove them from around her ankles. She pushed her shirt up to her waist as her hand gently placed the toy on herself.

"Please," she whimpered.

I want to be a better man. I want to be able to shut the link down. I want to say that I'm not hard, salivating, as I watch you.

I'm your mate. There is nothing wrong with us. Watch me. Her finger went to turn on the vibrator.

Stop. Pause. Not yet.

She released a shaky breath and wet her bottom lip with her tongue.

Listen to me very carefully. He sounded so strained, but it was so sexy.

She couldn't see him, but she knew that he was close to breaking and doing the same as her.

I want to try . . . something. He paused. *Put your hands above your head. Do not touch yourself. Close your eyes and let down all your barriers.*

She couldn't help the way her eyes widened. *If I do, everyone near me will be able to hear my thoughts.*

I'll handle it, he promised. *Let them down. And Aella, focus on my voice.*

She wasn't sure if she was able to finish from just his voice. Part of her was sure she'd be.

She listened, closing her eyes and lowering all of her barriers. A feather of a feeling, a sensation, flew across the skin of her stomach and up her chest. Fingers—it felt like fingers. It felt like his fingers dragging across her like she was a painting.

Keep your eyes open. I have to see you.

She opened her eyes, focusing them on her stomach.

Tell me to stop.

No.

Stubborn mate.

She gasped as she felt the similar sensation of her nipple being sucked beneath her shirt. Phantom touches—that was his phantom touch. Her eyes shut again as another eruption of pleasure washed over her, dousing her in heat, setting her world aflame. If it was like this, when he was in her head, she could only imagine what it would be like in person.

She felt the feather touches between her thighs. He palmed one and let out a surprised moan when she felt a soft yet firm lick to her core. Her heels dug into the bed. She writhed, her hands finding her breasts. They felt heavy to her, heavier now that they were filled with tension.

Suddenly, the image of Icarus came into her mind. He was in front of a mirror, naked and hard, stroking himself. His hand clutched the edge of the marble sink, his eyes closed. She knew he saw what she was doing. He groaned from his hand, from the image of her. It was all so much—too much—and yet not enough. She barely touched herself. Those phantom touches barely touched her aching pussy. And still, she was rising and then falling, blissfully.

Beautiful.

She saw him finish, his seed spilling out in beautiful white strands, coating the mirror he stood in front of.

* * *

The thought of the previous night consumed her. It distracted her. It turned her on. It was delectable torture, a preview. She ran a hand over her face as Machiavelli and Eveline spoke about the training measures to be taken to prepare for the games. She couldn't focus. She swallowed, remembering how his phantom touches felt and how his moan sent her over that peak. She wanted to hear it again. She wanted to hear it in person. She wanted to hear it forever.

She thought about what it would be like in person. Would he be dominant? Loving? Would he take her hard? Would he make love to her?

She imagined him as dominantly passionate, the type of man to hold her tight but give her what she wanted. She imagined finishing her paperwork to be rewarded by him, and his hands would trail up her spine, slipping off her shirt, his mouth devouring her breasts. She'd moan. He'd take off her skirt and fuck her hard, passionately, telling her how good she felt, how long he had waited, and how he thought about her. She imagined him marking her. His lips parted, fangs elongated and piercing her skin. She wanted it. She wanted to be claimed by him.

If you keep thinking like this, you're going to make me come in my pants.

She was startled by the voice but didn't show it.

She wanted to smile. *Do you think I could?*

Yes.

Pride—that was what she felt.

You're hungry. You need to eat. I can feel it.

He was right. She was starving. She'd skipped breakfast and lunch and had a feeling she would skip dinner too.

Eveline set a candy bar on her desk.

Aella smiled. "Thank you."

Thank you. She knew he had mind-linked with her sister to bring her something to eat.

* * *

Later that night, Aella was startled awake by the sensation of fear, dread, and pain. She gasped, sitting up in her bed. She heaved a sigh, unable to breathe. She realized as her mind cleared that those feelings weren't hers. It was his. He was having a nightmare.

Her stomach fell. She'd never felt such despair or turmoil in her life.

She focused hard, forcing her mind link as far as she could. She realized that whenever they linked, he was the one carrying the weight of the thread. He was stronger and more experienced. It should come easier to him. For her, it felt like she was running a marathon.

She felt the link between them solidify, and she pulled that dream away. She didn't look into it. She wouldn't invade his privacy like that. She thought about him, how she saw him just as he had done with her. She forced these thoughts—these bright, loyal, impressive thoughts of him into his head. She showed him how she saw him: a protector, a warrior. He was Atlas to her. He was an Adonis. He was brilliant. He was breathtakingly beautiful.

As she lay back down, she stayed awake, sending those good thoughts to him, filling his head with pleasant dreams.

CHAPTER TWENTY-THREE

Pack games were apparently a big fucking deal. This week was the only week of the entire year that male mates were allowed on Luna Council lands. So besides the increasing amount of testosterone, it was a time of walking on eggshells for Aella. Lunas were territorial when it came to their mates in the same way alphas were over them, and she didn't have the innate understanding of what was acceptable and what was not because she was not raised under such customs.

She elected to simply stay away from men who weren't in her pack. It was easier, and she didn't want to make enemies or offend lunas who were, for the most part, quite kind to her.

Aella could see from her porch squadrons of cars passing through the golden gate, each waving the flag with its crest. After studying packs for three months, she was able recognize them based on what flag was displayed. One by one, cars slowly made their way through the gate and to their respective pack house.

Icarus was on edge. Aella could feel it. They left their links open to each other in the event that something happened, but everything was going smoothly. She doubted anything catastrophic would occur between the time when Icarus landed in Sweden and the time when he got to the pack house.

Her cheeks burned with the memory of what had happened a few nights before. She wanted him in her head again.

She wanted to feel his hands on her even if it was all in her head. She heard him swear in her mind.

Aella.

She tried to hide her shocked expression from Eveline, who was next to her.

Would really like to land without a hard-on.

Her heart seized in her chest. She readjusted her stance as heat pooled between her thighs.

"Why do you look constipated?"

She rolled her eyes from Eveline's quip. Silence took over between them, and Aella opened her mouth to say something before shutting it again.

"I think Icarus is changing his mind."

"About mating?" Eveline perked up. "That's amazing! I'm so happy for you."

"You have always been my number one, my person. It means so much more to me than you will ever understand, Eveline." Aella reached her arm around her sister, pulling her to her side.

Eveline grinned.

"You're gonna kick ass," Aella remarked. "You're far superior to all the other gammas."

"Do you think so?"

For once, Aella saw a hint of insecurity in Eveline's expression.

"Yes, of course." She pushed back at Eveline's fly-aways. "You have trained every day for six hours a day, not including your dynamic stretching. You've trained with Machiavelli and Icarus, who both are revered fighters. Icarus is the best fighter among all wolves. If he doubted your abilities, he would have never sent you with me."

"Thanks, Aella."

* * *

In their regalia, each woman waited for their pack to be announced. They were in the familiar municipal hall, the one where they had come to the first time. They were the last pack to be announced.

One by one, lunas ascended those grand stairs to their packs waiting for them in anticipation. This was like a showcase of all the hard work put into their lessons and training, and every luna was enthusiastic about their progress. Aella was too, but she knew only half of her pack valued her.

She felt Celest fidget on her feet beside her. She knew that everything she felt, Celest had been feeling it for years.

"You know, the pack has bullied you into submission, into thinking you are undeserving because of what you were born as," Aella started, not quite looking Celest in the eye. "But you were born as the mate of the Great Kaius. It is your destiny. This position is and has always been yours, regardless of your species.

"And in the short period of time that we have taken pack responsibilities, you have excelled, both as a friend and as a beta female. You are not the human mate of Kaius. You are the beta female of Pack Superior who so happens to be the mate of Kaius."

Her sentence was quickly followed by the sound of a trumpet throughout the hall and the boisterous voice of a woman cheering for Pack Superior. The doors opened, and Aella became suddenly acutely aware of how heavy the crown was on top of her head and how the brooch pinned on her bodice was slightly crooked.

She ignored the stares on her as she walked forward onto the terrace and waved graciously at the crowd. She stood for a moment, Celest slightly behind her to her right, Eveline to the left. They were in matching gowns, although Aella's was much more ornate with the sash of the pack on her. In her right hand was the scepter of Pack Superior, and in her left was the orb. Both of which were carried only by the alpha or luna of this specific pack.

Carefully, the trio descended the stairs in silence and walked to where Kaius and Icarus were standing, on the highest podium in the hall.

Aella's eyes trailed up the length of Icarus, and she inhaled deeply. He was wearing a gray tuxedo, one that was fitted to his broad, muscular frame. She had never seen him unclothed, not even shirtless, but she could clearly tell from the way his white shirt hugged his torso that he was well-defined. He was by no means a slim man. He was robust, a formidable statue of a male.

His hands were clasped together neatly in front of himself, and she couldn't help but notice how those veins popped. She wondered if his arms were just as veiny. By the time she reached his eyes, she could tell by his knowing smirk that he had caught her checking him out.

She blushed as she stopped in front of him. Celest went to Kaius' side while Eveline went next to Icarus but left a space for Aella. She was hesitant to continue the tradition. Her eyes hesitantly glanced at Kaius.

It's okay, Icarus sent to her.

She nodded, not to him but to herself.

"Welcome, mate," she said in Romanian.

She gasped as a rough hand wrapped around her wrist, pulling her closer to him. He leaned toward her, and she almost passed out thinking he was about to kiss her. Instead, his lips went to her forehead as he took the scepter from her hand. He pulled away, and he gently guided her to his side.

She couldn't help but stare at his perfect profile. *Damn.*

Soon.

She could have sworn she saw his mouth turn upward.

You . . . you look beautiful. His voice sounded strained in her head.

She tried to hide how much she liked that he thought so. She tucked her hand in the crook of his arm as he led the processional forward. Looking closer, she realized he donned his very own crest, which was in the shape of a steel diamond with a wolf insignia carved within it. On top of his head was a crown similar to hers.

He is an incredible man.

His silver eyes met hers unexpectedly. *Hardly a man.*

What do you mean? She looked away abruptly. *Oh.* She could have sworn she heard him chuckling in her head.

They continued to lead the pack back to the house.

Icarus' voice filtered through her head. *The other night, my nightmare turned into a . . . dream.*

Her face remained pleasant, shying away from showing her true emotions. She had hoped he wouldn't have known, and she didn't think he would say anything about it here.

That's good.

He looked down at her.

I know it was you.

Looking forward, she shrugged. *You know if I could do anything to ease your suffering, I would.*

You stayed up all night.

And I would again.

His steps faltered slightly.

As they reached their pack house after the promenade, Icarus led everyone into the foyer where those who had come from Romania took in the space.

"This is actually nice," someone said.

Aella smiled. "All of you have rooms. The youngest ones will be in the basement. Any mateless individuals will occupy the second floor while all mated couples will have the third floor. Breakfast is served at 8:00 every morning. Lunch is at 12:00, and dinner is at 6:00. What is mine is yours, so please make yourself comfortable. If you have any questions, Edeline is your point of contact. However, my office . . . well, my office is now Icarus' office, but please come to me if you need anything."

To be frank, she wanted to take her dress off. It was starting to become uncomfortable.

"Eveline and Machiavelli will talk more about training," she added.

Her stomach growled. She was starving. She forgot to eat in the morning because she was already running late, and she desperately regretted it.

She felt a hand on her lower back, and she knew immediately it was him. She looked up at him. *Oh God, those silver eyes.*

A boyish grin spread over his face. "I didn't know you liked them."

"You really need to teach me how to put my barrier up around you." She looked above his eyes in embarrassment and put her hand on his chest. She was sure this was almost the closest they'd been.

"I thought you preferred the contacts. I thought the silver eyes would be off-putting to you."

"Not at all," she admitted.

"Come. I can hear your stomach." He pulled away from her slowly, gesturing with his head to the kitchen.

"Lunch isn't prepared yet."

"I know."

She followed him into the kitchen, where some others were playing cards. She was greeted as she sat down at the island.

Icarus went to the fridge, pulling out milk and strawberries. Then, he went to the cabinet and retrieved honey and oats.

"You're making oatmeal?"

"It's your favorite." He didn't look at her as he put a pot of water on the stove.

"How do you know that?"

He gripped the edge of the counter, gazing at her. "Do you think I know nothing about you?"

"No, not nothing. Just not the small things, like what I like for breakfast."

"You like strawberry oatmeal because you think it's healthy."

"It is healthy!"

"Not when you put a cup of brown sugar on top," he responded, a small grin on his face.

"Listen, not all of us hate sugar, sunshine, and puppies."

"I never said I didn't like puppies. Would be ironic if I did, wouldn't it?"

She laughed. She laughed hard from her belly and attempted to cover her mouth to give off a facade of grace. "Was that a joke?"

"If you have to ask, it wasn't a great one."

"No, it was. I just wasn't expecting it from Grumpy Superior."

"Grumpy Superior?" His eyebrow rose.

"It's your nickname. Ask Machiavelli. I've ordered everyone to call you that." She shrugged.

"Really?"

She leaned forward on her forearms, giving him a look. "You think anyone here would call you Grumpy Superior? They all think you want to kill them."

"I don't want to kill them." He moved to the stove and poured a cup of oats into the boiling water. "Well, not all of them."

"Was that another joke? You're on fire, Alpha Superior."

The room turned icy. Icarus' back turned to stone, and she could see every vertebra snap into place. His hand gripped the handle of the oven.

Did she say something wrong?

"Icarus?"

"One second."

What? She nodded to herself, swallowing her other questions.

A moment passed and then he relaxed, turning to face her again.

"I'm sorry," she mumbled.

"What for?"

"I don't know."

"I wasn't prepared for the effect that would have on me of hearing you say that."

She watched as he investigated her expression. Something crossed his face, but he shook it away, turning back to the stove. She squirmed in her seat, the sudden urge to orgasm consuming her.

"Holy shit," Eveline grunted as she entered the kitchen. Her nose twisted in disgust. "Can you go handle that? I can smell you from down the hall."

"I'm going to kill myself," Aella muttered. "You mean you can smell—"

Eveline nodded, and Aella shot from her stool, the suffocating long dress catching around her legs. She couldn't look at him, not even as she felt his burning gaze on her. She was so embarrassed.

"Aella, wait."

She didn't stop even as she heard Icarus call her name, and she found herself outside, behind the house, with a twig scraping against her leg.

She gave a frustrated grunt as she lifted her dress and pulled the branch from under her dress. She didn't think this through: rule number seven, when running away from your mate and sister in embarrassment while dressed in a ball gown, don't run into the forest.

She held herself against the tree as she slipped off her heels. "Fucking hell, Aella. You stupid whore."

Stepping onto a root of a pine tree, she reached up and wrapped her arms around a thicker branch. She hauled herself up, sitting against the trunk as she contemplated if she could hang herself with the train of the silver dress.

"Stupid, stupid," she chanted, knocking her head against the tree.

"You know," a deep voice started from behind her, "I'd suggest, if you want to escape the prying ears of lycanthropes, you go farther out or farther up. But"—Icarus tilted his head as he came to the trunk of the tree—"I have a feeling you won't be able to escape your security brigade."

She looked at him and hated how he took her breath away every time. She stayed quiet. She noticed him looking at his hand that held a small bowl before she heard him sigh, pulling himself up with his free arm. She had struggled to get up this high, but to him, this was child's play.

He sat in front of her, his thighs cradling the thick branch. She swallowed. Her eyes squeezed shut as she turned her head. Her stomach coiled and then released.

"You still haven't eaten."

She turned to look at him, her eyes drifting to the bowl in his hand. She took it enthusiastically. "This is so good," she said, humming at the sweet taste of strawberry, sugar, and oats in her mouth.

He stayed silent, and she watched as his Adam's apple bob.

"I practiced."

She tilted her head in confusion.

He continued albeit with hesitance, "When we were moving to Romania, I knew you would have trouble adjusting, so I learned your favorite meals and left them for you. Oatmeal, grilled cheese with fresh tomato soup, rosemary chicken with mashed potatoes—which . . . are awful."

Her heart stuttered in her chest as she recounted the number of times she'd gone into the kitchen and found a plate waiting for her. She had always assumed it was Celest making her food, but it wasn't. It was him the entire time.

She laughed. "Have you ever considered that your opinion is wrong? Potatoes are easily the greatest vegetable—"

He snorted.

"Oh, come on! Baked, grilled, smashed, sliced, diced, deep-fried . . . you can cook them in literally every way, and they turn out delicious. You have no sense of—"

"How's your playlist," he interjected, a grin prying on his lips.

"You ass, do you know how unsettling it is to be listening to soft indie one minute and then the next—"

He laughed. It was a deep-rooted, from-deep-within-the-belly cackle of a laugh that most people did on a regular basis, except she had never seen him so carefree before. She had never seen the way his eyes light up when he looked up trying to contain himself, or how he had a cute small dimple on his left cheek. It was beautiful, beautifully tragic as well. There was a reason he'd never laughed like this.

"If it makes you feel any better," he said, trying to catch his breath, "I had to explain to an alpha that those romance novels weren't mine."

She felt the laugh bubble up inside her. "What did you say?"

"I said they belonged to the luna who had a strange affinity for such books."

She loved hearing him call her such a title.

She was brought back to reality. "We need to talk about one particular book."

He raised his bushy brow. "*The Alpha's Conquest*, really?"

She laughed, throwing her head back. "I didn't think you would meticulously look at the title of every single book." She shrugged. "What can I say? I have a thing for alphas."

She loved the look on his face from such a brazen response, but his shock was quickly masked as he leaned forward just slightly, his hands settling a few centimeters in front of her on her dress that covered the branch. She grew self-conscious from the way he analyzed her. His eyes roamed her face, scanning for something. She wasn't sure what.

She redirected the conversation, asking, "How did you find me so easily?"

He gave her a look. "Well, finding women in silver ball gowns in the middle of the woods is actually easier than it looks."

"Was that another joke? God, you should be a comedian. I'm starting to think you may actually be funny."

He gave her a small smile, and she was breathless again. She could feel her heartbeat in her chest, from nerves? Anxiety? Something else? She didn't know. She didn't need to figure it out.

"I want . . . I want to try something," he spoke again, his voice raspy. "Push me away. Tell me no."

It was a small whisper, a plea.

He leaned forward, his hands splayed in front of him. His brows were knitted together as he looked into her eyes and down to her lips.

"You know I could never—"

"I've tried so hard, Aella." His eyes shut as his forehead gently set on hers.

She could smell that familiar scent of pine and mint on his breath, and she wondered if it was his toothpaste or cologne. Did he wear cologne?

He's so close.

"You are disastrously tantalizing, and every part of me craves your attention in every way. I am a monster. You are so much better than I am. You shouldn't be damned. I had to fight like hell to survive, and fighting turned me into what I am."

She could feel his hands fist between her legs, an attempt—she speculated—to keep himself from touching her.

She breathed him in. "And what are you?"

"Selfish." His lips found hers with such ferocity that it almost startled her. It would be overconsuming if she wasn't just as starved for him.

She gasped as his touch lit her skin aflame in fireworks, and he took the opportunity to take her further. It turned slow, contemplative—the calm after the first taste of his mate.

Time slowed. Her hand wrapped around the back of his neck, and they briefly disconnected. She felt his strong hands on her hips as she surged forward. He wouldn't let her fall; he never would.

She climbed on top of him, straddling him, the dress tangling in their legs. She was sure it couldn't get much better than this. He wrapped his arms around her, securing her to him. His one hand slithered to the dip in her back as the other fisted her hair at the nape of her neck. She felt him between her legs, hard and straining against his suit pants.

She couldn't help herself. She leaned into him more, letting her legs fall around him, her aching core softly stroking his hardness. She moaned into his mouth. She could have sworn she heard him curse, but she was too wrapped up in the way he seemed to be moving her hips against him.

"Again," he ordered, pulling away for the briefest second. "Do you know how your moans turned me into a madman? How I heard you coming in your room all those nights? How I heard you finish yourself thinking about me? Do you understand what it does to a man?" He connected with her again, taking her mouth. "It makes him insatiable."

He pulled her hair back, just enough to expose her neck to him. He kissed a pathway down her skin as his hand gently kneaded into her thigh.

Another moan escaped her, then she felt him smile against her.

"Good girl."

CHAPTER TWENTY-FOUR

As Aella signed the formal announcement of the next pack deal between Pack Superior and Pack Earheart, she noticed Machiavelli and Eveline arguing over who would get the last cookie that was left over from dinner.

"Actually," she interrupted, "none of you get the cookie. Give it to me." Looking between the two adults, she realized how closely they resembled children fighting over the last sweet. She bit the smile back. "Okay, then share it. I'm trying to do work, unlike you two."

"We're providing moral support."

"Thanks, Ev, but you all have games tomorrow. It's 11:00 PM. Go to bed."

"Don't have to tell me twice," Machiavelli agreed, throwing the file back on the desk, then he shot out of the office.

Aella was grateful that he took the time to gently close the door instead of letting it slam shut.

"You know"—by Eveline's voice, she could tell she was about to drop some juicy information— "birdy told me you and a certain alpha got frisky in the woods today. I don't know why I'm surprised. You've always had an affinity for dramatic—"

Aella's head spun. *What if Kaius saw?*

"Relax." Eveline crossed her arms as she grinned at her sister. "I also know someone made sure Dad was preoccupied."

She sighed in relief. "Thanks, Ev."

Eveline put her hands up in defense. "Nope, not me. Mom distracted Dad, and Luna Earheart was coming to find you to hang out when she ran into you two."

"Please, don't let—"

"Yeah, I know. Dad won't find out. You know, you call Mom Celest and Dad Kaius now. You call them by their first names. Do you feel like they're not your parents anymore?"

She wasn't sure if that was the case. Honestly, it was confusing for her. She felt a strong bond with them, and she respected that they raised her. They loved her, and she knew that. They cared for her, gave her a home, watched her grow up, and she would always be appreciative.

However, at the same time, since training with Celest at the Luna Council, their bond had become different. They were still religiously protective of each other, but Aella didn't feel like her beta female was her mother but a friend.

As for Kaius, well, she was angry at him. She hated how he thought he could be happy but she couldn't. She didn't hate him. She could never. Kaius was the father figure in her life for the longest time. He'd taught her how to ride a bike, how to change a tire, and how to defend herself against boys. He taught *her* her first sentences of Romanian. He was a great person and a better lycanthrope.

Yet, a part of her resented him. A part of her didn't understand how anyone, especially a father, would want her to live as unhappily as she did. He was important to her and loved by her, but she didn't know if she considered him her father still.

"That's not it. I love them as family, and I love them as the people who brought me up, but"—she shrugged—"I don't know. Does that make me a bad person?"

"No, not at all. It makes you human, ironically. Good night, Aella."

As Eveline went to leave, she stopped by the door and lightly tapped her hand on the trim. "Alpha is still up too. I saw him sneak some of your work into his room."

"That explains why it seemed like I had very little to do," she mused.

"And I think he left a box of Cheez-Itz in your drawer. He must know you get too busy to eat sometimes. You know, I think his room is soundproof." She said with a suggestive tone.

Aella dazedly opened her drawer and took out the box, almost missing what Eveline was implying. She looked at her sister, and Ev shrugged with a teasing grin before disappearing down the hall. Her stomach growled, and she realized that she did forget to eat.

I wonder if . . . aha!

There were potato chips in her other drawer, Granola Bar in her purse, and Pretzels in her filing cabinet. He had put them all there. Her heart swelled. Looking at the pile on her desk, she quickly calculated if she could take the rest of the night off. If Icarus and she both pitched in, they could both take the night off and work normal hours the next day.

She shut the drawers and stood up, then turned off the lamp.

* * *

Aella knew that he knew she was outside his door. Even she could hear her heartbeat in her ears as she hesitated to knock. It was eerily quiet for her pack house. Usually, even after everyone retreated to their rooms, she could hear the pitter-patter of steps, but not this time. All she could hear was the sound of blood pumping in her head.

Kaius was just down the hall. Maybe even he sensed her standing there. Maybe he would act like he didn't, or maybe he would lash out. Maybe he would be furious and come haul her ass away.

Maybe Icarus would reject her. Maybe the plan she had in her head was futile and childish. Maybe she was stupid. Maybe he wouldn't want what she had to offer. Maybe he wasn't stressed. Maybe she'd be bad at it. Maybe he wouldn't like it—maybe, maybe, maybe.

Fuck it.

She knocked, and the door opened. He was standing there, not shocked to see her but confused as to why she was there. They knew not to speak. They knew that the slightest utterance of each other's name would let everyone in the hall know she had come to his room at such an ungodly hour.

He moved out of the way, closing the door behind her as she walked in.

"Your room is soundproof," she blurted.

He nodded.

She played with her hands. Looking around his room, she noticed the lamp turned on in the corner next to the large recliner. Papers were scattered across the small coffee table. The bed looked neatly made, and seeing it made her suddenly realized how large he looked compared to a king-sized bed.

"I should have given you my room. It's larger. I didn't think . . ." Her eyes found the pile of papers stacked on the table again. "Do you plan on finishing all this tonight?"

"It's manageable."

"It's a lot. Do you always do so much at night?"

"Yes."

"That's absurd." She flushed the stack in her hands. "If I take half and you take half, we can finish early, and you can sleep." She knew that he had moved closer to her, but she ignored his presence.

"Aella," he called, grabbing her wrists. "Why did you come here?"

"Are you stressed?"

Maybe she shouldn't have blurted it out that way.

His brows knitted together as he stared down at her with those silver eyes and angular face. "What does that have to do with anything?"

When she didn't respond, he answered, "Yes. When the packs compete tomorrow, if anything happens, I am prohibited to intervene, unlike every other alpha."

"But why would you—" She stopped as she realized. "You're worried about them."

Judging by how he lowered his gaze, she was correct. He cared about his pack even though it was rare of him to show any type of emotion other than anger toward his pack.

"You have added great wolves to our pack. I might even like some of them."

She smiled. "You know, it wouldn't kill you to let them know."

He remained motionless but continued, "If a pack member breaks game rules, alphas and lunas are allowed to step in. In this case, if something were to happen, I wouldn't be able to intervene because I am forbidden from participating."

"Is the only reason you never participated because of your physical advantage?"

He nodded, removing the items from her hands and setting them back down. "That, and my position in the world is unquestioned. Pack games exist to establish an unofficial hierarchy. My pack has always been at the summit of it."

She nodded. "Yes, but mine isn't." She was ashamed to admit it. "Even you questioned my position."

"No. I have never ever questioned your position. I was against human-lycanthrope bonds for a while, but so was Kaius."

"What?"

"He loves Celest, and I have never questioned his fidelity to her, but I had brought up that she could learn her position. I told him that there would be adversity and that he'd have to fight like hell for both of them when they first mated. He said he didn't want to put her through that; that he could make her happy outside of pack relations. I didn't push. I didn't care that much. I'm sure it was a discussion he had with Celest too, so then I assumed that if she was unwilling to accept the responsibilities, all humans would be. You're different. You're the change."

He looked at her with such confidence and faith that she had to swallow her emotions. She suddenly became hot. He inhaled and visibly struggled to open his eyes.

"I read in that book that alphas are volatile creatures—that they are hyper-emotional, overly aggressive, and incredibly sexual. Part of a luna's job is to be the calming force in his life, the person that can be what he can't. The person"—she swallowed—"that relieves his stress."

"Aella," he rasped, "what are you saying?"

"I'm saying," she started, her hands itching to touch him, "that I am doing my responsibilities as a luna when relieving your stress."

She could see his Adam's apple bob from anticipation, and it was nice to know that she could make the alpha a bit more emotional than he usually was.

"And how would you do that?"

She shook the hair—which had fallen out of her ponytail—from her face. She didn't answer his question explicitly. "You said you haven't been with anyone since finding out we're mates."

"What did you think? That I would touch another woman who wasn't my mate?"

"Well, yes. We couldn't be together, not in that way. And, you have . . . needs."

He shook his head. "After I realized what you were to me, I didn't want anyone else."

Turned on was certainly what she was. He'd waited that long for her.

"Would you have waited until I was twenty-six?"

"Yes. Touching someone else is infidelity."

She took a breath, her hands reaching his chest. She laid her palms flat on it as she contemplated her next words.

"I want to touch you," she whispered.

"Aella," he murmured, his voice hoarse and raw with need.

"If you don't want me to, I won't, but I want nothing more than to please you, and no one will ever know. This can be the last time until you are ready for more." She went quiet for a moment. "You're stressed," she pressed, and her tongue started delving out to wet her lips. "You made the choice to wait to mate, and I accepted that graciously."

He gave her a look.

"For the most part," she rectified. "Waiting is your decision. I want to make a choice for myself. I want to." She waited for disagreement as her hands worked off his belt. She was vaguely aware of the clink of the buckle on the hardwood floor.

She broke his gaze for a second to unbutton his black dress pants. She tried to slow herself, ease herself away from the excitement that bubbled in her stomach. She wanted to see him—she salivated to taste him. She had never experienced such a visceral, physical reaction to the prospect of seeing a man naked. She knew that it was because Icarus was hers. He was made in her perfect vision. She had been with men before, had sex before, given head before, and been given head, and it was all well and nice, but it was never like this. She never quite literally felt herself quake at the prospect.

His cock sprung up as soon as his pants fell to the floor. He was a briefs man.

She inhaled to calm her nerves, her excitement. She looked up at him, asking for permission. The subtle nod gave her the confidence to palm him through his dark briefs, and they both took a deep breath as she touched him. He was very hard underneath her small hand.

"Do you feel that?"

She wouldn't have heard him if he weren't so close to her. His voice was so quiet.

"Years of pent-up torment, all because of you."

Her breath hitched. She rested her head against his chest as her hand slowly ran along with the imprint. She felt his cock twitch under her palm.

She pulled away from him and pulled down his briefs before standing once more. She locked in his gaze. She didn't see *him* yet; she didn't look. Her eyes slid down his dress shirt until they reached the hard large member pressed against her stomach.

Fuck, he's bigger than I thought.

Am I not what you desire?

She jerked back, startled by his voice in her head. And then she saw that flicker of insecurity in his eyes. Her expression softened from fucking horny to "I'm about to tell you how great you are."

"There is not a single man or lycanthrope that could ever compare to you." Her heart skipped a beat. "I'm going to take you in my mouth now."

He was motionless as she descended to her knees. She looked up at him, watching his eyes brighten to that familiar shiny silver. His jaw ticked.

In her head, she prayed that all the other times she had done this would pay off now. She grabbed him at his base and ran her tongue up his length, circling his head. She could hear him utter something faintly, but she didn't think too much of it.

She did the same once again. He smelled like mint, pine, and something masculine. She knew she was a fiend for that scent. She took him into her mouth, tasting his excitement on the tip of her tongue.

"Fuck."

It was Romanian, his native tongue.

She took him further, which was not even the majority of his length, but she knew any further would hurt her stomach. So she took him slowly, bobbing at a deliberate pace. Her hand worked the rest of him that couldn't fit within her mouth. She felt him shake, and pride swelled inside her.

Her tongue maneuvered expertly around his head. She felt saliva fall from the corner of her lip. She popped off. She didn't wipe her mouth. Using both hands, she stroked him, enjoying the view of his member swollen and hungry for her. It glistened from her work, jumping just slightly as her thumb ran underneath his tip.

"Look at me."

She did so without argument.

His hand gripped her chin. "Such a good girl. You're doing so well."

Oh fuck.

That might have been the hottest thing ever said to her.

As he released her, she took him again. His grunts of approval were music to her ears. She learned he was a vocal male, something that always turned her on.

"Aella."

She knew that strangled voice—that sound every man made before he was about to finish. She continued at the same pace. His hand gripped the bedpost, and she knew he had splintered it from his tight grip.

He let out another grunt, a gasp. His cock went rigid in her mouth as his seed coated the back of her throat. She swallowed.

* * *

Pack Superior was seated next to Pack Earheart. Each pack had its own designated section with viewing stands and eight chairs seated on a scaffold. Aella sat next to Icarus, and on either side of them were Kaius, Celest, and Eveline. The empty chairs would one day be held by Eveline's mate, Aella's delta, and the delta female.

The field was bustling. Aella could hardly hear her own thoughts, so she couldn't imagine how loud it was for the wolves. It was a bright, sunny day out, the kind of day that would make her smile as soon as she woke up.

The sun beat down on her, and she fidgeted, feeling a bead of sweat run down her cleavage. Thank God, she put deodorant underneath her breasts that morning.

"The first few matches are between the all-female and all-male groups."

She nodded distractedly at Eveline.

Stop it.

She tilted her head toward Icarus, frowning.

You're picking your cuticles.

She was. She still couldn't drop that bad habit. She flexed her hands, a shallow breath leaving her chest.

It will be alright.

She nodded, returning her gaze to the field before her. The teams lined up, and alphas and lunas rose as their fighters were announced.

"Edeline, Rowena, and Katrina from Pack Superior."

The area around her erupted in applause while Eveline howled in praise. It seemed as though Aella was the only one nauseous with nerves.

She forced a smile on, her hand clutching the bodice of her gown as her chosen fighters took their place on the field. It was clear—by the size of Rowena's eyes—that she was more nervous than the other women. Edeline was smiling, reveling in the attention. Katrina was laser-focused on her task. Eveline had told her that Katrina was the most advanced fighter of the three. She would take logistical point.

Aella could feel Icarus was staring at her. She didn't look at him; she didn't want to show him just how concerned she was.

As the sun beat on the heart of the Luna Council lands, and the birds flew high above them, the games began with the blare of a trumpet.

* * *

The games continued in the sweltering heat, and watching her pack fight filled Aella with apprehension and pride. Yet, she couldn't resist the wince that consumed her whenever someone landed a blow on her pack mates.

They enjoy the fight, she reminded herself; this was their Olympics.

"Let's go, Eveline!"

"That's my gamma!"

"Kick their ass!"

Aella leaned her head to the side as her pack screamed in applause. They were proud of their gamma, who seemed as if the brutality of it all was natural to her. It was no secret that Eveline had and would continue to face adversity. Female gammas were uncommon. If a gamma had a daughter first, they would often forfeit the position to their brother. Eveline was the first female gamma in Superior history.

Aella looked at her mate, who was watching the fight with a bored expression. If she didn't know him so well, she'd believe he wanted to be anywhere other than there. That frown he wore was a facade. He was worried.

He gripped the end of the chair tightly, controlling himself. She knew that he could splinter that wood easily. It was a reminder of the sheer strength he had.

Aella closed her eyes in discomfort when Eveline was punched hard. Kaius had to look away, and Celest winced. Icarus remained pointed, his eyes narrowing as if he was speaking to her, willing her to do better.

Fuck, was what she heard in her head. It was Eveline.

You're so much better than that, Eveline.

That was Icarus' voice, and Aella didn't expect him to encourage Ev.

They're ganging up on me.
Eveline, you know what to do. I trained you.
I have never been successful.
Eveline.

She heard him sigh harshly beside her.

You can do it. If you couldn't, I wouldn't have made you gamma. He paused, then continued, *do you know how many people told me not to?*

There was another pause.

Eveline remained steadfast against her opponents' attacks.

Do you know how many times Kaius told me to go easy on you?

Ev got hit again.

I never did. I never doubted you.

Silence descended before a whisper resonated through Aella's head.

You can do it. I trained you.

Drowning in emotion, Aella looked at Icarus. She shifted her eyes to the field to see Eveline dodge and then attack. The burst of energy and resilience caught her opponents off guard, allowing Eveline to destabilize them. She was excelling. She was winning. She had the upper hand.

Icarus' focus never wavered, not even shifting to Aella. He was motionless. He was concerned. Whether he realized it or not, he had shown emotion; he had motivated his gamma. That facade cracked, and Aella was proud of him.

Finally, as Eveline regained her composure, Icarus' silver eyes met Aella's again. The master of ceremonies walked onto the field and lifted Eveline's arm up. She was declared the winner, her chest heaving and blood dripping down her neck.

The pack erupted, and for the first time, Aella was linked in with every single person, every lycan in her pack. The emotions she felt weren't just hers but everyone's. She belonged to them as they belonged to her.

She grabbed Icarus' hand, her palm wrapping around his fingers. Her mate looked at her, hardness clouding his eyes.

She sighed and squeezed his fingers. "You can smile. She won, Icarus. She did it."

He shrugged, his eyes moving toward the field, where the pack was throwing Eveline in the air.

Aella saw it. She saw it in those silver eyes—he was proud.

"I never doubted she would," was all he said.

A new hunger consumed her. All she wanted to do was feel him. She watched his profile as he gazed at the crowd. They were happy. They were motivated. They were having fun, loud and boisterous.

Suddenly, sadness fell on her. She saw longing. She held out her hand, standing up. Her gown pooled around her in waves.

He looked at her hand skeptically.

Rolling her eyes, she pulled as hard as she could, but he didn't budge.

"What have you been eating? You need to start a diet," she teased.

"And you need to start going to the gym. You get winded from walking upstairs." He let her pull him to his feet.

"That's hard cardio."

A ghost of a smile appeared on his face.

She tugged him toward the pack on the field, but he hesitated to follow. He looked at her, at them, and back at her.

"I don't think they want me there."

Her brows furrowed, and her heart lurched. He thought he was unwanted, unloved by his pack, but he was so silly. The people she brought into the pack loved him. They loved her too. They were good, loyal, and kind people.

"They want to be with you," she said. "They talk about it a lot, actually. They feel you don't want them around."

"It's not that." He shook his head. "I just . . . I didn't know how to be in happiness when I was so unhappy."

"Are you still unhappy?"

He looked at her, something crossing over his features. A breathless laugh left his mouth. "No."

"Here's to Pack Superior!" Machiavelli announced in the middle of the celebration. He locked eyes with Aella, a smile plastered on his face. "Tell him not to kill us, please."

She knitted her brows, confused. Before she knew it, she was drenched, doused in the coldest water she'd ever been in. She felt an ice cube fall down the bodice of her dress, her hair becoming a curtain over her eyes.

She turned toward Icarus, who was also wiping water from his eyes. His hair was sleek against his forehead, his gray suit darkened by the water.

He smiled and then let out the loudest, sloppiest bark of laughter she'd ever heard from him. And she was breathless, consumed by him, drowning in his laughter as the others joined happily.

Machiavelli slapped Icarus' shoulder and stood next to him as Edeline snapped a quick photo with her phone. Icarus wasn't upset, not in the slightest. He was bright. He was relaxed. He was having fun.

And oh God was he loved.

*   *   *

Icarus sat on the couch, leering over the documents in his hand. Aella remained at the desk even though she had insisted they swap. He said he belonged at that desk; it was hers.

She was agitated. She knew she had barked at everyone, frustrated. By what? She didn't know, but she was annoyed. Everyone was walking on eggshells around her. She tried to stay quiet, biting her tongue, but people kept picking. They kept talking, speaking, and saying stupid shit.

Malia ran into the office again, laughing. Usually, Aella would laugh with her, but she was simply not in the mood.

The girl climbed onto her lap and played with Aella's curls.

"Don't pull," Aella reprimanded. She was stern, but she managed to keep her temper at bay.

But then the girl climbed off, and Machiavelli strolled in with a ball, tossing it to her. Malia caught it and tried to throw it back, but she was just a child, and her aim was poor. The ball hit the lamp on the table beside the door, shattering it into pieces.

"Everyone out, now! Malia, go to Edeline. For fuck's sake," she sneered after Malia ran out, "you're a grown man, Mac. Can you please start acting like it?"

She didn't see Mac's surprised expression. She'd never yelled before. She was never upset, not in this way. If she didn't see the way Mac's eyes filled with sadness, Icarus did.

"I'll clean it, Luna," he said.

"No, just go."

He listened, leaving the office and shutting the door behind him.

In silence, Icarus watched as his mate ignored the mess and returned to her desk. He stood, buttoning his jacket, then walked to the closet. With a broom and dustpan in hand, he kneeled before the pile of shards. He was meticulous in his ministrations as he cleaned up the mess.

"It's just a lamp," he reminded her.

She looked at him, staring daggers. "Not the point."

"Isn't it?" He stood and threw away the shards in the garbage can beside her desk. He crossed his arms. "You bit their heads off."

"They shouldn't be playing in the office like that."

"They were having fun, Aella."

"Are you trying to make me feel bad?"

"I'm trying to get you to calm down."

"You're doing a shitty job." She stood up. "You're allowed to act like a dick to everyone, but I'm not?"

His eyes narrowed dangerously. "You aren't me."

"Obviously."

Silence reigned.

"What is wrong?" he finally asked.

"Just . . ." She sighed, holding her hand out. "Leave me alone."

His gaze became impossibly sharp, but his small smirk gave away that he was onto something—something he knew about her that she didn't know about herself.

He rounded the desk, stopping beside her. "What's an alpha's job?"

Her brows knitted. "What?"

"What's an alpha's job, Aella?"

She scoffed at the rudimentary question. "To look after the pack."

"Wrong." His hands found her waist, turning her toward him.

She didn't fight much as he cupped her thighs and lifted her onto the desk.

"What are you doing?"

"The job of an alpha is to first make sure his luna is happy."

"What are you saying, Icarus? Look, I have work to do."

He looked at her like he was furious with her. His hands went under her pencil skirt behind her knees. He watched as her face contorted in confusion and shock.

"Icarus?"

"Are you so upset because you're horny, Luna?"

"I—what?"

"It's natural. Most lunas would feel the same being around their mate without being touched." His hand trailed down her cheekbone. He sighed deeply, grabbing her chin. "I'm going to *taste* you, Aella. I'm going to make you finish. Any issues?"

Her heart was in her throat, with trepidation and excitement. His fingers found the sides of her panties, and he pulled them down. She lifted herself to make it easier for him. He held her gaze as he folded them and laid them on the desk next to her. If she weren't so nervous, she would have found how organized he was humorous.

His hands found her calves, and he wrapped her legs around his waist and lifted her effortlessly and then carried her to the other end of the desk. He sat her down, gripping her waist once more, and pushed her further up the mahogany.

"Icarus, you don't have to . . ."

Words died as he kissed her calf, setting her leg over his shoulder. A singular firm hand rested on her chest, gently forcing her back. She lay down, her hands fumbling through his dark hair as he laid kisses between her legs.

"Really, you don't have to. I'll be in a better—"

His tongue flicked over her clit once. She moaned, concluding her sentence, as her head turned into a frenzy of thoughts. She felt his arms encircle her waist, pulling her to the edge and holding her down. She was trapped, his tongue buried in her.

Her hips bucked against him, but his strong hand reached up to her chest and gently pushed her back. She grabbed his hand as she rode his face. Soon, that sweet peak was so close to her that she begged for him to keep going.

"Oh God." She felt his hands tighten around her. Her stomach flipped as her climax swelled inside her.

His lips found her thighs before he pulled away. The sight of her wetness on his lips made her quake on that desk before him. She was struggling to breathe as he stood to his full height. Her eyes raked down his strong form, widening at the sight of his soaked black pants.

"Fuck," he growled in annoyance.

"You came?" she said, shock lacing her voice.

"You don't know how good you taste."

* * *

Aella had a moment to herself. When she did, she usually spent it with Icarus, but he was meeting with the Alpha Council. Similar to the Luna Council, they congregated to discuss multilateral political issues. Unlike the Luna Council, they did not have their neutral territory, and they were not nearly as efficient. They often had to suspend meetings due to aggressive episodes.

Aella found herself in a spot she'd never been to. She knew the Alpha Hall existed, but she'd never had the time to stroll down the corridor that had the portraits of every active alpha.

She walked down the hall. The sound of her heels relaxed her as she looked at the perfectly hung portraits. Honestly, she was just interested in seeing Icarus' and feigned interest in the others'.

She found Icarus' portrait at the very end. While the others' were hung on the sidewalls, his was on the farthest wall, between them. Underneath was *ALPHA SUPERIOR* inscribed on a silver placard. It was higher than her, so she had to strain her neck to look.

Icarus looked younger, more regal compared to how he looked now—put-together but on his own terms. In the portrait, he looked like he was stuffed in his regalia. The gray suit was decorated by the sash of Superior, his crest proudly painted on his chest. His eyes were stern. There were no dreams in them, only duty. It was always about his duty.

"This was made two hundred years after I was turned."

She closed her eyes as she felt a ghost of a hand on her lower back. When she opened them, he was leering at the portrait. He looked, in part, disgusted by it.

"You don't like it?"

He tore his gaze from the painting. "No, I don't."

"Why not? It's uncanny. The painter did a fantastic job."

He agreed. He opened his mouth as if he was going to speak, only to close it. His brows furrowed, his face crumpling into pain. He stumbled forward, but her hands found his waist. Her chest pressed against his as she stuttered back to hold the majority of his weight. Fear gripped her.

"Icarus? Icarus," she panted, her back hitting the wall.

With the strength he could muster, he put his hand beside her head. And when he lifted his head, his body seized again from the clear pain running through him. Her head raced. There was a disease—a pandemic—and he wasn't immune to the sickness. The mortality rate was 21 percent.

She couldn't breathe, suddenly. "I'll get help."

"No," he grunted.

She felt his hand turn into a fist beside her, his other hand relaxing around her waist. She knew he was trying to force himself not to hurt her, not to use her as a way to lessen the pain.

"It will go away." He groaned.

She realized that even though his expression morphed into clear agony, he was completely silent. As his head was buried in her neck, she realized that this pain was normal for him. He'd learned how to cope. Still, she didn't understand what was happening.

"You're scaring me," she admitted after a minute. "Let me get help."

He shook his head.

She tried to soothe him, running her hand up and down his back slowly, then she started reading *Les Mis* to him. She'd memorized the first chapter. She recited it to him in a low voice.

Eventually, his breaths returned to normal, and he slowly lifted his head. She looked at him, expecting an answer. A sheen of sweat coated his head. His eyes looked sad, exhausted.

"Champion of Lycanthropes," he started low, his voice hoarse, "whenever wolves die, I am reminded of my failure."

She realized that his "failure" was not protecting them.

"You feel it whenever someone dies?"

He nodded. "And it tears me apart."

Her eyes started to water. She looked away from him for a second, trying to contain her emotions, but they all happened at once. They erupted around her, making her feel helpless. Before her, this man—this wolf—took such pain on behalf of his wolves. He was forced to feel their physical and emotional anguish every day of his life. And suddenly, she hated Artemis.

Who would ever condemn a man to such a fate?

"Whenever you feel the pain"—her eyes shifted to him—"tell me. You will never go through it alone again."

That was a promise.

When he was finally able to walk, she didn't take him back to the pack house but to that vault where her jewels waited, polished and beautiful. She took him to the connecting library and grabbed his favorite book and read to him.

After hours of silence, he spoke to her as he settled his head on her lap: "The only time I experience peace and the only times I could sleep peacefully are when you are near me, reading to me, speaking to me. Your presence is everything I yearn for."

CHAPTER TWENTY-FIVE

The games continued. The delta matches had taken place hours prior. Pack Black won. Now, it was the beta matches, which Kaius would not participate in.

Aella watched as males entered the field, stripped themselves of their shirts, and stood in a circle. A male, tall and broad, stood on the farthest side from her. She realized quickly that it was Beta Cyril. She couldn't control her gasp as she saw the marred skin of his chest and back. It looked as if he had been burned. It looked as if those scars were vibrating, as if something beneath him slithered and contorted.

She swallowed, a feeling she couldn't decipher washing over her. She looked at Icarus. "Do you feel that?"

He cocked his head to the side. "Feel what?"

That answered her question.

Before she could speak again, the loud horn blared, and the fight began. Cyril was an accomplished fighter. He was strong, resilient, and quick. He was the best on the field. He was dangerous, practically feral.

No. He was truly vicious when displaying his skills, going for the kill without finishing them. It was brutal. It was grotesque.

She turned her head away from the sight. Cyril won. Pack Samir dominated the beta match.

They didn't show their triumph, which was unusual. All the packs celebrated after a victory while Alpha Samir didn't even look impressed. He said something to the beta, and Aella could have sworn she saw Cyril wince.

"What did he say?"

Icarus looked at her. His eyes were bright with anger. He didn't answer her, but he stood up and re-buttoned his jacket. "Kaius."

"Yeah, I heard."

She watched as Kaius stood.

"Icarus, what did he say?"

"Alpha Samir used his alpha command on Cyril. He ordered him to beat the wolves of the pack that lost their matches."

Her mouth went dry. "What?"

"He can't disobey the order, Aella. He has to do it."

She stood, shaking her head. "They don't deserve to get beat."

"I agree."

"You can stop it," she argued.

"If I intervene, Alpha Samir would have the right to challenge me."

She wanted to say, "You could beat him," but she bit her tongue. She shouldn't force her mate to fight, not only fight but to kill. An alpha would lose, and a loss meant death. And she was damn sure Icarus' reign wouldn't be the one to fall.

Something intangible pulled her away from the dais. She needed to follow that beta. She needed to see him, to stop him. And the prospect of him hurting others made her sick.

"What is going on in your head, Aella?"

"I don't . . . I feel . . . I feel connected to him as I do to you but without romantic interest. It's—"

"Go."

Her eyes widened.

"Go," he said again. "I'll stop him, but you follow that feeling. Aella, go."

She hesitated for a moment before picking up the skirt of her dress and running off the platform.

Pack Samir didn't have a pack house. They didn't have a luna, but they were given a plot of land near the grounds to set up tents. That was where she found Beta Cyril, shaking against a tree. He convulsed. A growl escaped him as his hands gripped around the trunk of the tree, his head against it. He punched it hard enough to splinter.

She didn't understand what was happening until she looked behind the tree and saw a male standing in front of a cowering woman. The male who was protecting the female looked horrified—terrified—and whimpered, his hand extending toward the beta, who was foaming at the mouth.

Beta Cyril seemed to lose whatever battle he was going through and tore himself from the tree, stalking toward the male.

"Wait!"

That was her voice.

Cyril continued onward.

"Stop!"

She hardly recognized her voice, but she knew she was using her luna command. She could feel it tightening around her, snapping into place.

Cyril went rigid, then he turned toward her.

She could see it—the picture of sadness. She had seen it in Icarus too, but this was different. This was helpless, pathetic, enslaved.

"Help," Cyril whispered.

Her eyes locked onto his, and her world slowed. It felt like a thread tying itself around them, and a deep-rooted feeling of familiarity and protective duty seemed to drown her.

She gasped as the revelation startled her: "Delta."

She rushed toward Cyril, only to be stopped by Icarus.

"He won't hurt me."

"You don't know that."

"He's my delta."

"I know that." Icarus took a steadying breath. "I felt it too, but I won't risk it, Aella." Whatever patience Icarus had had must have depleted because he looked at Cyril, rolled his eyes, then barked out another command. "Your previous alpha command is broken, Cyril."

Cyril collapsed to the ground.

Icarus loosened his grip on Aella and walked in front of her, placing himself between her and Cyril. She moved past him and kneeled down, Icarus protecting her from behind.

"Cyril?"

"Alpha Samir is coming," Icarus muttered. It wasn't exactly dread in his voice but annoyance at what would happen next. His attention went to Cyril. "Would you ever hurt her?"

Cyril's wild silver eyes locked onto Icarus'. He shook his head.

"I believe you," Icarus affirmed. "I will not command you because I know it's hell for you, but if you touch her, I will kill you. Do you understand me?"

"Yes, Alpha Superior," Cyril gasped out.

"Kaius, stay and guard."

Aella's eyes went back to Cyril as her mate focused on Alpha Samir stalking toward them.

"I am so sorry this happened to you," she whispered to Cyril. "You don't have to stay. You never have to listen to his command again. You're my delta." Grabbing his hand, she swallowed her emotions. "Do you recognize Pack Superior as your new pack?"

Tears welled behind his eyes. He gulped, nodding. "With the utmost sincerity, Luna."

Looking up at Kaius, she asked him a silent question.

He shook his head. "Celest is not coming here, not with alphas fighting."

Celest was the missing piece to adding a new pack member. Without her, Aella could only partially fulfill the ritual.

She looked at him spitefully. "You always tell her what to do. That's going to kick you in your ass one day." She shook her head, returning her gaze to the other man. "It is with the greatest confidence that I welcome you into Pack Superior. I will protect, care, and provide for you as I can. I will treat you as a comrade and as my child, and with the utmost sincerity, I appreciate the promise you make today. For any wolf willing to give their life for their alpha and luna is a wolf I am willing to do the same for. I thank Artemis for providing me with another wolf. You may rise."

It seemed as if something new washed over him—something akin to a fresh start, a new wave of enthusiasm, a second wind. He stood easily, his gaze penetrating hers, then he bowed before her. There was a sickening snap behind her, and she went to look.

"Don't," he said, stepping in front of her gaze. "Alpha Superior wouldn't want you to see what he just had to do."

"Is Alpha Samir . . . ?"

He nodded. "He's dead."

Hearing the sound of steps approaching, she didn't hold her breath for someone else to start speaking.

"What the fuck is going on?"

"Eveline—"

"Actually, wait, it doesn't matter that much. What does matter is that the pack games are still happening, and the pack match is now. If we don't get our asses there, it's an automatic forfeit. We will handle this fuck fest later."

The final game was packwide. Every single member would fight, excluding the Superiors, children, and pregnant women.

* * *

Aella sat, once again, next to Icarus. The memory of what had occurred moments earlier made her mind race. She watched as Cyril stood from his seat in between Kaius and Icarus. She realized then that he had planned on fighting once again.

She shook her head. "Cyril, you don't have to."

He looked confused, shocked even. "You're giving me the choice?"

"Yes, of course. You don't need to fight if you don't want to. You have free will."

His brows knitted, but then he nodded and stepped off the scaffold, taking his place next to Eveline.

Eveline regarded him for a second. "I take point."

"You're a gamma?"

She nodded.

"Women weren't allowed power in my last pack."

"Must be a weak pack, then."

A small grin played on his lips. "Some would say."

"Do we have a problem?"

"Can you fight?"

"After this, I'll fight you and kick your ass."

He nodded. "Whatever you say, I got your back," he relented.

"Ah, look at you, becoming a feminist so quick!"

Aella was nervous, but she was above all else proud of those who stood with her. So when the sound blared as a signal to start the competition, she tried to relax. Pack Superior had great strategists. They had a plan, a formulation the inner circle had created for this precise moment. She and Celest had little to no input in it; they didn't want to. They had neither experience nor wolves.

Eveline was in front of her pack, the first to take a hit. Mac and Cyril were nearby. Then, the world froze, and Aella felt Icarus lurch forward, a grunt parting his lips. He threw his body in front of her, collapsing on top of her. She didn't understand. There was chaos. Shouts of pain, sounds of bullets, and screams of horror—all of which were blocked by his massive form. She lowered both of them to the ground. A hand gripped her arm, and she screamed.

Icarus yelled out her name, his eyes wild. He was motionless, a bullet wound in his chest.

That didn't make sense. He'd heal. He was practically immortal.

He'd heal.

She was hauled up from behind, and she watched in horror as Icarus tried to clutch her. Every time he looked as if he could stand, he was shot. She was turned and found the eyes of a man she'd never met. Behind her, the screams died to a murmur, and the sounds of bullets finally quieted.

It was eerily quiet. Her heart raced. Her feet dangled from the ground. She bit back her whimper of pain from the claws that dug into her skin. She realized, as she looked around the man, that there was an entourage of men with weaponry and gloves. And then she made the connection: the bullets must have been laced with wolfsbane.

Icarus wouldn't be able to heal, not from the bullet wounds that littered his skin. Wolfsbane was toxic to them, a painful sedative. It would render any lycanthrope powerless. They couldn't move. They couldn't shift, and they lost their strength. Alita had given a lesson about it, saying it was monitored closely and illegal to grow in all packs.

"What did you do?" she asked, shocked and confused. She hated how her voice came out as a pathetic whimper.

"Keep shooting if anyone regenerates. Keep the Superiors cuffed, including Eveline. Don't hurt Celest, not yet."

The man who held her smelled of dust and mold, a scent that nauseated her. He wasn't looking at her while he spoke. She knew someone else was behind her. When she looked around her, she saw Celest. She was also being held, but she was screaming now—screaming for Aella, screaming for Kaius, screaming for Eveline.

Aella was carried on the scaffold next to Celest. Her hands were bound by a rope, and the rope was strung from the wooden beam above her. The same happened to Celest. She was hung next to her.

Kaius was dragged in front of her while Icarus was placed in front of Aella and was shot again when he thrashed against them. Aella realized in horror that bullet holes laced his chest. They covered him, his blood seeping through the material of his shirt. She wept. His eyes met hers, something she couldn't read crossing them.

Eveline was brought in next and thrown beside Icarus. Her breaths were ragged, and her eyes couldn't stay open. The man who had held Aella—the man who barked orders—came in front of her.

"Do you know who I am?"

Aella spat in his face.

He smiled, wiping it off.

Bastard.

"My name is Ansan."

"Fuck you."

"Your mate killed my mate."

"Fuck you," she repeated.

"Aella," Celest warned.

Aella quieted. If she was going to die, if they were all going to die there, she was damn sure not going to go without a fight.

There was no doubt in her mind that Icarus had killed Ansan's mate, but he always had a reason, and that reason was always justified. Icarus did nothing that didn't have a point. He didn't do anything punitive to innocent people. She hated herself for not pestering Icarus more about it.

"What do you want?" She seethed.

"That's a great question." His finger gently traced over her cheek.

She winced back. Ansan's voice was higher than Icarus' and more boyish but still menacing. His eyes weren't silver. They were all black, not a speck of white in them.

"So, you are her, huh? The mate of the Great Superior." He turned to Icarus. "I must admit, I was expecting . . . more."

"Sorry to disappoint," Aella said sardonically. "What do you want, Ansan? They will kill you for what you've done."

"Seems to me like they're a little preoccupied. I'm going to make them feel what they put me through. Do you understand what that means?"

She tried to choke back the bile that rose in her throat. She didn't want to die. She was terrified.

"Icarus told me the story. He killed your mate, not Kaius."

Celest's eyes sought hers, but she ignored them. She trained them on Ansan.

"Are you trying to save your mother?"

"And Eveline had nothing to do with it. None of the new members in my pack had anything to do with it."

"Innocents always die in war."

"Think about it." She had to take a breath to be able to force the next words out. "Having a mate is all Ic—Superior wanted. Imagine the pain you'd put him through if he had to live, knowing his beta was happily mated still. Imagine having to watch your gamma find their mate as well, all the while yours was"—she tried to hide the hiccup in her voice— "murdered."

"Aella," Celest pleaded.

Aella shook her head. She looked intently at Ansan.

He neared her, running his nose against hers.

She held her breath, the stench of him turning her stomach. There was nothing more revolting than that. She tried to ignore the sound of Icarus fighting, thrashing, only to be shot to keep him from moving.

"Persuasive." Ansan suddenly moved away from her, turning to Celest. "Your luna might save you after all." He stuffed his hands into the pockets of his jeans. "Make sure your mate keeps his eyes open," he ordered, smiling. "So he can watch, of course."

"Watch what?" Celest froze. Her gaze morphed into sadness and concern, a chilling mixture in her brown eyes. "No," she pleaded. "Aella doesn't . . . she's not . . . She's innocent! She has never done anything to you."

"Maybe. Maybe not. But your mates deserve to suffer. And she is important to both of them, a two-for-one deal."

Aella looked upward, trying to hold back her tears. She knew she was shaking, and a sob left her lips as she realized what would happen in the next few minutes. It was like she couldn't catch a break in this life.

Startled, feminine dark eyes met hers. Celest cried, shaking her head.

"Close your eyes," she said.

She wasn't speaking to Icarus. She was speaking to Aella.

Aella choked back her sob.

Ansan walked over between Kaius and Icarus, kneeling down to meet their gaze. They were awake, but they were not in control of their bodies. All they could do was listen and watch.

"You made me do this." He looked at Icarus. "If you close your eyes, I will make it worse for her. Do you understand?"

Aella's eyes squeezed shut.

Ansan jerked back, nervous, as Icarus thrashed again. Ansan laughed, going back to her. His hand ran up her abdomen. His touch wasn't like Icarus'. It made her feel cold instead, causing her to tighten everywhere.

His hand roamed over the bodice of her gown. She thought it couldn't get worse until he started speaking. She knew that even though he was looking at her, he was speaking to her mate. He pulled her arms down from the rope to lower her hands.

"You are . . . pretty," he whispered from behind her as his hand unzipped her gown, and soon she was clad in her underwear before him. "And I heard," he drawled out, harshly cupping her breast over her bra, "that Alpha Superior never mated you."

She heard a growl, then another shot. She felt her stomach drop. She forced her face into her shoulder as he continued to assault her. She tried to stay strong; she really did. But then he ripped her underwear off, then she heard the sound of his zipper from behind her. She couldn't look at Icarus. She wouldn't let the last time he saw her eyes be as they were.

"No." She heard Celest say softly. It was like she was in denial of what was happening. "No," she repeated.

Aella heard the rope croak as they were pulled against the beam.

"No," she continued to chant, her arms thrashing against their binds.

But then, somewhere within the tirade of nos was a growl. It was soft at first but loud enough to turn everyone's heads as Celest's eyes changed colors. Her skin turned into fur, and her arms quickly broke the rope from the beam, her hands breaking free from their confines.

Canines—those were canines. Aella was sure of it.

Another growl—louder, stronger, and more determined— filled her ears. With both trepidation and awe, Aella realized that Celest was no longer human, and Ansan wouldn't survive long enough to force himself onto her.

Icarus' eyes didn't go to Celest but met Aella's.

Celest was smart. She removed the threat of being shot first, going after the wolves with guns. As Ansan fumbled to get his weapon out, a hand snapped around his throat, hauling him off his feet. Celest was terrifying.

Aella watched with both pride and nerves as Celest snarled, exposing her canines at the only male still standing.

"How dare you?" She squeezed tighter. "How dare you lay a hand on my luna? How dare you attack my pack and expect to live through it?" She smiled crazily, dangerously. She looked toward

Kaius and Icarus. "Are you watching?" Not waiting for a response, her teeth tore into Ansan's neck.

His jugular vein spewed coats of blood onto her, decorating the scaffold. It somehow missed Aella as her world turned fuzzy, and she became light-headed. The lights around her flickered, morphing between colors, and right before her eyes fell shut, she realized she was having a seizure.

* * *

Aella didn't know where she was, but she was calm. She wasn't scared. She felt serene as if she was in a dream. It felt like she was in the clouds or a dreamscape. She felt her limbs but could hardly hear anything past her breathing. It was warm, white, and tranquil.

Something bright shone in her eyes.

Putting a hand up to block the annoying ray, Aella could see a shape in the distance. As it neared, she remained motionless.

"Hello," greeted a woman. She radiated grace, and her heart-shaped face conveyed maternal instinct.

Aella gulped. "Hello."

"Do you know who I am?"

Aella shook her head.

The godly woman gave a sweet, soft smile. "Your people call me Artemis."

She faltered in her stance, taking a defensive step back.

"Be calm."

"Why am I here? What have I done?"

"It is nothing you have done." Her expression saddened. "It is I who has to apologize. I have made an error."

Aella looked at her, confused yet intrigued. A fresh wind washed through her hair. "A goddess doesn't make errors."

"Even the godly make mistakes," she countered. She took a moment. Her eyes left Aella's and then returned, skeptical. "Icarus was never supposed to be given a mate. You were never supposed to exist."

She didn't know how to respond.

"There is a choice you must make, and it is yours to decide. The way the lycanthrope world works hinges on one unequivocal truth: there must always exist one lone wolf."

Enlightenment surged through her before dread consumed her. "Icarus."

Artemis nodded. "This needs to be amended. In order for mates to exist for all other wolves, there must be a lone wolf without a mate. However, you may choose your mate, but if you do so, the bonds of all the other lycanthropes will be forfeited, broken."

No, no. She took another step back as bile rose in her throat.

"I am sorry, Aella."

"No! This isn't fair! You are a goddess. You make the rules."

"Not when it comes to this type of fate. This is a rule determined above me."

"Nothing is above you." Aella couldn't help but sneer at the woman. "I have to choose between having a mate and others having theirs? I-I can't do that. I won't."

Artemis stayed silent.

"The choice is you can choose to stay on Earth and mate with Icarus," she spoke again. "In this choice, there will be no other mate bonds. Or you could elect for Icarus to forgo a mate and save the other bonds—"

"No," Aella yelled. "No, I can't . . . I-I won't." With hands on her ears, she backed away from the woman, tears threatening to escape her.

"You have to."

She shook her head, falling to the ground, where she stayed for hours. Artemis remained standing, watching her until she finally had enough.

"If you do not answer soon, every other wolf will die. You must make a decision."

Bloodshot eyes looked up at the woman. Aella scoffed in disdain. Her knees came to her chest. "First, you tell me I need to make an impossible decision, and now you're putting a timer on the said decision. Fuck you!"

Artemis kneeled beside her. "Choose."

Aella's eyes shut again, a tear rolling down her cheek. "I want to choose Icarus."

"But?"

"No buts." Aella looked away. "You have forced that man to live in agony, in pain for centuries, having to watch his loved ones be loved while never being able to love and be loved in the same way. You beat him. You tormented him. You gave him, arguably, a worse lycanthrope life than his human life. And for that, I will never ever forgive you. He says he's a monster, and even if he is, you made him one. You are the monster. I choose him."

If she was affected by what she said, Artemis didn't react. "You're saving your bond with him, forgoing the others?"

Aella shook her head. "No, I can't. I can't damn anyone but myself."

"What are you saying?"

"I will take his spot."

Artemis' brows knitted.

"I will take his spot as the lone wolf. You will ease his suffering. I will damn myself, not him or anyone else. You will give that man a great afterlife, one where he has a mate and is happy."

"You'd do that for him? For them?"

"I love him."

It was such an easy thing to say. It was an irrevocable truth.

"But why then do it for them? Why save theirs when you can have yours?"

"Because I love my sister too, and she's always dreamed of having a mate."

"You love them disastrously so."

"And I will continue to love Icarus even when he's gone. I will always remember him and how he made me feel."

* * *

Aella gasped awake on that field, Icarus beside her, moving, healing, and gazing at her. He was worried, distraught even. He called her name again.

She couldn't breathe. She couldn't bear the way he looked at her like she'd brought light into his life. His silhouette appeared in front of her as the sun shone behind him. His angular jaw was set, his beautiful silver eyes bright with fear—fear that she was hurt. He didn't know how badly she was, but not in the way he thought. It was a pleasant sight, the last one—she realized—she would ever see of him.

Tears streamed down her face as she pressed her palm on his jaw. He didn't nuzzle her; he was on high alert, his hand supporting her neck as he helped her sit up.

"Aella," he breathed.

The relief in his voice made her throat constrict. He cared so deeply for her, and it broke her heart. She couldn't help but bury herself in his arms. He was the utmost protection. He was her safety, her tranquility.

"Aella?"

Pulling away, she looked up at him, and his brows furrowed in confusion.

"Aella, I am so sor—"

"You know I love you, right? And I always will."

He had apologized, and she wanted to scoff. He shouldn't be the one apologizing. She was well aware of the audience forming, but she didn't care, not now.

He was so focused on her. "Yes."

"And you know that I truly think you deserve happiness. You didn't deserve all the shit life gave you."

"Aella—"

Her hands fisted his shirt as she looked up at him.

"You're so handsome," she murmured. "And being your mate is the pinnacle of my existence. I have found so much beauty in your darkness. I was never supposed to exist," she gasped. "But I am so glad I do, and I've learned that even when fate fucks up, even when you aren't supposed to love and be loved, you love anyway. You love harder."

"I'm okay." His hands found her jaw. "It's over. It's over."

She smiled weakly. She trembled.

"I had to make a choice," she said shakily. "I had to choose between our mate bond and everyone else's. I chose the latter." She never prepared herself for the look of betrayal etched onto his face, followed by the realization of what it all meant. "But I refused to let you live that life of solitude. I refuse you let you live in pain any longer."

He sucked in a breath. "What did you do?"

Shocked, pained, and in disbelief—she felt the same way.

"Little Luna, what did you do?"

"I can't let you live in pain, and I can't take away Eveline's chance of being happily mated. She deserves—"

"What did you do?"

She shut her eyes as pain flooded her senses. "I'm taking your spot, Alpha Superior."

"No," he snapped. "No, I would never let you live that life. I . . ." His gaze wavered. His silver eyes dimmed to a dark brown. His knees fumbled, his hand reaching for the ground to steady himself.

"No!" Lowering him to the ground, she was above him, cradling his face. "No! I need more time," she screamed. "Please give me more time," she pleaded.

His hand reached up to touch her face, his thumb stroking her cheek. There were so many unsaid things on the tip of his tongue, but his strength betrayed him, and he elected on the only thing that he needed her to hear.

"The odds of you existing were slim. The odds of me ever existing with you were even less. Maybe I was never cursed. Maybe Artemis was merciful because she gave me the chance to fall in love with you, and it is a privilege to love you, Luna Superior."

She screamed for her mate and for the life she never got to live with him. *I can do this, but even if I can't, I must.*

CHAPTER TWENTY-SIX

The thing about cries is that if one sobs long enough, eventually they become silent. Aella's pain was silent as she held her dead mate against her. She couldn't breathe. She still felt the bond—unsevered—but she knew it would be broken soon.

She had always wanted to be a lycan but not this way. She wanted to be a lycan with the man she loved. Now, her desire seemed moot, and she wished nothing more than to stay human and die. Now, as it was for Icarus, it felt as if her lycanthropy was a curse disguised as a blessing.

A hand touched her shoulder, but she didn't care. She didn't care who it belonged to. She didn't care at all—until that hand had the voice of her nightmares.

"Aella."

She froze. Hatred rose in her chest. She wouldn't leave her mate, not even for revenge. He was still warm, and she needed to savor it. For once, he looked peaceful.

"How can you look me in the eye? You killed my mate," she cried. "Don't I deserve mercy?" she asked.

"Yes."

The sincerity in her voice struck Aella.

"When I was a human, I had fallen in love."

"I don't give a—"

"He died, and I am . . ." The words on her lips went dead. She started over: "I never saw him again, but he is in a place I could never go. I was told there was a way for me to see him again, and I'd do anything just to see him."

Aella was almost sympathetic.

"But for me to do so, in order for me to be with him, I'd have to die. I am willing to do that, but my post cannot be unmanned." Artemis kneeled next to her. "For me to leave my post, I need to ensure my wolves would have the one that would always put them first—"

"I don't understand." Aella wept. "Please, leave me alone."

"I gave Icarus the same choice as you just now, and he chose you, Aella. I can't say I blame him. He had been alone for so—"

"What are you saying?"

"I'm saying that he couldn't take my place. He couldn't be a god. He couldn't be the deity everyone needs."

Hands gripped her shoulders, turning her to face the Goddess. "But you can."

She met Artemis' gaze. Her eyes were tired, bloodshot, and stung from the tears still in the back of her head.

"You love him. I can feel that love. You love him so much that you can't fathom the thought of living without him, and yet you chose your damnation instead of theirs. I believe you can take my place."

"I can't." Aella shook her head. Her eyes returned to her mate, who was resting just beside her.

Artemis' hold was firm, prohibiting her from cradling Icarus.

"You can," she coaxed. "You can with the help of your mate. I needed to make sure that you would choose them over him."

"I don't . . . I don't understand."

"Alpha Superior was not supposed to have a mate because he was connected to me. He was damned because I was. But if you take my position, that connection will be severed, and you could bring him back."

For the first time throughout this ordeal, Aella watched Artemis' brave facade break.

"Please, let me die." Her lips thinned as she pressed into Aella. "The underworld will give life if it takes one, and I want nothing more than to make that exchange."

* * *

She couldn't leave him. In his bed, she nuzzled herself into his side, her head on his chest. She listened to his heartbeat, unable to close her eyes and rest. He was alive, and that soothed the pain in her chest, but she wouldn't be able to breathe until he woke up. He had healed fully. His blood had been hand-washed away.

"He's alive, Aella."

Aella nodded. She had been vaguely aware of Eveline, who stayed in the room with her. Ev had never left her and never would.

Eveline said that every few hours, and Aella appreciated it greatly as it was what grounded her.

"Do you want to know something fucked-up?"

Eveline was shocked that she spoke but nodded.

"Artemis designated this role to me because I chose lycanthropy mate bonds over my own, because I'm selfless." She couldn't help the sour tone of her voice. "But if it weren't for you, I would have chosen otherwise. What does that make me?"

"A damn good sister."

She smiled tiredly.

"It makes you flawed," Ev continued. "And that's okay."

Aella stared at Icarus' face. She rarely looked away from him. She couldn't. He stirred. She sat up, waiting, hoping, and praying he would wake up—with brows knitted and eyes fluttered open, locking with hers. She felt like she'd been crying for days on end.

"You're awake," she whispered, dimly unaware that Eveline was getting up to leave.

His hand rested on her head, and she nuzzled it, closing her eyes.

"You're here," she said more to herself.

"You're an incredible woman."

"You're supposed to be dead," she muttered, trying to wrap his hand around her head.

"But I'm not. Open your eyes."

His voice was soft, but it was still a command she obeyed. She listened, unable to hide her relief, as he spoke, "Being both soft and strong is a skill very few have mastered."

"You're here."

"Aella." He sat up, pulling her onto his lap.

As she straddled him, he placed her head in the crook of his neck.

"You have been through so much. I refuse to allow you any more pain or suffering." He brought her head to his.

"Does that mean . . . ?"

He nodded, smiling at her. "I don't think I could have stayed away for that long anyway. You're so strong but so exhausted, aren't you?"

She nodded.

"I'm going to kiss you until you can't breathe and then lie here with you until you sleep. Is that something you would like?"

"Yes," she responded.

He kissed her softly. He kissed her like she was fragile because she really was. He cupped her face, his thumbs trailing over her cheeks as his lips met hers. It was peaceful and tranquil, the type of kiss that made her feel serene.

When he pulled away, he showered her cheeks and neck with kisses but never ventured further. A moan, an almost breathless sigh, escaped her as his mouth found the area just below her ear. She heard him inhale sharply.

"Your body is so reactive to me," he uttered. "I'm obsessed with you."

She had never thought she would ever find a person that would be consumed by her. She'd thought that things like this only happened in those silly romance books, but she was so wrong. They exist and only need to be mined; they don't just come.

"I don't want to sleep."

He stared at her, eyes ablaze, jaw set like he was biting his tongue. "In all my worst nightmares, you're dying. You're too far from me, fading away. I can't get to you, and I scream, but I can't save you." His brows knitted together. "I can't imagine what you felt, but I imagine it was somewhere along the lines of the worst pain you've ever experienced."

She felt the memory claw up her chest, and the thought that it could have been a reality made her eyes sting. She felt like she was always crying.

Her eyes closed as she breathed through the emotion.

He straightened his back, and he continued, "I promise you I will give you anything you want."

As her gaze found him, she realized she loved to see the hunger in his eyes, the sight of a man who would come undone before her and lavish her. She wondered if he'd ever looked at someone the same way, but then his gaze escaped her as he closed his eyes tightly. She understood then that he was trying his absolute hardest to go at her speed.

"I want . . ." she whispered. "I want you to touch me." Her eyes were caught in a loop between looking at his lips and looking him in the eye.

His jaw hardened, and he went rigid as her hands slowly moved up the vast, taut canvas of his chest. She grew uneasy, unsure. Her heart stammered on as her hand went to the nape of his neck, attempting to pull him closer. He let her, their noses inches away.

Then, there was a pause, but this brief moment of breaths and closeness felt like an eternity.

"I'm trying to control myself."

She could hear the need in his voice, and she pulled him closer, her lips gently grazing his. Something escaped his lips, something guttural, then her world exploded. He deepened the kiss, pulling her forward with his arms, as his tongue plunged into her mouth, toying with hers. He inhaled her greedily, hungrily, and impossibly deep.

Her world started to spin as she was brought onto his lap, straddling him. The feeling of his strong, muscular body consuming hers was enough to make her see stars. He was intoxicating, and she couldn't imagine being anywhere else than right there with him.

He ran his hands up her back but then stopped. The sound of fabric tearing caught her off guard, but she wasn't upset by it. She pulled away, her shirt discarded somewhere.

He took her mouth again. She felt him hard against her, straining, jumping for her touch. She slowly moved her hips against him, eliciting a subtle groan of approval from his chest. Without breaking the kiss, he lowered her to her back, his arm bracing her head. He disconnected from her lips, insatiably trailing a path down her neck. His hand gripped her jaw, forcing her to give him more access.

She let out another moan, his hardness between her thighs made her tremble from anticipation. His mouth moved down her chest while his one hand slid the strap of her bra down her arm. She couldn't tell how her bra came off her as she was too distracted by his mouth around her nipple, sucking just hard enough. She was hot, burning for him.

"Please," she begged. "Please."

His lips roamed up her neck. "Again," he ordered, his hand going to the button of her jeans. "Beg for me. It drives me crazy." Kneeling above her, he hastily slid her pants off. "Do you want me to stop?"

"Never." Finally, she was able to catch her breath. "You have too many clothes on."

His jaw tightened, and he inhaled, taking in the sight of her. "I can't believe you're all mine, Aella."

She blushed, glancing down at herself. *I have saggy breasts and a pudgy stomach*, she thought, not understanding what he saw.

Her internal critique of herself was short-lived because his hands went to the buttons of his shirt. He took his time undoing them, and she knew he did so to tease her, to drive her insane with want.

"If I wasn't going mad with the need to be buried inside you, I'd take my time." The shirt came off, displaying his well-defined body for her. He was akin to Adonis himself.

She sucked in a breath, trembling. She knew she was wet, so ready for him. He stood, pulling off the rest of his clothing, and she had never seen someone so perfect, someone so perfectly arousing to her. In every way, he was tantalizingly addictive, and as she stared at his physique, she was sure mates were made for each other. He was made for her, and she was made for him.

She grew nervous as she looked at his hardened length. Insecurity bloomed in her again. What if she couldn't take him all?

He moved to her again, kneeling by her feet on the bed, then removed her underwear. He rested over her, his arm holding his weight off her as his eyes trained on hers. His free hand slowly—painfully deliberate—trailed down her skin. Over her breast, down the contours of her stomach, and over her hip bone.

"This," he stated heartily, palming her pussy, "is mine."

"I need—" She gasped, her hips thrusting forward.

"You're not ready yet."

"I'm so wet, Icarus. I'm ready. Please."

His mouth was on hers again. Gently, he trailed his fingers over her thighs, teasing her, playing with her. "I watched how you touched yourself. I watched as you used that vibrator and came without penetration. I know you can't finish from penetration, so why would I force it upon you so quickly?"

"You're not forcing it on me. I want you inside me so badly."

"Let me make you come first because embarrassingly enough, I won't last long."

His chin dipped into her shoulder as a singular finger circled her aching clit. A flash of pleasure shone in her, her heels pressing into the bed and her back arching just slightly.

She had never been happier being naked.

She felt him inhale her scent, his mouth clasping around her nipple once again. The sensations of him were almost too much. She was by no means a virgin, but with him, she felt like the experience was brand-new.

"All those months pining after you, dreaming about you, fantasizing about you, seeing you from afar was treacherous. I'm going to memorize every beautiful curve of your body."

"Oh," she panted.

That familiar feeling of warmth grew in her lower stomach. Her body froze, unable to articulate her pleasure as she drowned in it.

"It's barely been a minute, yet here you are, coming for me like a good girl. I wonder," he mused, "did your dreams include this?"

He already knew the answer, but her head was fuzzy from her climax.

"Use your words."

Her clit pulsed, another wave of pleasure crashing into her. She nodded.

He ordered again: "Words."

"Yes." She felt the tip of his cock against her pussy, hard and ready to be within her.

"You must tell me if you need me to stop."

She nodded, becoming impatient. An annoyed grunt left her. "Please."

She felt him edge inside her, and they both gasped at the small amount of depth. His eyes shut, his frame rigid on top of her.

"Fuck," he cursed. "I love it."

"More," she whispered.

He obeyed, inching in slowly. She winced, the sharp pain radiating through her stomach. He immediately froze again, worried eyes looking down at her.

"I know it's a lot. You can take me. You're meant for me."

She never heard a truer statement in her life.

He continued until he was fully sheathed inside her.

"You're doing so well," he murmured. He settled a hand on her hip, and she could feel him shake as he slowly thrust himself in and out of her.

She felt his restraint resolving. She bucked her hips to meet his thrust, and he froze, his stern eyes filled with lust.

"Don't. My control is breaking quickly."

She wrapped her arms around his shoulders, pulling him down to kiss her again. "It doesn't hurt anymore." She wasn't lying. "I want you to lose control."

His eyes darkened to black silver. His hand came up to her neck, wrapping around it, his lips hovering just above hers. The entire situation was so hot.

"Open your mouth."

She listened, and as he thrust into her hard—harder than any other time—a band of saliva fell into her mouth. He took her mouth again, his tongue stealing dominance between them once more. She felt her pussy tighten around him, milking him. It was so primal. She'd never had a man do such a thing before to her. She liked it.

No, she loved it. It made her feel taken, claimed, marked.

He took her quickly, almost harshly, at a steady pace. He threw his head back, a growl tearing from his mouth as his hands gripped her breasts. She loved the sight of him getting lost in her.

Something arose within her. She knew that tingle of warmth, but she had never been able to orgasm from penetration before. She had tried for years to master it herself, but it had appeared to be a futile quest. She realized that Icarus was wrong. He would make her finish like this.

He must have sensed she was close again because his hands framed her head, maintaining the same pace.

"Fuck, you take me so well. You're going to make me come. Would you like that?" His lips found hers again. "You're so beautiful, so perfect . . . I love your body."

Well, that did it.

Her pleasure peaked once again and toppled, sending pools of pleasure through her in calculated shocks. Her toes curled. Her back arched. Her world brightened. She could feel her core grow even wetter, a phenomenon she'd never expected could happen.

She felt him go rigid inside her, his hands going to the sides of her head, fisting the sheets. He forced a hand to take his cock and remove it from within her, decorating her sepia skin with his seed.

He grunted his pleasure, sending her over the edge. It was easily the sexiest thing in the world. And as his orgasm waned, he gave a boyish smile to her. He put a hand out when she tried to sit up.

"Don't. Let me commit this to memory."

She was glad he stopped her. She felt like she couldn't move; she didn't want to. She wanted to bathe in the aftermath of their sex, but she started to feel guilty as his seed trailed off her and onto his bed. She didn't want to cause a mess.

"Does it make you uncomfortable?"

She watched his eyes fixed on her stomach. Her brows knitted. "No, but I don't want to make your bed dirty."

He laughed, shaking his head. "I can wash the sheets. Relax."

She listened, settling back down on her back. He settled beside her, nuzzling his nose into her neck. His hand found her lower stomach, and she tensed, knowing he would get dirty. He seemed to enjoy it. He enjoyed seeing her covered in him. He enjoyed feeling his seed on her.

"Why didn't you come inside me?"

"I didn't have permission."

"I'm on birth control. You always have permission."

His expression softened. "Do you want children?"

She nodded. "Not for a while, though. Do you?"

"I didn't," he admitted. "But I think it would be a crime to not continue your genealogical chain."

She smiled, shaking her head in disbelief. "Yours is 'Superior.' That sharp jawline, that body, those eyes . . . your children would be heartbreakers."

She was inclined to kiss him as he smiled again. Her eyes wandered down his frame to his cock, which stood just as hard as when they started. Now that she examined him, he never broke a sweat. He wasn't tired at all.

She thought for a moment. Was she sore? No, not really. Could she come again? She wasn't sure. She wanted to see, though.

She placed her hand on top of his that was on her stomach and slowly dragged it to her pussy again.

"I want you to come inside me," she whispered.

His eyes flickered, his fingers lightly trailing down her navel. As soon as he thrust his come-covered fingers into her, a moan literally tore out of her. He removed them, running them back through his come, only to bring them back to her clit. He wanted her pussy to be drenched in his seed.

"Grab the headboard."

* * *

It was time for everyone to return to Romanian pack lands as the season of the Luna Council was coming to a close. It was a bittersweet moment for the lunas, especially Aella. She'd grown there. She'd come into her own. For a while, this place, this community, was her solace. She'd been taught and nurtured into a good luna that could become a great one. She wasn't great—not yet—but she had all intentions of becoming that.

"What's with that glowy thing you got—"

Eveline stopped in her tracks. Her eyes jumped from her to Icarus and then back to her, a smile spreading on her face. She moved next to Aella, shifting the moving box from one arm to the other.

"Good job, sis." She looked at her alpha, a mischievous grin on her face. "Does this mean the stick up your ass is finally removed?"

Icarus' icy gaze landed on her. "Depends" he responded. "Are you still in my pack?"

Her brows bent down in confusion. "Yes."

"Then, clearly not."

Eveline's grin widened. "Was that a joke? I like it."

Aella looked at her mate, but her eyes shifted when Celest and Kaius came down the stairs. Kaius was holding another two boxes to bring out to the moving van.

Soon, the Luna House was cleared of the items that needed to be brought back. A feeling of pride and disbelief overwhelmed Aella as she stood in the elaborate foyer. She knew she could return whenever she wanted, but leaving for any amount of time made her sad. This house was built in her vision, and she loved it. The other house just didn't feel like home. She knew he was there before he touched her. She always gravitated toward him.

His arm wrapped around her shoulders as they took in the space. The furniture still decorated the home, but everything of significance had been removed.

"Remind me to teach you how to hold your barrier up even when you're not focused on it."

She looked up at him, wrapping her arm around his waist.

"I want you to feel as though Romania is your home, and I will do anything in my power to make that a reality." He removed himself from her, going into the pocket of his dress pants, and pulled out a black leather wallet. He took out a black card and handed it to her without argument.

Taking it, she raised a brow. "You're just giving me your credit card?"

"Of course not. That's a debit card. The pin is your birthdate, and the birthdate you gave me."

Her heart stammered in her chest.

"Buy whatever you want. Change whatever you want in that house."

"But it's your home. You decorated it."

He shook his head. "I did not decorate it, and it's not my home. A certain dark-haired woman with curly hair is my home."

Aella grinned. "I didn't know you felt that way about Celest."

She'd never seen a man turn green so quickly in her life. She laughed, throwing her head back.

"I think I might vomit. Not that she isn't . . . well . . ." He struggled to find the right words.

She laughed harder, patting his back. "I'm just kidding, handsome. Come on, let's go before Cyril hunts us down."

As she walked out of the Luna House with her mate to her side, she looked back and remembered a time when she was drowning in insecurity—a time when happiness seemed too far to reach—and she smiled.

Icarus paused to watch her nostalgia.

It dawned on her that she could have never become the person she was without accepting the person she used to be. And then she realized she was still the same person. She just had to grow.

    With a tear rolling down her cheek and a saccharine smile, she turned back around, ready to start her next chapter.

CHAPTER TWENTY-SEVEN

It was calm. For once, in years, she didn't feel like she had the weight of the world on her shoulders. She didn't feel the claw of guilt or shame. She felt appreciative, not toward Artemis—whom she still harbored ill feelings against—but for her life.

Humans walk this world aimlessly, learning, dating, and enjoying life. There are things that make them happy (she couldn't deny that), but they still walk alone, and if they do find someone they like, chances are it is not their soulmate.

Aella had hers. She had been through some shit to be there on top of his chest. He was alive, healthy, and for the most part immortal. So would she eventually. All the shit—the shame, the pain, the hiding, and the trauma—was so worth it for moments like this, moments where his heartbeat threaded steadily under her hand, where his fingers gently glided across her skin; moments that had passed, and moments that still would.

The relief and contentment in her chest were overwhelming. She had fought for her fairy tale and won. She closed her eyes. He shuddered underneath her. She lifted her head, and the sight surprised her. On the cheeks of her alpha mate were tears. They were gentle and steady, his eyelashes heavy. He didn't seem shy about it, didn't look ashamed. He displayed his tears to her.

"Are you in pain?" she asked. Fear crept up her spine, a feeling she was so tired of.

"No." His eyes wandered to her lips. "Goddess help whoever tries to hurt you." His hands slipped around her, slowly lowering her to her back. He leaned over her, his one hand brushing away her knotty curls.

"You are," he started, his voice thick with emotion, "the best thing I ever waited for." His hand moved over the valley of her breasts, one of his fingers gently caressing her nipple before retreating up her chest. His eyebrows knitted together as he looked at her.

"After Ansan ransacked that village, I was furious. I didn't protect them, and they were innocent. I didn't do my duty. And I thought that if I couldn't do my responsibility as their protector, what was the point of it all? The suffering, I mean. I—" His words caught in his throat.

"When I returned to the house," he continued, "there was a letter waiting for me, along with a recorder. Your voice was the single thing that kept me going. And then . . ." He swallowed, his eyes crinkling in thought. "And then when the pain set in from the genocide of my wolves, your voice was the only thing that got me through it."

Her gentle hand reached to touch his face, and he nuzzled himself in it. The tears that had fallen from his eyes dripped onto her palm, and as he fisted the duvet beside her, she realized that she cried with him.

"I want to mark you."

Her eyes sparkled with emotion. "What are you waiting for then?"

With narrowed, whimsical eyes, he said, "I want to show you something first. Has anyone explained what the Evanescent is?"

She tried to run her mind through her lessons.

Coming up empty, she shook her head.

"It's the time when the moon is the closest to us. It happens once every decade. We celebrate it." He fell silent, thinking. "It's next week."

"What day?"

He pulled his head back. "Your birthday." He let go of a breath that sounded like a surprised scoff. "Isn't that something else? How beautiful, how . . . sumptuous, how fitting."

"Tell me more. How do you celebrate?"

"It starts at dusk. The children light lanterns. And mates, well, they sneak off. Once the children go to bed, the event becomes rather erotic for many."

"Erotic?"

He leaned into her shoulder, kissing her delicately. "Yes," he hummed. He pressed another kiss—slow, hot, and intimate. "We worship the moon; it calls to our most primal side."

"And how . . . ?" Her mouth was dry. "How do you worship it?"

A warm trail of kisses traveled up her neck, landing just below her jaw, before his calloused large hand moved up her bare stomach, not touching the mounds on her chest but itching to do so.

She felt him smile against her.

"My sweet luna, we fuck until dawn. I intend on filling you until you're bathed in my seed or until I die."

"You're immortal." She gasped as his mouth latched onto her ear.

"Your cunt is enough to make even the immortal perish from pleasure." And he took her mouth hungrily like he was starved.

* * *

Dusk fell upon the castle, and excitement bristled through the dark, cold walls. Wolves traveled in and out, bringing food outside for others, laughing joyously as they anticipated the Evanescent.

Aella found herself with Hasina and Daria, preparing a Romanian dessert called papanasi. When she returned, she learned that the pack was growing more accustomed to her, although it was clear some were still opposed. They didn't say anything, however, too afraid of Icarus' wrath that would not be subdued this time.

It saddened her. She didn't want to be treated kindly because of their fear of punishment. Regardless, the pack was preparing for the celebration. And as the final pastries came out of the oil, Daria rushed the others to get outside: "Come, come! The kids are lighting their lanterns."

It was a chilly night as Aella stood in front of the pack house, watching the children light the stings under the paper lanterns decorated with their art. There weren't many children in the pack, but a good handful of them were eager to participate in the tradition. The oldest, Emilia, who was fourteen, had participated in the tradition only once before.

Aella took a breath and closed her eyes. She reopened them and gazed at the snow-capped mountains surrounding the palace. It was an exquisite sight, one she wished she could see better in the dark.

She heard the bright, untainted laughter of a child.

Looking toward the wondrous sound, she saw something she'd never thought she would see. Icarus was kneeling before a child, fixing the crinkles in their paper lantern. His brows were furrowed in concentration, but she knew he was in a place of contentment.

She knew only some of the horrors he had seen in his life, and he probably would never be able to be carefree without the memories, but she also realized that sometimes she would get these brief wisps of delighted, relaxed images of her mate. It elated her. She couldn't explain the kind of happiness that swelled in her chest.

His hair was tousled by the wind, a tuft falling onto his forehead. And then, if the sight couldn't get better, he took out a lighter and lit the bottom of the lantern. He looked skeptical for a moment as if he didn't know how to go about doing what he wanted, but then he held out his arm. The little boy happily went into his embrace.

Icarus stood to his full height, handing the lantern to the boy, and together they watched it fly to the night skies. The little boy smiled at him. Icarus smiled back—the only time she'd ever seen him smile at anyone else besides her. His eyes met hers, and he gave her a boyish smile.

Holy shit, she was going to combust.

His eyes went back to the boy, and he said something that she couldn't hear. Icarus turned and started walking toward her.

"Aella, this is Alexander."

She nodded, her eyes meeting the boy's. "Yes, I know. Hello, Alex."

"Luna! Did you see my lantern?"

She nodded, chuckling. "Yes, I did!"

"Do you want to know what I sent to Artemis?"

She lifted a brow.

"They write appreciations and wishes on the lanterns and send them to Artemis." His eyes settled on her for a moment.

"I writed . . ." Alexander fumbled. "That I am thankful for—" He stopped, struggling to find the words in English.

"What did you write, Alex?"

Her Romanian wasn't great yet, but she could get by.

Alex's eyes lit up. "I wrote that I am thankful for my mommy and daddy and my alpha and my luna."

The boy had replied to her in Romanian.

Fucking hell, she needed to stop crying at everything.

She swallowed her tears, nodding at Alex with a smile. "You know what I think?"

He shook his head.

"I think Alpha needs the biggest hug in the world."

Weary silver eyes met hers, and she winked as Alexander gasped. Mischief clouded the boy's eyes, and suddenly all the kids who were finished with their lanterns charged toward Icarus, latching themselves in his arms, on his waist, shoulders, legs, or any limb they could find.

"Group hug!" Alex screamed in his native tongue.

Laughter echoed throughout the field.

Aella watched from afar as Icarus stumbled, careful not to step on a child, and fell to the ground. She took out her phone and took a photo of that moment.

Icarus laughed. It wasn't delicate or fragile but was a soft, deep rumble from his chest. Her skin felt in tune with the atmosphere. The hairs on her arms stood for a reason that was not uneasy or uncomfortable. It was revitalizing. It was strange. It felt good.

Eyes landed on her, marveling at her. Icarus, Kaius, Celest, Eveline—everyone focused on her. She didn't understand.

Icarus stood. The children were also mesmerized by something behind her. She turned and was punched in the chest by the sight. The moon, bright and large, was the closest she'd ever seen it. She felt drawn to it and felt that it was drawn to her as well. She wanted to touch it, to drown herself in its luminosity. Even though it was still leagues away from her, it seemed reachable, raining light on her, dousing her.

She inhaled. Her heart fell in tantalizing joy. She felt her mate behind her, but she couldn't tear her eyes away from the sight.

"Aella, your eyes . . ."

She heard him whisper.

"They're silver. No"—he struggled— "they're brighter than mine. They're luminous. They look like the moon."

She was in a trance. She couldn't look away.

She shook her head at her mate. "I haven't shifted yet. They shouldn't be."

"You're right." He didn't say anything else, didn't give an explanation. He stayed with her.

Her eyes remained on the moon while his were fixed on her. They stayed there, standing side by side. She didn't know for how long. She didn't care. It called to her. She was somewhat aware that the pack lingered there too, witnessing the miraculous sight.

As the moon started to drift away, her heart deflated.

"No, no, no," she muttered, taking a step forward. "I need more."

He gripped her elbow. "Aella."

Her eyes met his. "Please."

He looked at her intently for a few moments. He nodded, then turned to Kaius. "Get the kids to sleep. We'll be back."

As Kaius nodded, Icarus grabbed Aella. Hauling her on his back, he whipped through the forest.

It only took a few minutes, and they were already on the peak of the highest mountain within their sight. The cliff overlooked the forest below, the moon sitting large and proud on the edge. She was glad for the boots and tactical jacket she was wearing for the weather. It was freezing, but she needed it—needed this.

His arms wrapped around her waist. She knew it was to keep her warm and to make sure she wasn't an idiot and jump off the cliff in her trance.

She turned in his arms. "What's happening to me?"

He knitted his brows. "The transition from human to lycan happens relatively quickly. It takes one defining moment and several hours for the physical transformation, but you're not transitioning into lycan." He kissed the top of her head. "You're transitioning into a goddess, and that transition will take much longer. Your transition just started, and your fixation on the moon is natural. It's your domain."

For a moment, his gaze went to the orb behind her before returning to her. "I think I finally know my favorite color."

Her face contorted in confusion.

"It's brown."

"Brown?"

It was an unusual choice.

Nodding, he played with a tendril of curl that fell on her shoulder. "Your eyes used to be brown. They reminded me of coffee. Your hair is dark brown. Your skin . . ." He sucked in a breath. "I love it."

"Do you not like my eyes now?"

His gaze narrowed. "One day I'm going to fuck that insecurity out of you. I love your eyes now too."

Heat pooled between her legs. She looked up at him under her lashes.

"If I remember correctly, you wanted to mark me."

He shook his head. "It's too cold here. You'll freeze."

"I want you to do it here under the moon before it leaves us." She turned to gaze at it one last time. "Please?"

He was pensive for a moment. "But then I will carry you home, do you understand?"

She nodded.

"And we won't stay a minute longer than necessary. You're already shivering."

"Not from the cold."

Then, his tongue slowly ran along her bottom lip, softly asking for permission—which she granted easily. It was a slow, intimate kiss.

"Will it hurt?" She could feel his hand wrapped around the back of her neck, bracing her as she had to look up at him.

"You'll feel a pinch at first, like when you get blood drawn, but then it's ecstasy."

"And when I get my wolf, can I do the same to you?"

His eyes brightened, and he stiffened for a moment. She could feel his length against her stomach. Pulling away, she ran her hand up his length and hid her surprise from feeling wetness against the pads of her fingers.

"Did you . . . ?"

He nipped her bottom lip. "The thought is a lot for me to handle."

She smiled against him. "You're still hard," she whispered. "I want you to do it."

His hand trailed up her side and wrapped around her neck, tilting her to the side, exposing it. He dipped his head, and she forgot how to breathe as his nose ran up the muscular indent of her skin. His hand was on the small of her back, holding her as she arched against him.

"You're tensing," he whispered. "Are you nervous?"

"A little about the pain, but I think it's more because I don't know when it's coming."

"Do you want a countdown?"

"A countdown?"

He hummed against her.

She felt his hand move down, cupping her ass.

"Five . . ." He kissed her down her collarbone, his hands still on her skin. "Four . . ." His hand went under her shirt, fingers gently running over her hardened nipple.

She moaned, eyes shut as she reveled in the man that found religion in her body.

"Three . . ." He kissed her slow, deliberate. "I thought about marking you between your legs, but I want your mark to be seen by everyone."

"Icarus, please . . . I'm so—"

"I know. Two . . ."

"Yes," she whimpered.

"One." His lips returned to her neck.

He was right about the sharp pain that would run through her as his canines pierced her skin. Her eyes flew open, and she stiffened. His arms were strong around her, protecting her, holding her up, before pure bliss consumed her. It submerged her, taking away any other sense but touch.

She said a prayer, not to Artemis but to Icarus. She felt his teeth within her, felt his lips suck in her essence, and felt her body take from him. They connected on another level that she couldn't start to comprehend.

He groaned against her. His hand fumbled to her pants, unbuttoning them and shucking them down crudely.

As he tried to get his pants off, she realized he wanted to be inside her as his canines were. She helped him, her hands going to his pants, unzipping them and pulling them down, before she stepped out of her pants. He didn't lower her to the ground as she thought he would. Instead, he gripped her thighs and hauled her up. He settled himself within her, destroying her world and rebuilding it.

She had never orgasmed so quickly in her life. His cock stiffened as his seed found home within her.

If she had been more coherent as he removed his canines, redressed them, and carried her back home, she would have noticed when the snow melted around them and how the trees looked singed. If she had been smarter, she would have realized that on Icarus' back were two scars equidistant from each other in the same spot where wings would have been.

CHAPTER TWENTY-EIGHT

She was huffing, breathless, as her mate lay on top of her. His arms cradled her head, keeping most of his weight off her. She felt him chuckle into her skin.

"Does it ever go away?"

"What?" he asked, dazed. He didn't lift his head. "The sex? Never."

"No." A chuckle escaped her. "The constant need to have you inside me. Not the sex, just the persistent turn-onnery."

"Turn-onnery?"

"Yes."

Another laugh ensued, this time from him.

"Does it go away? I mean, when does it stop?"

"It doesn't. It won't. I'll spend eternity fucking you, Luna Superior."

Her stomach twisted. Her hands found his chest, pushing him off her and onto his back. She straddled him. Her hair, a mess of curls and knots, cascaded over her breasts.

Those stern silver eyes and angular features were filled with lust once again. She hovered over his cock—which was wide awake, hard against his stomach. She reached a hand in front of her, gripping him at his base.

He hissed, his hips thrusting forward. His hands shot above his head, fisting the metal railing of his headboard.

"Shit."

His cursing in Romanian turned her on so fucking much.

"Again," she ordered (in Romanian).

His eyes shot to hers. His member pulled in her grip, and she gave a feline grin.

"You like it when I speak to you in your native language?" she said, and his hips bucked.

She continued in his native language: "Very well. Do you know how often I sat with you in your office, listening to you speak Romanian and fantasizing about how I could take you? Years," she gasped. "I spent years thinking about it."

"And you think I didn't? You don't know how many times I watched men in the office staring at you with fuck-me eyes. You don't know how hard I used to get behind my desk as you filed."

"I want to fuck in that office, in front of those large windows."

"I can't go back," he gritted out, becoming frustrated that she was moving her hand so slowly.

She raised an eyebrow.

"I almost lost you there. You almost—" He stopped, pinching his eyes together. His hands loosened on the metal rod. "You almost died."

It was like there was a switch that flipped on in his head as if somehow the memory opened something else within him, something carnal. He was strong and fast, forcing her onto her back, hooking her leg over his arm, and entering her with such speed and depth that her breath floated away from her. His hand rested on her abdomen as he tried to get deeper in her—hard, rough, passionate, primal.

"Fuck," he cursed, baring his canines. "I . . ." He grunted. "Need"—he thrust again— "to get . . . deeper." He fucked her so hard that her body moved toward the edge of the bed.

She loved it.

He threw his head back, annoyed. "Not enough," he spoke through gritted teeth. "Fuck, you feel so fucking good, Aella."

His hands forced both her legs up around his shoulders, then his one hand fell behind her neck so she wouldn't hit her head on the wood of the bed. And he fucked her, relentlessly, quickly, not stopping until he got to the depth he wanted—which was, admittedly, in her throat.

And it was painful. She could feel his head at the entrance of her cervix, but in the mix with such pain was this deep pleasure that bounded within her. She had never been one to mix pain and pleasure until this.

His free hand found her clit effortlessly, and instead of rubbing her like he was trying to win the lottery, he circled his thumb slowly—a stark contrast to the pace of his cock going in and out of her.

How the fuck did he have a better rhythm than her?

Doesn't fucking matter.

"All of it, Aella," he commanded.

Her eyes fell shut as her pussy flipped.

"Look at me." When she did, he nodded. "You can do it."

She came hard, fast; it came so suddenly. A sob escaped her. And then he stopped, and more sobs shook her.

"Aella, did I hurt you? Aella."

"No," she gasped. She opened her eyes to see his wild with concern. "No," she repeated. "You make me come so fucking hard that I don't know how to handle it."

He kissed her slowly, tasting the tears on her lips. He sucked them. Still inside her, he lowered her legs while kissing her down her neck as she softly whimpered.

"Sometimes I look at you," he began, "and I'm so overcome with awe that I almost break down."

"Almost? What stops it?"

"I remind myself that I can't show weakness around anyone because if I do, it could get you hurt."

"You can show weakness around me."

"I've cried around you before."

"You have, and nothing about you changed in my eyes. Your masculinity stayed intact. It was actually hot."

He went quiet, his eyes flickering to her chest and then back to her eyes. "Sometimes"—he swallowed—"I imagine you . . . swollen with my . . . pup."

Judging by how long it took him to finish his sentence, it was a hard thing for him to tell her, as if she was going to be upset by it.

She had thought about it too, but they both knew it certainly was not the time. Still, the thought—to be filled with his seed and carry his offspring, birthing his child—was sexy to her.

Her hand went to her stomach. "One day I will be. One day, I'll nurture our child."

He cursed again. His cock stiffened inside her and then released, pulsating within her. He went rigid, eyes shut, hands around the sheet as he finished within her.

"Wow, you really do get turned on by that." She smiled. "I can get down with a breeding kink."

They showered after.

She enjoyed sleeping, at times with his cum trickling down her thighs, but this time she wanted to wake up clean for the morning.

They settled back in bed next to each other.

"Why do you think I have seizures?"

He turned on his side to look at her. His hand was lazily holding his head. "Why are you thinking about this now?"

She felt his fingers trail up the valley of her breasts, but she forced herself not to get turned on. "I had an episode when I met Artemis."

Nodding, he sighed. "If I had to guess, something to do with divinity. You are, or will be, a goddess. Something tells me it was always your fate to be one. Maybe it was your body's way of channeling such power. I don't know. Could also be you're simply epileptic as a human."

"But Celest and I both are." She tried not to think so much about the divinity thing.

"Maybe it has something to do with lycanthropy, then." His ministrations on her chest stopped. "You'll have to come to terms with it someday, you know. You can't ignore it forever."

"I know," she whispered. She turned on her side to look at him. "I just don't want to yet. I don't know when or how I'll take on the powers of Artemis. For now, I just want to be my alpha's fuck toy."

"Aella," he growled.

"We are not having sex again." She laughed. "Cyril informed me today that the southern packs seem to be getting better. The virus seems to be dissipating."

"There has never been a cure."

It wasn't new information to him. He'd received the report probably before she did.

"Then why do you think it's getting better?"

He was silent.

He shook his head. "I don't know. It's concerning. I am glad it's getting better. I can't imagine the pain some of my wolves went through. Well, your wolves now."

"No. You were always their protector, their champion. You lived in agony so they could live in happiness. They're yours."

"What does that make you?"

"I don't know."

Comfortable silence filled the room.

"Icarus?"

"Yes, my princess?"

"Fuck. We are not having sex again. Stop turning me on." Her smile turned somber. "Tell me about Ansan's mate."

He inhaled deeply, turning onto his back. His arm was slung over his forehead as he went pensive.

"Her name was Harper," he began. "Kaius and I rescued her from a brothel. Back then"—he sighed—"when packs weren't formed, we responded to requests for aid. There were no alphas besides me, hence no law and enforcement. Rumors would pass from one wolf to another and somehow get to us. Anyway, Kaius received a note that there were lycanthrope women being forced into prostitution in what is now Wales. We responded, and the leader of the ring was another male, not Ansan."

He answered the question that had been on her tongue.

"Or so we had thought."

"What do you mean?"

He breathed deeply for a second, then he looked at her. "We were wrong; we underestimated how evil a woman could be. We were blinded by our own prejudices." He shook his head again, looking back up at the ceiling. "We killed the man and the others that helped organize the brothel. The women were freed and returned to their families.

"Harper didn't have family. She was allowed to travel with Kaius and me. We pitied her. She struggled, or seemed to struggle, with getting through her trauma. She took care of us. She'd cook, fight, clean, and bathe us."

"Bathe?"

He nodded. "She performed the tasks of any maid, though we didn't force her. A few decades later, we were called to another urgent matter in what is now Finland. That's where we met Ansan, who had organized a pack there and was labeled 'Alpha.' They were mates." He shrugged. "I wasn't that bothered. Something always rubbed me the wrong way about her, but women are always my weak spot—"

"You've threatened women in front of me."

"Because I've learned that women are not only just as capable of evil but sometimes perform it better than any man could. I learned that the hard way."

"Fair."

He grinned. "Fair? That's it?"

"Part of me is happy you realized women can fuck you up."

He rolled his eyes. "It is very difficult to fight a woman for me, but I will if I must. I will if I have to protect my pack. Regardless, once she moved away from us and with Ansan, I started hearing about missing females in the northern packs."

Her stomach twisted when she connected the dots. "Oh God—"

He nodded. "She was the one who organized that ring and forced women into sexual slavery. You should have seen what she forced those women through."

She could tell by the way his hand turned into a fist that the thought still infuriated him.

"She turned Ansan too. Before her, he had been a decent, well-equipped alpha." He looked at her as if he was thinking if such a relationship could make him do something as cruel. "I never understood it until now. I like to think I wouldn't do anything you ever wanted, but—"

"You wouldn't," she affirmed. "You're too selfless."

"He helped her. He never did the dirty work, but he ignored the hints. We tracked the leads back to her and went to speak with Ansan. I was so close to making him see clearly, so close to making him understand why Harper couldn't continue to be in that position of power."

"What happened?"

His eyes surveyed the ceiling. "She found us speaking with Ansan and showed him pictures."

"Pictures? Of the women?"

"No, of us." He didn't look at her.

"Us?" Her heart skipped a beat. "Oh," she said, inhaling. "You and her . . . ?"

"Yes." He shook his head again. "Well, I didn't remember it, but the pictures were proof. She showed him to make it seem like I was going to take away his mate."

"And no male can think straight at that prospect," she concluded.

"Yes. We fought. I killed her. Kaius crippled Ansan. We took sovereignty of the pack. We left him powerless, without a pack, without a mate, but . . . we kept him alive, and that was out of mercy. We thought we were merciful. So he spent his years planning our demise."

"Why didn't . . . you know?" She winced from how harsh it sounded. "Why didn't you remember sleeping with her and why couldn't you hear her thoughts? You can hear the thoughts of every lycanthrope."

He sat up, his back turned to her, those scars as apparent as ever. She made a mental note to ask him about them one day.

She sat up with him, sensing something brewing within him. She stayed silent.

"Icarus?"

"Do you remember when I told you there are other species?" He didn't wait to continue because he knew she did. "Some of them are incredibly powerful, and I was a young lycanthrope. She met someone who could block her thoughts, and at the time I didn't realize that when I looked at her, I couldn't hear anything. And"—he rubbed the back of his neck—"she would feed us. She slipped magnesium into my meals. I was never suspicious of her, so I never thoroughly checked them."

"Oh God, that's why you always sniff your fork before eating and insist on tasting my food before I do."

He nodded.

"She drugged you," Aella concluded. "And then she . . ." Her stomach churned.

"It's not a huge deal," he said nonchalantly. "I should have checked my meals. I should have been more cautious."

So many thoughts and retorts filled her head, but she couldn't say how much she disagreed because he spoke again: "So many more women were tortured, raped, murdered because I had been a fool. That's why I killed his mate. That is why he hated me."

"Stop." She reached toward him, resting her hand on his shoulder. "That wasn't your fault. What she did to you . . ." She tried to mask her anger. "What she did was fucked-up and not at all your fault. You were not responsible for her wrongdoings."

He laid his palm on hers. She could tell by the way his shoulders slumped that he didn't believe her.

"I'm so sorry," she added.

There was silence, lengthening.

He turned to her, gave her that pathetic excuse of a fake smile, and lay back down. "Let's sleep."

* * *

It wasn't a scream. It was a deep, guttural grunt. It was so quiet that it almost didn't wake her up. Lifting her head up, she looked at Icarus, whose face was etched in pain. His brows were knitted, and his teeth bit into his bottom lip so hard that she could have sworn she saw blood. He had shredded the blanket. His breath came out in spurts of pain—a whimper; he'd whimpered.

And then, just as she was about to reach for him, his eyes snapped open. But he didn't look at her, not before he threw himself from the bed and into the bathroom where he collapsed in front of the toilet, emptying his stomach.

There was a moment of silence once Icarus finished dry-heaving.

Aella found herself walking into the restroom, dread consuming her.

In between his fits of wrenching, she found herself behind him, her one hand on his back and the other on his shoulder. She stroked his spine gingerly, making him tense from her touch.

A moment passed, and she was about to leave. She didn't want to make him feel even more uncomfortable.

As she pulled her hand away, she heard his soft yet firm voice: "Don't."

He proceeded to vomit. She stayed with him, rubbing his back, kissing the nape of his neck, giving everything she could to remind him he wasn't alone—not anymore, not ever.

He fell back from the toilet, exhausted. He was sluggish as he propped himself against the cabinet of the sink. She flushed and realized neither had brought water to bed.

She left, only for a second, to get a glass. When she returned, he looked at her shocked, as if he wasn't expecting her, like he thought she was leaving for good. His eyes were red.

"I wasn't," she started, unable to find the words. "I just . . ." She sighed, holding the glass up. "I got you water." She kneeled before him, her hand cupping his jaw as her lips went to his forehead.

"I'm sorry."

"You have nothing to apologize for." She handed him the glass. "Drink some water. I debated on getting you milk."

"Milk?"

"Yeah. I read this thing that water actually makes the bile in your mouth spread after throwing up, and that milk cleanses the pallet, but I didn't want to be weird."

He gave her a soft, tired chuckle.

"Drink and then we will brush your teeth. We should shower again too, but I'll understand if you are too tired."

"Aella?"

She stood up, grabbing his toothbrush and toothpaste. She coated his brush and wet it and then handed it to him, crouching in front of him.

"Aella," he called again. "Usually it lasts for hours, the vomiting."

She looked at the toilet and then back at him, brows furrowed. "It's only been a few minutes. Do you feel sick again? We can put blankets in here and sleep on the floor."

"No." He shook his head. "I think . . ." he started but shook away the sentence. "The only time I felt peace before, when the pain became too unbearable, was when I listened to your recordings. And now, now I don't think I could have gotten through another night of puking without your touch. Your presence is everything I yearn for."

She ran her hand through his hair, and he closed his eyes, a serene expression crossing his features.

"You've turned your pain into power, and that is remarkable, but I wonder what you could turn your happiness into. Now, brush your teeth so I can kiss you."

He smiled. He finished brushing, then stood up.

She went to the shower, turning it on. He hated baths.

When the water was warm enough, she undressed them both. Her alpha was far too tired to do so himself.

As they stepped into the shower, he hissed with a chuckle.

"You like your temperature somewhere between Texas and hell."

She threw her head back in laughter, turning on more cold water. She found herself eventually sitting on the tiled floor. Icarus was lying, his head on her thigh. The shower was large enough that the water didn't directly land on them.

She was humming to him.

"You've always loved singing."

"Too bad I suck," she replied humorously.

"Believe me, you're not the one who has to hear it—"

She swatted his chest, and he laughed. It punched her in the gut. It was a beautiful sound.

"I'm joking. The only reason you think you aren't good is because of that recital when you were fifteen, and that boy said you were tone-deaf."

She gawked at him. "How do you know about that?"

He ignored her. "Haven't you wondered why he transferred schools?"

"Icarus! He was sixteen years old."

He shrugged, his eyes closing again. "He liked you, you know—that's why he said that."

"That's what Eveline said too."

"You don't believe us?"

She shrugged, pausing her hand in his hair. "No, it's not that. I'm just not sure."

He went silent, closing his eyes.

"I read something in that book you gave me about a male that locked away his mate because he feared for her safety."

"The story of Acrisius." He twisted in her lap so he was on his back. "He's an alpha in the south."

"He's still alive?"

He nodded. "He regrets his decision every day. His mate killed herself."

"I know," she responded solemnly. "Would you ever . . . ?"

His silver eyes opened, regarding her heavily. "The only time a man locks his woman away is when he fears he can't keep her safe." His brows furrowed. "I have no doubts that I can protect you."

Heat pooled between her thighs. This time it wasn't due to the water that fell on them.

His eyes darkened with hunger. He cursed, his eyes closing. "You smell divine. I've been thinking . . . your story is the only one that makes me want to live."

"Don't say—"

"But our story is one that elates me," he interjected. "And the fact it isn't over gives me such profound happiness. I can hardly breathe when I think about it."

His hand reached up to play with a curly tendril of hair that was soaked against her shoulder. Slowly, he wrapped a hand around her neck—a possessive act, one she didn't mind—but he needed to ground himself. It reminded him she was there, alive, well, and happy.

"Instead of reading stories, we should write them," he said.

"Write them?"

"Yes, ours. We can read them to our children one day, read them to the little ones of the pack. It would give me great joy to write the story of my salvation. It would be the greatest story I would ever read."

And as she leaned down to kiss him, she silently agreed.

THE END

The Correspondence between Icarus and Aella

February 23, 2013

Atlas,

I've decided to call you Atlas because you look like you have the world on your shoulders. I think it suits you. My father says you probably won't visit us again, and a part of me believes him. I hope he is wrong. Anyway, you made me calm when I was really scared, and I hope this recording can do the same for you when you're scared or stressed. I was thinking maybe we could read the rest of the story together . . . when we have time. Maybe it's a stupid idea, and maybe you're way too busy, but I've read the first few pages of it. I hope we can read, together, War and Peace *by Leo Tolstoy—all 500,000 words of it.*

– Aella

January 20, 2014

Aella,

I fear you give me too much credit. Atlas was the name given to a titan who was punished to hold the universe up with his bare hands. This is not what I do. In any case, I do not mind if you call me Atlas, but please be aware that I am no titan. Do not fabricate a person of whom I am not.

Thank you for the recording. It was nice to listen to. I will send recordings when I can, but War and Peace *is a very long novel. Are you sure we can finish it?*

Happy Birthday, Aella.

– Atlas

Atlas,

I think we can finish it, maybe not this year but within the next few. I've never finished the entire thing because I always get bored, but this will make me finish it.

Do you know a lot of Greek mythology? I think it's cool.

I'm not sure what my name means honestly, but I'm confused why you won't tell me your real name.

Dad says our family is complicated. Why is that? He says that you're complicated.

Thank you,
– Aella

March 14, 2016

Aella,

Perhaps I haven't been zealous in our efforts to finish it. My apologies. I was busy with work, and life became difficult. I've read War and Peace *multiple times*. It's one of my favorite novels over the many, many years of my life.

I'm sorry I missed your birthday. I hope this next present makes up for it.

To answer your question about Greek mythology, I studied it when I was much younger. It was fascinating to me just like it is to you.

My name is not of importance. The simple utterance of it reminds me of something that cannot exist. I prefer Atlas.

As you can see, "complicated" is putting it lightly. Kaius is correct; our family is intrinsically complex. Most of our relatives live in Asia and Europe but, in recent years, have migrated all over South America and to some parts of the US. We have a large family.

Aella—a whirlwind; a Greek Amazon who fought Hercules to protect her land.

– Atlas

April 2, 2016

Atlas,

You're a few centuries old, which explains how you had the time to read War and Peace *so many times. Now, it seems like we don't have to finish it, considering that you've read it already.*

Thank you for the birthday wishes. When is yours?

I have to admit, all of the new information is . . . insane to me, but part of me is glad that fairy tales are real. Do vampires exist? What about wizards, and pixies? What does being an alpha exactly entail? And how good is my dad's hearing?

You said you were cursed . . . why you?

– Aella

April 10, 2016

Aella,

To be frank, I do not remember the day or the month of my birth. I do not know exactly how old I am. All I know is that your father is younger than me. Birthdays are unimportant to me. However, yours is a different case. Each year you grow older, smarter, and bigger; each year, you get close to the inevitable. Your birthday is important because your days here are numbered. Your father's lifespan—if his mate weren't human—would last centuries longer. When one mate dies, the other does as well, so when your mother passes on, so will your father.

I have read the book many more times than I remember. It's been years since the last time, so it's fine to continue it. After all, you do have to read it.

You have taken everything we told you really well. It makes me wonder just how wild your imagination is.

Vampires are very few and far, but they do exist in small numbers. Wizards do not exist, although some have unusual powers. Pixies do not exist, either. But faes do.

Your father, Eveline, and I can hear a sound of a tree falling from miles away if we focus, so your father has very good hearing. Why do you ask?

An alpha is a pack leader. We are responsible for the protection, financial advisement, and security of all pack members. There are many alphas and lunas in the world, many of whom organize their pack however they wish. Honestly, it's a tedious job; one might think it to be boring.

I'm considered the oldest lycan because when my species was first created, I was chosen by the Goddess Artemis as their protector. It's a long story.

— Atlas

June 9, 2016

Atlas,

I think we should choose a birthdate for you. How does April 19 sound? If we don't celebrate, it makes each year less valuable, right? Just because you will live for a very long time, it does not mean that time isn't important.

You were right all those years ago—action is not my favorite genre. Can you guess what is?

Thank you for visiting me that day. Somehow you made all the fear go away. It was like you were fighting off all my bad and scary thoughts.

The fact other species exist is super cool! I want to meet a vampire so badly. You said some people have powers. What type? Faes exist?

I asked how far you can hear because sometimes a girl just doesn't want her father to listen in. It's embarrassing. It's invasive.

Lunas? What are lunas? You mentioned alphas and lunas in your last letter. I've read many books explaining this topic somewhat, but they were considered fiction, and I probably shouldn't get my information from those.

You became protector of lycanthropes. I hope one day you will tell me the story, even if it's long. I have time, even though it's much less than yours. So what do you say? Can we finish War and Peace *and the story of Atlas?*

— Aella

January 20, 2018

Aella,
Happy eighteenth birthday.

You are persistent in learning about my past and the story of my existence. In every letter, you ask, and in every other letter, I tell you that I do not want to tell you. However, it has come to my attention that an eighteenth birthday is important these days. It signifies a coming-of-age event. So, I will tell you, but only in person.

Have you decided where you will attend college? What will you study? What gives you joy?

— Atlas

March 8, 2018

Atlas,

A couple of years ago, I chose a birthdate for you, April 19. You said you didn't want a gift. This year will be different. Your birthday is in a few weeks. Be prepared for the celebration. Hopefully, you can also tell me your story.

I've decided to stay close to home like Eveline. With Ansan still around, Dad won't let me go too far. I have also decided to study animal behavior and biology, with plans on attending veterinary school.

You asked me what gives me joy. I'm not quite sure.

Atlas, I have been having dreams about a man. Is it normal to have such vivid dreams most nights?

— Aella

Letter from Luna Alita, High Luna of the Luna Council, to Luna Superior

Luna Superior,

It is with the utmost excitement that I welcome you to the Luna Council. However, I am saddened to be writing to you under the circumstances outlined in your letter. I have the greatest respect for Alpha Superior and Beta Superior.

Kudos to you and your beta female for being exceptional. Please send my formal acknowledgments to Beta-Female Celest and Gamma Eveline. I am upset to have just been notified of Celest's existence; there was never an announcement that Beta Superior was officially mated despite the rumors.

Your letter leads me to believe that you may not know much about me or the Luna Council. My name is Luna Alita Sok. I am the High Luna of the Luna Council. I am mated to Alpha Sok. The majority of our pack lands are within Cambodia.

The Luna Council is a global congregation of all lunas and is headquartered within neutral territory in northern Sweden. This is where upcoming pups and pack mates are trained for their respective duties. This is also where wolves who disaffiliate from their pack are allowed to seek a different pack. It is where your delta, who will be in charge of your training and protection detail, will be chosen.

There are fifty lunas within the council (you can find their signatures at the foot of this letter). All of us are very enthusiastic to meet you. We want to extend an offer for you, for Beta-Female

Superior Celest, and for Gamma Superior Eveline to come and be apprentices under me, my beta female, and my gamma female. It is important to note that your respective mates are not allowed on the territory at this time.

The Luna Council is under the sole protection of lunas. No mates of upper ranks are allowed within the lands. However, in three months, the pack games begin, and for a week your mates are allowed to attend and meet the new additions to their packs.

I understand that the distance and time away are difficult for mated pairs. This will be exceedingly difficult for Beta Superior Kaius and Beta-Female Superior Celest since they have consummated their mate bond. However, there is a solution, and I hope that you consider this. Below is the recipe for a remedy that will assuage the effects of the mate bond caused by distance.

I think it would be an excellent experience to train and learn. I am also selfish and would love to meet the first human mates.

In this envelope are three brooches. These are yours. They are your pack crests. Wear them with pride. Your mates were already given theirs centuries ago. These were crafted in his image when Alpha Superior created his pack, but more importantly, Luna Aella, he specially made yours by hand. Your crest has been regularly cleaned and protected by the most secure vault within the Luna Council. Your brooch is not only a sign of your status but also a note to Alpha Superior's unwavering fidelity to you.

We had always thought that Icarus would not be given a mate. Artemis had explained that he had to live mateless for all of us to live with ours. He is and always will be the protector of our species. Because of the reality of his being mateless forever, Alpha Superior spent decades building a library and jewelry collection that would, in theory, please his mate. I believe he did this to ease the pain of never having a mate because—to him—his mate existed within the contents of his library.

If you choose to come, all the other lunas will be in attendance, accompanied by their brigade. You will be given your pack lands and pack house here, and new members will be added to your pack if you accept them. The entire council is protected—with twenty-four-seven security provided by a neutral squadron of wolves. Arguably, this is the safest place for a new luna, beta female, and gamma. Please know that your arrival to the Luna Council would remain strictly confidential and only those within the council would know of your presence. Only upper-rank wolves will know, and their secrecy will be bound by my order.

Please consider this offer. Affixed to this letter is my phone number and email address.

*With love,
Luna Alita*

Do you like werewolf stories?
Here are samples of other stories
you might enjoy!

LUPUS DEUS

SOPHIA MOORE

PROLOGUE

As the gods looked down at their creation, they looked with worry and caution. He was no longer the same. They'd lost control over him decades ago, and now he'd become a real problem for them. No longer was he just the "Messenger of the Gods." He was now a god himself. He'd won the title fair and square, showing all those who'd stood against him that he wouldn't hesitate to shed the blood of those accused of disloyalty.

He was cruel.

The gods looked down at him as he fought his way through the bodies of his enemies. He wasn't even in his full form yet, and to him, they were already nothing but a bunch of toys to play with; and he made sure that he killed them in a way that would leave a mess—a bitter sight even for those foul enough to appreciate a kill.

He was vicious.

As they watched, the female gods all gave each other knowing looks. His appearance had been expected to be as ugly as his personality and reputation, but it was the opposite. His looks equaled those of the male gods in the room, and he knew it as well.

He was seductive.

As they watched on, they became horrified at the amount of power that he'd been collecting daily. Not only was he dangerous and out of control, but his power was also becoming too much for even the gods to handle. They feared that if he returned to them, he'd be able to take them out—all of them.

After all, it wasn't a secret that they couldn't have been more neglectful and devious when it came to the boy. They'd taken him from his home, when they'd seen a purpose for him, and turned him into what he was now. The gods sat around the glass table, all heads high and eyes cold. Finally, one spoke. It was Alstha, Goddess of War and Knowledge.

"Something must be done immediately! He is slaughtering hundreds every minute, some not even guilty!" she exclaimed, outraged, her godly features twisting into something dark.

"We cannot do such a thing. We made sure of that when we made him, that he be indestructible and that his powers be undiminishing," Eccasto, God of Intelligence and Instinct, spoke, his voice marked by regret.

"And whose bright idea was that? We've all seen what the boy can do, and I swear on all that I know that something ill will happen to us if we do not find a way to stop him," spoke Fate.

The gods froze. His name was simple, and he spoke only when needed. His words were basically law, and if he worried about their future then this was graver than they'd thought. They all looked around the table and pondered what to do.

The boy had trained with Alstha, so he knew much of war, among other things. He'd trained with Eccasto, so he knew how to react to anything. He'd trained with Fate, so he was prepared for almost everything. The boy had trained with all of them . . .

Almost as if the same thought had passed through their heads, discussions halted. The boy had trained with all them . . . but one. There was one god whose power they'd thought he wouldn't need on his missions, so they hadn't prepared him for her, although he had mainly been in her charge and was of the same species as her: Luna, or as her people called her, Mother Luna.

All eyes went to her as she cocked her brow questioningly. Out of all of them, she was the safest. She hadn't interacted with the boy.

"What?" Her melodic voice passed through the vast room.

"You're the only one he hasn't prepared for," Fate spoke, his expression one of caution but also glee.

"And?"

The gods looked at Fate, curious.

"Mother Luna, what is the one thing you give your children that none of us can give?" he asked, standing from his chair and making his way to her gracefully.

"A mate," she answered proudly and without hesitation.

The other gods gasped as they realized where Fate was going with this. Fate tsk-tsked and took her hand in his, lifted it to his mouth, and kissed it softly, lingering just as bit.

"No. I can both give a lover and take one away in a simple 'accident.' " She snatched her hand back forcefully, and her beautiful features shifted into an animalistic expression, her lips parted, teeth bared, and angry eyes narrowed in warning.

"Be calm, Mother Luna. I will not harm any of your . . . innocent children."

Her features returned to normal, but the wild look in her eyes was still present, active.

"Hope—you give your children hope, of having someone to cherish, someone to trust, someone to love."

"Yes, I do. But what of it?"

"The boy has nobody to love, no one to call his own, no family. Look at him. He goes and comes as he pleases. He's free—too free."

The other gods finally understood and agreed, but they didn't quite get the endgame.

"Send him a warrior! She will tame his heart!" yelled out Alstha, her eyes gleeful at the thought.

"No, send him a heartless girl! He will pine for her affection, and his instincts will let him do no more!" yelled out Eccasto.

The other gods also yelled out their thoughts and opinions about what she should be and why, but with a raise of a hand, Fate shut them right up.

"No."

The gods looked at him, flabbergasted, not comprehending how Fate couldn't see the brilliance of some of their ideas.

"So who shall I mate him to, Fate?" asked Luna, excitement clear in her eyes. Everyone knew she loved matching couples, even the impossible pairs.

"She will be gentle like the breeze of autumn, catching him off guard—so different from what he's used to. That will build up his desire to get to know her," Fate said with a pointed look at Eccasto.

"But she will also be stubborn and defend herself against him with a bravery no other has shown him in years. This will be great for others, for she will bring him down from his high horse and let his feet touch the ground again." Fate looked at Alstha.

"Her beauty will be inward. She will be beautiful, no doubt, but it won't be the beauty he's acquainted himself with. This will open his eyes and make him see people for who they are, not how they seem outside. She will bring him peace, joy, and hope for things he thought he would never get. She will tame him—his power, his heart, his spirit, his whole being."

The room was silent as the gods took all of this in. Then one god spoke, "But will she be his undoing?"

Fate stayed silent. "Can you do it, Mother Luna?" he later asked, apprehension clear in his voice.

She replied with a smirk. Her hands lifted from the table, and mist surrounded them. The sun suddenly set, and the moon rose. Luna chanted under her breath like usual, but this time everyone watched closely, knowing that their fate, ironically, depended on this event they'd always ignored or snickered at.

Luna also did something different: she brought her wrist to her mouth and bit it, then let the blood from her wrist seemingly float up. A grand amount had left her before the wound was sealed. Fate narrowed his eyes at this.

The blood slowly began to take a solid form, and next to it, blue blood appeared, making the others hiss—the blood of the boy.

"What are you doing?" yelled out Fate, alarmed by the gleam in her wild eyes.

Luna continued to chant, ignoring the others. Both orbs of blood began to come together, Luna's blood taking on a hint of purple just before it touched the boy's. They intertwined, clashing for a moment before they became one and suddenly vanished into thin air. Luna tilted her head to the side before blinking, her eyes clearing and facial expression turning into that of indifference, or perhaps boredom.

The other gods glared at her.

"What did you do?" Fate asked her again, with a sharpness to his tone.

Luna gave him a wide smile as she sealed their fate. "And thus Vivian Grey was born."

CHAPTER ONE

"He's looking at us."

"I know."

"I don't like him looking at us."

I snorted at my wolf. *"And what do you want me to do about it?"*

"Claw his eyes out."

I rolled my eyes at her.

When we hit another turbulence, my hands gripped the armrests tightly, my fingers becoming pale from the excessive use of force. I had no problem flying, but my wolf hated being off ground. It made her extremely easy to piss off, and our being connected to one another meant that I was well in tune with her emotions. She had been eyeing passengers ever since we'd got on and hadn't stopped trying to convince me to claw everyone's face.

"I'm not going to claw his eyes out just because he's looking at us. Calm down. We've only got a few minutes left until we can get off this plane."

I could feel her gleeful excitement at the idea of solid ground. She settled down without another word. I raised my window blind and tried to make something of the view, but we were still too high up. My thoughts floated around to the reason for my trip.

A few years back, werewolf packs were getting infiltrated by wolves from an unknown pack. It wasn't until these wolves had begun their full-on attack, taking members, that the alphas realized this wasn't random. Packs were being hunted down one at a time, from one corner of the world to the next.

The mystery was around the attacker. In the beginning, fingers had been pointed at one another, but soon we came to see that no pack was safe. Every pack was getting attacked, leading us to believe the last thing we'd wanted to believe and blame the last thing we'd wanted to blame.

The attacking pack had wolves faster than light and stronger than alphas, yet they'd never attacked at first, only sat around. That was until they were given the unknown signal for their attack. The packs had prepared as much as they could, but nothing could stop the attackers from coming and taking what they wanted. But what did they want? That was the million-dollar question.

These wolves appeared out of nowhere, only to disappear right after taking what they wanted when they wanted, and attacked like a trained hunting pack. They were as strong as enforcers yet functioned like middle-ranking members. Who was in charge of them? We all had a suspect, whose name no one wanted to lay on the table, because if anyone did and *he* heard, then their head would be on a table.

When my pack seemed to be next on the hit list, my parents decided to send me away, to make me stay with my cousin Lily from the Cusco pack. Many members did this with their daughters, seeing as it was young women that were being taken. The even-stranger thing was that some of those who'd been taken were later brought back, unharmed and without the slightest idea as to what had happened or where they'd been taken to.

My parents had been supposed to come with me, but my mom had gotten sick; and Dad, being the over protective mate that he was, had basically locked her in their room, after cleaning the house excessively, and said he wasn't going to risk her getting worse on the trip, even though she was barely snuffling. She bared her teeth at him for that. But Dad wasn't worried that they'd try to take Mom. She was, after all, mated and older than the girls that were usually taken.

Being away from my parents made me anxious, but I knew that they could take care of themselves and that after this whole mess, I would be back home with them in no time. After all, who was I? I'd probably just get returned. One thing was certain, though: Whoever this person was, they were not joking around. They wanted something. And, by the way things were going, it seemed they were going to get it.

* * *

A brown-haired woman was running to me with open arms. I wasn't one to avoid physical contact, but when you've been sitting in a plane for over a day, you tend to feel unhygienic. That was me at this moment.

"Hey, Lily," I said as I hugged her, aware that I was somewhat trying to keep my distance. But, because she was squeezing me so hard, it was impossible.

"Wow, you've gotten big since I last saw you!" she exclaimed—because that's something every girl wants to hear.

Lily was nine years older than me. Her long brown locks were actually controllable and framed her long face in soft waves, the sharp brows high on her face gave off the impression that she was easily surprised, her fine lashes framed her dark-brown eyes, and the crinkles at the corners of her eyes made her look younger, though her filled-in cheeks weren't helping. She stood at five foot five and was an energetic person, especially for someone who was at the ripe old age of twenty-seven.

"Gee, thanks. And, yes, I'm fine after being in a flying metal tube for hours," I responded sarcastically.

She shot me an apologetic look before grabbing one of my bags. "You know what I mean, Vivian. I wasn't calling you fat. I was just stating that you seem taller. No need to rip out my throat," she said defensively, putting her free hand in front of her throat as if to protect it.

I rolled my eyes at her theatrics.

We exited the airport and made our way to her car, where we placed my bags. Lily got in the front and began to drive. "You got your pack papers, right, kid?"

I nodded in response, then she hummed and continued to drive. She'd glanced over at me many times throughout the ride, until she finally said what was on her mind: "Now, don't be alarmed, but there's a bit more security around Cusco pack land. I'm not allowed to say why, but don't worry about it. Just listen, and stick to the rules."

This was new but not all that alarming. I looked at her but didn't ask anything. I suspected that this was their way of staying on guard against the attacks.

Every wolf knew better than to try to get information about a different pack. It was seen as suspicious and could start more problems than it was worth. When on another pack's land, the foreign visitor had to bring their ID, show their pack birthmark and a document signed by someone high-ranking allowing the visit, and obey all their rules and regulations. And alphas took trespassing and security more seriously nowadays.

Lily drove down a path in the forest that was easy to navigate but only for those who knew where to turn. The deeper we got into the forest, the calmer my wolf got. The scenery was different but close to what she knew.

Around ten minutes into the drive, we passed a sign that read, in big bold letters, *Private Property. Do Not Pass. Will Be Shot on Sight.* For any human, that should be enough to stop them, but most wolves knew that it was just a warning to humans. Werewolves, if they chose to pass, would be stopped at least a mile away from the pack land. And, as if to show me I was correct, two large men with weapons stepped out of nowhere and stopped a few feet ahead of the car.

Lily slowed to a stop and rolled down the windows. One of them walked slowly to the car, while the other stood still in front of us, his eyes steady on me and hand ready to pull his gun out if I made a wrong move. No matter how many times someone went through this, the knowledge that even if you were innocent, one wrong move would mean trouble would startle them.

"Lillian Grey, born on Cusco soil and still a member," Lily stated seriously.

The man right outside her window eyed her, then me, before inhaling and taking in our scents. Lily surely had this land's scents, but I probably reeked of humans, of a different land, and of uneasiness.

"What about her?" he asked, his voice gruff and suspicious.

I took that as my cue. "Vivian Grey, born on Defluo soil and still a member, granted permission for a visit regarding family matters, documents in place," I said as professionally as I could, my heart beating loudly against my chest, my hands shaking a little. No matter how many times I'd done this, it was still a bit nerve-wracking.

"Papers, mark, and ID."

I nodded; took out my papers, my wallet, and my ID; and gave them to him. He read through my papers, then looked back and forth between my ID and me as if I'd changed a lot in the two years since I'd taken it, although I still was brown-eyed, had a bit of baby fat on me, and had my brown hair cut at the shoulders.

He handed them back to me. "Mark?"

I unzipped my hoodie and pulled the left collar of my shirt down to show my mark. My pack's mark was kind of like the others': three slashes by claws but with a line going through the middle of it and two perfect circles underneath. I pulled my collar back up afterwards but left the hood unzipped.

His expression became blank for a moment, then he nodded at the guy in front, giving us the clear. Lily proceeded forward as soon as the other man moved out of our way. This had happened two more times before we were let in, passing the big gate that separated the pack from outsiders. Lily was right: security was tight.

While most might believe that werewolves guarded their pack land in wolf form, they actually only did that inside the gates. A pack's main concern was being seen by humans, hence the armed werewolves in human form.

"Okay, now we can start the fun," Lily exclaimed, breaking me out of my thoughts.

"Can I shower and, I don't know, maybe eat?" I asked her in an exasperated tone.

It was her turn to roll her eyes. "Okay, okay, I'll feed you before you call your mom and tell her I haven't been taking care of you in these first few hours that I've had you. She'd skin me alive," she said jokingly—I think.

After we'd pulled up to her house and she'd gotten me settled in, I took a much-needed shower and felt its effects immediately. I was no longer cranky. I'd also taken in my appearance before I went down. My short auburn strands fell right to below my collarbone, cut straight. My face had a slight flush due to the hot water. My large brown doe eyes paired up with my deeply arching eyebrows to make me look like a know-it-all. My pointy small nose made my chubby cheeks look childish and my face squarish. I wasn't fat, but I wasn't quite fit, either; and I was okay with that. My lips unconsciously turned up at the corners, and I skipped down the stairs and into the kitchen with this smile on my face. Lily looked at me suspiciously, but I just kept smiling.

"What did you break?" She put down the sandwich she'd been making to cross her arms.

I let my jaw hang and widened my eyes to feign hurt. "What? I'm offended, Lily. I would never break anything in your house," I said, putting a hand over my heart, knowing this was utter bullshit, because a few years back, I'd broken her living-room chair. To this day, I still say that it was just an old chair and that it wasn't because I was heavy at all. The corners of her lips twitched, letting me know that she was probably thinking about that, too; but she just shook her head at me and put a plate in front of me before taking a chair and setting herself on it.

"So, how have you been, kid?" she asked.

"We're all good—a bit worried, but good. How about you?" I answered, picking up the sandwich. I took a bite out of it while she continued to talk to me.

"I've been good over here, staying out of trouble. But between you and me," she whispered as if someone was listening, "I sneak out every Friday to head to the library."

I choked on my sandwich. "B-but you live alone. No need to sneak out." I looked at her incredulously.

"I know." She smirked at me.

It'd taken me a while to figure out she'd been joking, at which point I entered a small giggling fit.

"I like to live wild," she declared, throwing her arms up.

I shook my head at my crazy but missed cousin. She was an odd one.

We talked for a whole two hours, catching up on happenings and even talking about my stay here, but after a while, I began to feel exhausted and was itching to have some quiet time.

"I'm going to go to bed. The earlier I go to sleep, the more time we'll have tomorrow," I blurted out, already making my way out of the chair and up the stairs.

"All right. We'll go for a run tomorrow, if you want." She waved me off, standing and stretching her arms over her head.

"Yes! My wolf needs it. Night, Lily." I smiled at her.

"Night."

I finally went to sleep two hours after I'd said I would. I hate jet lag. My eyes slowly closed as darkness crept around my mind, then I was in dreamland.

That, however, didn't last long because a loud screeching suddenly blasted through the air, startling me out of my sleep. A few seconds later, screaming followed, from somewhere outside. I rubbed my eyes furiously, trying to remove the sleep from them. At first I thought I was imagining things, but then I noticed a red light was flashing outside the house along with another blaring noise. Loud stomps made their way to my room, scaring me. My wolf began to growl in my head, pacing in unease.

When my door was busted open, I stopped mid-scream, realizing that it was a panting, pale Lily. One side of her brown hair was frizzy, her eyes bright and wild with fear and panic. I leaped out of bed and moved towards her. When I got close enough, she suddenly gripped my shoulders tightly and opened her mouth to say something, but then a voice coming from what sounded like a megaphone boomed: "Code Red! All women and children: make your way to the safety bunker. We are under attack. I repeat, go to the bunker; we are under attack!"

It took us a while to realize what had been said.

"We have to go now!"

I looked over at Lily, my eyes widening at her words. Why was the pack under attack? Could it be . . . ? And why did it have to happen while I was sleeping?

She gripped my hand and dragged me down the stairs. She pulled open the door and peeked out, her eyes wide and fearful. My heart was beating like a hummingbird's. I was aware my breathing was loud, but I didn't care. A thin layer of cold sweat had begun to form on the back of my neck. I looked around with her. There were people running in different directions, in panic—most of them like me, in sweatpants and baggy shirts.

"Let's go" was all Lily had said before she took off running.

I took off with her, not wanting to be left behind. I sped up when I heard guns going off in the distance along with loud snarls. My blood coursed faster through my veins, my body heating up from the sudden workout. I had to remind myself to keep calm, because people make stupid mistakes when they panic . . . like trip.

"What's going on, Lily? What—" I stopped when I suddenly crashed into her back.

She turned to me, frightened, words rushing out of her mouth: "Your parents didn't know this. If they had, they wouldn't have sent you here. Shit, if we make it, they're going to kill me. I'm sorry. I shouldn't have let you come. My pack got a warning that we were next, but it didn't fit their pattern, so we didn't believe it could be true. Oh man, this is messed up." She looked around nervously. The alarm had stopped a while back, but the red flashes and gunshots were still going on.

"What warning? When?" I shouted at her. I felt like I couldn't breathe no matter how many breaths I tried to take. It seemed like the air didn't want to make its way into my lungs. I was too young to have a panic attack!

"I'll explain later, but we have to go to the bunker. Come on! Stay close!"

Once again, we took off running into a part of the forest everyone else seemed to be heading towards as well. I didn't like this one bit. I felt like I was just running around blindly. This wasn't my pack. I didn't know the layout of this land. And I'd come here to get away from the danger, not get closer to it! I scowled at the darkness that we were running towards.

The more we ran, the farther away the fighting and shots sounded, and we ran until I knew we were safe; but I didn't feel comfortable knowing people were still in danger. Ahead of us, I could see women and children going into the somewhat-large but flat building. So many people were trying to get in at once that when both Lily and I tried to get in with them, we were shoved around and separated.

"Lily?" I started to panic when I couldn't see her. This was all too confusing, and everyone was crying and talking at the same time. "Lily?" I cried out louder. I might not have been very close to Lily, but she was family and the only person I really knew here.

I felt a hand grasp my left one and spin me around. A relieved breath left me, my body sagging upon seeing Lily next to me. "Oh, thank fuck!" I exclaimed. I hadn't realized just how much it'd freak me out to lose her until I had her back in my sight.

"Sorry—I was swept away at the door." She hurriedly walked us over to a wall and slid down.

I followed suit, my legs hurting from the sudden run. I'd demand answers now that we were far away from the danger, and my wolf agreed with me. "What's going on, Lily?"

She looked up at me with a strange expression on her face, then I realized it was because she was holding back a sob. I snapped my teeth together and clenched my jaw. Tears scared the living daylights out of me, but I pushed my uncomfortable feelings to the side and put my hand on her shoulder, hoping it'd reassure her somehow. I wasn't exactly sure I was actually helping, though. She just took deep breaths for a while, then squeezed her eyes shut.

"Tell me what's going on. What warning did your pack get? Who's attacking?" *And why the fuck did you let me come here when you knew your pack was in danger?* I didn't say the last one out loud, but my wolf's annoyance was very much fueling my own.

She took a shaky breath but didn't open her eyes. "I can't tell you everything because I'm bound to secrecy by my alpha, but I can tell you this: *he* wants something—someone. I don't know! My alpha got a letter a few months ago saying we were next, but it didn't fit the pattern, so he paid it no mind. He said we would be safe. But *he* got offended. *He* didn't like it. We affronted *him*, insulted *him*. We were tactless. And now we're going to pay. Alpha thought *he* was a myth, a fraud. Alpha was cocky. Alpha was wrong," she whispered, seemingly more to herself than to me.

It scared me to see Lily act this way. Her speech had been almost childish and choppy, but that wasn't what concerned me. "Who, Lily? Who did . . . your alpha disrespect?" I asked, not knowing how to phrase my question better.

She looked up at me, her large brown eyes blank. "The one known as the Lupus Deus."

If you enjoyed this sample, look for
Lupus Deus
on Amazon.

QUEEN MATERIAL

BOOK 1 *of* ACE OF QUEENS SERIES

MARCY SWALES

CHAPTER ONE

Death had never phased Rye. She had already seen her grandparents, from both sides, pass away. It was something she always accepted as a part of nature.

But her father wasn't supposed to die. Well, at least not yet. Rye thought she had more time with him; thought he would be there clapping for her when she graduated from college or when she received her MCAT scores. God only knew her mother would be too busy with her werewolf diplomatic business or the twins, Chyna and India.

Rye honestly had no hard feelings towards her younger sisters. It was her mother she had an issue with.

Olivia Alden was always too busy for her firstborn. She claimed it was her job, but Rye couldn't help but feel it was because Rye was human. Olivia, being a werewolf, would have naturally wanted her firstborn to carry the wolf DNA but, being mated to a human, she had known the chances of their children carrying the wolf DNA was fifty-fifty. Lucky for her and unlucky for Rye, both of the twins carried wolf DNA.

Olivia had taken off for long periods of time for the twins, time she did not spare for Rye.

"You father couldn't have handled how a wolf changes and behaves as they grow up," she had explained to Rye. "You were the easiest to raise out of all my children."

"Easiest because you were never there!" Rye had screamed at her. It was a battle that they had both fought many times.

But Rye couldn't complain about the childhood she had with her father. Jacob Alden was a European history professor who taught Rye to dissect frogs during summer vacations. He would call her his little prodigy.

"My Rye is the greatest in the world!" he would often say.

Were Chyna and India envious of their father's relationship with their elder sister?

Perhaps. But unlike Rye, the twins were shy and quiet. They were obedient, and would never dream of doing half the things their sister did. Olivia always had her eyes on the twins and Jacob on Rye.

But now there was no one to watch over her. She felt completely lost as she sat still on that uncomfortable chair at the funeral parlor and looked around at the many faces in the room. She looked at Chyna and India both sobbing delicately, their blue eyes puffy and prominent on their round faces. Oliva stood next to the casket, her demeanor not betraying an ounce of emotion.

Who are these people? Rye thought. She didn't feel sad or hurt when she got the call about the accident two days ago; she didn't feel her eyes swell up with tears when they had her father laid in the cherry wood casket; and she most definitely didn't feel comfort when her mother pulled her into a tight hug outside the funeral home.

But she had felt angry. She had just let her arms hang by her side and held her breath, waiting for her mother to pull away. She was angered by her touch. How dare she cry? Her father deserved better. He deserved a mate that spent his birthdays with him. He deserved a mate that called him to just let him know she loved him.

Mates were supposed to be your better half. Rye would hear stories from her grandmother about how when you found the one, your whole world would move around them. They were the essence of your existence. But when Rye watched her parents, she thought it was all just a bunch of bull.

To her, it was an animalistic instinct that insured the survival of a species. It wasn't love. It was a sick, twisted form of lust that doomed two individuals to stay together for the survival of their kind . . . Well, at least for maybe one of their kind in Rye's parent's case.

"I am so sorry for your loss." A voice pulled Rye's attention away from throwing daggers at her mother with her eyes.

She turned to see an elderly gentleman standing in front of her. He had salt and pepper hair that was neatly trimmed and styled. His black suit looked tailored to perfection. She could see his irises were ringed in gold.

Lycan.

Rye had only met one or two pure-blooded lycans before, mainly friends of her mother from work. Only pure lycans had a ring of gold around their iris, too light for the human eye to catch. But given Rye's senses were heightened from her mother's werewolf DNA, she caught it.

Pure lycans were rare. Over the ages, they had mixed with humans, creating the werewolf race. Those werewolves mixed with more humans and either created werewolves or *misce*, human children with heightened senses, like Rye.

"Jacob was a wonderful husband and father," the man continued. This time, Rye noticed his thick British accent.

Rye looked into his eyes and blinked. "Do you say the same line at all funerals, or do you have different ones that you rotate between?"

The man struggled to say something else. He opened and closed his mouth like a gaping fish.

"How about, 'So what now? Are you burying him or burning him to a crisp?'" Rye suggested. "Maybe try that one out at the next funeral you're at. And please, do let me know how it goes. I've been meaning to ask someone that."

Olivia saw her daughter speaking with one of the Royal Councilmen from across the room and hurried over before Rye said something bizarre.

"Councilman Jude." Olivia approached the pair, eyeing her daughter suspiciously after seeing the baffled look on the old man's face. "Thank you for coming."

Rye sat back down and looked straight ahead. She couldn't help but let a tiny laugh escape her lips as she correctly predicted her mother's actions. Of course she was treating her father's funeral like a networking event.

Both the councilman and Oliva turned to look at the strange girl with dark hair sitting in front of them.

"I see you have met my eldest daughter, Rye," Olivia said in a polite voice. "Dear, please stand up. This is Royal Councilman Lawson Jude from Romania."

Rye pretended not to hear.

"Rye." Olivia's voice was laced with warning.

"It's quite alright, Mrs. Alden." Lawson sensed the tension between the mother and daughter and didn't want to be the cause of any further hostilities. "We were all so gravely shocked to hear about Jacob's sudden passing. King Dorin sends his thoughts and prayers to your family."

Rye was fed up with hearing the same sentence over and over again. She stood up with a stomp of her feet, making sure it was loud enough for everyone to hear. She looked at Lawson and Olivia, who were frozen mid-conversation from her sudden actions.

"Remember to ask if they're planning on burning the body to a crisp," Rye said to Lawson before turning on her heels and walking out of the funeral home.

Lawson and Olivia stood motionless, watching the young girl disappear around the corner.

With embarrassment in her eyes, Olivia turned to Lawson. "Councilman, I am s—"

"Mrs. Alden, I believe you have given birth to a luna. Possibly the queen luna we have been searching for two centuries."

If you enjoyed this sample, look for
Queen Material
on Amazon.

A ROYAL'S TALE

Mated to the Alpha King

JENNISE K

PROLOGUE

Dear Reader,

It is with great pleasure that I present to you a brief introduction of the new world you have decided to enter, a new life you have decided to live. Let it be known that it will only last for a number of chapters, but I hope you enjoy it while it lasts.

Let me, firstly, introduce myself.

Hi, I am Theia Anderson. I am just like any one of you, human, alive, and breathing—unless you are a zombie, in which case *I am not* alive or breathing, and I especially *do not* have brains!

Just putting it out there!

I am eighteen and currently a senior in Rosenberg High. I'm what they call a nerd, but let's face it, nerds nowadays are hot!

I have also only recently moved from the sunny state of California to a place called Piedmont, which is located just beside Seattle.

Needless to say it rains here—*a lot*.

When I moved here, I imagined finally living in a cold state and thought that it would be an amazing experience, although the fact that it was in the middle of the year and I would have to settle in as the "new girl" was very well placed in my mind.

New friends, new teachers, a new environment—everything was new.

But that all was well-known and understood. I had expected it.

However, what I certainly didn't expect was to meet the man who owns the castle I gazed upon from my window every morning and night.

Yes, a castle—a castle I am now living in.

This is my story—a story I am now willing to share, but only if you can keep a secret.

Do you remember the stories your grandma used to tell you every night about cursed beasts, village beauties, girls in red capes, and wolves in disguises?

Well, maybe, just maybe . . . they actually did happen. Maybe beasts do exist.

They do.

I would know; I am bound to one.

Who, you may ask?

Well, I am mated to the Alpha King.

How?

You will see.

You will live through it, with me.

I hope you enjoy the ride.

Best wishes,

Theia.

CHAPTER ONE

Done—finally!

Packing had never been my forte. In fact, I absolutely detested packing. Maybe it was because the amount of books and other things I possessed seemed impossible to place in tonnes of boxes.

After slapping duct tape across the box, I picked up a marker and marked it Theia's Books #3.

When the box was pushed aside carefully, I finally let out a sigh of relief as I wiped away a layer of sweat that had accumulated on my forehead, though it had only been two minutes since I had wiped it last. I lived in the warm state of California, and it was summer, so naturally, the heat was killing me.

A single thing one should always know about me: I am not built for heat. So when my dad came home one afternoon and declared that we were moving from California to a cold region on the outskirts of Seattle called Piedmont, I was actually very excited.

Well, that was until I realized that I was now going to have to join a new high school in the middle of the year and leave my best friend, Casey, behind. And with this being senior year—with prom and all—well, it sucked.

Had I been at my old school, Stinson High, I would have at least had my best friend to accompany me. The thought of being at home, all alone, on prom night only helped in making me sweat more.

My family consisted of my dad, Arthur Anderson, who was a professor of history and literature; my mom, Maia Anderson, who was a designer and entrepreneur—big word, I know—and me, Theia, currently a senior student in high school, hoping to become a criminologist or psychologist—whichever came first. I also had a very strange fascination with history.

I guess Dad's genes rubbed off on me that way.

Another soft puff of a sigh escaped me as I lazily picked myself off of the floor and dragged myself towards the bathroom. I had only two hours before we were to load everything and leave, and I knew, in this heat, I would need every minute of it.

Minutes later, as I stood under my cool shower and slowly looked around my bathroom for the final time, I let a few stray tears flow with the water as I washed the tiny ache in my chest away.

It seemed like a day had passed when I found myself scrubbed and fresh, walking out into my bedroom in a towel.

A loud yelp left my lips when I suddenly found myself on the floor, a heavy weight on me.

"Don't go!" Casey cried, hysterical against me. I would have cried, too, but the fact that I was currently sprawled on the floor with only a towel on and my hundred-something-pound best friend on top of me was a little . . . suffocating. I was merely five foot something after all.

"Need . . . to . . . breathe, Casey!" I managed to gasp as I writhed under her, trying to escape her deadly grip.

Immediately, Casey stilled above me.

"Oh, I'm sorry!" she muttered hurriedly, becoming beet red, as she got off of me and stood, before giving me her hand and helping me stand up.

On my feet, I sighed as I brought her in for a hug. "We will talk every night on Skype or FaceTime. And then there is Messenger! We will always talk. It'll be like I'm not even away, I promise," I said to assure her as I pulled away and, losing my towel, put on my clothes.

Casey sighed, too, her sigh a little heavy—a little scared. "What if we don't?"

I smiled—a broken small smile. My hand found Casey's again, and I gave it a comforting squeeze. "No matter what happens, whether we talk every day or not at all for months, when we do talk or meet, we will always be the same: best friends."

A small tear dropped down Casey's cheek, and she nodded, chuckling against the moisture on her face.

"You better tell me everything when you get there!" she blurted out, smiling a bit, as she folded and placed my towel in a plastic bag before packing it in my suitcase. My room was nearly empty. It was literally stripped bare except for the built-in bookshelves and a few boxes and suitcases that were still lying around waiting to be hurled into the moving truck.

Smiling, I nodded and pulled Casey in for a final hug. "We'll visit each other on the breaks. I'll miss you, you know?"

Casey nodded. "I'll miss you, too, Thi."

The loud stomping noises alerted us both of someone coming up the stairs, and soon enough, there was a knock on the door. "Theia, are you done?"

"Yeah, Dad, come in!" I replied as I picked up my jacket—just in case it got cold—and slipped into my flip-flops, which seemed like an irrational choice considering the contrast between the two. But I wouldn't need my shoes in the car anyway; I'd probably just have them tucked under me throughout the ride.

The door opened instantly, and in walked my dad with two bulky men. Smiling at me softly, they strode towards the boxes and picked them up before leaving the room even barer.

Again, Casey and I stood in my empty room—a room we'd had dozens of sleepovers in; a room we played with our dolls in; a room we gossiped, planned, and plotted in; a room we did our homework and fangirled in.

I sighed.

"I think we should go now . . ."

"Uh-huh."

Casey and I walked downstairs hand in hand. I took a deep breath as I stood in the living room.

The place had a lot of my memories. I had basically grown up in this area. Well, that was until I turned sixteen and got the television set up in my own room. My eyes closed, and I let out a deep breath and whispered, "I'll miss you, home. Goodbye."

"Theia, sweetie!"

My mom's voice rang out to me like a fire truck's siren, and I instantly opened my eyes and walked out of the threshold, letting Dad lock the door and hand over the keys to our real estate agent, Vanessa, who had managed to sell our home for a very, very reasonable amount.

The day outside was bright, happy, vibrant, and warm. The heat suddenly didn't bother me anymore. I looked around my neighborhood and smiled. I would be taking all the good memories with me as I went. As much as I was sad, truth be spoken, I was also secretly excited.

I didn't know what it was, but I felt like something was waiting for me in Piedmont—an adventure waiting to be lived, maybe a mystery waiting to be unraveled. The little knowledge of the new feeling in me made it all the more alluring, and somehow . . . secretly, I couldn't wait to reach Piedmont.

"Bye, Cas! I'll call you when I get there, okay?" I muttered, suddenly holding back my tears, as I was pulled into a hug.

"Uh-huh, we will always talk! And if we can't, we will at least message when we can," Casey said to assure me as she hugged me.

Smiling slightly, I pulled out of the hug, and with a final wave, climbed into our SUV, then watched my best friend stand in my yard, in my neighborhood, for the last time as my dad drove off.

It felt like I was leaving a part of me here. But then again, I was becoming whole.

* * *

"Are you excited, darling?" Mom suddenly asked me, cutting the silence that had been building up since we left seven hours ago. The ride from California to Piedmont was fifteen hours and thirteen minutes, and already in these seven hours we had stopped twice to fuel up the SUV and buy some snacks for along the way.

"Yeah, Mom. Are you?" I murmured back, knowing full well that both my parents were extremely excited for this "new chapter" in their life. Dad would not stop talking about the amount of brilliant literature the new university he had managed to attain a job in had, not to mention the immense raise in wage and position. He was ecstatic. As for Mom, her boutiques and salons around California were still running, but although she would have to fly back and forth every once in a while, her excitement about opening a new boutique and salon in Piedmont was especially overwhelming.

"Oh, I am so excited!" she squealed, clapping her hands together, before turning towards Dad and placing a loving kiss on his cheek.

It was normal for me to witness their weird romance, so I just rolled my eyes and looked at the passing view.

"The new house is bigger, Theia," Dad said with a chuckle, looking at me through the rearview mirror.

I knew he was trying to make me feel better about moving and leaving my old friends and life behind, so I just grinned at Dad and spoke the first thing I thought would make him worry less: "I get the room with the best view!"

Dad chuckled again and nodded, making my grin widen. It wasn't hard to notice that I was a papa's girl, and with me being the only child, he doted on me. I was his little Fuzzybottom—not that my bottom was fuzzy, but . . . just because—and, well, he was my hero.

"One of the best things about the house is that it has great views for all the rooms. But you'll receive the one with the best view, we promise. We should be settled by tomorrow. Hopefully, the day after, you and I could go shopping!" Mom squealed as she turned to look at me.

Not excited at all, I somehow managed to produce a fake smile and plaster it across my face. Nobody messed with Mom when it came to shopping—nobody.

Once her attention was elsewhere, I turned around to see how far behind us our moving truck was. Before turning back around, I brought out a book from my backpack, plugged my earbuds into my iPod, and played "Davy Jones Music Box and the Rainy Mood." Somehow, the rumbles of thunder and the soft sound of the tune playing together created a better reading mood for me. Shoving the iPod inside my pant pocket, I flipped through the pages of my newest read, *Indiscretions*; slumped back into a more comfortable position; and began journeying once again, into a different time, a whole different world—this time, into the world of Lord Lockwood.

* * *

"Thi, we are here!"

I mumbled a few incoherent words before turning in my bed.

Need sleep.

"Thi! Wake up!" Dad's voice urged, before I was being shaken by the shoulder and lightly tapped on my face.

What the heck?

"Alright, alright!" I grumbled as I sat up on my bed and opened my eyes.

I gasped, my face becoming warmer by the second, as I finally realized that I was in our SUV and a couple of people were staring at me, smiling like a bunch of weirdos—my folks included.

My cheeks burned as my eyes rested on a blond-haired guy smirking at me, an axe in his hand and resting on his shoulder.

What was he? A huntsman? I rolled my eyes in my mind as I pushed any budding crush away. I was more of a *Beauty and the Beast* girl anyway.

Finally managing to look away, I smiled back at the rest of the folks smiling at me, who were two slightly elderly couples.

"Oh, she's so beautiful!" the red-headed one of the two gushed as I shoved my iPod and book into my backpack and got out of the SUV.

"Thanks," I mumbled back, knowing full well that the blond was still staring, smirking at me.

"Hello, dear. Welcome to Piedmont! I'm Jane, and this here is my son, Alex, and my husband, Hugh. We live just there, beside your house. Those there are Mary and her husband, Grant. They have a son, too, Matthew. He is good friends with Alex here," Jane told me excitedly, and I smiled back brightly, mirroring her excitement.

"It's nice to meet you all. I am really excited to be here," I replied happily as I extended my hand towards each one of them. I shook their hands softly but only waved awkwardly at the smirking blond, Alex.

That boy seemed as beautiful as he seemed arrogant—beautiful nonetheless. But then again, arrogance trumped beauty any day.

My new home stood tall and proud, with red bricks and a posh-looking french door. It seemed to have at least three floors, taking into account the small attic on the third floor. Even the front yard seemed beautifully cultivated. I waited for Jane and Mary to start talking to Mom, for Hugh and Grant to start helping my dad, and for the movers to place all our stuff into the house before picking up one of my smaller book boxes, then I made a run for it.

Dashing into the house as quickly as I could, I stopped only to grab Dad and drag him away, begging him to show me my room.

He grinned excitedly and, exchanging a knowing look with both Hugh and Grant, led me upstairs until we came to a stop on the very end of the hallway. He unlocked the room and opened the doors, motioning me to walk in.

I walked in . . . and froze.

There in front of me was the most amazing view of a castle perched on a mountain, surrounded by pine trees and fog. Beyond it, I could see water. Maybe a lake? Maybe the sea . . . It was actually hard to say through the fog.

I turned around, already readying myself to leap on Dad, but frowned when I noticed that I was now alone in my room, and the blond, Alex, was standing at the doorway with the usual smirk on his face, his axe missing.

The urge of just smacking his smirk away seemed quite strong at the moment. And it would be easy too.

Bam! And voila—smirk-less!

"That is the castle Dovelore, owned by His Grace, Alexander Whitlock—His Grace because some say his grandfather was a Duke and that has now been passed down to him. He is also very rich—if the castle isn't proof enough—but not by heritage. Most of it is self-made and all. We are supposed to visit that castle this year, you know . . . Mr. Whitlock is providing one lucky student with a full scholarship to any university he or she wishes to attend and another lucky student a chance to stay in his castle on the breaks, with full access to his library and a full tour around the castle—if he or she wants, that is," Blond spoke, his gaze not once shifting from the castle, which although it looked quite brooding, looked equally inviting, as if charming me into visiting. There definitely was something about that castle.

Suddenly very curious, I turned towards Blond and asked, "What would you like?"

He turned his attention towards me, and for the first time in the fifteen minutes that we had known each other, he smiled at me—a real smile.

"Although the most brilliant literature is available in the castle library and I would love to roam the dungeons and secret pathways where the pirates were slain and beasts held hostage, I want the scholarship."

I nodded and turned back to look at the castle.

What beasts was Blond talking about?

The feeling of my feet pushing themselves forward registered slowly before I found myself staring at the castle, my hands sliding the window open.

Is someone living there right now? How many rooms could there be?

I swept my gaze along the windows of the castle but stilled when I saw someone staring back at me. It seemed like a he. His bulky build made sure to show no confusion, even if he was so, so far away. It was quite distinguishable that he was wearing a white shirt, but that was all that could be made out; the rest was a blur.

"Hey, Blond, come here!" I whispered, motioning Blond to move forward.

" 'Blonde'?" Blond whisper-yelled, sounding outraged, as he made his way to me.

The man was still staring. His stare seemed so intense, it made hairs stand on the back of my neck.

I turned towards Blond, wishing he could see the strange man just like I did. Castles were always haunted, but truly, the one I would be seeing day and night . . . could not possibly be haunted, could it?

"Can you see the man?"

"What man? I see no man?" Blond whispered back, narrowing his eyes, as he looked in the direction of the castle.

I turned towards the castle again.

The man was gone.

"He was just there, I promise!" I whisper-yelled, putting my palm on my heart.

Blond looked at me, frowning, for a second before his smile came back—the friendly one.

"I can help you decorate your room," he said, looking as if he really were interested in sorting out my mess.

I smiled as I brushed a strand of brown hair behind my ear, silently thanking God for Blond's sudden offer. Decorating my bedroom would have taken me all day and night otherwise.

"Let's do this."

If you enjoyed this sample, look for
Mated to the Alpha King
on Amazon.

ACKNOWLEDGMENT

I'd like to acknowledge Sunshine, my editor

AUTHOR'S NOTE

Thank you so much for reading *Igniting Icarus*! I can't express how grateful I am for reading something that was once just a thought inside my head.

I'd love to hear your thoughts on the book. Please leave a review on Amazon or Goodreads because I just love reading your comments and getting to know you!

Can't wait to hear from you!

Julianna Wrights

ABOUT THE AUTHOR

Julianna Wrights is an author for the readers who find love in between pages. After establishing a following on popular reading platforms, Wattpad and Inkitt, Julianna decided to embark on the journey of professional publication. Her favorite genre to read and write are dark romance, paranormal romance, and adult romance. At the moment, her favorite book is the Love Hypothesis by Ali Hazelwood. Julianna is an Undergraduate student with four cats named Lucifer, Cedric, Genesis, and Hades, all of which drive her crazy with affection. When they're not writing, you can find them in your local coffee shop reading or scrolling for hours on TikTok.

Made in the USA
Middletown, DE
21 November 2022